She Who is Hidden

The Savannah Coven Series by Suza Kates

Whisper of a Witch
Conviction of a Witch
Binding of a Witch

Romantic Suspense by Suza Kates

Hallowed Eve

She Who

ICASM PRESS

Savannah

is Hidden

SUZA KATES

Published by Icasm Publishing LLC
5710 Ogeechee Rd. Suite 200 #278, Savannah, GA 31405
www.icasmpress.com

Library of Congress Cataloging-in-Publication Data
Kates, Suza
She Who is Hidden / Suza Kates
p. cm.

ISBN-13:978-0-9849030-2-3 Hardback
ISBN-13:978-0-9849030-3-0 Paperback
ISBN-13:978-0-9849030-4-7 Ebook

I. Title

Printed and bound in the United States of America
10 9 8 7 6 5 4 3 2 1

For my father

A man who valued books, history, and strong women

1

Imagining the sweet, cold drink waiting in the break room fridge was the only thing that kept Erica going as she struggled with the huge box. Her afternoon ritual included raspberry vitamin-tea and a quiet corner in the weapons room. She found the silent menace of swords and war hammers hanging on the walls to be oddly soothing, and as soon as she finished the task at hand, she would slip off for a brief retreat.

Slipping her fingers between Styrofoam and cardboard, she pulled until she grunted and a thick lock of black hair fell into her eyes. All thoughts of her daily respite fled as sweat trickled down her neck. The cinematic equipment that had just arrived at the museum was refusing to slide out of its packing, and with the workers she'd hired busy elsewhere, she was left to set up the aquatic section by herself.

She let go of the box and wiped her brow. Randie, her assistant, was on the phone now with the heating and air service. For what the system had cost, the thermostat should at least be calibrated correctly. Kicking on at what felt like eighty degrees was far from acceptable.

Just as Erica decided to attack the box with scissors, Randie rushed in with eyes wide. "You have a call," she whispered with her hand clasped over a cell phone.

"That's your phone."

"I know, I know. Just take it."

Erica's brow furrowed as she accepted the tiny silver device. "This is Erica Conner."

"Dr. Conner." The male voice on the line seemed vaguely familiar, his tone brisk with the sound of London. "This is Daniel Monroe. I hope I've not caught you at a bad time."

Erica's mind raced, but she could think of only one person she knew by that name, the famed archaeologist. "I'm sorry, Dr. Daniel Monroe?"

"Yes. I'm sure this is quite a surprise. I'm sorry we've never had the chance to speak before, but I've recently been made well aware of your impressive credentials."

"Thank you," Erica stammered, still confused. "I've attended many of your lectures."

"I realize that this is unexpected, but I was hoping to meet with you to discuss something of some importance. I am in town and could make arrangements for this evening."

"Of course." Erica tamped down on her curiosity and struggled to come up with a suitable venue for the likes of Dr. Monroe. "There is a wonderful Italian restaurant..."

"Actually, it would be better if I stopped by your home," Monroe said, cutting her off. "I'd rather not explain now. Say seven o'clock?"

"Oh...fine. Sure. I can give you directions."

"Seven o'clock then. Until this evening, Dr. Conner."

The digital display let Erica know the call had been ended, leaving her in a state of bewilderment. Daniel Monroe? He was one of the world's most highly respected archaeologists, known not only for his genius and dogged persistence, but also for his exploits many had hailed foolhardy at best, suicidal at worst.

What could he possibly want with her? Maybe he'd heard about the museum and wanted to donate some artifacts. No, now she was letting her imagination run away with her.

She hadn't even had time to ask him how or why he'd called her on someone else's personal phone. It was all a little too strange, but there wasn't the slightest chance she would have refused. Daniel Monroe was a man she'd been hoping to meet for years, but thus far, that had been impossible. He still traveled and kept a tight schedule, a lifestyle belying the fact he was in his late sixties.

Her eyes flew to the watch on her wrist. It was almost five now, and Erica needed to pull something together for tonight. There was so much work to be done, but meeting Monroe was a once in a lifetime opportunity she couldn't miss. If his visit could benefit the museum in any way, Dr. Monroe would be priority number one.

Erica glanced down the empty corridor that would soon come to life with underwater imagery. The gallery of artifacts meant much more to her than a life's dream or hard-earned success. The pieces here represented the many expeditions her father and grandfather had taken. And they were all she had left of the two men who'd raised her.

What she was building here was much more than a museum. It was her family's legacy.

The reminder was enough to assuage any guilt she felt leaving the boxes piled on the floor. Calling over her shoulder for Randie to lock up, Erica practically ran to gather her purse from her office before dashing out the rear entrance to her car.

Once the air conditioner was on full blast, she slapped the button to kill the radio and dialed her friend Karen, hoping she wasn't tied up with some crisis. Karen answered on the fourth ring.

"Hey," Erica said. "I want your expert advice. I need a really good wine."

At six forty-five there was a staccato knock on Erica's front door before it swung open to let Karen in. "Where are you?"

Erica was in the kitchen, bent over a tray where she arranged hors d'oeuvres. "In here. Did you get it?"

"The best money can buy. I brought a lighter option, too, since you're going all out." Karen's boots clomped across the burnt-orange, Mexican tile.

With a smile of gratitude, Erica took note of her friend's clothing, a polished version of her work attire. Karen always had to be ready to run. Or, to be exact, ready to chase. The sleek, black pants and gray top were stylish and most likely comfortable. Law enforcement evening wear.

Neither tall nor petite, Erica saw nothing special about her looks, but the same couldn't be said about Karen. The two of them had raven-black hair and light-colored eyes in common, Karen's a rainwater gray and Erica's pale blue, but that's where the similarity ended.

Karen was the product of a Chinese mother and a father who was a tough, tall Texan. The combination had resulted in a dangerously beautiful woman, long-legged and exotic.

Erica was surprised fugitives even ran from Karen, since most men fell into a hormonal stupor in her presence.

"So who exactly is this guy?" Karen asked as she snatched a *Prosciutto Crostini With Lemony Fennel Slaw,* out of the catering box that declared its contents.

Putting the Chardonnay in the stainless steel fridge where it would chill, Erica said, "Let me put it this way. He's one man I've been dying to get alone for a long time.

"Hmm."

"So I can pick his brain."

Her friend looked disappointed. "Oh. Then it must have something to do with a bunch of old bones."

"You put it so nicely. Yes, he's in my field, and I have absolutely no idea what he wants."

"He didn't tell you?"

"No, it was a short conversation." Erica placed the finishing touches on the exotic, teak wood tray. One of her first purchases when she'd bought her house, the tray was etched with ancient calligraphy and gave the impression of culture and sophistication. "As a matter of fact," she added, satisfied with her display, "he was almost evasive."

"You mind if I stick around? I have to admit, you've made me curious."

"You mean suspicious?"

Karen opened the Pinot Noir to let it breathe. "A little of both, I guess."

"You're welcome to stay. Besides, you might actually find yourself interested in our discussion." Erica sent a sidelong smile to her friend.

Karen gave a non-committal shrug. "I'll stay over after. We might as well make the best of it and break out the chick flicks."

"You know, you'd lose all credibility with the men you work with if they knew you preferred tearjerkers to blow 'em up movies."

"Just one of the many mysteries that guys will never understand about the superior sex. I can cry over a love story and shoot the wings off of a fly with the tears still in my eyes." Karen drew an imaginary gun and blew off the barrel.

Erica rolled her eyes. "And you wonder why you're still single." She knew though, that her friend's levity was an effort to shake Erica out of the nervousness assaulting her stomach. Despite the fancy food, drink, and trappings, Erica was still twisting her mind into a knot, trying to make sense of Dr. Monroe's mysterious call.

"Look who's talking about singledom," Karen said with a smirk. "Besides, you should be grateful. Not everyone has their very own U.S. Marshal to spend the night in case of emergency."

"You trained me well, Marshal. I can take care of myself."

A subtle, sonorous chime rang out, startling both of the women. The doorbell seemed to have a more distinctive ring, as if it knew the caliber of person waiting on the other side.

Brushing her long bangs away from her face, Erica made her way to the foyer while Karen took the tray to the living room. With a last deep breath for calm, Erica opened the door.

Dr. Daniel Monroe was a tall man, distinguished in appearance with silver hair and moustache. A few drops glistened on his brown trench coat announcing another night of rainfall. Perfect, white teeth moved in time with his British accent. "Dr. Conner, I can't tell you how pleased I am to meet you at last. I hope you'll forgive my abrupt self-invitation."

Erica stepped aside to wave him in when she noticed he wasn't alone. A man stood behind Monroe, just outside the illumination falling from her porch light. Her first reaction was fear, as if he'd crept up in pursuit of her guest.

Before she could comment, Dr. Monroe pitched over his shoulder from the foyer, "I hope it's fine that I've brought company. I assure you it was most necessary."

Erica's normally perfect manners failed, leaving her to watch in silence as the stranger moved into visibility. Her gut feeling was one of suspicion. Something about the shift in his position sent a shiver up her neck, but that sensation was overridden by another when he came to a purposeful stop in front of her.

Erica was not easily affected, but what she experienced now was abject awe of the male specimen. He stood about six feet in height and carried himself with the unintentional ease of an athlete. His jaw was set while intense brown eyes stared at her from under a clean cut styling of black hair. His body language was almost militant.

The man stepped closer and gave her a thorough onceover. Scrutinizing. Judging.

And any feeling resembling attraction fled from Erica in an instant. He hadn't said a word, yet she felt insulted.

"And you are?" she asked as her brow arched of its own accord.

Instead of answering he looked to Monroe. "You didn't tell her?"

Karen chose that moment to join them as they all stood there studying each other. "Hello, you must be Dr. Monroe. I'm Karen Fields, a friend of Erica's." She shook Monroe's hand. "Can I get you something to drink?"

"Yes, yes." Monroe took the opportunity to slip out of his coat. "A brandy would be nice."

"Oh, well, we only have wine. Erica's not really a drinker."

"That would be perfect," he said with a nod.

Since he stood still holding his coat, Erica moved to take it and put it in the closet. She turned back to see that the stranger had slipped past her and into the living room. He surveyed the room before depositing himself on the leather couch.

Erica moved to take a seat in one of the chairs opposite and gestured for Monroe to do the same. "I hope you don't mind if we skip the small talk, Dr. Monroe, but your call this afternoon was unexpected, and now I'm a little concerned about whatever it is you haven't told me."

He put his hands on his knees and stared at the floor as he gathered his thoughts. "You are acquainted with the eighteenth dynasty?"

"Yes, I did my master's thesis on symbolism in architecture and décor of the tombs from that time period. I assume you're referring to Egypt?" A spark of pleasure ignited in Erica's once shaky stomach. She would be on steady ground with this conversation.

"Exactly. I'm sure you are familiar with Pharaoh Hatshepsut."

"Yes, the queen who would be king. Her story is fascinating."

Karen returned with the wine. Dr. Monroe took it with a smile, but the stranger refused with a lift of his hand.

"Whose story is fascinating?" Karen asked, taking a seat beside the silent man on the couch.

Monroe smiled graciously. "Why don't you tell it, Dr. Conner?"

Erica nodded and sipped her wine before launching into history. "Hatshepsut was the daughter of King Tuthmose, not to be confused with the more well-known Tutankhamen, or Tut for short. Tuthmose sired both Hatshepsut and her husband Tuthmose II."

"Wait," Karen interjected, "you mean she married her brother?"

"Precisely. Half-brother technically, but yes. You see, the royal blood was presumably passed through the mother, so Tuthmose II made a good political move by marrying his half-sister who carried the royal blood of their father."

Karen looked disgusted while the stranger looked annoyed, giving Erica good reason to finally say, "You never did introduce yourself, Mr..."

Monroe intervened. "I'm sorry, where are my manners? Matthew Pierce, a colleague of mine. I've asked him to be here tonight for professional reasons."

"Which are?" Karen asked, showing her support of Erica.

Matthew's dark gaze landed briefly on Karen before returning to the lady doctor. He'd been given a picture of Erica Conner, but the black and white version didn't do her justice. He'd never seen eyes of such a light blue, and the contrast of dark hair was electric. She wore a starched shirt and one of those knee length skirts women liked that had something to do with a pencil. The professional attire was fitting, but the straight lines couldn't completely disguise the firm but feminine curves beneath.

Matthew redirected his thoughts and remembered why he was here. His mouth parted to answer Karen's question, but Monroe interrupted before he could speak.

"I'll explain everything in time, if you'll indulge me a bit more," the older man said. "Please continue, Dr. Conner."

Erica smiled at the apparently well-intentioned Monroe and began again. "Tuthmose II and Hatshepsut produced only daughters, but Tuthmose II had a son by another woman, a commoner, Isis. The boy was named Tuthmose III."

"How original," Karen quipped, causing Matt's mouth to jerk with what thought about being a smile. The friend of the doctor's had kick. Too bad she wasn't the one they'd come to see. The one they needed.

He allowed his eyes to fall on the sexy doctor as she spoke.

Erica caught his stare briefly before returning her attention to Monroe. "It was decided that Tuthmose III would rule when his father died, since he was the only son. He was young at the time, so his step-mother, Hatshepsut, who was technically also his aunt, guided him as regent."

Another sip of wine. "It seemed that Hatshepsut was not inclined to wait for Tuthmose III to come of age. Since she was the daughter of a well-loved pharaoh and a beautiful, enigmatic woman in her own right, Hatshepsut declared herself pharaoh."

Erica waited for a shocked reaction from her listeners, but receiving none, she explained, "It was unheard of. A woman had never been pharaoh before, queen perhaps, but not pharaoh."

Karen took the bait. "Okay, so what happened?"

"Nothing for about fifteen years. You see, she had more than just her father's popularity on her side. Along with stating that her father had desired her to be pharaoh, she made a much more significant claim. She also claimed to be the child of a god."

"Which god?" Karen asked, moving to sit on the edge of her seat.

"Amun. Known as the god of many things, but specifically the creator of all. There was a story of how the god Amun came to Hatshepsut's mother disguised as her father, with the end result being the divine conception of Hatshepsut. This was enough to secure her position as pharaoh, but she still persisted in strange behavior, wearing false beards and male attire."

At this point Monroe jumped in, eyes alight with enthusiasm. "She ruled for fifteen years with the primary objectives of peace and productivity, which would have likely continued if not for the coming of age of Tuthmose III. Hatshepsut disappeared suddenly with no public explanation, allowing Tuthmose III to slide into position of pharaoh. It is assumed she did not die of natural causes," he finished with a meaningful tilt of his brows.

"This is all very interesting, but what does any of it have to do with Erica?" Karen probed.

Again Matt found himself thinking how useful the Marshal would be in the field, but another gun wasn't what he and Monroe had come for. They needed an intellectual with very specific information programmed into her brain.

He scanned Erica's stiff posture and serious expression before shifting his gaze to a photo sitting on the table next to her chair. Black tresses and cat-like eyes told him the girl in the picture was a younger version of Erica. She had ponytails in her hair and a skull in her hands. Her smiling father stood behind her as they posed for the camera, and he couldn't have looked prouder.

A noise drew him back to Dr. Erica Conner. The sharp point of her black shoe tapped on the floor as she waited to be told why the men had come to her.

Silence hung in the air for seconds until Monroe looked pointedly at Erica. "You've heard of the discoveries at the Deir-al-Bahri cache?"

"Some mummies and," she paused to think, "a canopic vase of Hatshepsut's." Her face froze before relaxing into a look of anticipation. "Dr. Monroe, are you telling me you have the canopic vase that held Hatshepsut's liver?"

Monroe smiled as if receiving the correct answer from a pupil. "Yes, in a manner of speaking, but not the one from Deir-el-Bahri cache. That was a decoy."

Erica pressed her lips together as a tiny wrinkle formed between her brows. "What? But, how do you know?"

"I know because the true container holds a very important clue, one that has been hidden for over two thousand years."

Erica remained silent, apparently dumbstruck by Monroe's revelation.

"Tell me, Dr. Conner." He leaned forward to ask, "How do you fare with riddles?"

2

The man made a sign from the window, letting the others know to come ahead. All was clear. He then turned back to look at the woman sleeping soundly in her bed.

She had no idea what honor had been bestowed upon her as the first chosen. The man knew she had deep brown eyes under the closed lids, in contrast to the fairness of her skin and blonde hair that fanned across her pillow.

The man's given name was of no importance, for tonight he was known only as the serpent. In English, the rough translation was *Serpent-Raised-Head*. This was a name he had coveted for many years, and the pain and sacrifice had all been worth this long-awaited moment.

He was the first to fulfill the role of the serpent in the ritual. He was a member of the first team to receive the blessing, and only the best had been chosen. There could be no mistakes. The Serpent had performed his duty well. He'd gained access and guarded the area, as well as the woman.

She turned in her sleep and sighed. Hope was her name, he remembered. The blinds were pulled and curtains closed to darken the room. It was ten o'clock in the morning, but Hope had worked all night at a local hospital.

She was a nurse. A healer. She was an appropriate choice for the first.

The others came through the door, drawing the Serpent's attention, each in clothes that matched the specifications. It had taken some time to ensure the requirements had been met, yet with clothing that would not draw any unwanted attention.

There were four of them. Each had been thoroughly tested and trained, and they were well aware of the importance of what they were here to do. The time had come. More than four thousand years ago, the days and the millennium had been prophesied and were now upon them. They were blessed to be alive during the time of the reformation.

During the initial struggle, each would help make sure the woman was subdued, to ensure that no alarm was raised and that her body remained unharmed. Bruised tissue was to be avoided at all costs. Though each man would lend himself to this end, only *He-Upon-The-Willows* would be allowed to perform the binding. His name was as ancient as the skill that had allowed him to create the thin, strong ropes made from willow leaves.

Hope was exhausted from the night's work, but woke instantly as four sets of hands fell on her arms, legs, and face. The hands didn't hurt her, but she couldn't move in resistance, or tear her mouth away for a scream.

She felt no pain, but fear surged to her core, greater than the terror of waking to find strange men in her bedroom. Their serious faces showed no trace of emotion, and a warning inside her cried out that they were not there for any common crime.

Something was happening to her feet, then her legs, a quick movement that wrapped twine or rope around them, circling again and again. Just as suddenly, the hands were gone, but she still couldn't move. She was tied so tightly, encased from ankles to knees.

One of the men who'd been working on her legs moved to the bedside table. He struck a match then used the spurting flame to light candles. Those weren't hers. Why had they brought candles?

Soon she smelled sharp and spicy incense that overrode the sulfur from the matches. The thought of satanic rituals had her struggling again, but the men held her firm as hot tears rolled down into her hair, her ears.

The hand slipped from her mouth, but before she could scream, it returned to press something between her lips and past her teeth. Hope shook her head and tried to cringe away. Whatever was in her mouth was soft but firmly packed. It tasted like some sort of plant, maybe leaves. She barely had time to register this before they bound her left wrist with the same type of rope as her legs.

She looked up to see the hollow eyes of the man still holding her other arm. They impaled her with dark intensity and filled her with a fear she'd never known. She'd seen a lot in the blood, guts, and misery of emergency rooms, but nothing came close to the expression on the man's face as he looked at her, smiling.

Another man was beside him then, tying her right wrist as well. Once he finished she pulled her arm, only to feel a jerk on her other one. Her arms were linked to each other by a cord that ran up under the bed. Pulling would be useless.

The man with the depthless eyes removed something from her table. He held it up with both hands and began to chant. The words were foreign, but Hope recognized the flash of silver in the man's grip. It was a knife or dagger, the hilt embellished with beautiful blue stones.

How strange that she would notice the colors at a time like this.

Everything seemed to move in slow motion now as her eyes followed the knife, watched it cut cleanly through her shirt and underwear. Candlelight danced on her golden skin. She was completely exposed, completely helpless.

The intruder's deep voices melded together as they began chanting and gathering around her. The man with the knife stopped to look at Hope and say something in the foreign language before touching the cold, metal point to the hollow between her breasts. She saw his hand move downward but didn't register any pain; the blade's sharpened edge sliced so cleanly.

Hope stared at the shadows moving on the ceiling and thought of her mother. She thought of the innocent, screaming child she'd helped bring into the world hours earlier, the tears and laughter of all who'd been there. She would never experience that miracle for herself.

She could feel the knife now and recognized the sound of her own flesh being separated. The man's gentle touch was his worst cruelty.

As darkness crept in on her from all sides, the man raised the knife once more but stopped to lean over and stare into Hope's eyes. Her future, her dreams, and the meaning of her name were suddenly wiped away when the man caught her stare. And through the chanting of the others he whispered, "Thank you."

3

"Riddles? As in deciphering hieroglyphic messages?" Erica asked, thinking she'd found the real reason for Dr. Monroe's visit.

From an early age Erica had been taught several ancient languages and forms of symbolism. Her father had been brought up the same way, since her grandfather believed that in their line of work one could never predict when certain knowledge would prove valuable, possibly even save a life.

Monroe nodded. "That might certainly be part of it, yes, though in actuality it would be a bit more involved."

Erica's patience was wearing thin and her natural inquisitiveness had been stalled long enough. "Dr. Monroe, with all due respect, I do enjoy a good puzzle, but if you'd like my help you're going to have to come to the point."

His countenance grew somber. "Very well. I, that is, we need your assistance in finding some crucially important items, the canopic jars of Hatshepsut. When I said that I had one of the jars, I should have said that I have a good idea of how to find it. Sensitive information has been brought to the attention of certain governmental bodies, which is where Mr. Pierce comes in." Monroe turned to the dark-haired man as if passing an unseen baton.

Matt Pierce glanced at Karen then gave his full attention

to Erica. "One of the branches of government that Dr. Monroe is referring to is the National Security Agency, or NSA. It's responsible for collecting foreign signals and making sure that certain information gets to the necessary parties."

"You mean they spy on people," Erica put in with a sarcastic grin. She wasn't entirely comfortable with the way the agent was looking at her. He still seemed to be assessing her worth and displayed neither the courtesy nor friendliness of Dr. Monroe.

"Some might say that, but look at it this way, Dr. Conner. If you knew there was a person out there just waiting for the right time and place to kill you, would you like to be apprised of their plans beforehand or just take your chances and hope they developed a conscience?"

Erica's response was silence. She'd lit a lavender candle in the foyer before her guests' arrival, and now she focused on the calming scent. She would not let a rude stranger ruin her evening and the rare chance of speaking with Dr. Monroe about her life's passion.

"At any rate," Matt said, getting back to the subject, "the NSA delivers information on various terrorist groups or other organizations that might pose a threat to Americans or innocent citizens of any country."

Karen raised an eyebrow. "Again, what does any of this have to do with Erica?"

"For the last several years I've been handling information and tracking the movements of a group that was brought to our attention through the NSA's SIGINT section."

"The what?" Erica asked.

Karen honed in on another piece of information. "You're not with the NSA?"

He answered both their questions. "Actually, my position is with the FBI, and my job is to keep close tabs on a couple of religious groups that have the potential to be dangerous. SIGINT is how we refer to Signals Intelligence, information gained from various multi-functional technologies."

"Dr. Conner." It was the first time he'd addressed her directly, and the intensity of his bottomless, brown eyes was mesmerizing. "The society that concerns us now refers to itself as *Kherep Amun*. It's believed to have been founded sometime after the ruling years of Pharaoh Hatshepsut. Their name may have changed some over the years but is fundamentally the same as the original."

"Kherep Amun." Erica slowly tasted the words. "The word *Kherep* translates loosely to mean "be at the head" or "control." The second is a name. That of the god Amun, often known as He Who is Hidden. The word hidden is associated with his name, because it means he is the god that cannot be seen with mortal eyes. He is inscrutable to gods as well as men, ultimately representing the incomprehensible power that created the world."

"You mean he was considered the one and only god?" Karen asked.

"Not the only god, but rather the controlling god," Erica said. "At times his name was mixed with those of other deities. For example, he later became Amun-re or Amun-ra in combination with the sun god. Egyptian society held him in various levels of esteem at different times."

"But what is important to us is his position during the time of Hatshepsut and the ones who established Kherep Amun," Dr. Monroe pointed out. "This is a society that has persisted since approximately fourteen hundred years before the time of Jesus Christ. They are smaller in number than the three primary religions, but extremely devout in their beliefs."

"What are those beliefs?" Erica asked. "And why have I never heard of them?"

"They are not like other religions in that they do not openly recruit followers but are selective in allowing entry only to those whom they deem worthy. They accept only those who will commit their lives to the search for the hidden one, Amun."

"Searching spiritually?"

Dr. Monroe mulled over his answer. "A physical search that once completed will fulfill them spiritually. A large part of that search involves the canopic jars of Hatshepsut, the self-proclaimed daughter of Amun."

"So they believe that if they have the organs of Hatshepsut, or the symbolic vases that contained them, they will essentially have a physical part of Amun himself."

Matt started to say something, but Dr. Monroe beat him to it. "Yes, that's the essence of it."

Erica was still unconvinced. "It's been reported that the mummy of Hatshepsut has been found, but scientists were initially unaware of the identity. Why wouldn't Kherep Amun attempt to steal the actual mummy?"

A lazy smile crossed Dr. Monroe's face. "They know the mummy in question is not their lost queen."

"But they identified the remains with DNA analysis," Erica persisted.

"Another cover-up," Matt said. "This one compliments of several national governments working together. It is in everyone's best interest to stall Kherep Amun's activities."

Matt decided to withhold some details for now, but felt the woman in front of him deserved to be warned. "Dr. Conner, there is one thing we know for certain about this cult. It is fanatical, and it is extremely dangerous for anyone it sees as an adversary. If you choose to help us with this task, there will be risk involved."

"We had to take the utmost precautions contacting you," Monroe said. "Even our coming here tonight may prove foolish, but we felt it better to be secluded in your home where we would have been aware of any, say, unwarranted attention."

"So that's why you called me on Randie's phone today?"

"Yes, we weren't sure of the security of your own mobile phone or the lines at the museum."

Erica clasped her hands together in her lap. "Do you think

this group has actually gone so far as to tap my phones and those where I work? How would they even be aware that you'd contact me?"

"I'm sure it hasn't come to that," Matt assured her, "but we need to be cautious. It's not such a stretch to think they might consider contacting you themselves. They have dossiers on the top minds in all pertinent sciences, yours included."

"Why is it so important to find the jars before they do? I understand the scientific importance, but is it worth losing lives over?"

Matt remembered his agreement with Monroe. The two of them had decided to fill Dr. Conner in slowly, so he stayed quiet and let the archaeologist lead. Monroe had a natural rapport with her, but too much information up front might scare her. Despite his own reservations, Matt knew they needed her.

He clenched his fingers on his thigh. Correction. *He* needed her.

"Many more lives will be lost if they do find Hatshepsut's jars." Monroe answered, studying Erica with eyes that were suddenly shrewd. "And I haven't yet mentioned, if you find these jars, regardless of the aid you receive from myself or any government agency, the relics recovered will be yours to do with as you will. This includes the canopic vases of Hatshepsut. Quite a coup for your museum."

Not just my museum. Erica allowed the implications of the older man's promise to sink in. *For my father and grandfather. Hatshepsut's vases.* The enormity of the find would be news around the world. People everywhere would want to see the relics, and to do so, they would have to come to a quiet area just outside of Atlanta, Georgia.

They would come. And they would know of her family's accomplishments. Her images of glory must have shown on her face, since Karen made a surprised noise. Her friend, however, didn't share her excitement.

"Wait, Erica, don't jump the gun here. You still don't know

exactly what you're signing up for. God's sake, the FBI is involved." Karen set aside her drink and put the flats of her palms on her corduroy-covered thighs.

Erica considered the warning for a moment. "I have to ask, why me? Dr. Monroe, you're the one the government has turned to in this matter."

"You have the eclectic academic knowledge as well as vast experience with excavating a diversity of sites," Monroe told her. "This assignment will require someone capable of pulling pieces together from many areas of expertise. After myself, you are the next best candidate." A touch of regret passed his eyes. "I am simply not young and agile enough for what may lie ahead in this pursuit."

It was this last statement that decided the matter for Erica. Though she could help stop these Kherup Amun people, and having any of Queen Hatshepsut's artifacts would be wonderful for the museum, she had to admit her own selfish reason as well.

The sound of metal scraping into the earth, uncovering history's secrets. The thrill of the search and elation of the find. These were the things that made her blood pump faster.

And it was obvious that despite the perils, Monroe would take this errand if he could. So Erica would do it in his stead.

"It would require that you take some time away from your current project, but the outcome could be immensely more beneficial," Monroe said. "And you would have an FBI operative with you at all times, for security purposes."

Erica's excitement dropped like a stone. She knew what was coming next and turned to the now smugly smiling Matthew Pierce.

"I guess you're going to have to learn to like me," he said.

Her distrust of the agent must have been as apparent as his was of her. And she didn't appreciate that condescending smile. "Are you sure you'll be physically able to do what's necessary?" she asked. She tapped her shoe twice then stopped herself.

"The places we'll probably end up won't resemble a clean, white office with the FBI."

Matt scoffed. "I'm sure I'll manage." He gave her a head to toe perusal that was just as unflattering as her comment had been.

Erica suddenly wished for her cargos instead of the expensive heels and skirt.

"No offense," Karen said suddenly into air that had grown thick with tension, "but are you the only protection she'll have?"

Matt answered, but his dark stare was fixed on Erica when he said, "Don't worry. I'll be enough."

Erica wondered if she might not need protection from the agent himself. What had she ever done to make him so resistant? They had sought her out, not the other way around.

Monroe cleared his throat, "So is this a yes, Dr. Conner?"

Erica dismissed Matt Pierce and beamed at the older man. "It is. How could I say no? And I believe we've come to the point that you should call me Erica." She smiled at the seasoned archaeologist as if they shared a secret, which they did. They both knew the exhilaration of finding that which had been lost to humankind for centuries, even millennia, and being the first to lay eyes on it before its return to the light of day.

"Excellent. We should speak again tomorrow so that I may brief you on the data we have thus far. You should pack and make any needed arrangements this evening, as we'll have you both departing as soon as possible. You'll have no need of any research materials, since Agent Pierce's agency will supply us with communication devices. I'll be available to you both at any hour for conference."

"Why not let me get started tonight?" Erica rose with Monroe, disappointed he was leaving.

"Patience. Tend to your personal things tonight, and rest assured that your mind will be challenged to your content over the next weeks."

As Monroe reached for the door, Matt Pierce brought him up

short. "Before we go, there's something I want to clear up. Dr. Conner, or can I also call you Erica?" She gave a stiff nod as she studied him warily.

"Before we could approach you, we had to be sure you hadn't already been compromised."

"I don't know what you mean."

Matt headed toward the kitchen, stopping under the doorframe and reaching to pull something down.

"Son of a bitch," gasped Karen as understanding dawned on her.

He shrugged unapologetically. "We couldn't take any chances on this."

"What is that?" Erica frowned at the small object in Matt's hand.

"It's a bug," her friend supplied.

"But how…" Erica halted in mid-sentence, suddenly finding good reason for disliking Matt Pierce. "Who the hell do you think you are?" she demanded, furious now as she realized he or someone he worked with had broken into her home. They'd placed a listening device in her private space.

"Sorry, Erica, but you called it earlier. We spy on people, remember?" He winked at her. He actually winked. "I'm sure you'll begin to understand the necessity when you get past this initial anger."

Initial anger? Erica could feel her muscles tense as her mind worked furiously for words strong enough to flatten Agent Matthew Pierce against the far wall.

The man wisely knew when to make an exit. "We'll be in touch tomorrow." He followed Monroe out of the room but turned to smirk at Erica while she sputtered. "And all things considered, you can call me Matt."

4

A line of light shimmered across the gold medallion in Erica's hand as she read the markings. It was larger than similar charms used in fifteenth century BC, but the amount of inscription on the back was explanation for its size.

The busy sounds of Atlanta's Hartsfield-Jackson International Airport clouded the air of the lounge where she had ordered a now watered-down iced tea. Dr. Monroe quickly briefed her as they waited for Matt Pierce to return with boarding passes.

"This was recovered from a female mummy thought to have been Hatshepsut's wet nurse. Originally found in 1903, it eventually found its way into the basement of the museum in Cairo. A guard stole some treasures from the lower level storage rooms, assuming they would never be missed."

"How could they not be missed?" Erica couldn't imagine the Cairo curators being so careless.

"Over the years, many archaeological finds have proven plentiful in artifacts. Only the most sought after or meaningful pieces remain on display. The things that may be viewed are only a small percentage of what lies in storage. Ironic isn't it? We spend our lives bringing them up so that they may be returned to the ground."

"I don't think ironic is the first adjective I'd choose," she replied with a scowl. "How did you end up with this piece of jewelry?"

"Though illegal, the black market can be a wonderful tool for one who has connections. I purchased it in Scotland last year and have since been researching its origins. This is how the NSA was made aware of my interest. One thing led to another and, well, here we are."

"You were doing Internet research and the NSA tagged you?"

"Evidently I threw up enough red flags for Agent Pierce to make a house call, but this does not upset me. Now that I have been made aware of Kherep Amun and its activities, I'll supply your government with every possible assistance."

"You still haven't explained why the group is so dangerous."

Monroe pulled a black file from his case and slid it across the table. "Read this and it will give you more than enough detail." A frown settled on his face, further enhancing his age. "I expect you will focus on solving the puzzles presented, but remember that Agent Pierce is the authority on Kherep Amun. He will keep you safe if you let him."

Erica acknowledged this with a nod, recognizing his concern. "Speaking of puzzles," she added, "I'm sure you already have your thoughts on this necklace and where we go from here, since we're in an airport."

"As I said, the mummy that was wearing this piece was not positioned as one of royalty would have been. She was buried as a servant, so the necklace was not given much attention and probably went to the museum's basement almost immediately, its message lying undiscovered for another century."

His mention of the message brought Erica's focus back to the hieroglyphics on the amulet. The symbols of vultures, reed leaves, and other natural elements translated into sounds that were a second language to her.

"The first four lines of writing are fairly simple. *Habi,* which is baboon, *duamutefla* means dog, *imseti* is human, and *qebehsenuef,* the falcon. These represent the typical heads on the lids of the four canopic vases used in mummification. They stored the lungs, stomach, liver, and intestines respectively."

"Exactly. They, like the wrappings of the mummies themselves, served to protect the vital organs as one passed into the next life. Interestingly enough, the brain was sucked out and thrown way, as it was considered useless." Monroe laughed. "An incredible error for such a highly civilized culture."

"And you connect the jars with Hatshepsut," Erica continued, "because of the verse that follows. *She is hidden in the words of her lover*." She met Monroe's eyes. "Now you're going to enlighten me as to who her lover was, right?"

"No. I believe you already know."

Her doubtful look had Monroe holding his hands up in a halting motion. "Just think about it. With whom did Hatshepsut spend an undue amount of time? On whom did she bestow the privilege of tutoring her daughter?"

It took only seconds for Erica to make the connection. "Senmut."

Monroe waited.

"The same Senmut who was rumored to have fathered that daughter." Erica's smile was triumphant. "The very same Senmut who was the architect in charge of building Hatshepsut's temple in Luxor where her life's achievements were inscribed on the walls. A man known to hide puzzles and riddles among his very detailed work."

"Now you've got it."

Her sudden elation deflated. "Wait. It can't be this easy or someone would have solved all of this years ago." Erica took a sip of the tea and grimaced before reaching for a pink pack of sweetener to disguise the weak brew.

"Keep in mind that this very small but simple clue was purposely placed on the jewelry of a servant," Monroe said, still eyeing the medallion. "The supporters of Hatshepsut, mainly the priests, took great pains to hide her remains from her stepson, Tuthmose III."

"And they knew that even if found, the wet nurse's mummy would be overlooked. It was beneath him to worry about a servant," Erica said.

"The priests were right to take precautions, since after her mysterious death, Tuthmose assumed the position of pharaoh and ordered every drawing or relief of Hatshepsut to be destroyed and her name scratched out." Monroe frowned. "Luckily, his ego caused him to leave many inscriptions on the walls where he simply inserted his name where hers had been."

"The wet nurse was found in an alternative tomb, correct?" Erica wanted to check her facts before she and Monroe separated. As soon as she stepped on board the plane, her sole companion would be Matt Pierce. Good thing she had the file to read, because it would be hard to make small talk with the difficult FBI agent.

Monroe nodded as he spoke. "The alternative tomb lay a mile west of Dei-el-bahri, in the Valley of the Queens, but it was never finished. Most likely because Hatshepsut declared herself pharaoh. Her later temple was built at the entrance to the Valley of the Kings. A step up in hierarchy."

"The inscriptions we need are on this newer temple?" Erica asked.

"Yes. Look at the front of the pendant."

Erica turned it over. The simple name of *Ra* was written above more symbols that loosely translated into the word *reveals*.

"Ra reveals?" Erica worked it out. "The sun god reveals. The sun reveals."

Monroe smiled in the affirmative. "At dawn, as the sun rises, the frontal inscriptions will be lit in gold, plainly visible."

"How will we recognize the message? It must be encrypted somehow or it would have already been found."

"Either that or people have just never realized what they were reading." Monroe spread his hands in a helpless gesture. "I'm sorry I can't tell you more."

"It looks like Agent Pierce and I are going to the temple to begin the search. I wonder if it will lead to more than the canopic jars. Possibly to Hatshepsut herself?" The idea of recovering the lost queen, the Egyptian ruler who'd been missing for thousands of years, stirred the familiar longing in Erica's gut.

She wasn't normally greedy for fame or fortune, but she could imagine the attention such a find would bring. The Conner name would be cemented in archaeological history. Papers would be written. Scientific journals would document the quest, and Erica could share the love and respect she had for her father and grandfather with the rest of the world.

"We can't be certain what you will find," Monroe said, putting a stop to Erica's imaginings. "After moving Hatshepsut's remains, Senmut and the priests left the trail to the vases and most likely her mummy as well. At least, that is what I believe."

Erica put her hands on the file, wondering what she would learn about the elusive cult that worshipped the lost queen. "If they wanted to protect her, why leave clues at all?"

"The immediate need was to protect her body from Tuthmose III, but the ultimate goal was to make sure she was remembered. Hatshepsut's years of rule were very peaceful yet prosperous times. Her success certainly disturbed some men of that time, just as it might still today."

Erica smirked, well aware of the pros and cons of being an independent female. She refused to allow romantic relationships to interfere with her work. Her goals. By date number two, most men figured this out. She wasn't a femi-nazi or anything, she just knew what she was capable of and what she wanted to make happen.

As if conjured by her thoughts of antagonistic males, Matt Pierce appeared suddenly and dropped into the chair next to her. He shot Erica a tight grin and set two boarding passes on the table.

She picked up the tickets before sliding her eyes up to meet those of the man who would be dogging her every step until this excursion was completed. The man she didn't fully trust. "First class? I'm impressed."

He shrugged. "I didn't think you'd tolerate coach, and despite my best efforts, the powers that be want to make sure you stick with the plan."

With an edge to her voice Erica replied, "I would have been fine in coach." She leaned back and crossed her legs. "At least you're finally admitting you don't want me along. Care to tell me why?"

Matt shrugged. "I don't see the necessity. We'll have communication available almost anywhere. I could just as easily contact Monroe with any questions or discoveries. But as I've said, it's out of my hands." The air practically snapped between them as Matt burned Erica with an irritated stare.

She fired one right back.

Monroe took the tickets from Erica's hand and wagged them at Matt. "Dr. Conner's onsite presence is essential, so you two had better start getting along. You're going to be spending a great deal of time together, and you absolutely must work as team if you are to succeed."

"That's part of the problem," Matt said in a low voice. "I work better alone."

"And I work better when I'm not being questioned or doubted every five minutes." Erica met his hard gaze head on. "I don't have a crew to lead on this expedition, so the heavy lifting will fall to the two of us. But I'm not sure I'm comfortable going into risky situations with a man who admits he doesn't want me around."

"And I'm just as uncomfortable looking after someone who's better suited for a lab or classroom. You're a liability and a detriment. Plain and simple." Matt grabbed her tea and downed it.

"Then why don't you send another agent with me instead? If you don't think you can handle it."

Monroe held up his hands as Matt pointed a finger at

Erica. "You are the most appropriate team. Young, strong, and holding the necessary skill sets. You both have mutually exclusive knowledge regarding Hatshepsut and Kherep Amun. Learn to deal with each other." With an exasperated huff, the older man raised his snifter and smiled. "Cheers."

Erica did little more than settle herself into the soft, blue leather, snap on her seatbelt, and raise the footrest before diving into the file Monroe had given her. Completely engrossed in the workings of Kherep Amun, she paid no mind as they lifted off and soared over the golden-green canopy of forest.

It wasn't until she began rifling through the pages for a second look that she sensed his eyes on her. Matt Pierce's presence was a palpable force.

It was also annoying and unavoidable.

She stole a glance at him out of the corner of her eye before turning to face him. "Do you always stare at people?" she asked through clenched teeth.

Matt's laid back drawl answered, "Not usually." He waited a heartbeat before adding, "But I do often stare out airplane windows if the view is good."

Erica huffed and quickly returned to perusing the papers, afraid she might actually blush. She had sounded vain, not to mention rude. He dismissed her so easily, and his lack of courtesy brought out the worst in her.

When the flight attendant offered them a beverage, she eagerly ordered a drink. She'd once gotten a terrible headache while drinking champagne on a flight to Los Angeles, but if it settled her nerves, she was more than willing to risk a screwdriver.

As they waited for their drinks, Matt slid a hidden glance

to the woman beside him and commended his quick thinking. He had been watching Erica, but damned if he wanted her to know that.

She'd been so absorbed in the file, so intent on her purpose, that she hadn't noticed his perusal. At first he'd studied her with displeasure, hoping for the thousandth time that his superiors had made the right choice. Despite the appropriate clothing she now wore, and the boots that were most definitely broken in, Erica Conner still seemed out of place. She had a certain polish to her, even without the skirt and heels.

As he'd stared at her, his thoughts had begun to track a different route. He'd allowed himself to notice certain things. Like the way her rosy lips moved as she mouthed the words of something she felt was important. The loose strip of inky hair that had escaped her barrette. And the way she kept tucking it behind her ear. The delicate fingers that occasionally skimmed along the lines. Her hands were so small, he had a hard time picturing them working their way through dirt and stone.

The pretty doctor was hard to get a handle on. From afar she had seemed competent and defensive. After they'd met...she'd become even more defensive.

But it was clear she knew her business. They needed an expert in Egyptology who was also well versed in other areas, and even Matt couldn't argue with her credentials.

Dr. Erica Conner was the woman for the job.

Despite any misgivings he had, Matt had no choice but to make the situation work. His job was to coordinate in the field and watch for traces of Kherep Amun. In other words, it was up to him to keep Erica safe. He couldn't do that if she didn't trust him to.

Swallowing a huge dose of humility and taking a deep breath, he spoke to the woman in question. "Learned anything new, Doc?" He smiled in an offer of peace.

Erica looked up in surprise. It wasn't the question that jarred her but the amiable tone. And Matt Pierce was smiling at her.

Naturally and without spite. To her great consternation, she found it a hard smile to resist.

After a moment of hesitation, she decided Monroe had been right. She and Matt were going to have to get along, and she should do her part. She could start by thinking of him as a partner. Not as Matt Pierce or Agent Pierce. Just Matt.

She grinned back briefly before tapping the paper in her lap. "Yes, actually. I knew Kherep Amun was founded to keep alive the memory of Hatshepsut, the daughter of Amun. What I didn't know was that a man named Neils wrote an informational pamphlet about them in 1930. Why didn't anyone ever follow up on that?"

Matt shifted toward her in his seat. "Neils supposedly heard about the group from a local in Shanghai. The man claimed to be the son of a Kherep Amun member who'd fled from his father's teachings. He told Neils a story about their plan to take control of the world, or inherit the earth, something along those lines."

Erica quirked one side of her mouth. "It sounds pretty far-fetched."

"Right. Which is probably why Neils was written off as a kook. He also swore that the man he'd spoken with had disappeared, explaining why the story couldn't be corroborated."

"Shanghai." Erica shook her head. "It's not unheard of for someone to just up and disappear from there, no pun intended."

"Of course not," Matt said, but grinned anyway. "Neils and his booklet didn't come to our attention until we started looking into Kherep Amun for ourselves. After nine-eleven, when organizations of Arabic origin were being watched more closely, we stumbled onto some alarming messages, and I was assigned a new job."

"What type of messages?" Erica was beginning to relax and wanted to keep Matt talking. He wasn't as intimidating when he spoke at length. Probably because it left no time for that depthless stare of his.

Matt shifted again. Another inch closer. "Vague references to their group coming to power, preparations being made, and a mention of the end of days. It was enough to get our attention."

Erica felt the wrinkle form between her eyes that always accompanied her skepticism. "I'm sorry, but I have a hard time believing so many people would dedicate their lives to such a ridiculous notion. Why would anyone today honestly think Hatshepsut was really the daughter of a god and that her remains would lead to some sort of religious salvation?"

Matt looked at her with no readable emotion. "Let's say you have sound reason to challenge the existence of Jesus Christ, much less his divinity. You have irrefutable proof that he was just a myth. Or how about the prophet Mohammed? How easy is it going to be for you to convince their followers of that?"

Erica saw his point. "I guess because all of this is so new to me, and it's been successfully kept a secret for so long that it's hard to comprehend. It seems bizarre."

"The zealous way they've guarded the existence and purpose of their group gives you an idea how devoted they are and what a problem they could be." Matt's eyes clouded over as if vile thoughts battled inside his head.

Erica saw his jaw tighten and wondered what he was imagining. Or recalling. After a helpful gulp of vodka-laced OJ, she said, "At least they should be easily identifiable, if they're ever found. You're aware that once accepted into the group they have a tattoo put on their abdomen?"

He nodded. "Strange place for an affiliation marking. They're usually on arms, chests, legs, even inside bottom lips. I haven't seen one, but reports of the tattoos have cropped up occasionally. The most recent being the victim of a homicide in your own backyard, Atlanta. Did you see the picture in the file?"

"Yes." Erica flipped pages until she came up with the image of a bird. "This isn't exactly my specialty, so I'm guessing it's a bird of prey, considering its claws and the shape of its beak."

"You're right. An ornithologist said it was a falcon. Don't ask me how. It's not my specialty either."

Erica appreciated his attempt to connect. Maybe he wasn't as bad as she'd first assumed.

He reached over to point out something in the swirls located below the depiction of the bird. "Do you know what this means?"

"What?" Erica was caught off guard by his arm resting against hers. The unexpected warmth shot straight to her chest and made her breath catch. "Oh. No. I didn't notice that before. I can see the letters mixed into it now. What do they spell?" she asked him. She'd let him tell her instead of sorting the letters out for herself. He already knew the answer.

Plus, she needed a moment to settle down. Her reaction to his touch was unnerving.

"It says *Unis*. Monroe mentioned it was the name of another pharaoh."

"Of course." Erica sighed, glad to be back to an area in which she was well versed. Something else to think about. Other than the solidity of the arm still pressing into hers. "Unis was supposed to have ascended to the sky like a falcon on the wind. It makes more sense now."

She grinned at Matt but moved away, taking back a bit of control. "Do you know what his name means?"

"No, but I bet you can't wait to tell me." Matt leaned back in his seat as well, as if her retreat made him realize they'd been close to one another.

"It means he is one whose spiritual eye is opened."

Matt held her gaze. "So it has a religious connotation, but what's the relation between this Pharaoh Unis and the tattoos?"

"I don't know. It may just be the meaning behind his name rather than an actual worship of the man himself." Erica paused and looked up at nothing in particular. "Now that I think about it, there's some mention of Unis having sat with Amun while the God ate a meal, but I'm still not sure that matters."

"Speaking of a meal, here come the lunch trays." He gave her a look of distaste. "I guess you were the right pick for this job."

Erica was caught off guard by the mood swing and his shift to disgruntlement. She'd thought they'd been making progress. "Why is that such a problem for you? Is it because I'm a woman?"

He stared up the aisle, refusing to look at her. "You would think that."

She flipped her napkin open with a snap. "That wasn't exactly a denial. In fact, it almost supports my suspicion."

Matt just smiled at her obvious irritation.

Erica's now sour mood was conveyed by the bite in her words. "I don't understand the urgency. We've got a religious group that's a little off the charts, and they're looking for canopic vases belonging to a long dead queen. Plus, Monroe said there aren't that many of them."

"He said there weren't as many as are found in Christianity, Islam, or Buddhism." Matt let the statement hang in the air.

She narrowed her eyes at him. "What is it? Tell me what you're thinking of not telling me."

"Fine." He turned back to her in a sharp move. "We told you they don't recruit members, but there are still plenty that have found their way to the theology of Kherep Amun. Remember, this group was founded at least a thousand years before the time of Christ. That means the original members had centuries to pass beliefs to their sons and their sons and so on. You get the picture."

Erica didn't need to do the math. "So they've expanded their following exponentially and then some."

"They've been prolific. We're getting the idea that there may be a million or more worldwide."

"And?" she prompted.

"When they get what they're after, it will start a ripple effect. It will ignite cells all over the world that will in turn spread to the next. Whatever it is they've been planning to do will be set into motion."

"Why now? How long have they been looking for Hatshepsut, and have they made any progress?" Ice cubes shifted in her drink, startling her. In a reflexive action, she put her hand to her chest.

Matt didn't answer, but stared at her hand still resting below her throat. "What's wrong?" she asked, but he remained fixated on her hand where it clutched the material of her shirt. He was looking at her, but his gaze was far away.

Erica relaxed her arm and let it fall to her lap, studying him as he broke from his trance and rubbed the back of his neck.

"Matt? You never answered my question."

The eyes that rose to meet hers were cold and hard. "You're asking for information we just don't have, yet."

As the significance of that set in, Erica began to worry her bottom lip. She thought over what he'd said and all she'd read in the file. "You still haven't told me why they're dangerous."

"That's part of what you're here to help us find out. We'll know more after we search the temple." He turned forward to eat, telling her he was done with the conversation.

They finished their meals in silence. After their trays had been cleared, Matt tucked a pillow behind his head and settled on his side. He faced away from her.

A new sense of fear was burgeoning in Erica's gut, but she decided to close her eyes and try to get some rest as well. They still had hours to go before connecting to their final flight in London. Then they would be headed for Egypt.

Between the new information she'd learned about the cult and the way Matt kept changing gears, her mind would probably be running full speed for another hour. She plumped her pillow a little too harshly and wished for a sleeping pill.

She needed to rest her mind. To be prepared. There would be plenty of time to rehash everything they had said, as well as things she wished she'd asked when they made their final destination.

And she would be asking those questions, because out she

was certain of one thing.

Matt knew more than he was saying.

5

The reassurance that it was a dry heat meant little to Matt and Erica as they drove toward the west bank of the Nile River. The sun wasn't even a glimmer on the horizon, but the earth still seemed scorched from the previous day. Sand practically sizzled into the air.

A man had greeted them at the airport and led them to a black jeep before handing Matt a piece of paper and leaving. When Erica asked about the note, Matt gave her a terse, "Directions," before hopping into the driver's seat.

Erica ground her teeth and climbed in beside him. The man switched too easily between charm and bad-attitude. He seemed to forget they were on the same side. When she'd told him she didn't need directions to Hatshepsut's tomb, he gunned the engine and said, "We have to make a stop first."

Riding in silence, she observed the world around her. She took note of fresh signs of societal change while appreciating the things that remained the same.

Egypt had once been the most powerful civilization in the world, and the grandeur of that long ago society could still be glimpsed in the city of Luxor. Ornate décor struggled to shine through the dust that stirred from dirty streets. Since the tourist trade had died off considerably, Luxor was not as busy as in past, more prosperous days. A blessing or a curse, depending on how one made his living.

Matt stopped the jeep outside a building that emanated thick smells. Given the dank atmosphere, it might roughly be described as a restaurant. On a good day. But Erica knew they hadn't slipped into the darkened alley to pick up food. She waited in the jeep until Matt returned with a black duffel bag, tossing it in the back as well.

"I don't even want to know," she murmured while flipping through the pages of a pamphlet on Egyptian tours.

He shifted into first gear, muttering, "No, you probably don't," before speeding off into the warm night.

An hour later they were making their way across the rocks and sand near the Valley of the Kings. There was a steep semi-circle of cliffs surrounding the area that also served as a gateway to the royal resting place for those so revered. Outside of this area was where Hatshepsut's true temple could be found. It was one of many structures that were collectively referred to as Deir el-Bahri.

The name of her temple was *Djeser-Djeseru*, which meant the sublime of the sublimes, quite a compliment for a female pharaoh. The love Senmut had felt for his queen was evident in the elegant architecture he had designed for her.

Rows of colonnades reflected the vertical lines of cliffs in the background, and the harmony between land and structure seemed to expand the temple itself. Some of the best-known hieroglyphics in the most vibrant of hues could be found here, and many Egyptologists believed more tombs and treasures were still waiting to be unearthed.

Together Erica and Matt decided on the best vantage point. They would need a clear view of the temple's inscriptions when the sun rose to cast its revealing rays. She didn't know what to expect or how long they would have to find the words they were looking for. Would the clue be a quick flashing signal? Or a subtle glimmer easily missed?

She put her hands on her hips and stared. Assessing. One

morning's sunrise might not be enough. The construction was vast, and its walls were covered with various inscriptions that told the story of Hatshepsut. They couldn't say for sure which time of day would give them the angle of sunlight they needed. The perfect fragment of time could last for hours. Or minutes.

Matt studied Erica as he eased to her side. He could tell she was worried. If the wrinkle between her eyes hadn't given her away, the tackle-the-problem stance would have.

Though her face was stern, her features glowed pink in the light of dawn. The sun hadn't broken yet but was foretelling its own glory. He could almost imagine her as fragile, ethereal.

And he wanted her to be anywhere else than here with him. Why couldn't she have proven to be a coward?

"We need a plan." Her sharp words brought him out of his reverie. The formidable counterpart to her ethereal side was back.

"What kind of plan? We're here where we need to be, and it cost us plenty of *geneh* to bribe the guard to let us in early."

The money was unimportant, but he needed some excuse for his surliness. He'd have to find a better way to channel the protective urge she stirred up in him. He was almost out of excuses for why he always seemed pissed off. The silent treatment was getting harder to keep up, too.

Occasionally she spit out some random piece of trivia or an unexpected observation. And damned if he didn't find himself wanting to dive into a discussion. To make small-talk.

The way her brain worked was fascinating, and it caused the most bizarre comments to come out of her mouth.

Erica's hand flew back, slapping him on the chest. "We should split up. There are different terraces, and we'd be wasting time trying to cover them together. We can each take one, then signal the other if we find anything."

Matt grunted. "Signal. What were you thinking, maybe a flash of mirrors?" He just couldn't seem to control himself.

She huffed. A princess deigning to speak to a pauper. "No.

One of us won't be facing the sun, so that wouldn't work even if you had been serious. What do you have in mind? This is your supposed area of expertise."

He wasn't sure if it was the moving shadows alerting him to the sun's imminent arrival or the fact that she'd insulted his competence. Whatever the motivation, he found himself tossing the miniature radio up in the air so she'd have to lunge to catch it. "How about we use these?"

Matt left her gaping after him as he turned on one foot to head toward the upper terrace. He tossed a parting shot over his shoulder. "The talk button should be self-explanatory."

He was glad the sand smothered his stomps, so Erica wouldn't realize she'd gotten to him. She sure knew how to push his metaphorical buttons, so maybe staying pissed wouldn't be that hard after all.

Erica briefly considered nailing Matt in the back of his head as he marched away, but there was no way she was going to do something like that. She would need the radio intact.

She took three long deep breaths, trying desperately to remember why she'd come. And to remind herself of the prize at the end of the riddles. Hopefully, she wouldn't have to tolerate Matt Pierce for more than a few days.

How difficult could the clue be to solve? This was the new millennium, and people today loved their puzzles. Herself included. *Let's see what you've got, Senmut.*

A golden glow began to fall across the walls of the building, and Erica pushed aside her internal conversation. As usual, she was simply awed by the work of civilizations from so long ago. What they had been capable of was astounding. The temple seemed to take a deep breath of anticipation, and Erica found herself doing the same.

Then the gods opened a giant version of Pandora's Box. Sunlight broke over the horizon, instantly burnishing the valley. All around her sands threw off the slightest glisten of crystals, while crevasses etched into the landscape stayed hidden. Dark patches slithered along the mountainside.

But the temple was alight with the glory of the sun god. Ra had spoken.

Erica knew they had to work fast if they were going to cover all of Djeser-Djeseru before the sun rose too high in the sky. She systematically began working her section, moving from one back corner and around to the front, across, and eventually winding to the opposite corner.

She and Matt had agreed to leave the back side as a last resort since the sun wouldn't fall on the area directly. And by the time the light shone from overhead, the posterior portion would be blocked by the backdrop of mountains.

After a while, Erica glanced up and saw Matt working around the temple in a similar fashion. Sweat beads began to form on her upper lip and not entirely from the heat. She was beginning to worry this was not going to be as easy as she and Monroe had imagined in their dreams of discovery.

Nothing was ever that easy, she knew. Dreams might be the fuel that got you there, but discipline and determination had to kick in and do the rest.

The radio in her ear jolted her and interrupted her perusal of a battle scene. Matt's voice was controlled but held a hint of eagerness. "I think you need to come up here. There are some words that stand out."

Erica didn't need to be asked twice. "I'm on my way."

She wanted to run, but they had also agreed to remain as inconspicuous as possible. She calmly but quickly joined him on the second terrace where he was examining words she could tell were in the form of a quote.

"Where?" Erica asked, realizing she was panting a little from the controlled exertion.

He stepped back and to the left then indicated she should do the same. "Now walk slowly to the right and tell me what you see. You almost have to stare at it like one of those posters with a hidden picture. Don't take your eyes off it."

She did exactly as he asked but saw nothing. Then she did it again more slowly. Still nothing.

She jumped when Matt's firm hands fell on her shoulders. He moved in closer until she could feel his chest against her back. "Move with me," he whispered, then guided her in an easy glide. "Keep your eyes on the words and tell me when you see something change."

Erica swallowed against a dry throat, but held her gaze to the words as if her life depended on it. Matt's hands burned on her shoulders, the firmness of his chest a strange comfort. Almost before she could register it, a glimmer of bright gold slid over the words from top to bottom in a diagonal fashion.

"Wait. I see it." She moved back to the left and watched the flash again, but in the opposite direction. She laughed, almost giddy with relief. "It's wonderful. The chiseling of the stone must be amazingly precise to get that effect."

"Now we know why it's gone unnoticed." Matt stepped away and put on his sunglasses. "Even if someone saw the light, they would chalk it up to a trick of the eye. It was dumb luck that I happened to catch it."

Erica smiled at him. "It wasn't. You were meticulous. I saw you." She focused again on the script before he thought to wonder why she had been watching him. She would never admit she'd been noticing the way his arms filled out the sleeves of his shirt. Or the fit of the dark pants he wore. He was dressed like a black ops agent or something. In spite of the heat.

She'd only taken a few, quick glimpses. Of course.

Brushing her hand across the stone, she asked, "These are the words I saw flash. Do you agree?"

Matt peered over the top of his sunglasses. "Yeah, that's the line."

Erica read the words out loud. "You must have followed the path of the sun."

"We definitely did that." Matt rolled the girth of his shoulders as if shrugging off a burden.

Erica read the rest of the text surrounding the line. "It's part of a quote from the rulers of the land of Punt. The journey to Punt was one of Hatshepsut's most memorable successes.

"Just traveling to another place?"

"It's a little more involved than that. It was a trading expedition that brought back luxuries never before seen in Egypt. It was also a version of foreign diplomacy." Erica whispered to herself as she reread the entire text.

Matt blew out a pent-up breath. "Okay, so what does it tell us? Where do we go from here? This place called Punt?"

"I don't know." It pained Erica to admit it. "Punt is really more of an area. Its actual location is a topic of debate. In fact, it's often referred to as the mystical land of Punt."

"You must have followed the path of the sun." Her brows knitted as she tapped a finger to her bottom lip. "This is what the ruling king and queen of Punt said to Hatshepsut's people when they came from the river. They assumed that only those approved by the gods would have been able to find their exotic and bountiful land, so they lavished the explorers with gifts."

Matt remained quiet, letting Erica work it out.

And she did. "I guess we're back to searching the walls," she said with certainty.

Matt stood still, dark glasses reflecting the expansive sand dunes. "For what?"

"We should look for anything to do with Punt, other quotes, or texts of any kind, even actual drawings that depict the expedition or its results."

Matt looked around at the overwhelming tribute to the queen who would be king. "You're kidding. I was able to help you look for a flash of light, but I don't read hieroglyphics."

"I know. You can study images and scenes. Keep your eye out for anything featuring a boat." Erica realized the chore they had before them. "I vote we get some breakfast first."

For once she and Matt were in complete agreement. He

nodded once, decisively. "I'll buy."

6

They decided to cover as much of the outside walls as possible before the heat of the day became unbearable. The orange dunes and solid stone radiated heat onto anyone foolish enough to stand still for it.

Erica gave in first. She'd been determined not to crumble before Matt, but her tongue felt as rough as a cat's. Finally giving in, she spoke into her headset. "Matt. Come in."

The first thing she heard was a chuckle. "Erica, why are you whispering? No one can hear my earpiece."

She was so hot and tired she forgot to be insulted and laughed at herself instead. "I guess I'm suffering from delirium or heat exhaustion or both. I vote we mark our spots and move indoors for a while."

"Sounds good. Are you drinking water?"

"Of course," she snapped. He had reminded her ten times in the last twenty-four hours as if she had no experience with a desert climate. "I can take care of myself. I'm not an idiot."

Matt's grunt carried through the bud in her ear before he added, "You sound like my sister."

Erica grinned, feeling a sudden camaraderie with a person she didn't even know. "Then I feel for her."

"Why would you say that?" he growled.

"You don't know?" Erica chuckled. "I'll meet you inside, boss man." She ended the transmission and headed toward the entrance, wishing she could see his face right about then.

Instead she studied the temple as she entered. Archaeologists had first started investigating the tombs at Deir el-Bahri in 1881. Despite a century gone by, not one royal mummy had ever been found, though some of the more valuable artifacts had started surfacing on the black market.

Once the grave robbing had been harnessed, the tombs were dutifully excavated and emptied out by more official means. Today the ancient artwork carved and painted on the buildings was on display for tourists from all parts of the world.

Erica almost felt sad as she walked up the carefully built, wooden ramp. Gone were the days of crawling into collapsible tunnels with bits of earth falling down through flashlight beams. Deir el-Bahri had been forced into the modern world. But at least this included electricity, which would be of great help as she and Matt scoured Hatshepsut's inner sanctum.

Lights from below the walkway were splayed across jewel-toned paintings. The pictures must have been exceptionally bright in original form, considering their clarity two thousand years later.

Few people traipsed the hallways inside, since no tour groups were being led through. Erica imagined the nightmare of trying to keep her place and not miss anything as tourists flowed all around her. Strangers might also wonder why she was systematically reading each and every symbol, mumbling to herself along the way.

She spied Matt and approached. He held out a colorful booklet she recognized as a guide to the temple's architecture and history. "I've already eliminated the places we don't have to look," he said.

Erica's brows shot up. "How did you manage that?"

He smiled. "You were right about the trip to Punt being famous. Not only is it mentioned in the guide, but there's a list of all the references made to it that can be found on the walls."

"Brilliant." Erica was relieved by the news and charmed by the way the grin transformed his serious face. "I knew you'd be good for something." Laughing, she threw her arms around his neck and planted a kiss on his cheek before she realized what she was doing.

As embarrassment washed over her, she tried to step back but instead found herself locked in place by Matt's strong hands on her hips. "That's all I get for my contributions, Doc?"

"Agent Pierce, let go. I lost my decorum for a moment, and I apologize."

"You kissed me," he said, settling his dark eyes on hers with an expression that set off warning sirens in her head. "Told you you'd be a liability."

That was all it took for Erica to find her spine again. If she was such a burden to him, why was he still gripping her like a hard-won prize? She narrowed her own eyes and flashed him a wicked grin. *Time to turn this situation around.*

The last thing Matt expected was for Erica to rise up and meld her warm lips to his. The kiss was chaste but was more tempting than he would have liked. Than he *should* have liked. The sweet meeting of their mouths was enough to make him forget where they were and what they needed to be doing.

Erica slid slowly away. Arms crossing over her chest, she asked, "Are you always so easily distracted?"

Matt's jaw clamped down as he gave her a stern look. The kiss had been foolish, but he could only cast stones at himself. She'd simply been excited about his finding the booklet, but when she'd flung her arms around him, in complete innocence, he'd experienced a rush of raw and raging desire.

Dr. Erica Conner smelled sinful with a little desert heat added to her natural female scent.

Oblivious to Matt's errant imaginings, Erica flipped open the booklet as if nothing had happened. "I think we should just follow along the list, since it's organized by tiers already." Her big blue eyes flashed up at him. "Sound good?"

"Sure," Matt said evenly. Again he found himself trying to sort out what he knew about this woman, or what he thought he knew. She was as much of an enigma as the mysterious drawings on the walls around them.

As she took a determined right turn and traversed a long corridor, he followed in silence. But it didn't take long for him to realize the view from behind had its benefits. *Why did the leading archaeologist in this area of expertise have to be this woman? Damn you, Monroe, for not being ten years younger.*

Even with the guidebook in hand, looking over each depiction of Punt was a slow and tedious process. They were studying the third one mentioned in the booklet when Matt noticed a character in the drawing that resembled an insect. "We're not going to run into any scarabs down here, are we?"

Erica's hand stilled over a golden man with a wolf-shaped head, standing on a ship as others around him dropped their oars in the water. Surely she hadn't detected concern in Matt's voice. "Are you telling me that with your background and experience, you're afraid of bugs?" She tried not to smile, but couldn't contain it when he scowled down at her.

"No. I just want to know what to expect before I go poking my hand down into any dark holes."

She couldn't resist taking advantage of the moment and put on her best scientist face. "They are rare, but often come out when things get quiet. You know, when there aren't as many people around."

"Like now," he stated.

Erica nodded and leaned in as if about to share a secret. "They travel in packs, but usually give off a distinctive high-pitched sound when they catch the scent of meat, so at least you'll hear them coming."

She swallowed a grin as Matt's brow creased and knew he was probably imagining the flesh-eating scarabs portrayed by some adventure movies. Laughter finally erupted. "But you're trained in hand-to-hand, right?"

Matt sighed. "You're feeding me a big one, aren't you?"

Her answer was more laughter.

He just nodded and lifted one side of his mouth. "Okay. You got me." He went back to perusing the drawing. "But that did not help build my trust in you."

Stealing a glance out of the corner of her eye, Erica saw his mouth was almost smiling. His features were at ease. Stubble was beginning to darken his jawline, and the ruggedness of his handsome face made her stomach pitch. "There really aren't any living scarabs," she said, hoping to get her mind back on their mission. "Scarabs are symbolic creature representing rebirth, so they were often used in décor or jewelry. They're actually modeled after a dung beetle, which is classified as one of the species in *Scaraboidea*."

Matt dropped his hands and turned back to her. "Is that a made up word?"

She held up two fingers. "Scout's honor."

"Yeah. That's three fingers, and I doubt you were ever a scout."

She didn't care to analyze his comment. "You see, the dung beetle lays its eggs in a ball of dung and takes it down into the soil. The young emerge at a later date, and seeing this, people believed it was a dead beetle being reborn from the earth."

"That was enough to make it symbolic?"

"Rebirth and the afterlife were central to the Egyptian society. Mummification was a preparation for the afterworld, and that's also why a person's belongings and all of their riches were buried with them. Just look at the tombs we're surrounded by now."

Matt looked up at the ceilings, also covered in script and artwork. "They can bury me where I fall. That will be plenty for me."

"I agree. However, the ancient Egyptians felt differently. Even a lot of the writings in these tombs are directions for the deceased, sort of like a crib sheet for the afterlife."

He shook his head. "You should be in a classroom."

Stiffening, Erica stared hard at the lines drawn on the stone in front of her. "What do you mean by that?"

"Exactly what I said. You have a way of making dried up dead people and beetles interesting. It wasn't an insult."

"You can hardly blame me. You've made it clear you don't think I belong in the field, which is *very* insulting since I was pretty much raised there. I didn't play with dolls and dresses."

Matt spoke to the wall. "Look, it has nothing to do with you."

"You admitted you didn't even want me along, and every step of the way you've been determined to remind me of that fact." She brushed her hair back with an irritated swipe.

Matt met her determined stare. "This is a job. A life-threatening job with unbelievable consequences if we fail. I don't like having civilians thrown into the mix, especially when it's," he paused and let his eyes travel to her waist and back up before grinding out, "a woman."

Erica gave an abbreviated laugh. "I don't know whether to feel affronted or to swoon at your feet. Was that an admission of your lack of faith in me or the white knight poking his head out?"

"Neither, just the facts. That's what I deal in." And just like that, the militant side of Agent Pierce was back in place.

"Need I remind you that you came to me? You wanted my help and I offered it, for several reasons." Erica's hands went to her hips. "Yes, I'm interested in any artifacts I might acquire ownership of during this journey. I'm very excited about the thrill of the challenge as well."

She held up a finger, implying she wasn't finished. "However, Agent Pierce, I am well aware there may be ramifications. Big ones. Though you've been tight-lipped, bordering on downright secretive, I get it. The bad guys are really bad and are playing for keeps. Well, guess what, Agent Pierce?"

He cocked a brow at that.

"This is what I do. This is my job, and I'm good at it. So,

female or not, I'm what you've got to work with, and maybe you should be a little more grateful."

Fury warmed her face and had her pivoting to look in the opposite direction.

Matt returned to scouring the rock for anything helpful, but Erica was no longer paying him any attention. She stared intently at a wall at the end of the corridor.

"What is it?" Matt asked, as if he'd just noticed her stillness.

"I'm not sure, but there's something about that area that caught my eye. It seems familiar, and I can't figure out why."

He came to stand beside her to look at the scene. It was obviously the return of Senmut from the land of Punt. Animals, plants, and other unidentified packages were being carried from a ship and laid before the people of Egypt.

Matt pointed. "Is that a dwarf?"

"Yes. Supposedly they brought back pygmies as entertainment." Erica spit the words out in disgust. "As pets."

"Let's take a closer look." Matt walked ahead while Erica took her time and closed in more slowly.

The drawings were more intricate than the others they had seen and were embellished with gold and engravings. Some of the smaller pieces had been pried out, probably taken and sold long before the temple was protected from grave robbers.

Erica tapped her foot and worried her bottom lip. She concentrated on a shallow hole in the picture. "There's something wrong here, but I can't put my finger on it."

She then proceeded to do just that and ran the tip of her finger around its rim. "This portion of the drawing represents Punt, from where they had just returned. It's the story of the glories they had seen there, things that obviously couldn't be brought back with them." There were mountains in the background and various structures that told of another society with different beliefs. The hole that held Erica's attention fell in the middle of what appeared to be a building of some sort.

Time had been unkind, and a crack led to one side of the

indentation, ending in a spot where a large chip had fallen away. This is what had kept Erica from seeing what was so clear to her now. "Do you notice anything odd about this marking?"

Matt closed in and took a moment. "It's too perfect. It's as if it's supposed to be there, not like places where the stone has fallen or been broken away."

"Precisely." Erica reached down the neck of her shirt and pulled out the medallion Monroe had given her just before she and Matt had left the States. She held it up to the hole on the wall and slid it perfectly into place.

"Damn," Matt said on a breath. "I can't believe it." He waited while Erica turned the golden piece back and forth within the space. "What do you think it means?"

She didn't answer, too caught up in trying to make the markings on the amulet line up with those on the wall.

"Turn it over," Matt offered.

"What?" she murmured, still trying to get it to work.

"Try the other side."

Erica looked at the medallion and realized she hadn't thought to try the side with the inscription. She had automatically tested the one with the picture.

As soon as she turned it over, she knew Matt had called it correctly. It was like a puzzle piece her brain could tell had the perfect color and shape even before her hand held it just the right way. There was a mental click when the piece lined up and completed the drawing of what was in fact a temple. By looking at the edging of the pendant, they would never have seen how the simple markings could bring an entire picture together.

Erica held it in place and was able to make out an altar from the lines as well as the ancient symbols that spelled out a name. Another hidden name, like the one in the tattoo. A reference to Amun, the god who had to keep his identity a secret or have his power stolen.

"El," she said.

Matt lifted one shoulder. "What is it?"

"It's not an it, but who. El was another god, an Asiatic god also referred to as Atem in Egypt and Cronus in Greek," she said.

"Then why is the name El found in an Egyptian pharaoh's tomb?"

Erica tapped her bottom lip. "Senmut traveled to an area known as the land of Punt that we feel sure is East of here. While in this area he must have seen a temple dedicated to the worship of El. He also used that name in case the wrong people found this clue, so they wouldn't understand." Her brows knitted. "I'm trying to think about the time period and where this temple might have been. The general vicinity of what we think was Punt."

"That sounds pretty vague." Matt looked doubtful.

"When you consider we're talking about civilizations that were in existence thousands of years ago, it narrows things down considerably. The world was less crowded back then, but like I said, El had many names and was worshipped by as many different cultures." She breathed deeply, her mind racing. "I can't think clearly. I need a map."

Kneeling to the cold stone floor, Erica rummaged in her backpack. She pulled out an atlas and quickly found pages with Africa and the Middle East. "Amun supposedly turned his face to the sunrise, the East, where he created the land of Punt. Historians still argue about the exact location, possibly Somalia or the Petra region. No one knows for sure, but when we factor in what we know about the temple..." Erica trailed off. "Damn."

Matt knelt beside her. "What's wrong?"

She ran her hands over the surface of the map. "What if it's not there anymore?" Fear pounded in her chest as she lifted her eyes to his. "You realize that any one of these places we need could have been destroyed by now? In fact they all may be gone. What if we can't go on from here?"

Erica suddenly realized how much she wanted to succeed. She could almost taste the glory of revealing Hatshepsut's vases at the museum's opening. She could hear the sighs of her colleagues, impressed by the reputable collection built in her father's and grandfather's names.

Erica chastised herself as Matt kneeled as well, joining her on the floor. She didn't see doubt or loathing in his eyes now, but a strange sense of calm. Confidence. Her fingers stilled and she tried to concentrate through the haze of guilt that clouded her mind. *Stop being so selfish. Kherep Amun is searching for the relic, too, and the reason can't be good. Here I am thinking only of myself.*

"Erica. You can do this." Matt laid a hand on top of hers. "You can."

His faith in her made her feel even worse. She cleared her throat. "Maybe...I..." Focusing again on the map, she took a deep breath. "Okay, we're looking for those who worshipped El and used that name specifically. Temples, east of here, civilizations that flourished in that time with the means to enslave and build." She sat back on her heels and gazed up at the carvings on the wall, the clue Senmut left for the worshippers of Hatshepsut to one day find.

Suddenly the lines of the painted temple triggered a memory. "I think I know." She grabbed Matt's arm. "A friend of mine has been working at an excavation site in Jordan. We haven't spoken in a while, but he's been there for a couple of years. I'm sure he still is."

"You think he'll know more about where this temple is?" Matt asked.

"I think it may be the very one where he and his team are located. He told me all about it when he first got the assignment. He was excited because the structure turned out to be older than originally thought. It actually dates to about 1600 BC."

"So it would have been there when Hatshepsut and Senmut

were alive." Matt nodded. "Good."

"He also mentioned that the original building was built by Canaanites." Erica grinned and waited, allowing Matt to finish her thought.

"And I bet I can guess who those Canaanites worshiped." He hiked a brow. "Our good buddy, El."

Renewed hope bloomed for Erica. "Yes. I guess we do know where to head next." She stuffed the atlas back in her bag and stood, but before she could walk away, Matt held her by placing a hand on her shoulder.

"Erica." His fingers were heavy. And so was the tone of his voice. "Before we go, I need you to show me something else."

"What else do we need?" A trickle of instinctual fear rolled down her spine.

Matt released her from his grip. "It has to do with Kherep Amun." His eyes seem to shadow over before he said, "I need to see the Cannibal Text."

7

The nights were for children.

These words had chased each other in the darkness of his dreams the night before. These words were still on his tongue as the small boy rounded the corner like he did every day on his way to school.

The child had black hair and eyes, rounded cheeks, and a silver crucifix hanging on a chain beneath the white shirt of an academy uniform.

The man snarled his lip. What he did this day would make these foolish Christians quiver and cry, run for the safety of their locked doors. Maybe then the sheep would have less faith in their empty God and learn to take better care of their children here on Earth.

But this place, this country had been selected because of the number of practicing Catholics. The man and his fellow believers would bring their fists down on the heart of the false religion. Deal a blow to the church that had enslaved the world for so long.

Then all the children would be theirs for the taking.

Rural Italy was unlike America, where people watched their little ones like hawks, always on guard for the pedophiles. That was a truly sick crime that would finally be abolished when his people and his god came to power. How anyone could do that to a child was beyond him.

He knew people would say the same about what he and the others would do to the little boy walking toward him, but they could never understand. They were nothing but swine. Blind fools allowing themselves to be led to the slaughter.

He knew the moment he'd been spotted. Little Marco had seen him and walked right up, within arm's length. "*Buon giorno*. Mr. Beni, why are you here?"

Even though people were more naive in the small *citta*, the man had taken precautions. There could be no mistakes now that the awakening had begun. They all had their duties to fulfill.

He had taken a job at the school years before and was well known and trusted there. It had been an ideal way to find the perfect one. Now the innocent face of the chosen child smiled up at his favorite teacher with adoration.

"We are not going to the school this morning. Since you have performed so well this term, I made arrangements to take you somewhere special today."

The streets teemed with life as everyone around them rushed to be somewhere else. Vendors hawked fresh baked goods or fruits for those who'd left without a morning meal. The warm yellow sun seemed to fill the air with an energy that whispered over his skin.

Marco rose up on his toes in excitement. "Where will we go? To the zoo? I want to see the monkeys play and throw things at people." The delight in simple pleasures remained intact at such a young age. The boy's dark eyes danced with anticipation and the thrill of being singled out for a day alone with the man who made learning so much fun.

Mr. Beni always made the children laugh.

The man took hold of the small hand placed so trustingly in his. "I can't tell you where we're going. It will have to be a secret until we get there." He kneeled down, eye level with the boy. "Can you keep a secret, Marco?"

The child answered with an enthusiastic nod. He would do anything Mr. Beni asked him to do.

They walked up the street in the direction from which Marco had just come but turned in the direction opposite of his house. As they edged their way through the crowded streets and toward the outskirts of town, Marco skipped along the cobblestone street and held tightly to the man's hand. Soon long stretches of field and sky opened up before them, and the noise of city life faded.

A lone dog barked somewhere in the distance.

8

Complete physical and emotional exhaustion swamped Erica as she sat heavily on the sofa. The plush green couch curved in a crescent shape and was covered in pillows. Though elegant, the color seemed much too bold in contrast to the red silk that papered the cabin walls. The décor was decidedly middle-eastern.

She and Matt had opted to cross the Mediterranean Sea on a slow boat ride that would allow them a chance to get some much-needed rest. The day had been long and unsettling to say the least.

Erica removed her boots, folded her legs under herself, and waited while Matt tipped the young man who'd guided them to the room. The flash of several colorful bills and the promise of more ensured their dinner would be delivered quickly.

She found herself studying the man who'd been assigned to aid and protect her. His coal-black hair was cleanly clipped in the back, and she had to admire the curve of the broad, muscular shoulders. She was also pleasantly surprised by the Arabic that rolled deftly off his tongue. And a little bit excited. Matt was turning out to be much more than a body guard

Afraid Matt would read her dirty mind when he faced her, Erica feigned a yawn and stretched her hands above her head. That was when she realized how sore she was. Her grimace did not go unnoticed, and before she opened her eyes, strong, warm hands had landed on her shoulders.

Her first instinct was to protest, but her aches melted away under Matt's skillful kneading. With everything they were involved in, it felt so good to just relax into the heat of his touch.

His nearness also helped drive away the images that had planted themselves in her mind. Grotesque scenes she'd begun seeing behind closed lids after she'd learned how dark the evil they were fighting really was. *The Cannibal Text.* Her stomach churned. *My God. What are we facing?*

She stiffened and pulled away from Matt, aware she'd let herself fall back on his chest. Recalling the horror of what he'd shared with her today snapped her back to the unfortunate present. Back to a reality where she couldn't get close to Matt.

Bad circumstances. Bad timing. And definitely...bad juju.

Why would she think he intended anything in the first place? If she recalled correctly, she'd been the one to kiss his cheek. And then *she'd* been the one to kiss his sexy mouth.

But that sort of behavior was going to stop this minute. She and Matt were simply in a stressful situation that required close contact. They were of the same age and both single. No excessive math skills needed to figure out that one. They were simply looking for comfort. A distraction from the killers that were out there waiting to pounce.

But this was no time for a romantic pastime.

"What's the matter?" Matt asked. A scowl covered his face when she jerked upright.

"I just don't think that's a good idea." Erica shook her head.

"Getting kinks rubbed out after a grueling day when we still have plenty of hard work ahead of us? How is that not a good idea?"

She turned to glare at him. "You know what I mean. After that kiss today, I just want to make sure we still understand each other."

He gave her his annoyingly cocky grin. "You mean the kiss

that you gave me?"

"I was just making a point."

"You did a damn good job of it, but don't worry. If I wanted to follow up on it you'd know. I wouldn't try an adolescent tactic like a backrub. Sort of paints the picture of sleazy boss coming on to the young secretary."

Erica crossed her arms. "Precisely."

"Precisely," he echoed, his mouth in a grim line. "How about you take the first shower? And be sure to lock the door in case I can't control myself."

Erica decided not to respond to the last comment as she made her way to the bathroom. She knew she'd done the right thing, even if it had offended Matt. Then again, her practice of drawing breath to sustain life seemed to offend him. He had a perpetual bug up his FBI butt.

It was probably a scarab.

Pulling out the band that held her hair, Erica decided a hot shower and mango scented body wash would go a long way in making her forget all about the sordid discussion they'd had after leaving the temple. A little tropical paradise to disguise the dread filling her heart.

Outside Matt listened until the water began to drum against the shower floor. Then he pressed his face into his hands. His intention had originally been to ease some of Erica's pain, but damned if other ideas hadn't assailed him as soon as he'd laid hands on her.

Settling into the silken pillows, he imagined the woman on the other side of the door and how those small but strong hands would be smoothing suds away from delicate curves. Black hair would glide over her shoulders, sleek and shiny, while droplets on lashes surrounded the blue eyes he couldn't seem to get out of his mind.

Hell. He probably should have taken the first shower. And ice cold.

He knew better than to let someone in, and Erica was testing the chinks in his armor. Even if the interest was only physical, she was a variable he just didn't need.

Matt told himself that several times as he listened to the running shower. As he tried to force out the images of the irritating and intriguing female he'd been stuck with. *Damn you, Monroe. Old man with a bum knee.*

The food had arrived by the time Erica stepped out of the bathroom. Her hair dripped onto the white T-shirt she'd paired with gray shorts. After her conversation with Matt, she found herself wishing for full pajamas, though with the heat, they would seem out of place.

He slid past her on his way to bathe himself, pointedly avoiding contact. "The food's here. Don't wait for me."

Erica thought he'd been a little too brusque, but then again, maybe she deserved it. Shrugging, she moved to take him up on his offer and find out what was under the silver lids of the serving trays. Most of her previous meals in Egypt had consisted of sandwiches and snacks that could be taken to dig sites in coolers. Erica wasn't sure what the food before her was, but she was famished.

She lifted the first lid to find a warm, colorful dish with a delicious aroma. Next was a serving set that appeared to hold a steaming drink, possibly some sort of tea. She was surprised to find a deep red liquid with a light floral scent, one she didn't recognize. She noticed the small cards behind each offering. "*Karkady*," she said aloud, testing the word on her lips.

"It's made from hibiscus petals."

Erica jumped to find Matt right behind her. She was a little embarrassed to have been caught bent over the tray like a curious schoolgirl. "That was a fast shower."

"I only needed to get clean. That, and I'm starving."

The way his gaze lingered made Erica wonder if more was implied than a need for food. She smiled away her own nervousness. "I don't recognize the others either."

She noticed how good he smelled, clean and woodsy.

He took her hand and pulled her around the table, back onto the sofa, then pointed to the warm dish she'd wondered about.

"This is one of the national dishes of Egypt, *ful medames*. It's made with fava beans, garlic, olive oil, and other ingredients I don't remember. You take the bread and dip it into this or the *dukkah*, which is made from a mixture of chopped nuts and seeds."

He demonstrated by taking a piece of bread and offering Erica a taste of both dishes. The sensuality of being fed by a gorgeous man, on a boat, in foreign waters sent a shiver over her arms while fingers of pleasure unfurled in her stomach.

Matt held her eyes with his as she bit from the bread. She knew he was about to kiss her, she just knew it, and found herself more than ready. How quickly the steadfast had fallen.

He turned instead and began to fill a plate for himself, leaving Erica with no choice but to do the same. Had she been imagining things, or was he only toying with her? Hiding her disappointment, she concentrated on the glorious food.

She chewed slowly, reminding herself to keep an emotional distance from Matt. She stopped thinking clearly whenever he touched her. Or looked at her in a certain way. Or got so close she could smell him.

Man. She was in trouble.

When they were both finished eating, Matt removed their plates and pulled a computer from one of the black duffel bags. He set it up on the table and connected some other components Erica didn't recognize.

"What's all that?" she asked as she poured a second cup of the hibiscus tea.

"We're set up to use MILSTAR with MPEG4." He didn't bother to look at her but continued attaching cables and wires.

"In English, please."

Matt sighed as if dealing with a persistent child. "We're accessing MILSTAR, the military's version of COMSAT…um, satellite communications. We'll be doing so with MPEG4, a conferencing software that will allow us to stay in touch with Dr. Monroe, no matter where we are on the globe.

"Oh," was all Erica could think of in response.

"Our friend, the doctor, should get a message requesting a conference, and then we wait until we hear back from him."

"That's handy. I guess we're lucky to have your military connections. Especially if we get buried under a collapsed tomb."

His look said her humor was unappreciated.

"Matt, I'm sorry if I upset you before. I know you weren't trying anything. Believe it or not, I respect you, and I know you have a job to do. I shouldn't have made assumptions." Unsure where the sudden declaration had come from, she smiled gently at him, hoping for a truce.

The expletive shooting out of his mouth was the last thing she expected in response to her olive branch.

He rose from where he'd been kneeling by the monitor and walked to stare out the window and into the black of the Mediterranean night. His hands gripped the windowsill as he spoke. "Let's get one thing straight. I *am* a professional, and nothing is going to distract me from doing the job I was sent here to do. I've been tracking the movements of Kherep Amun for four years, and I will stop them, no matter what it takes."

Erica stuttered, caught off guard. "Of course, I..."

"Wait." He faced her again. "I want you to understand that this assignment is my top priority. My first concern." He strode toward her and pulled her up to meet him. "Do you understand?"

Erica wasn't sure if she should be afraid or not but managed to nod and whisper, "Yes."

"Good," he said before crushing her up against him and covering her mouth with his. His arms wrapped around her waist as she felt her own slide up to his neck, then back down to his shoulders. Their bodies were like magnets.

She trembled in response to the passion erupting, and it became clear she'd wanted and needed this from the first night he'd walked into her life. Despite her trepidation, something about this man unsettled her very being. Whether she would end up loving or hating him in the end, there was no question that Matt Pierce...*affected* her.

Fear and logic melted away as the two clung to each other, soft form pressed to firm, a burning sensation shooting straight to the dark places that cried out for more. They moved together, exploring and demanding, and the aching need grew stronger with each new discovery.

As Matt lowered her gently onto the velvety fabric of the sofa, his motions were a mix of tenderness and a barely suppressed urgency to have her. To take her.

He'd tried to make it clear he would never have imagined becoming involved under these circumstances. Or even under ordinary circumstances. But as he'd been learning every minute they'd spent together, Erica was no ordinary woman.

And he'd held himself in check for as long as possible.

Her tongue was hot and smooth on his, stirring up feelings he'd forgotten were even possible. A madness rushed through him. To get closer. Deeper.

He slid his hand slowly along the curve of her thigh and made his way over hip and waist to settle beneath the weight of her breast. There he paused, still making love to her sweet mouth, he waited, giving Erica one last chance to pull away and deny him.

She didn't, and with a groan he settled himself between her thighs, the heat of their flesh burning through layers of clothing. Erica threw her head back with a gasp and clutched him tighter to her chest, allowing him to explore the nape of her neck with his lips. He marveled at the feel of her, wondering if anything had ever been so intense, so consuming.

A shrill beeping filled the room, startling them apart. Erica flinched in panic and surveyed the room, searching for the source.

Matt reared back with a growl and muttered an oath as

the monitor on the table blinked to life beside them. Within seconds the image of Dr. Daniel Monroe filled the screen. The English gentleman blinked and cleared his throat.

Matt pushed aside his own frustration as he took in Erica's disheveled appearance and flushed cheeks. Somehow he managed a grin and asked, "Did I mention the conference would be in video?"

9

Erica practically shoved Matt off and sat up, smoothing her hair into place in the process. "Dr. Monroe." She coughed behind her hand and quickly put her business demeanor in place. She was a grown woman and wouldn't make things worse by offering apologies.

Of course, there was the slight chance the distinguished older man hadn't seen her and Matt wrapped up in each other when the monitor snapped on. Maybe there was a second or two of lag time in the connection.

A wolf whistle and familiar voice shot that assumption all to hell. "Looks like you two discovered something besides old bones and jars."

Erica sat up straighter as her friend came into view over Monroe's shoulder. "Karen? What are you doing there? Are you both still in Georgia?"

"Nope. I managed to wrangle myself an all-expenses-paid trip to the land of wine and snails." Her wrinkled nose accompanied the latter mention.

"You're in France?"

"Lyon, to be precise." This from Dr. Monroe. "Your friend possesses rare powers of persuasion." The look on his face was a cross between annoyance and admiration, both directed toward Karen.

Matt joined the conversation. "They're at INTERPOL headquarters," he told Erica before directing a question to Monroe. "Finding everything you need?"

"Yes. Yes. The authorities from various countries all seem to be cooperating, unlikely as that may seem. It's to be expected when criminal activity becomes an international concern."

Matt picked up on the implications. "International? What's happened?"

Monroe grew somber. "I'm afraid it has begun."

"What's begun?" Erica shot up straighter, more embarrassed than ever to be caught making out like an errant teenager. If Monroe meant what she thought he did...Glancing to the side, she saw Matt's features etched in stone and wondered if he felt the same amount of shame as she did.

Her father wouldn't be very proud of her behavior. She'd been given a vital assignment with more at stake than the recovery of artifacts, and Dr. Daniel Monroe, a man they'd both admired, had caught her with her pants almost down.

Even after she'd been given full disclosure regarding the Cannibal Text, she'd tossed her better judgment out the door to make room for lust. Her intelligent female persona had taken a heavy blow.

Monroe continued, and his next words held even greater impact. "We've had two reports of murder, both crime scenes displaying evidence that assures us it was the work of Kherep Amun. A woman in the states, Washington D.C., and a boy in a small town just outside of Vatican City."

Matt scowled. "So they're slipping political messages into their blood work as well." He inched away from Erica, a barely perceptible move, but enough to hint at his own discomfort.

"Evidently." This from Karen who stepped in closer and tapped Monroe on the shoulder. "Don't sugarcoat it. Erica's knee-deep in this now and should be prepared."

"You're correct. No sugar-coating." Monroe hesitated briefly and drew in a breath before continuing. "The killings had ritualistic elements. They did things you wouldn't want to see in your worst nightmares. We'll send you the photos and details. Where are you now?"

"On the water, but we'll be arriving in Jordan shortly. We plan to meet up with a friend of Erica's in Pella. I'd like to get the details as soon as possible."

"Who's the friend, and can you trust them?" Karen asked, her usual cautious self.

"Cameron," Erica said. "Did I ever mention..."

"Cam?" Karen interrupted with a devilish smile. "Wish I could be there." On the screen, she shifted her eyes to Matt. "The meet and greet should be interesting."

"You think he'll be trouble?" Matt asked, stiffening.

Karen tilted her head meaningfully. "That depends on your definition of trouble."

Erica shot her friend a threatening glare, but Karen simply shrugged and grinned.

Matt narrowed his eyes then turned his attention back to Monroe. "We already have an idea of what happened at the crime scenes and what we'll see in those photos. We checked out the text while we were in Luxor."

"Yes. Kherep Amun has taken it more literally than we had hoped." Monroe's face tightened. "Did you find anything in the text that differs from the copies we already had?"

Matt shook his head. "No. It was pretty much the same."

"Tell me about this text," Karen said, a whiff of anger in her tone. Apparently Erica wasn't the only one who'd gotten a coat of sugar.

Erica's stomach rolled with a surge of nausea, but she shared the gory information. "They're referring to the Cannibal Text that Pharaoh Unis had inscribed on the east wall of his tomb. It's a piece of what's collectively called the Pyramid Texts. And the contents of the writings are as horrible as the title implies."

Karen nodded solemnly. "I saw the pictures and what was done to those poor people."

"Even after what we read," Erica stopped to take a cleansing breath, "I can't believe they've gone after children."

"Why would they?" Karen asked.

"According to the inscription, and I quote, 'Their big ones are for his morning meal.' It goes on to say that middle-sized ones are for evening, and small ones are for nights. Obviously this refers to adults, children, and I suppose adolescents are the middle-sized, not quite children or adults." Erica closed her eyes briefly. "Let's just pray that they stop there."

Karen's forehead furrowed. "What could be worse than killing a child?"

"The next line spoke of the elderly," Matt said. "They are to be used as what they call incense."

"Oh my God." Karen blanched. "You can't be serious."

No one answered.

Monroe finally broke the heavy silence. "Erica, do you have any idea why they are acting out the text so specifically?"

"I believe so. Tell me if you agree," Erica said. "As you know, Dr. Monroe, the text is long, but certain points seem to fit into what we know so far about Hatshepsut and her supposed divine father, the god Amun. A line from the writings states that it is the pharaoh who will weigh what is said, together with *Him-Whose-Name-Is-Hidden*. Hatshepsut fills the role of pharaoh and her father, Amun, is the god whose true name is unknown. The one who is hidden. So Kherep Amun could easily apply the meaning of the words to their own purpose. Since the Cannibal Text is even older than Hatshepsut herself, they might even call it prophesy."

Monroe nodded his agreement. "Go on."

"In Egyptian history, there have been many references to cannibalism and the stealing of the consumed person's *ba*, or what we would call a soul. The text refers to removing shadows from their owners, again the soul or spirit, and how by doing so, the cannibal achieves the ability to last forever." Erica raised a shoulder. "At least that's the simplified version."

"It seems to be the only thing that makes sense." Monroe confirmed. "Bindings of willow leaves were found on the bodies. Those carrying out this abomination are following the text exactly. The rituals are disturbingly...organic."

Matt leaned forward, putting his elbows on his knees as he spoke toward the monitor. "Do you have any idea if the murders were performed by the same group?"

"Apparently not." Monroe shook his head.

"Damn. That means different cells are already beginning to operate." Matt took a moment to mull over the news. "I'd be willing to bet that they're still a segment of the initiators, though."

"Initiators?" Erica looked away from the screen to Matt.

He gave her the briefest of glances. "The most elite and highest ranking of Kherep Amun. Only certain members will be allowed to perform the ritual before what they call their day of triumph, which I can only assume means the day they've recovered Hatshepsut's remains. If they do find her, that's when all hell will break loose."

"Wait." Karen held her hand out in a halting motion. "Why now? You said they've been around for a couple thousand years or more, right? What's got them all worked up?"

Erica crossed her arms, an attempt to quell both her sick stomach and the clawing fear in her chest. "We don't know yet. Maybe when we do, we'll be able to move faster."

"Let's hope so, because the bad guys already know what's going on, and they've got knives. Big knives." Karen looked pointedly at her friend as if reminding her to keep her guard up.

Erica forced a grin. "Thanks for the reminder. And I will, Marshal. Promise." She knew how scared Karen was and how helpless she probably felt being out of the action, unable to watch Erica's back.

Karen's trust in Matt had probably been shaken by the earlier display. And who could blame her? If the Kherep Amun members were as informed and as vicious as Matt and Monroe seemed to believe they were, Erica needed to keep eyes up at all times.

That meant no more wandering to the back side. Specifically, Matt's back side.

She almost hoped he was beating himself up as much as she was. She might have kissed him first, but he'd come at her full steam. And she'd welcomed his heat with eager arms.

"Well, I'll try not to worry." Karen had her smile back. "It looks like Agent Pierce has got you covered. Or he's doing his best to."

Erica felt her face burn while Matt remained impassive.

Dr. Monroe simply chose to ignore the insinuation. "Please do be careful, both of you."

"We will. I promise." Erica smiled into the older man's concerned eyes. "We'll be in touch soon."

"Very well," Monroe said. "Matt, you'll find transportation and necessities waiting for you when you dock. Which will be where exactly?"

Matt looked toward the window and into the black night. "Haifa, Israel. We can make our way east from there."

10

Erica and Matt walked in silence as they neared the excavation site. What they'd learned in the course of the conference with Monroe and Karen had been a sobering dose of reality, so they'd both returned to their respective corners to sleep the night away on the boat.

Matt had not slept well, and based on Erica's constant flipping, she hadn't either.

Now patience was wearing thin for both of them, since they'd lost a day of travel time. The car that had been waiting for them in Haifa had broken down, costing them hours until a replacement arrived.

Matt ground his teeth. Kherep Amun was slicing people up, and he'd been stalled by a broken timing belt. Being on the move again was a relief, but every hour was precious. He didn't know how much Intel Kherep Amun had, but they'd been trying to find the mummy and her vases for years. If the cult had any idea Matt was on the move and Erica had been recruited, the danger quotient would jump to one hundred percent.

For all he knew, the cult's network could have members keeping watch at any historical site related to Hatshepsut or Senmut. Hopefully, the place they were headed was off the radar. The longer he and Erica could work undetected, the better chance they would find the relics before Kherep Amun.

And the fewer people would die.

They were close to the next location, and after reviewing the options again, Erica felt sure this was the only one that fit. The next canopic jar had to be here.

Erica's mood had fouled considerably since the night on the boat, not only because they'd been...interrupted and she'd been embarrassed, but because she'd had time to come to grips with the murderous cult.

Kherep Amun considered itself a religious order, but if you took away the ceremonial trappings, they could be seen for what they were. A bloodthirsty collection of delusional men who thought they could eat the flesh of others and gain power. Even dressed up with ancient words and willow leaves, they were nothing but cannibals.

Matt looked again at Erica as she trudged along. They didn't talk much about the killings, and neither mentioned the little boy.

All they could do was get on with the mission. And Matt had to start by keeping his hands off the doctor. He replayed stern instructions to himself one more time. Find the clues, locate the mummy, and get back to his regular life.

He knew too well the risk associated with letting people slip inside his structured existence. They tended to mess up his routine, derail perfectly good plans. And women who looked and talked like Erica were especially skilled at screwing everything up, whether they meant to or not. The proof was in his temporary insanity on the boat. Sex and business? Not a good mix.

So the madness was over. Besides, Erica was fire and ice. Stirring his blood up with her kisses then frosting over when her rigid code of ethics kicked back in.

Matt knew their being together was a bad idea, but not because it was morally wrong. Hell, he could take what he wanted from her at night and still perform his duty during the day, but he planned on making this expedition short and sweet. Ultimately, he just didn't need the hassle.

As they crested a hill and stood overlooking the valley before them, Matt couldn't hide his surprise. This was no rugged terrain. Not what one might envision for in this part of the world.

"Not what you expected, is it?" Erica asked, smiling for the first time that day as they looked toward the Canaanite temple site.

Hills sloped gently, their magical green color dotted with outcroppings of gray stones. Clear, cobalt skies fell as a backdrop for the archaic structures that still remained.

Matt shook his head. "Are you sure we didn't take a wrong turn and end up in Brazil?"

Erica laughed. "If you go by sight alone, you won't know where you are, maybe even think you're in Rome."

Earlier she'd given him a thorough history lesson about Jordan and how its history included many cultures and conquerors. Greeks, Romans, and Muslims had all left their mark, since Jordan was part of the bridge of land connecting Europe, Africa, and Asia. The ancient city of Pella was referred to in Arabic as *Tabaqat Fahl* and was believed to have been inhabited as early as 5000 BC.

As they continued their walk down and through the valley, the influence of other civilizations became more evident. They entered an area at the base where cream and white stones littered the ground in contrast to the lush grass of the hillside. Soon they rounded a curve in the landscape and heard voices and the sound of labor.

Archaeologists and hired hands milled around the worksite, located on a mild incline. Greco-Roman columns rose from the ground and the mostly-intact flooring consisted of tile. Matt noticed patterns that, oddly enough, were very popular in modern American bathrooms.

An ominous hole sat in the middle of the stone floor, the entrance to the underground portion of the temple. "This,"

Erica said, "is what an archaeological site should look like." Then she added, "I hope Cameron is here."

Matt was concerned as well. The only number Erica had for Cameron hadn't worked the previous night, and Monroe hadn't been able to get through to anyone from the Australian team. They'd wanted to contact Cameron as discreetly as possible. The fewer people involved the better.

Suddenly a voice boomed from inside the large olive tent to their left. "I don't believe what I'm seeing. Either I'm sick with the heat and angels have landed, or my favorite rock-grubber is in town."

Erica grinned. "I know that voice. Clever and quick with just enough Aussie to be sexy."

Matt frowned at her response before catching himself and smoothing any trace of emotion from his face. *Why should I care?*

Erica turned as a big, blonde man threw open the tent flaps and strode toward her. "Cam!" she cried. With a laugh, she took two steps and jumped into his arms, returning his bear hug as he swung her in a full circle.

Matt stood back in observation of the reunion. He didn't like seeing the other man's hands on Erica, or the fact that he was once again being called Cam. The shortened version sounded more like an endearment than a nickname.

No chance he was hiding his resentment this time, and *Cam* was the first to notice. The other man looked his way after returning Erica to her feet, and with a scowl of his own, jerked his head toward Matt. "Who's the friendly bloke?"

Erica let her grin slip as she stole a glance over her shoulder. "Oh. This is Matt Pierce. We're working together."

A smile returned to Cameron's face. "Good. I was afraid you'd gone and gotten yourself married away." His hands fell to her hips.

Friend or not, Matt wanted to knock the guy on his ass.

"Cam. Is there somewhere we can speak in private?" Erica

caught the attention of both men with her question.

"Sure. We'll use my tent. I'll get us some drinks." He cast a glance at Matt. "Will he be joining us, then?"

"Yes," Matt responded before Erica had a chance. "He will."

When the tent's flap closed, darkness and cool air enveloped them. The enclosure offered relief from the bright sun and its reflection off the exposed stone. While his eyes adjusted, Matt took in the books and implements decorating the interior. The place was the hybrid child of library meeting tool shack.

Cameron waved a hand to suggest they take a seat at the large wooden table while he opened a small refrigerator. He removed chilled water with one hand, a brown bottle with the other. "Pick your poison? I can do without every luxury but one. Cold beer."

"We'll have water for now," Erica answered for both of them.

"Right, then." Cameron straddled a chair facing away from the table and popped the cap from his drink. "Now tell me what's going on, and no need to dress it up. I know you well enough and can tell you're not here for the sightseeing."

"We're looking for something and have reason to believe it may be located somewhere in the temple. Or that it used to be." Erica glanced at Matt. "It's important. Enough that the U.S. government and others are involved."

Cameron also looked at Matt, as if seeing him in a new light. "Well, you know I'll help you, Erica. If you're the one asking, it must be legitimate."

She sighed in relief. She'd expected Cameron to cooperate, but it would be much easier, and quicker, without the third degree. "I've read that the initial research placed the age of the temple around the early Iron Age, approximately 1000 BC."

Cameron nodded. "True, but a couple of years more digging revealed another temple beneath, dating as far back as 1600 BC. We found a cult stand, about a meter high. We think it served as an altar in the most sacred area of the temple."

Erica leaned in and held his gaze. "Who do you think the

altar was used to worship?"

Cameron answered slowly, as if he weren't sure his answer would be what she wanted. "Based on the painted decorations on the stand and the people inhabiting the area at that time, I'd say the place was built for the god El. That's part of why it's now referred to as a Canaanite temple."

Erica licked her lips. "Have you found anything that might be considered a discrepancy?"

Cameron nodded. "We have found some objects that hint of other cultures, but we chalked it up to travelers or trade. As I'm sure you know, the area was a flourishing trade center with links to Syria and Cyprus."

"As well as with Egypt, where it was called Pihilium or Pehel," Erica said.

"Have you found anything exclusive to Egyptian culture?" Matt asked, tossing aside Erica's more subtle line of questioning.

Cameron took a swig from his beer and placed it softly on the table, casting his eyes between the two of them before settling on Erica. "Tell me specifically what you're looking for."

"It may be in the form of a charm or cartouche, but what we're really hoping to find is a canopic vase."

Erica's face caved subtly as Cameron pulled his mouth to one side and shook his head. "Sorry. No intact vases have been recovered."

"Intact?" Matt zeroed in on the description. "But you've found pieces?"

Cameron held up his hands in a halting motion. "Less than pieces. We've recovered a few shards and some odd disks that might have been part of canopics, but none verified. Besides, they're not even here anymore. They weren't given much attention or value."

Erica cringed. "Please don't tell me they've been discarded or sold off."

"You should know better than that," Cameron said with a frown. "We would never toss anything found at a dig that dated back." He shrugged. "We sent them to storage for perusal at a later time. There's been too much excitement around here since the older structures were unearthed."

Matt wanted to shake the two of them. Enough chit chat. "Where are they now?" He leaned forward and dared the other man to leave the direct question unanswered.

Cameron narrowed his eyes. "Who are you exactly?"

"Cam, please." Erica placed her hand on Cameron's arm in an attempt to derail the male hostility that was building between the two. It served to calm one, but not the other.

Matt responded, his eyes hard. "I'm the one who's got a job to do, and I'm the one who's going to keep Erica safe while it gets done. I don't trust anyone with too much information." He darted a glance at Erica. "Or with her. As for now, that still includes you."

Cameron studied Matt with a flat expression but finally spoke. "The shards and anything we believe related to them are being stored at the Jordan Archaeological Museum in Amman."

"Can you get us in?" Erica asked then held her breath.

With a wink and a grin, the jovial Cameron was back. "Sure I can. Anything for you." He cast a challenging smile at Matt then turned his attention to Erica, putting his hand on top of hers. "I'd love to give you my own tour of the Isle of Fire."

Erica stared at Cameron. "What did you say?" the wrinkle was between her eyes, so Matt knew her mind was working at a furious pace.

In his own head, words and images were flashing all at once as he tried to figure out what had her excited.

"You getting rusty?" Cameron teased. "The Isle of Fire. The land of Osiris. We're right in the middle of it."

"Matt." Erica looked at him with blue eyes alight with knowledge. She was about to make a connection. "Where is the copy of the Cannibal Text you said you have?"

Without answering, Matt opened a bag, retrieved some

papers, and handed them over.

Erica's fingers flew over the printed lines before stopping at a portion of the text. She read aloud. "*Pharaoh is the bull of the sky, who shatters at will, who lives on the being of every god, who eats their entrails.*" She paused and breathed deeply before continuing. "*Even of those who come with their bodies full of magic from the island of flame.*"

Matt asked, "What does this mean for us?"

"I'm not sure, but this is a reference to Osiris. The people who were full of magic could have been so because of their own acts of cannibalism."

Cameron had been listening quietly but now interrupted with eyes wide open. "What in the bloody hell are you two talking about?"

Erica tapped her fingers on the dark wood of the table. "I'm trying to make connections between all of this. Cannibalism, this area of Jordan, Unis, Osiris."

Cameron sipped his beer. "Osiris is often thought of in relation to cannibalism."

Matt and Erica both stared at him, prompting him to elaborate.

"Yeah, it was his great idea to make Egyptians stop eating each other and practice cooking up only those they considered enemies."

"What else?" Matt asked.

"He's also well known for being the god of plagues and destruction." Cameron sat back in his chair. "I'm sorry, but I don't really know what you're looking for."

"I wonder if the end of days would qualify as destruction," Matt said aloud, meeting Erica's cool and worried gaze. He wondered if she was remembering what he'd told her about Kherep Amun and what she'd learned from the file she'd read on the plane.

"All we can do at this point is go forward and see what we can put together." Erica turned back to Cameron. "I'm sorry to ask, but is there any way you can take the time off and let us in to see the things you recovered? I know it's asking a lot, but..."

Cameron leaned forward and took her chin in his hand. "We'll leave as soon as you want." His eyes softened. "I don't like the way any of this sounds, so I'll do whatever it takes to help you. Especially if it keeps you safe."

The Aussie released his hold on Erica and spoke in a hard voice to Matt. "At least we have that much in common."

11

The ride from Pella was almost as tense as the impromptu tent meeting had been. Erica was positioned in the front passenger seat while Matt drove. She wanted to separate the boys.

Matt considered what he'd said earlier to Cameron, about protecting Erica. An instinctive urge to convey possession to the other man had overwhelmed him, and now that fact was a roiling ball of acid in his gut. Jobs were always important, but emotions were to be kept separate. That was crucial, not only for expediency and performance but for the protection of all parties involved.

The guilt and self-recriminations were intense when an agent allowed someone to be hurt. But if the worst happened...

Matt grimaced as the memory speared razor-sharp claws into his brain. A white spot of pain always seemed to accompany the vision of her falling. The surprised form of her lips as she clutched at the spot on her chest, deep crimson blooming from underneath her hand.

His own hands tightened on the wheel as the face he watched became Erica's. As the blood became Erica's.

Shaking himself loose from the talons of the past, he slid his eyes over to take in Erica's beaming smile. She was listening to Cam tell a story of a mutual old friend, chewing her bottom lip as she listened to the humorous details.

It was a comfort to watch, and Matt felt himself calming down. He lent half his attention to the lively chatter but kept his eyes on the road. She and Cameron had spent most of the trip talking, laughing, and catching up. Now, the gleaming city of Amman unfolded before them as the jeep finally brought them to their destination.

The seven hills, or *jabals*, defined separate neighborhoods, where modern buildings fought for space alongside the remnants of ancient civilizations. White houses were blinding under the hot sun, and the smell of kebabs filled the air from the stalls along the roadside.

There was a feeling of tranquility here, as seemingly carefree people sipped the rich Arabian coffee from small cups. Jordanians in general possessed a more welcoming spirit than many other Arabic countries. No machine gun toting tour guides would be found here, as they had been in Egypt.

The oldest part of the city was considered the downtown area and held various sites of interest, including a temple built in honor of Hercules. There was also a grand Roman amphitheater, weathered by wind, water, and time, but still able to seat six thousand.

Matt considered sharing what he knew of the city's history then reconsidered as he glanced at Erica. Her ice blue eyes filled with humor and warmth as she nodded at something Cam told her. She probably already knew all there was to know about Jordan anyway. It was amazing and somewhat intimidating that her brain could retain as much knowledge as it did.

As if feeling his perusal, she subtly shifted her gaze to him before turning in her seat to face forward. Cameron had finished his story, and the two archaeologists now rode quietly, taking in the sights around them.

Erica let the warmth and energy of Jordan roll into her as she enjoyed the sunny day. She was glad they had the jeep, since the climb up Citadel Hill to the Jordan Archaeological Museum was especially steep. The museum, built in 1951, held displays ranging from prehistoric days to the youngest pieces from the late Islamic era, dating around 1516. Among its great prizes was a collection of Dead Sea Scrolls, one of which supposedly told a story of hidden treasure to be found somewhere along the west bank of the River Jordan.

Despite the reason for their visit, she was secretly delighted to have a back-stage pass to the museum. Some people could spend hours poking through bookstores, shopping for clothes, or even playing video games. Erica's version of escapism? Relics and artifacts. Each with its own unique tale and long-forgotten adventure.

As they drew closer, Cameron directed Matt to park in the rear of the building. Certain privileges accompanied his position as team leader of the expedition that had donated so many valuable finds from the temple in Pella. They piled out of the jeep then entered through a back door. Instant relief washed over them as they stepped into the climate controlled building.

Erica breathed in through her nose and sighed. It was a wonder and a comfort that all museum workrooms smelled the same, no matter where they were located. Dust, alcohol and the underlying hint of what can only be described as aged earth.

She gasped when Cameron flipped the light switch, and she became the proverbial kid in a candy store. The room was filled with antiquities from primitive times, all in various stages of preparation for display.

A sarcophagus lay on a table in one corner. Erica made her way to it and performed her own assessment without touching. She knew better than to lay her hands on someone else's work in progress. It would be an incredible breach of archaeological etiquette.

"This is amazing," she said to no one in particular. "I'd guess it came from the Iron Age, but sarcophagi from that time period are very rare."

Cameron grunted and walked to stand beside her. "Yeah, they are. This museum happens to have four."

Erica smiled in appreciation of the artwork before her. "It's brilliant. Imagine the patience, the dedication it took to complete this."

Matt cleared his throat, returning Erica's attention to their purpose.

"Cameron, you know we could spend hours in this room alone, but I really need to get a look at what you found at Pella." Erica turned from the artifacts with only a small amount of disappointment. She promised herself a return visit to the Jordan museum when she'd completed her present task.

Cameron nodded in understanding and moved to unlock a large wooden door, revealing steps that wound their way into the depths of a basement. The surroundings transformed immediately. Where the work area had been well lit and comfortable, bare bulbs covered with cobwebs showed the way down the stairs.

No expense was spared for the valuable pieces above ground, kept for exhibition in the polished museum hallways. And no penny was wasted to house the things deemed less than worthy by the current curator.

The air was musty once they reached the bottom floor. Again, Cameron flipped a switch and long rows of fluorescents lit up one at a time in a domino effect. The room was huge. It stretched the length of the museum above, with square concrete columns in place for support.

"Don't worry. I know where the boxes we need are. I brought them down myself." Cameron pointed to a card table that had seen better days. "Why don't you clear those newspapers off and start us some coffee?"

Erica looked around and cringed at the coffee maker she saw on a side shelf. The crusted, brown stains told her it hadn't been cleaned in a while. "Where can I find a sink and some soap?"

Matt and Cameron smiled in unison at the look on her face.

"Back corner," Cameron said with a short laugh. "Matt and I will get the boxes." He turned with the obvious expectation that Matt would follow.

Before he did, Matt walked back to the dark corner Cameron had indicated. He searched until he found a light, turned it on, and left to join the other man.

Erica watched him go, surprised by his consideration. She had been in plenty of dank, dirty places before, and would have fared just as well here. She had a distaste for filth in living spaces but really didn't mind making do when she had to.

Still, she felt a tickle of happiness. Matt hadn't needed to make the gesture. It's not like there was any danger in the small room. With a smile lifting her lips, she made her way to the dingy little utility room with a lighter step and a fluttering in her chest.

Then she reminded herself she wasn't supposed to be thinking of her temporary partner that way. The giddy-schoolgirl-butterflies-in-the-stomach way.

She allowed the routine actions of preparing coffee to take her mind off of Matt. Even if the deep, dark brown of the grounds did remind her of his eyes.

By the time Matt and Cameron returned, the smell of brewing coffee was escaping into the small lounge area she had hastily straightened up. When Cameron had mentioned more than one box, Erica hadn't imagined this vast storeroom or that it might take longer than expected to search for the clue. Since they weren't even sure what to look for, each item had to be inspected carefully.

Both men held two boxes. They set them on the floor by the table before Cameron said, "Two more trips should do it."

As they walked back into the shadowy recesses, Erica surveyed the containers and chose the one closest to her to start searching. Each piece was wrapped in the cheapest of packing material. Newspaper. It reminded her of moving day. She and her father had always packed quickly and lightly when going from one apartment to another.

Her childhood had consisted of constant relocation, but she'd been happy. Her father and grandfather had given her everything a child needed to grow up healthy and prepared for the world.

And she still intended to give them something back. No reason she couldn't outwit the bad guys and take home the trophy.

Surveying the boxes that were piling up, she reminded herself they were still at the start of the race. And winning would require diligence. Attention to detail. She plopped into a chair and blew out a breath. "So that's why he suggested coffee."

Two pots later Erica was really wishing she had some cream, or even milk, to cut the bitter film that seemed to be making itself at home on her tongue. It had been a long day since they'd met up with Cameron that morning, and a glance at her watch told her it was almost seven o'clock at night. Her stomach was telling her the same thing.

She fell back into her seat and stretched her arms out. The laughter suddenly ringing out of her was in stark contrast to the somber atmosphere, and the two men with her raised their heads to see what was so amusing.

Cameron's jovial mood was intact, even though they were all exhausted. He gave her a half-smile. "What is it?"

"Look at all of us," she said.

They did, and realized what she meant. Their hands, arms, clothes, and even the coffee cups were covered in black smudges from the newspaper ink. Cameron laughed along with her, while Matt only smiled and returned to his perusal of the shard in his hand.

Soon after, Matt dropped the piece of pottery into the box with disgust. "Still nothing." Frustration built inside him with every piece they dismissed. He was afraid they wouldn't find what they were looking for. Erica still studied each item closely, but she had to know this could be a dead end.

With the murders cropping up, pressure to find and stop the cult was greater than ever, and Matt felt a personal responsibility for each of the victims. He tried not to think of the agony they'd endured in their last moments, but the images, especially those of the boy from Vatican City, stayed with him. They would haunt every step he took until this was over and the work of Kherep Amun was brought to a standstill.

The secrecy of the murderous group had surely aided their ability to gather information, and once this was finished, he would make sure people were told about them. Citizens had a right to know what sort of evil might be walking alongside them every day.

Cameron's voice intruded on Matt's dark thoughts. "Hey, Erica. I think I found the stash." The Aussie's green eyes danced with excitement.

Erica and Matt each put aside the piles they'd been working on so Cameron could place his collection on the table. They each grabbed a piece and began to unwrap the goods.

"It's not particularly organized down here, but I try to keep similarly themed items grouped together." Cameron said. He looked relieved they'd finally located the fragments with the Egyptian characteristics he'd promised.

Silence and a renewed energy fell over the group as each began scrutinizing their pieces in earnest. The men gave anything in question to Erica, acknowledging without words that she was the authority in this arena. She was examining a scrap of metal that could have been an amulet or currency when Matt finally found something.

He handed her what appeared to be a portion of an urn or vase. Only a jagged edge remained, but it was still attached to a disc-shaped piece of gold that might have been the bottom. Without the entire object, it was hard to decide what was what.

Matt was no Egyptologist, but he knew what they were

looking for. As soon as Erica held the object close, he knew she saw it, too. The piece wasn't exactly like the amulet they'd used to complete the clue in Hatshepsut's temple, but the inscriptions on this piece were similar to the others.

"Definitely hieroglyphics." Her brows furrowed as she tried to make meaning out of the symbols. She shook her head and rotated the round object as if trying to see it from a new perspective. Finally, she flipped it over and began to do the same with the opposite side.

Erica performed this routine for several minutes before handing it over to Cameron. "Here, you try." She rubbed her eyes and then her temples.

Cameron glanced at the markings. "The symbols are clearly the Egyptian style of writing. What's wrong? You don't think this is it?"

"No. The good news is I absolutely believe that's our clue."

"And the bad news?" Matt asked.

Erica dropped her hands to her lap. "It's encrypted somehow, and I can't make out the pattern. Hell, I can't even detect a pattern."

"Oh, I see what you mean," Cameron said, now looking more closely at the symbols. "They don't come together to actually convey anything. It's the equivalent of our saying something like... cat, bow, did ,dog."

Matt narrowed his eyes at Cameron. "Huh?"

"Exactly." Cameron nodded like he'd explained himself fully.

Exasperated with the other two, Matt snatched the disc from Cameron, careful not to cut himself on the sharp edge. He knew he didn't have the same level of knowledge when it came to artifacts, but at this point he couldn't do any worse.

Anger was now churning around with all that frustration he was feeling. The two experts weren't making any sense. The woman he was responsible for was coming to mean more to him than she should and was in a dangerous situation that he'd helped put her in. And to top it all off he was starving.

So it was understandable when he snapped, "What the hell does this mean?"

"What the hell does what mean?" Erica shot back.

"This circle in the middle. Why draw it there?" Matt gave Erica a stern look. "Didn't you tell me the Egyptians didn't bother leaving a mark unless it meant something?"

Erica looked dumbfounded. "Why, yes, I did. How could I have missed what was staring me in the face?"

Erica and Cameron reached for the disc at the same time, but Cameron stopped himself and waved for her to take it.

Erica gave an impish smile in reply. "Thanks." Again she studied the inscriptions. "Okay. I should have seen this before." She glared at the coffee pot like it was somehow to blame for muddling her mind instead of sharpening it.

She continued. "The symbols on this side are informative each by themselves. See, in the four most opposite sides we have the markings that indicate directions, north, south, et cetera. I saw them, but I guess I was caught up in trying to make them all flow together in a sentence."

"That's not the side with the circle." Matt pointed this out in way of a question.

"No, but your mentioning the circle made me refocus on the entire piece. I have to say, Agent Pierce, you're good at keeping me on task." She favored Matt with a brilliant smile.

Matt's stomach tightened in response. Covered in ink, wrung out from a hard day, and grumpy with hunger, Erica was still sexier than any woman had a right to be. He shifted uncomfortably in his seat.

Cameron glared at Matt for a split second before clearing his throat with a ragged cough. "Go ahead, Erica."

"Oh. Yes." She nodded to the disc in her hands. "In between the directional symbols are the four representing canopic vases, the dog, baboon, human, and falcon."

"The same as the original medallion that led us to Hatshepsut's temple." Matt remembered what she had explained to him about the gold piece.

Erica nodded. "Only this time they were separated and positioned randomly with even more symbols like the scarab and sun. Each holds its own value, so that helped hide the real message. It would make the other side seem like a group of unrelated symbols as well."

"But you don't think it is." Cameron stated the obvious.

"No. The message is there but is encrypted. Any good spy or computer hacker will tell you that all you need to know is the method of encryption used and from there it's all downhill." Her brows beetled, indicating she was either frustrated or concentrating. Matt wondered what she was figuring out.

He was learning to read her. Every gesture or expression on her face was becoming familiar to him, and against his better judgment, he was enjoying the very unique language that was Erica.

At the mention of encryption methods, Cameron's expression went from perplexed to triumphant. He held out his palm, and Erica answered by handing him the disc.

Cameron studied both sides of the artifact before shaking it at Matt. "You got it, buddy," he said with a grin.

At first, Matt didn't realize he was the one being called "buddy." "What exactly did I get?"

"The circle you had to point out to us supposed academics." He and Erica shared an embarrassed look. "The circle tells us all we need to know to break the code and decipher the message. It's a *scytale*."

"Now you two supposed academics are going to tell me what a scytale is, right?" Matt was feeling a little less volatile since it looked like they might still be in the game.

Erica jumped back in. "It's a basic transposition cipher. The Greeks used it during war time to send secret battle plans or requests to soldiers in the field."

"Fitting, after what you've told me about the history of Jordan and the merging cultures," Matt said.

Cameron shook his head. "Looks like your Egyptian riddler had a sense of humor."

"The original author of the note would wind a piece of leather or something similar around a rod," Erica explained. He would then write out whatever message he wanted delivered. Once the strip was unwound again, the letters couldn't be read in the order they appeared."

Matt took a swig of coffee then grimaced at the cold bitterness. "I know what you're talking about, but I wouldn't have known the name. The circle. It tells us the correct diameter of the rod?"

"Exactly." Cameron chimed back in with the growing excitement of the other two. "That's why it's fairly basic. Once the diameter is known, breaking the code is simple. You still have to play around with the size of the letters, or in this case, symbols."

Erica stood. "We need to get back upstairs and find something we can write on and cut into a strip."

"I reckon we have something that will work." Cameron turned with an unspoken question to Matt.

For once, Matt's responded without challenge. "I'll look for a rod."

12

Finding a cylindrical object of the right size turned out to be the easy part. After a couple of failed attempts with paper of varying thickness, Cameron broke down and took off his undershirt. The fabric was much easier to manipulate, and they had learned enough from their earlier attempts to gauge what size the symbols needed to be when written.

With the eagerness of schoolchildren, they all gathered around as the white strip was carefully wound around a beat-up, yellow broomstick.

Erica whispered, almost reverently, "I think we got it." Then more loudly she said, "Quick, somebody write as I translate."

Matt reached out. "Here, I'll hold it in place so you can concentrate."

Erica began to speak, stopping herself several times to straighten out the cloth and rephrase the message. It wasn't an exact science and Cameron's pad was covered in scratch marks by the time they were done.

Matt and Erica gave Cameron a minute to rewrite the text neatly. When finished, he handed the pad to Erica to read aloud while he wrote the translation down, this time in English.

Her voice flowed with crystal clarity, entrancing Matt as surely as a siren did her prey. It seemed an Egyptian goddess was standing beside him, the exotic words right at home on her full, pink lips. When she finished and looked at him, he forced himself out of the daze.

He hadn't understood a word but could feel the silken vibe of her voice still coursing through him.

More gruffly than necessary he asked Cameron, "Did you get all of that?"

"Hardly." Cameron lifted a brow that clearly said, *No dumbass*. "Since she spoke in Coptic Egyptian."

"Oh." Erica laughed. "Sorry. I'll try English this time."

Matt knew they needed to know what the message said, but he'd also liked the other way she'd read it just fine.

Erica was about to start the translation when a glance at Matt gave her pause. Smoldering was the first descriptive word that came to mind. She would swear the deep brown of his eyes looked…hotter, almost molten. Swallowing hard, she took a moment before tearing her own eyes away and back to the script.

She spoke more slowly, allowing Cameron time to copy it onto the paper. They all gathered around to look at both the hieroglyphics and what they meant in modern English.

Cameron placed his finger on the words. "I'm not sure about that part, why they chose to write it that way."

"Show me." Matt gathered in close to Erica's side, his hip resting against hers.

She did her best to appear unaffected, yet remained where she was. Enjoying the connection and the startling electricity from his body, she stayed connected. They would make this discovery together.

"See here," Cam said, "in this part of the message is the symbol for water, and here it is again in repetition."

Erica knew the answer. "The symbol one time means simply water. The same symbol placed vertically and in multiples implies a body of water."

Cameron glanced up at Matt. "Looks like they picked the right woman for the job, eh, mate? Me, I'll stick to Romans,

Greeks and such. Latin is much easier to follow."

Matt grinned at the man's self-deprecation, and Erica felt a dash of hope that the two had finally lowered their swords. Then she felt Matt's hand on the small of her back where it rested firmly. Possessively.

She had to clear her head to continue explaining the hieroglyphics. "On this side of the disc is the symbol for red, and another for a finger. Some of this I wasn't sure whether to take literally or symbolically."

"What do you mean?" Matt asked.

"Sometimes a symbol means literally what it is. For example, a chick is a chick, or it can be part of another word entirely. Add to that the fact Egyptians only wrote consonants and you can see where it might get a little tricky."

"But you know what it says," Matt stated with a confidence in Erica's ability that swayed her more than the heat of his hand.

Erica pulled in a calming breath and met his dark stare. "Yes, once put into the correct context, only certain usage of the symbols would make sense."

Matt lifted one side of his mouth in a devilish manner. "Then let's see what we've got."

Cameron took this as his cue since he was holding the pad. He read the words aloud. "Where the river's magic finger feeds the body of water, the god of gods is written, and the red ones guard his name. Seek the water."

They all took a minute to think about the words before Cameron commented with his typical dry wit. "Great. A riddle within a riddle."

Erica was becoming more accustomed to the twists and turns that Senmut had orchestrated. He had been a master of puzzles, and no two clues would be alike. It was part of the difficulty. "We have to break it down line by line. Let's take the first, mentioning the river's magic finger."

Matt spoke up. "The writer is originally from Egypt. If it

were any other river than the Nile, he would have given us a lead."

"But we're in Jordan," Cameron said. "Couldn't he have meant the Jordan River?"

Erica held her hand up. "You're right, Cam, but look at the rest, specifically the mention of a finger. The branching of the Nile as it heads toward the Mediterranean resembles a hand, causing the individual sections to be referred to as fingers." She went to her duffle bag for the atlas she'd used in Luxor. A visual was always better.

Once she opened the book, Erica pointed to the area in question. "See the fingers?"

"Yeah, I see the fingers," Matt quipped, "but which one is magic?"

Erica laughed at his directly-to-the-point tone. "In ancient Egypt, each direction was also given other meanings."

"Of course they were." He lifted a moderately patient brow.

"The north direction equated to earth and funerals, the south to pharaohs and fire, and the east to theology." Erica supplied all but one explanation, allowing the men to fill in the blank.

"I assume the westerly wind equates with magic?" Cameron said, still playing along.

"Yes. Magic and water."

"Water, again." Matt rested his free hand on the table. "Have either of you noticed how often water is mentioned. The river, body of water, look for the water, and now the magic is also related to the western finger and water."

"The western branch of the Nile was also called the canopic finger. Could that be a coincidence?" Erica looked to both men for their opinions.

"I don't believe in coincidence where all of this is concerned," Matt said. "What about the next line? We go to where the western branch of the Nile feeds the body of water, obviously the Mediterranean, then what?"

"The next line reads 'the god of gods is written.' We have to assume the god of gods is Amun. Referencing any other god that way would be an incredible insult, and the whole purpose of this is to protect the divine remains of Hatshepsut, daughter of Amun. There's no way her worshippers would desecrate Amun's sanctity by calling any other the god of all."

Cameron agreed. "Right. By saying his name is written, they could have meant any kind of inscription, but what would be the point if it weren't on something permanent, like an altar or temple?"

Erica put her fingertip to her lips and eased away to pace.

Matt looked again at the map spread on the table. "Alexandria is located at the mouth of the western branch of the Nile. Do they have a temple for Amun there?"

Erica covered her eyes with her hand as disappointment landed in her stomach like lead. "It wouldn't matter."

"What do you mean?" Matt asked. "What's wrong?"

"I think the temple of Amun was farther north than Alexandria."

Matt put his finger on the map. "There isn't anything farther north."

Cameron groaned. "Not anymore there isn't."

Matt heaved a breath. "Damn. This is impossible. All of this hinges on places that were here over a couple of millennia ago." He stilled suddenly, eyes lighting on Erica. "Maybe Kherep Amun won't be able to find her either. Maybe they won't be able to come to completion."

Erica spoke quietly, overcome by her sense of failure. "The murders have already started." And now she was sure there would be nothing to stop them. Not her knowledge. Not Matt's gun.

Cameron's eyes flashed. "Murders? What murders? What the 'ell have you gotten involved in, Erica?"

She forced a grin for her old friend. "Calm down, Cam. Your accent is showing."

"I still want to know what murders." His look was adamant.

Matt filled him in briefly, leaving Erica time to contemplate their new problem. The two men were still discussing the latest victim when Erica had a flash. A jolt of memory that jumped the chasm of doubt in her mind.

She swiveled and pierced Cameron with a look while pointing a determined finger his way. "Do you have Internet access here?"

"Of course." He led them to an elaborate office and booted up the computer.

This room had also seen the better end of the budget. The smell of leather and citrus permeated the air around several wide desks and high book shelves.

"What's got you worked up?" Cameron asked as he watched her type the words *Menouthis* and *Herakleion* into a search engine.

"I just remembered something I heard when they started excavating the sunken cities."

Matt was by her side in a flash. "You mean they've found the ruins of where you think this temple to Amun was located?"

Erica's fingers flew as she typed in more specific search parameters. "It wasn't the temple that triggered it, but yes. I remember the mention of some things that had been discovered."

She found a site she liked and clicked on the hyperlinks, bringing up more detailed information. She read a few paragraphs. "I knew it. Read this." She pointed to a few lines.

Matt leaned in. "We are very excited to be finding complete cities…"

"Not that part." Erica interrupted him and read out loud. "The ruins of the great temple dedicated to Amun, jewelry, pottery, implements, colossi of gods and kings."

Matt frowned. "So?"

"Colossi are great statues."

"I'm aware of that," Matt growled. "What does that prove?"

"Look down here." She moved the cursor to highlight a

paragraph. "Colossi made of red granite."

That sly grin of his lifted one side of his face. "Well that part makes sense. You should have led with it."

"I guess." Erica's voice deflated as she stared at the picture she'd enlarged on the website. Divers posed beside one of their finds. She knew what had to be done, and fear congealed in her spine before spreading to her gut.

"What's wrong?" Matt studied the screen then put a hand on her arm. "You're thinking about your father and grandfather aren't you?"

Erica jerked her head to look up at him. "You know?"

"I told you. We had to check you out first."

She rubbed her eyes, hoping to erase the memory of what had happened. "I knew I would dive again one day, but this caught me off guard. I'm not sure I'm ready."

Matt swiveled the chair until she faced him, then kneeled down to her level. "You have to be. We can't risk my missing the clue because I don't know what to look for. You see this stuff through a different lens than I do." He gripped her knee. "And yours is the one that counts."

"It was in the Mediterranean, too. I can't believe the luck," she whispered.

Matt's insistent stare gave her the resolve to sit up straight and sweep the self-pity out of her way. Her father would have demanded it. "Okay. I'm going down with you. I won't let this beat me."

"I'll be right beside you," he said before taking her hands in his.

Cameron had been standing quietly but spoke up now. "Erica. Since you know who the red ones are, how do you plan to look for the water when you're already surrounded by it?"

She lifted her shoulders. "I guess we still have to work on that part."

"But not tonight." Matt took her hand to pull her up out of the chair. "I refuse to consider the hidden meaning behind one more thing until I get something in my stomach."

"I second that," Cameron said.

Erica rolled her eyes. One thing she could always expect men to agree about was the need for food. Then again, she was famished, too.

They printed off the pertinent information regarding the sunken cities and closed up the office. As they gathered up their makeshift scytale and the broom, Cameron announced he'd called ahead earlier to reserve some rooms. "Compliments of the Australian Archaeological Society. I thought you might want to keep a low profile."

Matt looked at him with concern. "We already have ways of ensuring we do, but why would you say that?" He stopped and held Cameron in place with a stare. "We didn't tell you about the murders until tonight. When did you book the rooms?"

"Let's talk about it over dinner." Cameron said.

"How about now?" Matt wouldn't be put off.

Neither would Erica. "Cam, what's going on?"

"Fine. I was going to bring it up later, especially since you told me about Kherep Amun."

Erica had a sudden chill.

"We've had some security issues around the temple lately," Cameron said.

"What kind of issues?" Matt pressed.

"We usually clear out at night, leaving a couple of guys in a tent and some dogs, just for good measure. We've never had any problems, at least, not until recently." Cameron met Erica's gaze. "Last week, the two left behind both woke up with strange headaches. The dogs slept through our arrival back at the site, and it was obvious someone had been doing some digging of their own."

"How could you tell?" Matt asked.

"Archaeologists keep very precise records of any excavating they do. They have to." Erica explained the reasoning to Matt. "Characteristics of the layers of soil can tell researchers a lot about the time period it's from and what organic material existed then."

Matt nodded. "They'd know exactly where their digging left off and an intruder's began."

"That and the dogs, the men, and some other strange things began to add up. Someone swears they saw a man up on a hill and the flash of what might have been binoculars. The curator here changed his passwords after he discovered a history of a records search that he didn't perform." Cameron shrugged. "We've tightened security."

Matt held Cameron with his stare as he asked the most important question. "Is there anyone working at the site you don't trust?"

"No. We screen our workers well. We can uncover valuables at any given moment. Most of our employees have been with us for years." Cameron paused. "We did have one woman disappear suddenly."

Erica stepped forward. "You think she was harmed?"

"According to gossip, she got married and was no longer allowed to work. I had heard talk of an engagement, but frankly, I had a hard time believing it until she left."

"Why?" Matt asked.

"She came from a poor family and was the youngest of several daughters."

Erica offered a different view. "Then the offer of a good marriage might be a very persuasive tactic."

"They got to her," Matt said.

Erica shivered and rubbed her arms. "I just hope she ended up with the promised marriage and not a grave."

Cameron thumped her on the shoulder. "Enough of all this. I thought we decided to get some food. I know all the hot spots of Amman."

Erica smiled her thanks for his attempt to change the subject. "I need a shower first."

Cameron leaned toward her and sniffed, then wrinkled his

nose. "Yeah. You do."

Erica laughed and slapped Cameron's chest before giving him an appreciative wink. He was concerned about her safety, and from the cagey looks he kept slipping Matt, her friend was also worried about her involvement with the agent.

His protectiveness was pretty funny, since she'd been around for a few of his more flamboyant affairs.

Maybe Cam knew her better than she realized, since she was still grappling with her own confusion over Matt. Her will power and work ethic always beat back any romantic interest she might have, but they were losing the ground against the clean cut Feebie with the no-nonsense attitude and hypnotic eyes.

Every time she took a logical step back, she ended up taking two physical steps forward. Add in his moments of tenderness that blind-sided her, and Erica saw a very dangerous equation. One that might equal a repeat incident like the one on the boat.

She chastised herself and shook her head. Nonsense. She was more resilient than that. She and Matt were under too much stress. Working closely under a highly intense situation. She probably just needed someone to lean on, and he happened to be around.

Erica smiled to herself. Yes. That was it. The stress. The situation.

Because she couldn't remember the last time she'd needed anyone.

13

The cluster of girls passed the men without notice. Their youthful laughter told the world they still possessed the special appreciation for living that turned even the simplest outing into an adventure. They were the type of girls born into love and comfortable lifestyles, whose confidence was only further increased by the burgeoning beauty of adolescence.

The night was made for memories. The kind they would one day yearn for, when childish dreams had been replaced by the monotony and strain of true adulthood. It was a warm summer night made easier by a full moon and singing cicadas.

Music pumped from the bar and grille. Its location was convenient for the several surrounding towns, and everyone knew Friday nights belonged to the teenagers. Still, there were enough wayward adults in the crowd to allow the men to blend in at a side table.

If anyone had been paying attention, the severity of one man's expression might have raised concern. He was the man who would be filling the role of *Khonsu*, the slayer, for the night's proceedings.

Though the ritual would not be performed until the following evening, the best time for action would be tonight, amidst the chaos, noise, and carelessness of the young. Teenagers thought themselves invincible.

Khonsu had great concerns for what the men were planning to undertake. He felt it unwise to bring attention to themselves before the day of triumph had been attained. They would be operating at full strength then, and that would be soon enough for the world to know of their uprising. They had chosen the next sacrifice for the wrong reasons, and her disappearance would not go unnoticed.

The girl was the daughter of a high-ranking general in the armed services. How unfortunate the man's long-fought for position would ultimately lead to the loss of his child. Some of the initiators wanted the first rituals to serve as insults to the powers that be, as warnings of what was to come.

Khonsu disagreed.

He also disagreed with the choice for the *Serpent* in his group. Something about the man was unsettling. He was missing an aspect of self-control, and Khonsu did not feel he could be trusted to abide by the rules governing the ritual.

Khonsu sipped his drink and cast a furtive glance at his companion. He watched the Serpent as the Serpent watched the young girl. Another reason he did not approve of the man's placement on the team. The Serpent did not take his eyes away from the pretty blonde, his twisted mind taking an apparent and sordid path.

Khonsu expected trouble. He surveyed the rest of the men assigned to his group and took a mental count of those he knew would stand with him.

They had all been trained and held the sanctity of the ritual in the highest regard, but Khonsu knew what sudden power and one corrupt man's influence could do. The girl would be in their possession for a full day. He would have to make sure the Serpent was under constant supervision.

His mind returned to the activities ahead, visualizing the plan once more. The youngest of their group was an attractive man and could pass for a college student. He would be known as *Kehave* for the extent of the operation. Kehave's job, in history, had been to lasso or capture the sacrifice.

Tonight Kehave would approach the group of young women. Regardless of their response, he would be sure to spill the blonde's drink before leaving the table. The replacement he brought back would be laced with a slow-acting drug, one that wouldn't completely incapacitate. In time, the girl would become drowsy and experience a dulling of the senses. Her judgment and ability to react would be impaired.

The men knew she was supposed to go back home tonight, and her father's instructions had been explicit. She was expected to be there before her parents' return. This left more than enough time for the men to carry out their duty, and the girl's fatigue would ensure her decision to call it an early night.

She might not notice the porch light was out, though it was always left burning until the last family member returned. She would make it to the front door. They would allow that. As the girl focused on unlocking the door in the dark, Khonsu's team would close in quickly. The effects of the drug and the shadows of night would aid them.

Activity to his right pushed Khonsu back to the present. Kehave was on the move. The young man strode over with the kind of surety so often possessed by attractive people. The girls eagerly welcomed the handsome Kehave, his dark good looks disarming.

All of the men watched the unfolding plan from their discreet position in the bar. Except for the Serpent. His greedy eyes roamed over the well-shaped form of their quarry, tight blue T-shirt and white shorts that barely covered long, tanned legs.

The blonde chose that moment to toss her hair back and flash a sweet, yet inviting look to Kehave as he moved closer to her in the booth. He grinned back.

The girl never saw it, but from the darkened corner where the team sat, the Serpent also smiled. Then his hand disappeared under the table.

Khonsu saw it all and narrowed his eyes.

Yes. The Serpent would have to be watched.

14

Erica inhaled deeply and let the warm wind pass over her. Gentle gusts brought rich smells from the city below. Though most of the markets had closed for the night, the aroma of their wares still moved in rhythm with the scent of blooming jasmine, dancing up to tease and tantalize. Magic could be found here, if only one stopped to take it in.

Erica realized how much she had been missing her hectic but tranquil life back home. Murder and mutilation filled her thoughts now, and she knew how it felt to be wrapped up in the deaths of others. To bear a partial responsibility for their suffering.

Maybe she was being too harsh on herself, but all she could think of now was finding the next clue. The next vase, or whatever might be left of it. The longer it took her and Matt to complete the search, the higher the risk of another innocent person falling under the knives of Kherep Amun.

Damn those evil bastards for taking what could have been a challenging and exciting quest and turning into a nightmare. And any fantasy she might have of being with Matt was tinged at the edges with guilt. Morbidity.

Her growing interest in the FBI agent seemed lurid given the circumstances, and if any real emotion were to exist between them, it would forever be marred by the horrid memories of this trip and why they were really here.

Gazing up, Erica couldn't avoid the truth. Even with death and destruction all around, life still continued. Good, peaceful memories could still be made. And romance could still be found.

She considered the love affair between Hatshepsut and Senmut. The two had lived during a time when safety and security could change in a moment. Power was taken by force, just as Hatshepsut's nephew had taken from her. One day a queen and pharaoh, the next...vanished, with deceit and murder the most likely explanation.

Yet Senmut's love for his queen had persisted. So much that he went to extreme measures to hide her body. To protect her from those who would desecrate even her memory.

Erica sighed. The Jordanian night sky was beautiful, and romantic imaginings came easily. She wondered what it would be like to have a man love her like that. A man who would care for her and respect all facets of her personality. Love did strange things to normally rational people.

Just look how she'd changed her opinion of Matt.

Oh, no. That line of thinking was dangerous. She berated herself for even contemplating a future with Matt Pierce. The two of them weren't just living during hard times. They bore a responsibility to make the killings *stop*.

Sure the physical connection between them was undeniable, and it was reassuring to have human contact in the midst of all the horror, but he had made his position abundantly clear. Their predicament was temporary. No matter what happened between them, he was an agent first.

The man who made her melt second.

Erica tried to imagine what he was doing right now. Checking the weapon he always kept strapped to his ankle? Planning egress routes? Reading her e-mail?

No, that was unfair. He and Monroe had come clean about the spying. Still, there was a chamber inside Matt she just couldn't reach. She knew she could depend on him for protection, but what about the rest?

The whisper of his hand against her skin or the burn of his gaze when he looked at her with desire, these were things that could lead her down a rocky and treacherous trail. At least for her heart.

No, she couldn't be sure what Matt was doing right now, in any sense.

Cameron had made arrangements for three separate rooms at the hotel, so Matt was out of sight for the time being. While he was most assuredly on her mind, she appreciated the opportunity to be by herself for a while. To consider her clashing emotions, and the desires that would have to go unfulfilled.

She had taken a long, hot bath before making use of the complimentary scented lotion. The hotel provided every luxury, including a sauna and gym in the building that was a huge gray column rising above the Amman skyline.

A knock sounded on the door, drawing her in from the balcony. Erica wasn't expecting room service, since she and the men were planning to go out to eat. It had to be one of them, checking on her.

Disappointment crashed over her when it wasn't Matt standing on the other side of the door, and the sudden realization of that was even more of a reality-slap. She'd wanted it to be him. Her treasonous heart had practically leapt at the sound of the knock.

Instead of her newfound object of desire, one of the attendants from downstairs was standing there, holding out a white box to her. "Dr. Conner." He bowed his head, indicating he knew the delivery had been made to the right person. He backed away and disappeared down the hall, leaving Erica holding the box, adorned by a burgundy velvet ribbon and matching rosebud.

A mix of emotions collided as she walked to the sofa. It was a gift, obviously, but she was wary. Her imagination had been running wild ever since Cameron had told them about the intrusions at the dig site.

If Kherep Amun had been watching, there was a very real chance they'd seen her and Matt arrive. And seen them leave with Cameron.

Refusing to let the gorgeous box be a source of dread, Erica peeled away the ribbon and laid the rose gently to the side. Then she swept away sheets of transparent paper to reveal the contents. A swirl of glimmering white satin unfolded as she lifted the dress from its holdings. After a moment of awe, she stood and held it against herself, knowing it would fit perfectly.

Delicate beading trimmed the bust line, adding just enough sparkle. Leaving her arms and shoulders bare, it would hug her figure and fall to her knees with understated but sexual elegance. Erica wondered who was responsible, surely Matt or Cameron. She doubted this would be Kherep Amun's form of a scare tactic.

Laughter bubbled up, and she twirled with a sense of giddiness. She felt carefree for the first time in days and all because of a pretty dress. She was acting like such a girl.

Nothing could be done until she and Matt departed for their next destination, so she refused to feel guilty for taking some time away from the fear and worry. Besides, she might improve her focus if she let off a little steam.

On the heels of her rationalizations, Erica ran into a major stumbling block. More like a boulder. She only had practical shoes with her. Boots, to be exact. She worried her bottom lip and wondered if there were any way on earth she could find something appropriate at this hour.

Her hurried planning was interrupted as another knock echoed through the suite. Eagerness overrode caution as she rushed to the door, expecting the deliveryman to be there with the rest of her outfit.

He wasn't.

Matt stood fiercely in the doorway, a pair of white, strappy heels dangling from one finger as if he weren't sure what to do with them. A scowl darkened his too-handsome face.

Erica went warm and tingly inside. The romantic gesture combined with his warm chocolate eyes were almost her undoing. He'd shaved for the first time since they'd left Egypt, and Erica longed to run her fingertips over his firm jaw line and full, tempting lips.

"Thought you might need these." Matt held up the shoes.

Erica cocked her head. "What gave you that idea? You know something I don't?" She was teasing him, and her eyes said so.

"You can't take a girl to dinner in hiking boots. Kills the sex appeal of the dress." He handed her the heels. "I'll be back in half an hour." He turned to leave but stopped as if reconsidering.

After a long look of inspection, he leaned in and pressed his lips to hers. "You smell good," was all he said before walking away, leaving her wanting more.

In a daze she closed the door, reveling in the new awareness fluttering her heart and tingling her skin. She'd been attracted to men before, but nothing had ever come close to this.

She abruptly stopped smiling to herself. Could she really be crushing on serious Agent Pierce. The man of a million foul moods?

She shook her head and scoffed. *Surely not. It's way too soon. Impossible.*

Her uncontrollable smile popped back out. What did it matter for tonight? She would have a cherished friend with her on one arm. And a gorgeous, smart, reliable man on the other. They were in a mysterious and exotic land with a night of entertainment and camaraderie ahead of them.

Whatever might happen tomorrow, she was going to enjoy this evening. Under the stars of the Jordan sky, Erica Conner was going to allow herself to live a little.

Even during the hard times.

Stepping down from the jeep in her new outfit, Erica looked nothing like a woman who'd gladly scrounged through dusty boxes in a grungy basement only hours before. Matt took her hand to help her descend to the sidewalk. Her skin gliding over his was no particular hardship, either.

"Looks like we're not the only ones looking for a little distraction tonight." He said, tearing his eyes from the curve of her calf and gesturing to the crowded streets. Every square foot was covered by people laughing and talking as they headed for various destinations.

Cameron had agreed to park the car, leaving Erica and Matt in front of the building as the vehicle slid off into traffic. The door was lit on both sides by lanterns, and dancing flames created a welcoming entrance to the restaurant Cameron claimed was the best in town. The wood sign was unreadable, but appeared authentic and all the more alluring for its hand carved writing.

"We have a table waiting." Matt slipped his arm around her waist as they walked in, shooting down the interest of an approaching man. The stranger's bold assessment of Erica put Matt's back up, and he felt no compunction about threatening bodily harm with a single look.

Matt would swear a growl had started to form low in his throat, and the very real need to lay claim to the woman beside him was beginning to feel exactly right. He'd never found it necessary to mark a female as his personal territory, but an urge to cover Erica's lips with his own rose up in him with a fury.

He wanted to taste her right here in the middle of the restaurant, so no other male would even consider her an option. Not if they expected to survive until dawn.

The situation was too surreal. How could such conflicting demands coexist for him? His surprising attachment to Erica kept clashing against the burden of making sure she stayed safe. On top of that was the issue of the diabolical cult that could literally be around any corner.

And here he was taking her out to dinner. In a public place.

His face must have reflected his unease. Erica squeezed the hand she still clung to. "None of that tonight. We're closer than we ever thought we'd be at this point and make more headway every day."

With a curt nod, he led her inside and to their appointed table. He motioned for her to take the chair he'd pulled out for her then took the seat to her side. His back was to the wall and all entrances to the room in his line of sight.

He wouldn't frighten Erica needlessly, not tonight, but Kherep Amun's presence in Jordan was a given. They had staked out the dig site and that told Matt the group knew more about the vases and their hiding places than he and Monroe had realized.

The question now was how much did they know and what would they do about Matt's and Erica's involvement?

Matt knew they were a calculating and innovative faction, so they could easily decide to keep tabs on Erica, watch where she and Matt went next. Or they could try to take them down and steal any vases or clues they'd uncovered.

Or the cult might just decide to kill them.

"Do you want to go back to the hotel?" Erica asked, touching Matt's shoulder lightly. Her pretty blue eyes were shadowed with worry, and that's exactly what he didn't want. There would be plenty of dark truth to deal with in the morning.

He put on a smile that he didn't feel. "No. Just planning."

"For tomorrow?" she asked, still with an expression of anxiety.

Damn. He didn't want her thinking about that either. "For next week, actually. When I'm back in the States enjoying a decent burger."

Erica smiled then. "Cam promised we would love the food here. And if not, I think I saw steak on the hotel menu."

"Did I miss something funny?" This from Cameron as he

joined them at the table. "I'm gone for five minutes and you two start the party without me." He winked at Erica before looking over her shoulder to hail someone.

He'd obviously been here before as the waiter greeted him by name. "Cam. Good to see you again. Should I bring the *Nargileh* now, or would you like a meal first?"

"What's Nargileh?" Erica asked, giving Cameron a look that asked what-have-you-been-doing-you-bad-boy? "Should we be expecting an appetizer or another type of dish entirely?" The devilish raise of her brow made the implication clear.

"No worries, Erica. I'll save the pretty girls for another night." He leaned farther in. "Unless you've got some belly dancing skills you've been keeping secret. I might be up for that."

Her responding gesture was less than ladylike, and this time Matt's grin was for real.

After small talk about the city and the restaurant's reputation, they ordered drinks and several entrees to share. Cameron followed up with a request for strawberry Nargileh. He didn't correct Erica when she assumed it was some kind of dessert.

Matt knew better.

He finally relaxed but continued to survey their surroundings. The place was pretty upscale, and he was glad to know he'd made the right call with Erica's dress.

A candle sat in the middle of their intricate, mosaic table. Walls were draped in silks, richly colored in crimson and purple with gold stitching, and the soft music echoing in the background conjured visions of women in sheer fabrics sweeping and swaying with navels exposed.

"I find myself feeling extremely envious of the two of you." Cameron's sudden statement brought a look of surprise then concern to Erica's face, while Matt steadily watched him and waited for him to continue.

Matt was sure Cameron was about to admit he had feelings

for Erica. If a challenge was issued, he needed to be prepared. But what could he say? He had been holding Erica at an emotional arm's length. He had no real claim.

And that bothered him.

Cameron lifted his glass and drank before saying, "I've been tossing something about in my head for a while now."

"What is it, Cam?" Erica asked.

He let out a deep breath and met her eyes. "I've been thinking of making a jump."

Matt remained quiet. This didn't sound like what he'd been expecting. Erica also seemed confused. "What do you mean?"

"I think I'm going to switch areas of concentration."

After a few seconds, Erica chuckled and reached over to put her hand on his forearm. "Is that what you're all worked up about? You wouldn't be the first. Why are you hesitant?"

Matt could no longer contain himself. "What are you two talking about, and why do you seem to have your own secret language?"

Ignoring him, Erica asked Cameron, "What are you thinking of?"

"Marine," was all he said in response.

"Of course, you always did enjoy the ocean."

Understanding dawned on Matt. "All of this over a career change?" His barking laugh told them exactly what he thought of all the drama. "Isn't it all pretty much the same?

The responding scowls from both Erica and Cam made him throw his hands up in surrender. This was obviously not a joking matter. "Sorry. Please continue." He chose this time to partake of the food that had arrived and decided to leave the archaeology to the two of them.

Cameron shook his head. "I feel like I've wasted time, not only my own, but that of my professors."

"You'll still use the knowledge you have. You'd be surprised how often the fields cross over." Erica smiled encouragingly. "Besides, everything recovered from shipwrecks somehow came from terra firma in the first place."

Cameron gave her a small smile. "You're right about that." Twirling the contents in his glass he spoke to no one in particular. "I've been offered a spot studying under Dr. Nichols. I just hadn't quite made up my mind, yet."

"And now?" Erica prompted.

Placing his palms down on the table, Cameron took a moment before answering. A wealth of emotions crossed his face until he settled on a wide grin. Looked like he'd made a decision.

Cameron put the flat of one hand on the table with a *thump*. "I think we'll make that a celebratory Nargileh. And you'll have to have some, too." He waved over the server to let him know they were ready.

"Sounds good," Erica said, sitting up straighter in her seat. She was probably anticipating a nice strawberry confection.

"Do you think that's wise?" Matt asked Cameron. "We've already brought her out at night, and in a leg-baring skirt."

"No problems here, mate. Why do you think I chose this place?" He winked at Erica. "We may get a few odd looks, but as far as the skirt, I'm enjoying the view."

Cameron glanced at Matt as if judging his response to the comment.

Matt refused to give any hint of how badly he wanted to pull Cameron out of his chair and to the back alley. He blinked once to clear his mind of the violent imaginings. What the hell was wrong with him? He protected and served.

He didn't drag guys into dark places to pummel them. Especially semi-decent friends of a friend. He steered his gaze to Erica instead. There was the guilty party.

Firm, shapely legs crossed each other under the table, and he remembered how they'd looked beneath the sway of white satin. Her raven hair fell in a wave to her shoulders, and those intelligent eyes were alive with humor as she chatted with Cameron.

Strong yet curvaceous. Independent but sweet. And her skin

glowed golden in the candlelight.

All of the reasons he had for keeping his distance suddenly lost their strength. What had once been impenetrable steel now had a million holes shot straight through. His unbending will had been perforated. Weakened.

And it had all started with a skirt named after a pencil.

Erica had layers, more than he'd seen when they'd first met. But at the time he'd been furious about his orders to take her along on this risky mission. She could still be a pain at times, and he was still haunted by what could go wrong. What he'd seen go wrong. First hand.

But he had to admit Erica had been less of a burden than he'd expected. He also knew she possessed more than book-smarts. Courage, grace, and a slicing intelligence. A combination that had taken a seasoned Special Forces vet turned FBI agent and turned him into a hormonal teenager.

But what could he say? She did look good in that dress. His eyes fell to her legs again. Then her bare shoulders.

Erica misunderstood his stare. "I don't know why you would be worried about my dress." She tossed her hair back in a defiant gesture. "Jordan is one of the more liberal places in the Middle East, and I'm hardly the only woman here tonight."

"No," Matt responded. "But you will be the only American woman, with two men, in a short skirt. And now smoking Nargileh."

"Smoking?" Erica blanched. "Cam, you haven't ordered some type of opiate or something, have you?"

"Way to go, Yank." Cameron waved a dismissive hand toward Matt. "He's making too much of it. Nargileh actually has a spiritual base to it."

Matt snorted. "So does peyote."

Erica's eyes widened, and Cameron chuckled. "Don't listen to him. It's only a fruit-flavored tobacco that's smoked with a water pipe."

"That looks like a bong," Matt added with a smirk.

Ignoring the comment, Cameron continued. "It's actually gaining popularity in the states. All nice and legal."

Erica sighed, shooting an uncertain glance toward Matt. "I'll give it a shot. I guess."

"Good," Cameron replied, "Because here it is, now."

The waiter set down a tray with an elaborate wooden box. He opened it to reveal a mother-of-pearl inlay under the lid, while the pipe and other accoutrements nestled in a bed of green velvet.

Erica lifted the beautiful pipe. "This is not your ordinary bong." It was ornately decorated and glistened with gemstones that almost lent credence to its use.

Matt took the pipe from her and lit it. "Cameron is right. Some Arabs take their smoking very seriously." He offered it back to her. "Ladies first, or would you like a demonstration?"

Her smile was definitely mischievous now. "Just walk me through it." She raised the pipe ceremoniously. "If this is supposed to be ritualistic, then I say we make a toast."

"A toast with tobacco?" Cameron looked at her in doubt.

"Why not?" She cleared her throat. "Here's to good friends. Old friends that can always be counted on." She nodded to Cameron.

"And new ones, who hold a wealth of surprises." With this she gave a meaningful smile to Matt before moving the pipe to her lips.

Caught up in the moment, they'd all forgotten she was new at this sport. Erica inhaled deeply then abruptly brought the pipe down from her lips, holding in the smoke as if unsure what to do with it.

"Um." This from Cameron as he valiantly tried not to laugh. And failed.

Matt fared only slightly better. "You can let it out now." At the look on her face, he said, "And I suggest you do."

Erica exhaled on a cough, strawberry scented smoke swirling out and over the table. Keeping a straight face in front of the two laughing men, she managed to blink the tears out of her eyes and croak, "Does it come in chocolate?"

15

Warm night air flowed in behind them as they swept through the glass doors of the hotel lobby. The evening had been as relaxing as possible, given the surrounding gloom and conditions that had brought Erica and Matt to Jordan in the first place.

Other niceties than Nargileh had been consumed, and Cameron was walking a little sideways after several glasses of a dark and potent drink. He punched the elevator button several times, then cursed and performed the ritual again before realizing he'd finally hit a glowing arrow. Just the wrong one.

When they exited onto their floor, Erica breathed a relieved sigh as Cameron kissed her on the cheek and said goodnight. She wasn't sure what would happen between her and Matt, but whatever the case, she felt it would go more smoothly without an audience.

Matt had sent darting and appreciative looks at her all night, and as the evening waned, she'd begun to burn deep down in her stomach. A yearning that had spread and tormented. Matt wouldn't put his hands on her while others were nearby.

But she could tell he wanted to.

Now she felt the return of those fiery butterflies to her belly. Cameron was gone, and she and Matt were alone. Funny how things had changed. Only this morning she'd been isolated in the countryside with him, but somewhere in the hours since, she'd become acutely aware of every move he made. Every gesture and nuance of his expressions.

And every heated gaze as his eyes traced the outline of her face and body in equal measure.

Now he walked her to her door and waited as she swiped the card to open the computerized lock. Erica swayed a little as she turned to face him. "Are you sure there wasn't anything else in that pipe?"

"I'm sure." His gaze fell to her lips. "You're just not used to it." He grasped her gently under the chin and kissed her. "And because of that I've inadvertently ruined my own plans for the night."

Erica studied him, still dazed by the night's activities. "Which were?"

His warm breath whispered over her ear as he leaned in, one hand slipping up to curl around her nape. "To seduce you and finally do all of the things you and I have both been thinking about."

Erica had a hard time drawing a breath. Her body had grown tight with a sudden and suspicious ache. His chest was so close to hers, and all she could think to say was, "Oh."

Matt continued before she could recover. "I'm not going to do that now, because I want you clear-headed and in control when I make love to you." He leaned forward and kissed her again, but this time he sunk deeply into the act, holding her firmly with the one hand as if he didn't trust the other.

Erica was flushed with a full-on lust attack by the time he quickly pulled away. "Good night, Erica."

He trailed a finger over her collar bone and walked away, leaving her to stare blankly at the hallway wallpaper. Wondering what had just happened. It wasn't the flavored smoke making her heart pound like a sledge hammer. The only intoxication in her blood now was Matt. One hundred percent pure.

Something had changed between them since their last kiss on the boat. This time had been deeper, more consuming. The intensity held her there, standing in the hall and wanting to call after him.

Instead she sighed to herself and brushed her fingertips over lips that could still feel and taste his warmth. It looked like she'd be tossing and turning tonight, but not due to fear.

Closing the door behind her she turned and made her way across the suite, considering a nightcap to help her sleep. After her fill of tobacco, she decided against it and continued to the bedroom.

Erica went to the window and gazed out at the Amman nightline, thinking of Matt and how they would continue from here. What could she expect from him once this was all over? Was she setting herself up for failure? For heartbreak?

Mentally kicking herself for worrying about things she shouldn't be, she decided to go to bed and hope for sweet dreams. Slipping off her heels, she crossed to the bed's canopy, enshrouded by feather light materials. She pulled back the satin comforter.

And screamed.

Matt was in his room opening the small refrigerator at the bar. He definitely needed a drink. Walking away from Erica had been torture, with the trust in those blue eyes wreaking havoc on his control. But he was still conflicted.

Not a bad idea to take some time to clear his head. To figure out just what he was thinking. What he was doing.

The woman made him crazy. Why else would he toss aside his most ingrained values? Follow the rules and don't get attached. Especially to anyone who was or could be a mark.

The thought of Erica being the target of those madmen stiffened his spine with rage, the can of beer bending under the strength of his hand. They would have to come through him first.

Cocking his head, Matt held still and listened.

The sound had been faint, but it crystallized his blood into ice. He dropped the can where he stood then bolted. *Erica.* The cry had come from her room.

Bursting into the hallway he almost collided with a now sober Cameron. No words were needed as both men ran down the corridor, Cam's face as hard as Matt's determination.

Matt's training and patience were both tested when he kicked in the door to Erica's suite. He wanted to rush in but knew the foolishness of allowing emotion to rule action.

Both men stopped once inside, ready for anything. Matt stood still, listening. There was no sound, no movement.

Cameron breathed heavily beside him. "Where?"

Without answering, Matt held up the gun he'd drawn as second nature movements took over. He moved quietly to the open bedroom door and cleared the room. Seeing Erica alone, relief tried to take hold. Until he took a good look at her face.

Cameron made a move to go in, but stilled at Matt's raised hand. Both men looked at the woman they cared for then followed her frozen stare to the bed.

At first they didn't see anything, since one corner of the bed sheet had been pulled back and was tented, hiding the area behind it. Then there was the slightest movement on the bed, and Cameron knew in an instant what it was.

"Erica. Don't move, don't speak." Having grown up in Australia, Cameron knew the natural dangers of his homeland. They could be found in the sanctity of one's home as often as they were found in the field.

And this one was definitely out of place.

"It has good eyesight and smell, so just try to stay calm and breathe normally," Cameron said easily, imbuing his tone with the very calm he'd mentioned. The serenity that would save their lives.

Matt's eyes narrowed as he studied the bed. "What kind is it?"

"I can't tell for sure from here," Cameron rasped. "I need to see more of its body."

At that moment the creature shifted again and the rounded snout of the snake came into full view. It rose slowly in a sinuous dance, flicking its tongue into the still air.

Erica sucked in a breath.

Cameron looked into the mirror behind Erica and caught a more detailed reflection of the snake. "I think it's a taipan." For Matt's ears only he added, "Shit."

"Deadly, I assume." Matt was zoning in on the location of the snake, scoping out his options. "Can I drop it?"

"It would be risky. Its attention is on Erica and may respond to anything by striking out at her. If you miss..." Cameron didn't finish. He didn't need to.

Matt stiffened and spoke to Erica. "I'm going to come in closer. Don't look at me, and try not to jump when I shoot. It will all be over in a few seconds."

As he crept closer to their side of the bed, with the snake facing Erica, Matt aimed the gun at the most massive part of the serpent. The coiled positioning would allow him to hit several parts of the creature at once.

"Wait." Cameron stopped him, then spoke to Erica. "Whatever happens, when Matt shoots, get the hell out of there and around to the end of the bed. Head toward the door."

At Matt's questioning look he added, "Even if you hit it dead on, it might be able to fight back. I think her odds are better if she's not standing in the vicinity."

Matt nodded and zeroed in on the thick brown coils once again. With the silencer attached, the whooshing sound of the pistol filled the room. The snake's body jerked from the impact as Erica leapt away and ran to the opposite corner of the room. Trembling she crowded in behind Cameron, grasping his arm. "Did you get it? Is it dead?"

Matt answered with a couple more shots. "It is now."

Erica exhaled and covered her face with her hands. She stood that way for several seconds, shaking.

Cameron turned around and enveloped her in a hug. "You gave us quite a scare."

Laughter bordering on hysterical bubbled from her throat. "Did I? Sorry, I'll try not to do that again."

Cameron seemed to sense more than feel Matt standing behind him. Erica's eyes moved and softened in a way that told Cameron this was one battle she'd have to fight for herself. She was done for and there was nothing he could do to protect her.

Love was a shadow in the night, slipping in undetected and settling inside before you could stop it.

Cameron's lips quirked up as he looked at his old friend. He wanted her to be happy, and he could see how she felt about the man she'd been thrown into the kettle with.

Even if she didn't know it, yet.

He'd also seen the alarm on Matt's face when Erica had been in danger. That along with the possessiveness the man had shown since the moment they'd arrived at the dig site was enough to tell anyone looking closely that there was something brewing. Something strong, that would go one of two ways.

Rocking-chair buddies or the scar that never healed.

"What was it?" The question from Matt snapped Cameron back to the situation at hand. He cleared his throat and walked away from Erica to take a closer look at what was left of the reptile's body. He grabbed the tail and pulled, stretching the length of it across the bed.

"Ugh. Do you have to do that?" Erica rubbed her arms.

Cameron dusted his hands, feeling the invisible filth of treachery on his palms. "It's about two meters. And see how the color gets lighter on the underside, more yellow toward the head? It's an inland taipan, from Australia. It definitely doesn't belong here."

"Yeah." Matt's eyes were cold. "I'm sure we know who's responsible. I'm just surprised they knew where to find us, especially since you got us the rooms."

There was no accusation or suspicion in the comment. All of them realized that Kherep Amun was on to them and had tracked them here, despite any attempts to lie low.

"Ancient Egyptians revered the serpent," Erica whispered. "But they also used them for horrible deeds. Suicide." She lifted tense blue eyes to Matt and Cameron. "Or murder."

Things had changed. Cameron knew Matt would have to contact his associates and reinforce the need for precautions. They were all in danger now. "We can't stay here, but I have an idea where to go. If you feel safe doing that," he told Matt. "I can handle the hotel, too. The presence of the snake will explain the bullet holes, but I'll let them work out the rest for themselves. No need to share more than we have to."

Matt agreed with a nod and turned to face Erica. "It's time to go."

16

Daylight washed its way into the room and across Erica's eyes. Unfamiliar yet sweetly pitched birds called to each other just outside the window, ensuring she would wake up in case the sun failed at the job.

Once she'd swept the fog out of her eyes, she sniffed two times. Someone was cooking. And it smelled delicious.

She stretched her arms above her head only to realize she had a crick in her neck and that she was in the same position she'd fallen asleep in. The previous twenty-four hours had worn her thin, and all things considered, she counted herself fortunate to have gotten any sleep at all.

Remembering a flicking, forked tongue, she winced. Who was she kidding? She was lucky to be alive.

Pulling herself up to sit on the side of the bed, she worked what kinks she could out of her shoulders before staggering to the bathroom. Through sleepy eyes she took in her surroundings, tastefully designed with several antique pieces scattered about. She noted a rich shine on the darkly wooded floors, offset by walls painted slate blue.

The bedroom also boasted a sitting area with what she assumed were hand woven rattan chairs gathered around a stone fireplace. The collection of luxuries told her Cameron's reference to his friend having "a little money" had been something of an understatement.

The man in question, Steve, had connected with Cameron through a mutual acquaintance who worked at the dig site. As fellow Australians, the two had formed a rapport. Knowing Steve was out of town for a couple of weeks, Cameron had brought them here to bunk down at his friend's house for the night.

The members of Kherep Amun who had tracked them to the hotel would never know where to look. Cameron had argued the entire time as they'd sped through the night. He didn't want Erica to pursue the clues any longer. He thought she should get out.

She put the issue to rest quickly and firmly. Intent on seeing it through to the end, she rationalized that any possible risk to herself paled in comparison to the bloodshed that might be released if the religious group succeeded.

Besides, she and Matt would be extra vigilant from now on.

In addition to a stealthy getaway in the middle of the night, Matt had also made a quick sweep of all their belongings to ensure no tracking devices had been planted. After the snake incident, they couldn't afford to underestimate their enemies.

Erica wondered why they wanted her dead. She was the one deciphering the clues, and it made more sense for them to follow discreetly. Or steal the relics and puzzle pieces she and Matt already had.

Maybe Kherep Amun was way ahead of them, but if that were true, why were they still lurking around the dig site at Pella? Perhaps they weren't sure if the Egyptian pieces had been found and taken to the museum?

Regardless, the bastards had decided Erica was a variable they didn't want factored in. *Hmph. How would Hatshepsut feel about that, boys?*

As she made up the bed, her feminist anger was chased into hiding as the ugly replay of the snake's rising head flashed in her mind. Flesh raised in a tingle as she recalled the paralyzing fear.

Another shiver rolled over her and she decided to wash the distasteful sensations away with some hot water. But even with the jet stream massaging her shoulders and steam rising across the mirror, it was a long time before she felt warm.

After the shower, she found her way down to the lower level, following the aroma of baking. Fresh, warm bread called to her, teasing her nose and awakening her stomach.

In bare feet she padded down the wooden stairs, grinning when Matt's attention flew to her poppy-red toenails. He met her raised brow as she came to the kitchen door. "Nice pedicure, Doc."

Erica shrugged. "A woman's got to keep her spirits up while fighting evil maniacs."

Her casual delivery pulled an odd expression from him, as if he were surprised by her carefree attitude. She wouldn't spoil it by telling him she was still shaken up.

Instead she patted her hands on his hips and laid her lips to his before breezing past him into the kitchen. The simple gesture was casual and short, but sent her blood zinging to her head, chest... and other areas.

"Mmm...what are you making?" This she directed at Cam while helping herself to some of what was probably the best-smelling coffee in the world.

Cameron cast a look over his shoulder while swirling a frying pan. "My mother's breakfast specialty. Eggs with ham, cheese, and tomatoes."

"We call that an omelet," Matt said, but his comment was met with a laugh from Cameron. No barbs evident this morning. The two had somehow become comrades in the span of twelve hours. Brought together by a smoke and a snake roundup.

"Yeah, but you've never had my mother's omelet, mate." Cameron continued working ingredients into the pan. "Add to that home baked bread and chutney, your tongue will beat your brains out."

"Appetizing." Erica smirked at her friend. "Stick to cooking and skip the anatomical references, if you don't mind."

After doctoring her coffee, Erica turned to take in the large kitchen. Sunlight filtered in over an oval table roomy enough to sit eight. A clear glass vase, bottom the size of a bowling ball, held giant leaves resembling elephant ears. Set against their emerald green were bright red birds of paradise and white lilies.

Her eyes were drawn to the laptop sitting on the table, its black color a stark contrast to the lush flowers. Or maybe it was just a reminder that their mini-vacation was just that. Mini.

Erica would wait until after breakfast to think about awful things. She'd like to squeak out two cups of coffee's worth of peace.

The birds were still serenading each other outside, drawing Erica's attention to the sunny window. The home overlooked a mountainside below, white houses dotting the landscape amidst deep green vegetation.

"What a view your friend has here." She closed her eyes and leaned against the windowsill, letting the sun wash its cleansing warmth over her.

A moment later, her lids popped open as a piece of freshly cut bread waved under her nose. She faced Cameron as he sniffed and wiggled his brows. Taking a bite of the bread, he said, "Let's eat."

They ate like kings and laughed like loons. A full stomach, pleasant atmosphere, and trusted friends did wonders for her spirit. An hour had passed this way, and the three understood the time was necessary. Erica and Matt needed recharging.

It had only been a week since Dr. Monroe and Matt entered her life, but so much had happened since. The images of glory and fame for her museum had faded drastically. She still wanted to honor her family's name, but realized this might not be the appropriate way to do so. If she were honest with herself, she might not want ownership of the vases.

Every time she looked at them, she would remember a nurse, tortured and murdered in her own bed. An innocent child, lured to a grisly death.

Erica sought Matt's gaze, seeking reassurance and the strength he always possessed.

His answering smile did just that, soothing her with a single glance. Strange how this morning they could communicate without saying a word, and seven days ago they couldn't seem to speak without insult.

Their silent conversation was interrupted as Cameron leaned in to gather their dishes. Erica stood to help him wipe off the table as Matt began setting up the connection that would once again bring them eye to eye with Dr. Monroe. Virtually, eye to eye.

As the screen flickered to life, Erica pulled a chair to Matt's side, allowing them both to be in the field of vision for the parties on the other end. The last thing she expected to see was the kind Dr. Monroe with an angry red face, head cocked to the side as if lecturing a wayward student.

Matt barely hid his shock when another man came into view. "That's Gus," he told Erica. "My supervisor." He was also the one receiving Monroe's reprimand.

Monroe did a double take when he saw Matt and Erica's faces appear. He appeared flustered and cleared his throat before addressing them. "Matt. Dr. Connor. I am eager to learn what has transpired since our last…"

"Agent Pierce." Gus interrupted Dr. Monroe and nudged his way into the screen's view.

Before he could continue, Monroe was back. "You really should have more respect for your elders."

"And you should have more respect for authority." Gus faced forward and held his ground. Or about half of it.

As the men continued to debate, Karen's voice rung out in the background. "It's been like this since the new man got here and took over." Her face appeared between the shoulders of Monroe and Gus, eyes rolling to show her opinion of the territorial dispute.

Erica lowered her head in an attempt to hide the smile creeping out. Karen, however, was not bound by such modesty. Bobbing her head, she made the symbolic Rock On Horns with both hands behind the two men.

The scene was so comical Erica couldn't bite down on the laughter, earning her a chastising glare from Matt.

"Ahem." Karen cleared her throat in mock seriousness. "You were saying, Erica."

Deciding to bow out for the moment, Guy nodded to Monroe, but was obviously impatient to have his say.

Erica smiled in gratitude at her friend. "We've got a lot to report."

Karen brought a pretzel stick up to her mouth from somewhere off-screen. "You've made some progress in the search for old Hattie?"

Lolling her head to the side in consideration and humor, Erica gave the nickname some thought. "It is easier to say."

"Really." Monroe clucked his tongue at Karen. "You should also have more respect, young lady."

Karen only winked at him. She and the older man seemed to be bonding.

Regretting the loss of the light-hearted mood, Erica swallowed her smile and grudgingly returned to the topic of history, blood, and sacrifice. "We were able to recover the next clue, though only a portion of the vase remained intact."

Monroe grimaced. "It is to be expected. The more important matter is that you discovered more of what's needed to find Hatshepsut. Have you solved it, yet?"

"We believe so. With Cameron's help and access to the museum here, we were able to get the piece and decipher its message. Unfortunately, it was in an entirely different type of encryption. We should expect each puzzle to be unique."

"How was this one hidden?" Karen found a seat and rolled

up alongside Monroe.

"It was in the form of a scytale code," Erica said.

Karen stopped mid-chew. "A what?"

Monroe glanced at Karen. "I'll explain it later." He turned back to Erica. "Where did it lead you?" The older man's eyes gleamed in anticipation.

Erica sighed. "It was cryptic, obviously, but we're pretty sure the next vase was hidden in or around Herakleion."

Silence hummed from the monitor as both Karen and Monroe stared back, though each for different reasons.

Monroe finally found his tongue. "I'm hoping I've misheard you, Erica."

"I'm afraid not." Erica had been expecting this reaction and understandably so. "But we're still optimistic. Let me explain."

"Please do." Monroe said with a disgruntled crossing of the arms.

Erica sat up straighter, hoping to express her confidence in their plans. "I know you're all hearing this for the first time, and believe me, we were right there with you when we realized the city is now under water."

Karen sat forward in her chair. "Under what? And you're still optimistic? Sure you don't mean, oh I don't know...out of your mind?" Now both parties at the other end of the satellite feed looked unhappy.

"Relax." Erica continued. "There was mention of red colossi, some of which are still intact, leading us to believe there may have been similar ones in that area at an earlier time. Builders and artists tended to use the natural resources of an area for architecture and sculpture, and that means the red granite had probably been utilized before." She nodded as if agreeing with herself. "Many artifacts have been found there."

Gorgeous Asian eyes narrowed on Erica. "Found underwater, you mean?"

Erica zapped Karen with a look. "Do I tell you how to run an investigation?"

Inclining her head in acquiescence, the Marshal waved for her to go on.

"To answer your question, yes, underwater, but not that far down." Beside Erica, Matt shifted, but when she turned to him in question, nodded for her to continue. "Many of the statues and buildings that are large enough have been left in place," she said.

Monroe's took his turn with skepticism. "But Herakleion was built well after the time of Hatshepsut and her lover, Senmut. How could he have possibly had one of her vases hidden there?"

"Herakleion wasn't there, yet, but maybe another city was. You know how common it was to build new dwellings on top of old foundations. Plus..." Erica held up her hand before he could interject. "Plus, the clue alluded to the written name of 'the god of gods,' who we feel sure is Amun."

Enlightenment dawned and Monroe's eyebrows lifted. "Yes, the temple of Amun. I believe you are on the appropriate course."

"There are still some areas of concern. Water is used more than once, and you know it has a specific meaning each time." Erica felt her I'm-thinking-wrinkle form. "We may have to scout the area and get back to you. The more heads involved the better. I'll send you the copies of what we have so far. Maybe you'll have different insight."

The older man perked up. "We'll be here anytime. I'm beginning to appreciate the toys all these feds have at their disposal."

"Speaking of us feds." Matt finally spoke. "Do you mind if I brief Gus?"

Monroe's mood seemed much improved by the idea of a clue coming his way. He was almost jovial. "Of course. I'm sorry to say he hasn't gone far."

Soon Gus took his place onscreen, with a stubborn Karen maintaining her seat, refusing to be kept out of the conversation.

"Any sightings of Kherep Amun?" Gus wasted no time on

formalities.

Matt's face might as well have been made of stone. "You might say that. Except they were the ones who found us." He filled them in on the suspicious activities at the dig site as well as the computer hacking at the museum.

"They were actually there before you then." Gus made the observation with a clench of his jaw.

"Not surprising, really." This unexpected outburst came from Cameron. "It was well known that we'd unearthed some Egyptian items from the time period you're concerned with. If this Kherep Amun is as organized as you think, they probably investigate any pertinent finds."

After putting forth his theory, Cameron tossed a wink and a wave Karen's way. "Good to see ya', girl. Still keeping them all in line?"

Karen responded with a sly grin.

"You know." Erica brought them back to the subject at hand. "If those pieces had been given any more attention than being wrapped in newspaper and stuffed in a cardboard box, they might have been found before we got there."

Cameron nodded. "Yep. They would have been catalogued and shelved, making them easily accessible to whomever was fiddling around in our database. Thank the devil for alternate priorities."

"Gus, there is one other thing." Matt's lips pressed together as he stared at Karen, as if he didn't want to say whatever he was about to in front of her. "Kherep Amun tracked us to the hotel. I don't think they were around in Luxor, but they definitely made us by the time we got to Amman.

"What happened?" Gus asked.

Matt told them about the snake.

As expected, Karen erupted. "Oh, hell no. I think the time is right for you to pull out. This is getting out of control. Either you're coming out, or I'm coming in." She threw the ultimatum at Erica.

Before Erica could respond, Matt did. "Look, we know we have to be more careful now, and as far as we can tell, there is no reason for them to have Herakleion on their map as a possible location. We have the clue that points to it and are still having a hard time believing it."

Slightly defused, Karen ran her hands over her ponytail. "I still think you could use more backup." She added to Matt, "No offense."

"None taken."

"I need you there, Karen." Erica cast pleading eyes toward the screen. "I worry enough about what might happen to... us." She caught herself in time, but slid her eyes to the left to peek at Matt. Too many people around to allow her feelings for him to be so transparent.

Gus spoke up and broke into Erica's thoughts. "Matt, if you think they're close, let me know. I'll send in a team to track them. You're the lead on this and should stay with Dr. Conner. We need her to finish this."

Karen took exception to the comment. "And if you didn't need her? She's not expendable, you know. At least not to me."

"Or me." Dr. Monroe's voice echoed from the background.

Matt found Karen's eyes. "Or me." The meaning behind his words was clear. After a moment, Karen nodded reluctantly.

Erica looked over at Matt, then back to the others. "I guess we'll be in touch when we have more to share. Dr. Monroe, please contact us if you discover anything we overlooked."

The man peered over the shoulders of Karen and Gus. "I will, you can trust." He smiled encouragingly.

Matt needed one final clarification. "Gus. The SCUBA equipment?"

Karen's eyes widened at the mention of the gear. She looked to Erica but said nothing.

"Already working on it," Gus said as he stood. "Get to where you need to go and let us know where to bring it. The less anyone knows about your specifics ahead of time, the better."

With all parties in silent agreement, Matt flipped a switch and the screen went black.

17

Slapping sounds rose as the high speed boat collided with dancing sea waves, lulling Erica into a daze. Several hours ago she had still been in the relative luxury of the house in Amman, now she was fixated on the compact but deadly machine gun stored under the bench across from where she sat.

It seemed an odd contrast to the hot pink float and floral towel covering it in an effort to disguise. The nose of the gun stuck out, prompting her to nudge it back under with the tip of her tennis shoe. Having a pistol for protection at home was one thing, but the less she had to touch this cold black peacekeeper the better.

Erica and Matt had parted ways with Cameron amid promises to use caution and to be in touch via Karen and Monroe. Erica had tried to convince Cameron that he would only endanger himself if he kept in contact with anyone involved, but he'd been immovable.

Hugging her goodbye at the airport he'd given her no choice. "I'm either kept in the loop or I come with you."

She cared too much for her friend to allow him to accompany her and Matt. It was enough of a concern that he'd already been made by Kherep Amun. Staying in Jordan was no longer an option, and a replacement had been contacted to take over his dig site in Pella.

Guilt plagued Erica. Getting Cameron involved and forcing him to leave the excavation for his own safety was all her doing. He assured her he would have it no other way, considering what he now knew.

Cameron was leaving on a separate flight, heading back to Australia for a brief visit home. He would then join up with the professor who had offered him a spot on a team planning marine excavations near the coast of France. Cameron was going after his dream.

Footsteps interrupted her musings as Matt descended to the galley, a room equipped with every modern kitchen convenience. "You okay? Not getting seasick are you?"

Erica offered a weak smile in return. "No. Not seasick, just thinking."

"Good, because I got us some lunch." He laid submarine sandwiches on the table with chips, diet drinks and— bless him— chocolate.

Stomach growling in response, Erica dug in. "Monroe was right. You feds are handy to have around."

The boat was well-stocked. With American food and American bodies. Matt had been serious about increasing security. If other boaters looked closely, they would see chiseled muscles beneath the intentionally benign Hawaiian shirts of the men above. Three agents, one a former Navy Seal, took up their posts on deck as the vessel made its way out into the Mediterranean Sea.

Between chews Erica questioned Matt. "We're using the GPS coordinates Monroe sent us?"

Mouth full of food, Matt grunted in response.

She was referring to the data they had been graciously given by the lead archaeologist who'd originally found and mapped the sunken city of Herakleion. Since Monroe was already there in France and a professional colleague of the Frenchman, the two had met in person, saving both time and suspicious inquiries.

The man had been happy to help after being told a terrorist group had an interest in his beloved underwater city. After leaving many of the structures as an aquatic tour for divers, he was adamant about protecting the ruins.

Matt took a long drink of soda and reclined on the bench that served as seating for the table, both affixed to the floor for safety. "We've got a little time to kill. Why don't you tell me more about where we're going."

Erica nodded. "Only a little time. Herakleion is less than four miles from Alexandria."

"That still seems like a long way from the modern coast, meaning a large chunk of land just up and fell into the ocean." He swept a finger over the corner of her mouth. "Had a little mayo on your face."

Embarrassed by the idea, Erica used a napkin to wipe again, just in case. "There are a couple of theories as to how it might have happened. Theory one is an earthquake, as you might imagine. The other is a flood."

"A flood?" Matt asked skeptically. "You mean one the size of the forty days and nights kind? Wouldn't that be on record somewhere?"

Erica's grin dripped sarcasm. "As a matter of fact it is. A few major floods were recorded in this area." She casually took a chip, then another drink before continuing. "The sister cities of Menouthis and Herakleion sat only a few feet above sea level and were flooded yearly by the Nile."

"Begging the question as to why anyone would have built there."

Erica inclined her head. "True, but access to water and the advantages of having ports for trade helped settlements prosper. The good and the bad always went hand in hand. Floods were expected and dealt with accordingly. Landlords of that time kept accountings of anything that might have affected crops and revenue for the year. That's how we know there were at least two significant floods."

"Enough to wash away that much land?" Matt chomped into his sandwich.

"Not really washing away from above as below. Consider that the ground underneath was already wetter than normal due to a location near the sea, and liquefaction is not such a stretch."

"Liquefaction of the soil. From buildup and pressure."

"Precisely." Erica beamed at him, surprised by his familiarity with the concept. "The tumbling waters of a flood can carry much more sand and silt than normal river flow, plus the added pressure of the water can cause the soil below to fail."

Matt took a moment to consider it. "I'm betting on the earthquake."

"Me too." Erica stood to clear the trash. "Time for dessert?"

"Wait no argument? You actually agree with me, just like that?" The lopsided grin and teasing tone earned Matt a damp towel flying toward his face. He had good reflexes, so it breezed past his ear instead.

Erica smirked. "Whatever it was, it happened fast. Skeletons were discovered inside some of the homes that remained intact."

Even the hardened agent in Matt grimaced at that thought. "Let's hope they cleaned all of those out."

Grabbing one of the chocolates, Erica began to unwrap it slowly. To savor the experience. "I bet it was an earthquake, but either way, the Canopic branch of the Nile is no more. We know where it was, but as a flowing body of water, it's now defunct."

"I'm glad you know your history, or we would never have thought to come here." Matt grabbed a peanut and nougat bar. "So why an earthquake? Any fault lines nearby?"

"Yes, that and other things lead geologists to believe a quake was the likely culprit."

"What things?"

"There are two faults that could have contributed. The first parallels the northern coast of Africa, just offshore, and the second runs from the Gulf of Suez to the Mediterranean. Both could have shaken the area enough to cause liquefaction, even if they didn't directly force the area to the ground."

"Now we're back to liquefaction again." Matt shook his head.

"Liquefaction occurs any time water pressure builds up between grains of sand or silt. Like gumballs in a bag, tightly packed, there are still air pockets in between. Whether by shaking or forces of flooding, if the air pockets fill with water, the particles no longer touch each other. One push and everything can move. What was once land, now acts more like quicksand."

"Right. Picture the gumballs tightly packed and how hard they would be to move around each other." Matt leaned in. "Now fill the bag with water so that they float over each other and the entire bag is malleable."

Erica popped a piece of candy in her mouth and leaned forward as well. "You get an A plus."

Before she knew what was coming, Matt moved in and gently wisped his mouth over hers, savoring the sensitive flesh of her lips, before testing for entry with his tongue. The taste of him after the sweet candy was unexpectedly erotic. Erica found herself responding unabashedly, hands gripping the silkiness of his black hair.

Matt rose, never breaking contact, and pulled her up to meet him. Hands roamed wildly over her skin, covered only by a bathing suit and shorts. His palms branded wherever they touched.

A gruff voice calling down the stairs halted their fervor like a splash of water. "Hey, Pierce. We're there." The sound of engines slowing to a halt accompanied the announcement.

"Damn," Matt growled, his warm breath still on her neck, her cheek.

Sighing, Erica pulled away to meet his eyes, darker than ever with pent up passion. His dragon wouldn't be held in check much longer.

And she was ready to have it released. On her.

"One thing's for sure," she told him. "We'll have plenty of buildup if we ever get more than one minute alone with each other."

Matt groaned and lowered his forehead to hers. "Yeah, but the building up is about to kill me."

Erica laughed and headed toward the small set of stairs that would take them up into the sunlight and oceanic breezes of the main deck. Ascending with an intentional sway of the hips, she tossed over her shoulder, "Don't I know it."

Rising from the relative darkness of below, Erica shielded her eyes from the sunlight reflecting off the water and blinding white of the boat. The weather was beautiful. Gentle winds, not a cloud in sight, and calm seas. Perfect for an afternoon dive.

But afternoon seeped into dusk. A night dive. And dark waters.

Feeling Matt beside her at the railing, she vocalized her worries. "We're getting a pretty late start. We'll have only a couple of hours before the light begins to fade." Like a hundred other times, her imagination took her to another place. Another dive. She envisioned her father's last moments. Had he suffered? Had her grandfather?

Or had the collapse killed them instantly?

Matt didn't touch her, but his tone was gentle. "Erica. I know this is near where your father and grandfather had their accident. Are you sure you're up for this?"

She took a deep breath and leaned heavily onto the railing.

Her lack of response prompted Matt to give her an out. "You know, maybe one of the guys can dive with me. If we find anything that makes us feel we're on the right track, we'll come back up and fill you in." When she lowered her head, Matt leaned against the rail, too. "You don't have to go down."

"Yes, I do," she whispered.

"I can't afford to have you panic. With two stories of water over your head, the chance is too great."

She stood straight again, wiping her cheeks to catch a runaway tear. "I have to. We have to get the next clue and fast. My being up here will only cost us time. I have to do this for myself, because I enjoy diving."

Her blue eyes locked with Matt's steady brown. "I have to because my father taught me to dive, and he would never want his death to rob me of something we shared. That we loved."

Matt didn't offer lame comfort or reassurances but spoke with assertion. No questions. "If you're sure, then let's do it."

Casting his stare toward water that would deepen from turquoise to pitch black in several hours, Matt said, "We will have flashlights, but there are other reasons we should be back up by nightfall. The approach of another vessel might be more difficult to detect, if they're quiet and black out their lights."

Erica's muscles froze. "You think the cult will find us this quickly?"

"They won't track us any time soon, but the area could be on their watch list if they have information we don't. They may already be here."

Erica frowned. "Thus the need for the three bodyguards."

Now Matt did touch her, rubbing his shoulder against hers. "And me." His smile was half-tease and half-promise. "I'm not leaving your side."

In an attempt to shake off the somber mood Erica gave a nervous laugh. "Good, because we've got a whole city to inspect thirty feet down, and I need somebody to watch my back."

"I can assure you I won't take my eyes off of your back. Side."

His dry wit lifted Erica's spirits. "You just made a joke. And flirted at the same time." She shoulder bumped him. "Not bad, Agent Pierce. Not bad."

"But seriously," she added, "even with the coordinates we'll still be doing a lot of searching. We don't even know what 'seek the water' actually means."

Matt stood straight. "We'll do what we can. We have a good

lead with the mention of the red ones that guard his name, and the red granite statues have been found here. Amun's temple was no secret, so we can assume the statues guard his name. Or at least his spiritual name."

Matt gave her an odd look.

"What?" Erica asked.

"I've been around you and Cameron too long. I'm starting to sound...stuffy."

Erica huffed. "You've got your own brand of stuffy going on, I can assure you. Anyway, the statues down there now date to the time of Herakleion, but since Senmut mentions red ones, they could have been modeled after others that came before."

"You mean these might not be the right colossi?"

"No. The vase is here. The clue definitely pointed to this city, and the mention of the red granite just brought it all together for me. Besides, the real message was to look for water. The statues may have just been a direction to this area."

Gesturing toward the helm, Matt said. "Whatever the case, we have all the equipment to locate large granite structures and specifics regarding the colossi."

Erica studied the echo sounders, side-scan sonar, and magnetometers. They were top of the line and similar to what the original scientists used to map the site. With the differential GPS, the machines allowed archaeologists to paint a picture of what lay under the sea. Sound waves bounced off the sandy ocean floor and whatever relics were found there. Divers pinpointed the location of items of interest and marked them for future reference.

And granite magnified the earth's magnetic field differently than other objects, allowing the mineral to be detected more easily. An advantage for Erica and Matt.

"We stick with the plan." Erica spoke aloud, reassuring herself. "We'll focus on the areas that contain the statues. They wouldn't have been mentioned in the clue if they weren't crucial to the location of the next vase. The creator of the disc and its message wouldn't have wasted what little space he had to work with."

"At least here we have free access. No tourists, guards, or locked doors."

Erica lifted a dubious brow. "You're trying to put a good spin on the fact that we have to look for a hidden message on an object that may only be three inches in diameter. Something we're *fairly* certain was here a couple thousand years ago but was wiped off the face of the earth by either flood or earthquake. Oh, and it's under a whole lot of sand and water."

He peered into the depths. "I like our odds."

Not fully convinced, Erica followed his stare but shook her head.

"What else is down there?" Matt asked.

"Much of the surrounding walls still exist and stretch over three hundred feet. Repairs were once made to the walls, suggesting a history of destruction, possibly from earlier earthquakes." Erica gestured to the murky water. "The infrastructure of the port is largely intact. Streets, homes, more statues, temples, sphinxes, you name it. If they were structurally sound, portions of them are probably still down there."

"Like the Alexandria lighthouse." At Erica's quizzical look, Matt shrugged. "I did my research and read about the other ruins in the area."

"Too bad this isn't a pleasure dive or we could head over to that site next."

"Some other time," Matt said, still looking across the seas.

Erica tried not to read too much into the comment. Would she and Matt see each other when this was over? Clearing her throat, she said, "There's always the chance we'll run across pottery, jewelry, or coins. No excavation finds everything."

"Coins?"

"Sure. Those found before were proof the city had been in existence until at least the seventh century AD. Herakleion and Menouthis were well known for their wealth."

When thunder sounded in the distance, Matt gazed toward the ominous clouds appearing on the horizon."Looks like we'll be waiting until tomorrow. But maybe we'll get lucky."

Erica turned once again to stare at the water, as if she could see through the blue, straight to the hollowed out remains of Herakleion. The sunken city that could save lives. She offered up a small prayer. "Maybe we will."

18

"We should go down and orient ourselves to the area. The best we can, anyway. Visibility may not be great." Matt glared at the sea. "It's calm now, but judging by the amount of debris on the surface, things are still churned up after last night's storm."

Hands on her hips, Erica squinted against the morning sun. "You're right. We have the time, we need to use it." Finalizing the decision, she zipped up her dive suit with purpose and watched as Matt did the same. Both wore shorties, suits that covered torso only, leaving arms and legs exposed. The only difference between their suits was the color, Matt going with a sedate black in contrast to Erica's royal blue.

Matt twirled his finger, indicating he wanted her to turn around. Catching sight of the box-shaped device he held, Erica stopped herself mid-swing. "No tanks?"

"No." Matt shook the gear impatiently, spurring Erica to turn around with a grunt of displeasure. "We're using re-breathers. Less bulky and more efficient. I take it you've never used one?"

Erica made a non-committal sound as she slid the shoulder straps into place. "I haven't gone diving in a while."

"No problem." He gave her a quick tutorial on the pack, then went on to include their masks. "These are diver transceivers. The one-piece mask and headset allows us to communicate with each other underwater."

An impish grin crept across Erica's face. "Excellent."

Once suited up, the pair made their way to the stern then signaled to Clint, one of the three men who'd joined them on the excursion. Clint waved back, giving them the go ahead.

"See you down under," Matt said before falling off the edge.

Erica swiftly followed, not as fearfully as he'd expected.

He hoped this expedition healed her in some small way. Getting her back into field work. Into diving. Maybe she'd take away a positive from the depths of the Mediterranean. Something to help balance the horrible accident that had robbed her of her only family.

Matt took a moment and closed his eyes, floating in the gentle liquid caress, hearing the sound of his own breathing.

A tap on his shoulder bolted his eyes open. "You falling asleep?" Excitement was evident in Erica's smile, even from behind her mask.

"Just enjoying." He looked around. "I was right. I doubt we can see two feet in front of our faces." The water was a foggy green from below, light drowned out by the seaweed and other small particles. He motioned with his fingers. "Try to stay close."

Matt held the GPS device in his hand, a thin coaxial cable exiting from one end and disappearing above their heads. The cord was attached to a float overhead that encased the receiver. The satellite could send its signal through miles of space, but had trouble with a little water.

Erica followed as he swam in the direction indicated by the handheld gadget. He came to a stop, and if the coordinates were correct, they were close to the first statue.

"We're going to have to work the circle." He swiveled to face Erica. "Base or search?"

He was asking which job she wanted. Because of the low visibility, they would have to search for the exact location of the granite giants. Though they had GPS coordinates, they had to factor in a twenty to thirty foot margin of error. The float receiving the signal could be slightly off course from their position below, as its placement was dependent on the current.

"I'll search." She reached for the rope looped at her waist. Handing the end to Matt, she ran her fingers along the twisted braid until she found the ten foot mark. "Do you think this is too much?"

Matt shook his head. "If they're as big as you say, you should come across some portion of it. I think we should even go to twenty."

Working the circle was a search method often used by divers. One person stayed in a single position with the rope, acting as the base, the starting point of the area to be explored. The other diver searched while holding onto the other end of the rope at a designated distance. Swimming in a circle and keeping the rope taut allowed the team to cover the vicinity in degrees.

Matt positioned himself in the spot indicated by the GPS and watched Erica fade away. The olive water engulfed her before she was more than five feet from him, and he was glad to have the cord. It made him mildly nervous to have her out of sight in the gloomy abyss, but relief returned when he felt the line go tight. She had reached twenty feet and would now start circling him in a clockwise direction.

After a minute or so, he felt her pause. "Find it?" he asked into the head set.

"No," she answered. "Just a portion of the wall, I think, or remnants of a building. It's really hard to see."

They fell into silence as she continued around, Matt turning in a slow circle, following her lead. Once he found himself facing the red flag, floating but held in place by a weight, he knew they had made a full turn. "You want to go out another ten?"

Her voice echoed in his ear. "Might as well."

Matt waited for the rope to tighten again then followed her movements. He heard Erica grunt and said, "That sounded significant."

"That's because it was." Erica gave a nervous sigh. "This is huge. It practically jumped at me. Came out of nowhere."

"I'll be right there." Matt swam in her direction, taking up slack as he went. A large face suddenly appeared in front of him. "I think I found the head."

"I'm at the waist and can't see you. That gives you some idea how big he is." The delight of the discovery was evident in her laugh. "You take heads. I'll make my way to tails."

"Okay, I'll pull in the rope. Just stay in contact with the statue."

She made a *tisking* sound, and he could picture her stubborn face. If they weren't underwater, she'd probably be pushing the hair out of her face in frustration.

"I'll be fine," she said. "Let me know if you find anything unusual."

They covered the rose-colored sculpture inch by painstaking inch, constantly clearing dirty water wherever their flashlight beams met stone. In just under an hour, they found each other somewhere around the giant's lower back.

Erica looked crestfallen. "Nothing. You?"

"Nothing remarkable. Do you want to move on to the next one?"

"How long do we have with these re-breathers?"

Matt grinned. "We could make it to lunch long before they run out."

Erica gave a thumbs up. "Okay. I've got another in me."

They moved to the next area indicated by the coordinates and repeated the search process, this time with Erica as the base. Their first attempt led Matt to the outstretched arm of another figure with a solemn face.

"I found it," he reported to Erica. "Only, I don't know why they referred to these as the red ones. They're pink."

"Perhaps it's in reference to the name of the stone. Plus, it will be distorted down here." She floated up beside him. "Ready?"

"I'll go in this direction and meet up with you on the other side."

After twenty minutes Matt's patience and optimism were running thin. The natural light was fading, and the surface of the statue alternated from visible to undetectable every few seconds. "I'm having trouble making much out."

"Same here." Erica said, holding her light close to the stone. "I'm not even sure I'm covering all of it. It's hard to tell what I've already looked at."

Her sudden and short yelp made Matt's hackles rise. "What is it?" He stayed frozen in place, waiting for her response.

"I'm not sure, but something big and gray just went by."

Her whisper told Matt more than her words. "Stay put. Where are you?"

"I don't know. Somewhere near the shoulders."

Matt followed the length of the overturned figure until he could make out Erica's shape. "Have you seen it again?"

She nodded and pointed a finger in the direction behind him. A large dark mass was barely discernible, but was growing in size, moving toward them. They huddled closer to the statue, waiting for the animal to close in.

As the massive wings stirred the water above them, Erica and Matt ducked instinctively. "Damn," Matt said. "That was close."

"A devil ray. I can't believe we saw a devil ray." Erica had gone from fear to exhilaration in one smooth stroke. "They're almost extinct."

"It seems interested in us." Matt indicated the path the enormous creature had taken. "Maybe it will come back."

"They're not particularly dangerous, but I don't want to accidentally brush up against it." Erica shone the light up at her own face. "It's getting dark. There must be another storm blowing in."

Matt turned his own flashlight off and hooked it to his belt. "Ladies first."

After a meal of steamed vegetables and fresh-caught fish, the group of four relaxed around the table. Clint was on watch above, part of a proficient and ever-vigilant team.

"Thank you for providing the main course, John." Erica tapped the arm of her new companion. Being surrounded by the men felt like having a very muscular safety net, and cooking dinner had been a small token of her gratitude.

"It's a hard job, but...well, you know." He grinned.

The other man on protective duty was Dan. He reached out to pluck an ear of corn off a platter. "What better way to look like average Joes on a fishing trip than to fish?"

"Sure." Matt winked at Erica over Dan's head. "You take your undercover seriously."

About that time Clint walked down to join them. "You guys got me a plate? It's time to head out."

Erica stopped clearing the table when John and Dan rose in unison. "Wait. You're not leaving, are you?"

Clint tipped his head to Matt. "Captain's orders."

"Don't worry. They won't be far." Matt drew Erica's attention. "They'll be able to watch us from a distance. Any other craft will be spotted before they too close.

The rev of another boat sounded from outside. "That's our ride," Clint said, tossing Erica a wink before disappearing again.

She tugged on Matt's elbow and hissed. "Why didn't you tell me?"

"Forgot to mention it." Matt extracted himself from her grip. "Besides, you were busy cooking. The food was great by the way."

She snorted. "Kiss-up."

Watching Dan and John follow Clint, Erica felt the first pang of apprehension. She and Matt would be alone, completely isolated and adrift on the night sea. She wondered why she was more nervous about being with him than the possibility of assassins in the area.

"I'll see them off. Why don't you clean up?" Matt called over his shoulder, exiting without a backward glance.

"Why don't you clean up?" Erica parroted his less-than-romantic parting comment. Her case of nerves was suddenly cured.

She dumped the leftovers into a plastic bag and ungraciously stacked the dishes. Filling the sink with hot, soapy water she concentrated on the task at hand and forced herself to push aside disappointment.

What did you really expect? She scrubbed the frying pan as if it were to blame. *You're in a life or death race against time. He's got more important concerns than romancing you and helping with dirty dishes.*

By the time Erica had wiped up the table and counters, she felt duly self-chastised. Hearing nothing from above, she decided the other men had gone. Climbing the stairs without a sound, she eased onto the back deck and looked for Matt. There was no sign of him, so she called out his name.

"Up here." The words floated on the wind.

He'd answered from the front deck, so Erica moved in that direction. There she found him in a relaxed stance against the front railing, a beer in his hand. He lifted it in offering. "Sorry there's no candlelight, but they were a real bitch in this wind."

Erica walked to him and took the bottle, noticing the full white moon over his shoulder and the cool depth of his eyes. "This light is better. Thank you."

She took a small sip, watching Matt watch her. "It's good. When did you have time..." She broke off when he stepped closer.

In one motion Matt had her drink and was setting it aside. "I can't seem to remember why I shouldn't want you so much," he said. "Or why I should keep my distance." His dark eyes were determined and seemed to burn straight through her. The unwavering strength she saw there made her heart thud wildly before her stomach dropped. Then a smooth, liquid ache spread down from her stomach to her core.

Matt wrapped an arm around her waist and slid his other hand up to the side of her throat. Her pulse pounded against his palm, proof of her own driving need. She wanted him. Now.

She let her head fall back, offering herself freely.

And Matt took.

Removing his hand, he pressed his mouth against the same soft spot, pressing his tongue against her sensitive skin. Pleasure shot through her when his moist heat met her flesh. Her legs caved, so she leaned against his wide chest, unaware of the sounds she made in response to his gentle assault.

Matt was fully aware of her response, and was having a hard time staying upright himself. Not because he was felt weak, but because he had to lie Erica down and cover her. Have her. Completely.

The deep purr in her throat, the soft whimpers, it was all he could take. He lowered her to the cushioned chaise behind him.

Holding himself above her, he studied the silken wave of her hair as it shone in the light of the moon and waited for her eyes to open. He needed to look into that crystal blue before making her his. Needed to know she was there with him, wanting this as much.

Erica lifted heavy lids to meet his gaze, and Matt stroked her cheek, neck, and over her shoulders, telling her in his way that she was more to him than just a job. An assignment. More than a convenient female.

He lowered his head again to take her lips. And hoped she knew.

As the sweet, exotic wind swept over them and moonlight cast a pale glow on their bodies, they came together, gently at first, then with a fury. The boat rose and fell beneath them, moving in time with the waves and adding another layer to their rhythm.

It was the most overwhelming, most sensuous moment of Erica's life. The exact moment the earth dropped from beneath her. The moment she started to fall.

She had built a wall in the beginning to keep her feelings safe. Bottled up. Her independence served as a dam against unpredictable emotions, but now it broke apart, allowing tenderness for Matt to wash through her. Warm and soothing, it drowned any fear or doubt that might have remained.

How could caring for him be wrong? She wouldn't allow what was building between them affect her judgment or commitment. And she was sure he wouldn't either.

Matt pulled away suddenly, rasping out her name. His breath came fast and harsh as desire grew. Holding himself above her, he said her name again, but his tone held a whiff of question. Of doubt.

In answer, she reached up to cup his cheek then slid her fingers into his hair, pulling him down to meet her. Warm breath intermingling, she skimmed her lips over his and answered, "Yes." Her tongue slicked against his as her hips rose to meet him. "Yes."

As her insistent hands pulled blindly at his clothing, Matt plunged his hands into the thickness of her hair, gripping with controlled force, telling her how close he was to the edge.

Delicacy was gone, replaced with an all-consuming demand. The most basic of instincts, fueled by the hours they'd spent doubting what they felt.

There would be no stopping this now. And Erica was no longer ashamed of the thrill shooting through her.

Caught up in the sinful way his mouth worked, she was only vaguely aware of his other movements. The sudden heat of his bare flesh as his shirt disappeared, the linen of her dress being pulled up her body and over her arms. Matt's skillful hands were everywhere, and she found her back arching. Her arms lifting in invitation.

Soon she wore only a small swatch of white cotton, her chest rising and falling. Matt was above her now, the solid lines of his face lit on one side by the moon. He traced his hand over the curve of her hip before slipping a finger beneath the thin white string. "You're amazing."

The sincerity of his words floored her. Unable to speak she drew a ragged breath and intertwined her fingers with his, gripping tighter as he lowered himself to her.

Together they removed what was left of her clothing. And his.

They moved against each other, relishing the sensation of steel meeting silk, uniting with both urgency and revelation. Erica's skin came alive under Matt's attentive fingers. Under his mouth. His lips were everywhere, leaving a moist trail that cooled in the breeze.

Unable to wait a moment longer, Erica wrapped her legs around Matt's hips, pressing her breasts against him. His strength was evident in the sculpted shoulders, arms, and chest. His stomach flexed when she lowered her hand to take him in hand, and the thrill of her own power rushed to her head.

She stroked him, caressed him, until his fingers found her to offer the same sweet torture. So quickly the pressure inside her built. Releasing the thickness of his erection, she pulled his arm out from between their bodies and kissed him lightly.

Instead of rushing, Matt gathered her close and waited until she relaxed beneath him.

Her eyes fluttered open and connected with his. Their gazes locked, saying what couldn't be expressed in words. He took her swiftly then, sinking into her and groaning his pleasure.

Erica's head fell back as she gasped, and a surge of ecstasy flooded her. She was afraid she'd drown in it.

Sighing Matt's name, she shifted to give him more of herself. His strokes matched her own as they pushed against each other.

Kissing between rapid breaths and sounds of satisfaction.

Lost in the discovery of Matt, the sweep of the wind and swell of the tides were forgotten. No thought or concern remained for anything other than the storm building inside her. Only she and Matt mattered. Locked together and adrift on the sea.

She heard her name burst from his lips as she threw back her head. Lost in the shattering and blinded by the stars...she let the world fall away.

19

Matt couldn't sleep. Though he and Erica had finally relinquished their place on deck for the more comfortable bed below, rest eluded him. He studied the soft female form curled against him, one lovely leg thrown over the sheets and his thigh.

He'd crossed the line all right. Broken the rules. Yeah, more like he'd demolished them into an almost unrecognizable form.

Since their wild ride above deck, he and the lady doctor had been literally joined at the hip. Or some other acceptable body part. But their physical insatiability wasn't what had him grinding his teeth as he studied her as she slept, long lashes resting over closed eyes. He'd been in lust before, strong, overwhelming lust.

But he'd never found himself eager for a bedmate to wake back up once the party was over. To flash ice blue eyes at him as she verbally cut his legs out from under him. To overcome any rising ire with a soft and sweet smile. A kiss.

As if sensing his interest, Erica began swirling a pattern across his chest with her fingers. Paying special attention to the parts she liked, just as she had the file she'd read on the plane. He knew now that those small hands were strong and capable. But that they could be equally gentle. Loving.

Matt grunted. Loving. Love. There's a word he truly tried to avoid, along with any of its synonyms.

The more he cared for something, or someone, the more vulnerable he allowed himself to become. And in his line of work, being weak could quickly turn into being dead.

Still, he couldn't seem to stop touching her.

Matt caressed Erica's back and was rewarded by her sigh of contentment. Her face turned up to his in response. "I thought you would be sleepy."

"No, but I am seriously relaxed." His eyes closed to emphasize the point.

Erica lowered her head to his chest and resumed rubbing his skin, his stomach, and lower. Muscles rippled in response to her greedy touch. He covered her hand, stopping the exquisite agony. "Easy, or I might get...well...less relaxed."

Mischief was in her smile. "That was my intention."

Matt tossed her on her back and covered her so quickly it surprised a squeal out of her. He took advantage of the silence that followed and kissed her soundly.

Left breathless, she stared at him when he pulled back. "That's so unfair."

He tasted the spot below her chin. The place he now knew made her go liquid in his arms. "Have to use everything I can to my advantage," he murmured against her jawline. "But before you start on me again, I need some sustenance." He rolled off her to a standing position beside the bed.

As he walked away, her pretend gasp of insult followed him. Then so did a pillow, hitting him squarely in the back of the head.

Smugly, he raised his hand in a calming gesture. "Don't worry, Doc. I'll take care of you when I get back." The second pillow whizzed past his face, and he laughed his way down the corridor to the galley.

Moments later he returned, snacks and drinks in tow. Nestling in beside her, he offered her a fruit tea and a handful of spicy cereal mix.

Erica munched on his offerings before lifting a dubious brow. "You know what else is unfair? You seem to know a whole lot more about me than I know about you." Her head cocked to the side as she waited. When he didn't say anything, she cleared her throat and said, "Spy much?"

The reference to Matt's placing a bug in her home caused a dull flash of guilt, but he responded by putting a thin, navy blue pillow behind his head and reclining against the wall. "Sorry. Full knowledge of your activities and affiliations was imperative. And I would do the same again."

She blew an affronted breath through her nose. "Okay, I get it. I do. But it's not your average when-we-met-story." The bag of snack mix crackled as she grabbed it from him. "And there's no reason to get all agent-like on me."

His tone *had* been clipped, as if he'd been saying the words by rote. No emotion or sensitivity. To break the tension, he gave her a bawdy wink and rubbed her hip. "Well I certainly have full knowledge of you now." He leaned in for a kiss, but she dodged it.

"Not so fast." Erica held him up with a pointed finger. "I'm thinking it's time we were on a level playing field."

"What, you want full disclosure now? Previous girlfriends? What I eat at night when no one's around to see? Fetishes?" He lifted one side of his mouth in a sardonic grin.

"No," Erica said softly. "Let's stick to the basics. Where were you born? Do you have any brothers or sisters? Your parents?" She paused, looking down at the sheets then back up at him.

Without speaking, he put his arm around her and pulled her close. Those rules still lay in a pile on the floor, but now he had to decide if he truly wanted to let Erica in. Truth wasn't always a warm and fuzzy discovery.

But if he went cold on her, she might shut him out in return.

And if he opened up, shared a little, they might both start down that road. The one that inevitably led to affection.

To vulnerability.

His heaving sigh probably caused waves to roll from beneath the boat. Then he began. "I was born in California, an Air Force brat. We lived just about everywhere, so I don't call any place home. Two siblings, David and Rachel, both younger, and my parents are retired in Montana. They love the mountains."

"I've heard it's beautiful there. Big sky country." She set aside the tea she'd been sipping and returned herself to Matt's side. Resting the lines of her body easily against his. Putting her cheek to his shoulder.

He liked the way that felt. Damn it.

"And Rachel is the sister you said I sounded like. But only because you boss her around, too."

He felt the curve of her smile against his arm. "I never admitted to being bossy," he said, palming her backside and tucking her in closer. "And yes, you remind me of her. She's too independent, and that scares me. She's at college now, unsure what she'll major in but sure she'll do something great with her life."

"Do you doubt it? If she's anything like you..."

"Bite your tongue." He laughed. "And no, I don't doubt her a bit. I just hope she makes smart decisions. Stays safe."

Erica lifted her head to look at him. "She's at college, not a battlefield."

Again, he grunted. "Same thing. Any place can be dangerous if you're foolish. Naïve."

"Is Rachel those things?"

Pausing to consider his reply, Matt pictured his kid sister, who always seemed to be into anything that meant trouble. "No. Rachel is simply...adventurous."

"Then I like her already. And I'm sure she's just fine."

Was she? Matt wondered. Would she continue to be? He felt his forehead begin to furrow and stopped his dark thoughts in their tracks.

But not before Erica noticed the change.

She pushed herself up and propped on an elbow. "What's

going on? Is there a reason for you to worry?" She held his gaze, even though he'd hoped the hard look he gave her would shut the inquiry down. But the doc was too smart. Much too smart. " Does your worry for your sister have anything to do with why you were so against my being involved with this expedition?" Her face was set, telling him she would be satisfied by nothing less than everything.

Matt closed his eyes and remembered. The days after the girl's death and how he'd tortured himself going over every possible instant, every step, trying to figure out where the plan had gone wrong. He and his partner at the time had covered every angle. Or so they'd thought.

"Two years ago I was out of the Denver office, and we caught a case. Nothing too exciting. Running down some tips we thought could lead us to a local drug runner. A small fish that might catch us something bigger."

"What happened?" Erica asked in a level but supportive voice.

"An old girlfriend of the guy we were after had decided to help us out. She was hiding the fact she'd had a baby by the man. A boy. She was terrified he would find out and take her son from her and raise him in a drug culture." Matt thumped his fist into the mattress lightly. Then again.

"It turns out the guy we thought was just a runner was actually the heir apparent to a Colombian cartel." He paused before barreling ahead. "They were on to us and caught us off guard. We were transporting the girl and her son to a safe house."

"The girl?" Erica asked.

"Yeah. All of seventeen years old." Disgust laced his tone. "He evidently liked them young. Easier to control."

Erica let the silence fall between them, giving him room to confide in her at his own pace. He hated that she knew this about him, and that his memories were a source of pain. Regret. That they were a crippling weight dragging on him wherever he went.

He didn't want her to think he was inept. Or weak. After all, it was her life he guarded now.

"We picked the girl and the baby up at her apartment, thinking no one knew she'd contacted us. Gunfire came out of nowhere. My partner was holding the baby and dropped to the ground, covering the child."

Matt swallowed hard then took a sip of his drink. "I tried to get to the girl, but she was screaming, looking around for her son. I'm not sure if I heard the shot first or saw the impact. Logically one came before the other, but in my mind, all I can remember is the spread of crimson over her shirt. The round hit her in the chest. Immediate kill."

"I'm so sorry." Erica's heart was in her eyes as they glistened. He could see she honestly ached for him. "I know you did everything you could," she said.

He barked a laugh, anger suddenly lashing out at her for being so close, himself for letting her get there, and at everything in general. "How could you know that? You have no idea what I might have fucked up. If I accidentally gave something away."

Erica pressed her hand against his chest, as if her will alone would hold him. "I do," she whispered, "because I know you."

Resentment leaked from his shoulders as he ran a hand over his eyes. He didn't deserve such blind faith. "I haven't worked with a witness since. I got myself a job where the only person I ever had to worry about was myself."

"That's not true. Your actions keep people from harm every day. Even if you don't physically stand in front of terrorists, you stop their operations. You prevent them from going through with their plans." Erica took a breath and forged ahead. "You're protecting me. You have since before we even met."

Matt looked at her, a dry laugh rasping from his throat. "Is that how you see my home invasion now? I'm officially forgiven?"

She sighed, like she was relieved to hear the humor in his voice again. "Only because you didn't break anything. If you'd damaged any of my artifacts, well..."

"It would have gotten ugly, huh?" he asked, trying for casual.

Instead his chest tightened then released. The shadow of that young girl's falling body would never truly be gone, but here on this flat-ass mattress in the middle of the Mediterranean, he'd removed a little of the gray bastard's power. Just a sliver, but still...it was a first.

Matt cupped her cheek in his hand and pressed his lips to hers. "Thank you."

"For what?" She clung to him now, bottom lip quivering slightly. Then she chewed on it to get it under control.

"For listening," he told her, rubbing his thumb over that bottom lip. "And for making me talk."

In return, she nuzzled his neck, tenderly tasting and nipping her way down his shoulder. The tiny bite of her teeth was enough to erase any lingering weight from their conversation. Her open mouth on his nipple had blood rushing through him, and yeah, he'd been right. They couldn't keep their hands off each other.

When he reached up under the sheet, she opened her mouth to let him take. And she shoved the sheet away to let him explore.

A large swell rolled under the boat and made them both lean for a moment. Erica lifted her head. "The waves are getting a little rougher."

Matt rolled her on her back like a man with a dirty plan. He trailed one finger up the inside of her thigh. "They can get as rough as they like." He moved farther up, testing, teasing. "Because I promise, in a few minutes," he mouth followed the path of his hand, "you won't notice the waves."

A while later, Erica was recovering with one of Matt's strong arms draped over her midriff. His body and a portion of the sheet were all that covered her. "Water," she whispered. "I need water."

Matt lifted one arm to nudge her. "I went last time."

She slid one eye to the table beside the bed and grabbed the leftover tea. "This will have to do. I don't have the energy for walking just yet."

Matt shifted his head just enough to give her a satisfied look. "I'll take that as a compliment."

She tried to think of a sharp retort but couldn't really contradict him. Satisfied was definitely the word for how she was feeling, and judging by his determination to stay bed bound, Matt was equally content.

A shrill beeping filled the room. Erica knew that sound. With a stride like a gazelle she leapt and ran for cover in the bathroom. "Shit. Shit."

Matt's laughter rolled in her wake. "It's all right. I took precautions."

Dressed now in a T-shirt and pulling on shorts, Erica peered around the corner, looking for the voyeuristic laptop. She found the screen covered by a towel, blocking the room from view for those on the other end of the connection.

Relieved, she sauntered back toward the bed. "Precautions my ass."

Matt patted the bed beside him in an invitation for her to sit. "And what a nice ass it is."

"Hey, we can still hear you guys." Karen's chipper and completely pleased voice carried out from the speaker.

Erica groaned and fell back on her pillow. "I quit."

"We'll be right there." Matt stifled a laugh and struggled to put on his serious face.

Strangely unconcerned and with a newfound composure in the face of awkwardness, Erica pulled off the towel and came eye to eye with the screen version of her best friend. "One word." The lift of a singular brow said more than any verbal threat ever could.

Karen lifted her hands in supplication but couldn't quite lose the smirk. "Just checking in."

"At this time of night?" Erica swept her hair back from her face.

"It's only ten o'clock." Karen's face changed perceptibly. "We were going to check in tomorrow, but something's happened."

Matt and Erica were both paying attention now. "Is everyone else there?" Matt asked, referring to Monroe and Gus.

"Gus should be here any minute, but the good doctor is in the library. He's been researching every detail you've uncovered so far. He's trying to put together locations, people of importance who were present at the time the vases were hidden, anything that might form a pattern. He thinks he's missing something."

"Did he say more?" Erica wondered what Monroe was on to. Had she missed something? Maybe she was too distracted. Realizing this right after cozy time with Matt had a pin prick of guilt wedging its way back into her conscience..

"No. He says it's just a sense he's getting, ahem, *a niggling in his brain*." The last was said in a tone that imitated the British man.

"Please contact us as soon as he has anything that may shed light on all of this," Erica said.

"Will do," Karen replied. "As long as you keep your clothes on. My sensitive eyes can't take much more." She winked then turned her head as if something had caught her attention out of camera range. "Here comes Gus." Karen's face fell into somber lines as the man joined her at the computer.

Erica was overcome by cold dread. The expression Gus was wearing didn't bode well either. He and Karen knew something, and it was bad.

Gus shot hard and straight to the point. "There's been another." No one needed clarification of what he meant.

"Where?" Matt asked the question. His entire body tensed, arms corded with sinewy strength, as he gripped the edge of the table in frustration.

Erica was afraid he was taking each murder personally. After studying Kherep Amun for so long, he'd been waiting for exactly what was now happening. But he hadn't been able to stop it.

At least not yet. Erica fumed inside but held her physical appearance in check.

According to Matt, Kherep Amun was different from other terrorist organizations. They kept their plans close to the vest and trusted no one in the lower ranks with crucial information. They were shadows.

"Here in the States again," Gus stated with his temple pulsing. "A young girl, daughter of a high ranking general. The family is devastated as you can imagine, and it's been hard keeping this all under wraps. The general can pull strings in a lot of high places, and he is."

Gus shook his head. "This is a nightmare. Only those closest to this operation have full details. The general is good friends with the Vice-President, and the last thing we need is a military presence showing up when they have no idea what we're fighting."

"Surely the President is aware of a threat as large as that posed by Kherep Amun." Erica looked at Gus incredulously.

He stonewalled her with no verbal response and no telltale body language.

Beside him, Karen shrugged. "That's Washington for you."

Matt still stared at Gus with narrowed eyes. "When did this happen?"

"She was reported missing early yesterday morning, and by evening her body had been found. Dumb luck really. A homeless woman wandered into a shack out in the woods for shelter. She found the girl and went straight to the police.

"It was like the others?" Matt asked.

Gus paused. "Yes."

"What else, Gus?" Matt lowered his forehead, putting his stare directly in line with his boss's. "I need to know."

Gus closed his eyes for a heartbeat then said, "The girl was raped."

Erica inhaled sharply just as Karen whipped her head in Gus's direction, eyes glittering with a newfound fury. It was evident the agent hadn't shared everything with her or Monroe either.

Matt lowered his head, but Erica heard him curse with barely-contained rage. He looked back up at the screen. "That's completely out of line with the Kherep Amun protocol. What the hell happened?"

"Who knows? Evidently a rogue who's letting the power go to his head. It was after the ritual had taken place, so either he came back and committed the act, or the rest of his team didn't care to stop him. They may have even encouraged it as a final act of desecration."

"No. that doesn't add up. Despite the obvious wounds, the M.E. said the previous bodies had been treated carefully. Respectfully. And I can't believe a whole crew would go along with something so sacrilegious." Matt pulled over a chair and sat, running his hands back through his short, black hair.

"Gus." Erica addressed the agent. "You said it was done after the ritual? What do you mean?"

"The medical examiner reported that the rape occurred peri-mortem or post-mortem, either during the time of death or after. There were signs that blood flow had already decreased to the tissues that received damage. Those other than the ritualistic sites."

Erica seethed. "So she had her abdomen cut open and was then raped, possibly before she was completely dead?"

Gus only nodded.

Erica paced the small cabin, fists clenched at her side. "I want to stop them. I want to kill them."

My God. My God. How could I have been so self-centered? So blind and foolish?

Even after the first murders, she'd still seen the recovery of relics as a benefit. The lost queen's canopic vases and maybe even the mummy for her museum. Her family name would be celebrated. And all for collateral profit.

A gain that was nowhere near the cost of the collateral damage. That poor girl and the others.

Oh, Daddy. Forgive me.

She slammed both palms onto the table supporting the monitor and stared hard at Gus. "What was her name?"

He shook his head. "It's not wise to release..."

"I only need her name. Her first name."

He sighed, shoulders slumping. "Her name was Allison. They called her Alli."

Erica closed her eyes, vowing to herself she would always remember.

Matt rejoined the conversation. "This could be good or bad."

Rounding on him Erica hissed, "How could this possibly be good?"

Crossing his arms across his chest, Matt tensed. "I don't like this anymore than you do." He turned back to Gus and Karen. "You implied there was only one rapist, so you must have reason."

Gus nodded. "Yes. Only one man's secretions were recovered from the body."

"Oh, God," Erica whispered before sinking down to the edge of the bed, her shoulders and arms chilled, popping up with gooseflesh. She felt ill.

Matt spared her a glance of concern but continued with Gus. "So you're on it?"

"If his DNA is in any database in the world we'll find it."

"You'll find it." Matt hardened his eyes and said in a voice that would flash-freeze, "If the bastard couldn't control himself during a time as important as his first ritual, you can bet he's raped before."

Karen agreed with a nod of her head. "If we're lucky it could lead to a name, a place, and acquaintances."

"We could identify the first living member of Kherep Amun," Matt said.

Erica remembered what Matt had told her on the plane. The corpse found in Atlanta. They had never identified the body, so it had been a dead end.

"We'll stay on it. Just do your best to find the next vase. We're running out of time, and the general's involvement is making things sticky." Gus frowned. "As I'm sure Kherep Amun intended."

"We're diving again in the morning."

Karen tapped the screen on her end. "You two be careful."

Neither Matt or Erica said anything, only looked into the eyes of their friends with firm resolve. The stakes were getting higher, and they all had work to do.

Please, please. Erica huddled on the end of the bed, arms around herself for warmth and comfort. *No more.*

The screen went blank.

20

The farmer was blessed. It was a gift that after all the years spent in this very same place, the bursting color of his homeland still amazed him. The slow dance of the grasses surrounding his rice fields still brought him peace. Surely there was no truer green on earth, no place closer to what the creator had intended for himself as well as those he allowed to live here.

Yes, he had his own beliefs and chose to follow the teachings of the Quran. The true Quran, the one that taught kindness and love. He cared not for the adjustments made over the years by presumptuous men, distorting the book into one filled with hate, vengeance, and murder. Nayong, his home in the Philippines, was filled with both Muslim and Catholic followers, and he feared for the future that the younger, angry generation seemed to be creating for themselves.

The man breathed deeply and replaced the worries with serenity. It was easy to do with the sweet wind and gentle sun. A neighbor called to him and waved a greeting from the wagon he was taking to the local market. This man lived near the coast. His *carabao* now trudged slowly over the dampened ground, hauling the load of coconuts. Nothing here moved very quickly. Nothing needed to. Life here was still simple and honest.

The farmer raised his hand in return and watched until

the cart was lost among the shadows of distant trees. He then turned to appreciate the terraces where his own livelihood grew in abundance. The rice had always taken care of his family, providing food and income. His son had left to pursue business years ago, and now the farmer's grandchildren were college educated. The youngest lived in America and was on her way to becoming a doctor, the kind that helped women have babies.

Things had certainly changed. Women used to bring life into the world on their own, with a sister or other relative to offer whatever help was needed. He remembered the birth of his own child and how his wife had endured the suffering. For hours only small whimpers had escaped from the bedroom until the proud, lusty cry of the newborn boy filled the room. Announcement of his arrival. It had been a hard labor and the last his wife had gone through. They had never conceived again.

The thought of his gentle wife made him smile. She was now in their home, cooking for the next meal and probably working on her little *Visayan* dolls. Her delicate but strong hands could turn out five of the colorful figures in a day. The small female dolls wore traditional wrap-around skirts called *patadyongs* and *sinamay* blouses, both created from hemp fibers of the abaca tree. His wife sold her dolls to tourists and also made shipments to their granddaughter in America, who supplied them to shops there and made a little bit of extra money.

Everything the farmer needed could be gotten from the land. He respected the choices of his son and grandchildren, but he was happy to live out his days here, in his own paradise.

A strange noise caught his attention. The sound was like that of an animal, but none he was familiar with in this area. The noise carried on the wind from over the hills behind him, from the direction of his home.

The man steered himself toward the sound, his walking stick hitting the ground at a faster pace than normal. He heard the cry again, and something in the tone pierced a hole in his gut.

It had sounded human.

Moving with more speed than he would have thought himself capable, the farmer fought his way through heavy foliage to get home, abandoning the clear trail that would have taken him on a longer route. He wasn't sure when the sense of urgency had gripped him, but sweat was now streaking into his eyes, his breathing a painful staccato.

Another scream and he panicked. His wife's face flashed before him. She would never cry out unless there was danger.

Or pain.

He finally broke free from the thickness of the bushes and was met with silence. His house appeared normal, and he saw no one as he scanned the landscape around his home. The farmer swallowed hard and started for the door, feeling as if his heart were about to pound its way from his chest.

He pushed open the door and stared into the darkened room. The furniture was in its normal arrangement, nothing out of place.

Except there. The floor mat was turned up at one corner. It was not such an odd thing, but today it gave the man a cold fear. He made his way back to the kitchen, not knowing what to expect.

He could never have imagined the scene that greeted him.

Men were there, strange men, dressed in dark clothing. He saw his wife then. She was laid out on the floor, her ankles and wrists bound together with some sort of rope, her mouth stuffed so she could only moan. Her eyes found those of her husband and with recognition, a new sort of keening strained from her throat.

The farmer lunged forward, crying out his wife's name. He would save her from this. He couldn't let any harm come to her.

How beautiful she looked with the flowers in her hair, as she became his life mate. Her laughter rang in his ears as they watched their son's clumsy exploration of the green fields. He felt her hand on his as she woke him for the new day.

The images faded as the present horror tore apart his recollection of a precious life. Of better days. Erasing the images he had cherished for so long. One of the men kicked his walking stick out from under him, so he fell to his knees beside his wife. Someone came behind him and began to bind his feet and hands together as they had hers. How quickly they had it done, before shoving him down on his stomach.

The farmer adjusted so he was as close to his wife as possible and turned his head to look at her. Tears stood in her eyes alongside absolute terror. He willed her to be strong. If they stayed quiet, maybe the men would take what they wanted and leave.

Noise clattered outside and soon the back door opened to let in two more men. They spoke to the others in an unfamiliar language and made some sort of agreement. The farmer was still looking at his wife when the men began dragging her away and out the back door, leaving muffled cries in her wake.

The farmer tried to crawl after them but a foot on his lower back immobilized him. The man spoke, but the old farmer didn't understand the foreign words.

With the back door still open, the farmer could make out some of the sounds he'd heard before. Sharp snapping mixed with a low but steadily growing roar. The men had built a fire in the back yard. There was a pit out there, but the farmer couldn't think why these men would need it.

One of them returned to drag the farmer out, and the man who'd held him down followed. Thankfully, the farmer would be near his wife again. He searched for her and with no luck, turned his head to the other side. He was still on his stomach in the dirt, so it was difficult to see above ground level.

Then he couldn't make sense of what he saw. The men had his wife affixed to a large stake and some type of markings were drawn on her naked body, the blue paint stark against her light brown skin.

The men lifted the stake and carried her toward the pit.

High-pitched shrieks fought to get past the leaves filling her mouth. But the farmer couldn't hear his wife's screams over the sound of his own.

It was an unbelievable nightmare. The farmer was jolted from sanity for the first few moments as his mind scrambled to find a way out. Then the look on his wife's face stilled him. She was in agony, holding her head up in a pitiful attempt to escape the heat of the fire.

The farmer couldn't speak. At some point one of the men had shoved some of the green material in his mouth as well. He couldn't talk, but he knew he didn't have to. He knew he would be heard.

He began to pray.

The farmer didn't pray for his soul or his wife's. Their pure lives had seen to that.

He didn't pray for himself to be set free. That time would come soon.

Now when he prayed, it was for his wife. Never taking his eyes away from her face, he spoke the words in his head, hoping they would be answered soon. He pleaded for his wife. He begged.

That she would die quickly.

21

The morning was glorious. Gazing across the calm blue of the sea, Erica waited for daybreak. The dawning sun was only a bright line of orange on the horizon, teeming with ready-to-burst rays of light. She loved a good sunrise, and this one promised to be exceptional.

Of course, her newfound bliss could be enhancing the experience, as it seemed to be affecting everything else. The coffee was more flavorful, the breezes more aromatic, and her skin all but tingled.

Rubbing her sensitive arms, she thought, I could get used to this. Though she and Matt had alternated many times between making love and sleeping, she felt better rested and more energetic than ever.

They had discovered new aspects of one another, shared dreams and memories. She could have talked with him for hours, and sleep had been nothing more than a thief, stealing time from her that she could have spent with Matt.

Erica was as giddy as a schoolgirl and considering possibilities that had rarely entered her independent mind before she'd met him. Marriage? Children? Were they things she actually wanted?

The bigger question was, did Matt want those things?

The thought of children brought back an entirely different

set of images from the night before. A grieving general and a lovely young girl who had been defiled in the most heinous ways. The world could be such a cruel place, wrought with pitfalls and monsters waiting around the next turn.

Erica felt her mood shift. So many hopes and fears at war with each other. The thrill of discovering Matt and all he was awakening in her, followed by the crushing void when she imagined a society overrun by Kherep Amun.

She was becoming a swirling mass of conflict, capitulating between emotional extremes as often as the wind changed directions.

Gulls rode the breezes above, circling the boat in hope of a morning treat. So this simple pleasure is where she would focus. For now. Turning to retrieve some bread from the galley, she saw Matt behind her, seated at the table on deck and wearing her favorite lopsided grin. Something about him was different this morning as well.

Her answering smile was spontaneous and as promising as the bright, pink dawn. "How long have you been there?" she asked.

He sipped his coffee. "Just enjoying the sights."

"So was I." She sat with him and gestured toward daybreak. "It's gorgeous."

Matt was looking in the same direction but had eyes only for her. "Gorgeous," he said in a timbre that made Erica throb deep in her belly.

The silence between them was easy. Natural. They waited and watched as the sun broke free from its resting place to throw brilliant beams over the water. A million shimmers of light began their dance among the waves.

Shortly the sound of another boat's motor drew their attention. Clint was at the bow waving, letting Erica and Matt know the approaching vessel was friendly.

Erica regretted the loss of the tranquil scene she'd been sharing with Matt but was excited about the day's dive. If the surface was any indication, the depths should be much clearer than yesterday. The storms had churned things up...then swept it clean.

As the Clint and the others boarded, Erica stood to stretch while Matt downed his java fix. Then the men took up various positions on both boats, and Erica and Matt prepared their gear. An early start was essential, and Erica prayed they would find what they were looking for today.

The odds weren't good, but she'd been trying to convince herself they were. She'd played the optimistic card for Matt, too.

Every new clue could be the one that brought them to a dead end, but with tons of water covering the appointed search area, this was probably the one. Earth had to be dug up for most excavations, but dirt was manageable. Water, on the other hand, usually moved things from their original resting place then covered them up again. Nature's tricky magician.

Hopefully the vase or some portion of it could still be located, but the place they were searching had still been high and dry when Hatshepsut's lover had used it as a hiding spot. If the ocean weren't a big enough problem, there was still the suspected earthquake that had rearranged everything in the first place.

Hefting on her BCD, Erica looked grimly into the sea. *Only one way to know for sure.*

Matt and Erica took their positions on the back of the boat, spurring Dan to give them a playful look before saying, "Dive. Dive. Dive." The sound of her own laughter followed Erica into the cool water and bubbled out around her mask.

Regaining her upright position, she took a look around and was instantly elated. What a difference a day could make. Yesterday the murky green had encapsulated her in a type of blindness, but today was a diver's dream. Luminous blue water and perfect visibility. They were still positioned above the ruins, and an entire underwater city beckoned for her to come and play.

She did love diving, and was thrilled to reclaim the joy of it. No more fear.

And Matt had been a huge help in taking it back.

She stole a glance and saw Matt's tranquil expression. Deferring to Erica's expertise and her obvious excitement, he fell into SCUBA sign language, motioning with his hands for her to lead. He spoke the words as well. "I'll follow."

While she longed to investigate every piece of the hidden streets and walls, Erica knew they needed to focus on the area of the temple dedicated to Amun and another god, Heracles-Khonsu. The joining of deities and their names often bled over into a shared celebration as well.

Kherep Amun would most likely view it as sacrilege.

She and Matt followed the direction indicated by the GPS, briefly taking in the sight of a sphinx made of black granite, oddly out of place resting in the sand and surrounded by darting fish.

"Definitely not red," Matt pointed out.

"No. We should focus on the red ones first, although the clue didn't say they necessarily held the next vase, just that we should look for the red ones that guard his name." Luckily they would be much easier to spot without the ocean debris that had been filling the water on their last dive.

Erica pointed out another statue, smaller than the colossi, but still abundant in size. The young man's expression was disgruntled, as if he didn't care for the mossy growth covering his arms and face.

The remnants of a civilization long past were frozen in time, held hostage by the sea. Faces of stone forever trapped beneath the waves, where they had once stood proudly in the Egyptian sunshine.

Erica slowed to a hover. "We're close. There's Hapi."

Matt smiled at the familiarity with which Erica spoke, but to her, the figure was like a long lost friend.

"Is that one of the statues we searched yesterday?" Matt asked.

Erica shook her head slowly, the water making her movements slightly heavier than normal. "I don't think so. I would have recognized the form."

They glided up to the great physique towering over them. The beard and long hair bespoke of Egyptian origins and dignity, even though portions of his body had broken away.

Erica spoke with wonder in her voice. "Hapi, the Nile God." She rubbed her hands over the large cheeks and nose, great and serious eyes staring back at her. "And remaining upright as if still in control of the river and all the human lives that depend on it."

"Look for the water?" Matt speculated. "Could it be referring to the God of the Nile?"

Erica continued her study of the massive face. "I'm not ruling anything out." With a flurry of bubbles she turned in Matt's direction. "We should still search it together. One of us may miss a sign, so two sets of eyes are better."

"Right. I say we only go back to the statues from yesterday if we're unsuccessful with everything else."

"Okay." Erica flipped over and dove toward the granite feet below. She knew Matt would take his cue to start at the top.

With painstaking attention, they began their search. The last clue had been ambiguous, and they weren't sure what to look for. They couldn't be too careful. Even in the brightly lit water they carried flashlights. A good decision, since the colossi were so huge they cast shadows upon their lower portions.

They neared each other during the inspection, and Matt gently stroked the back of her calf as she passed. Her heart rolled over. Again the instant reaction to his touch.

"Hey. We're working here," she said, though her voice carried no real censure.

"Fine. I'll get back to work but will expect a gratuity when I find the next clue." Matt waited for her response. She said nothing. "Erica?"

She surprised him from behind with two hands around his waist. "Does the same go for me if I find it first?" she asked, stroking forward until her fingertips touched just below his navel. Through the head set she heard him rasp in a breath.

He turned to stare into her eyes through the plastic mask, the threat of retribution in his eyes. A kind of payback she could hardly wait for. "You've got a deal, Doc," he told her.

She placed both hands on his solid chest and pushed back. "Then I'd better start looking."

With the passing of another twenty minutes, they had thoroughly searched the body, with no luck. Neither took it as a blow to their positive outlook, as they were just getting started.

They took the time to consider the statue of a woman holding an infant to her chest. The pair had barely escaped a falling pillar that rested a couple of feet behind them. The scene was ironic. The two had survived being crushed but had been sentenced to a watery grave.

"Almost sad, isn't it?" Matt asked.

Erica nodded. "They seem so real."

"You're not going to cry, are you?"

She lifted her brows without comment then gestured to the mother and child. "They aren't the right color or composition. I'm not even sure they're granite."

Matt agreed. "The scale is off, too." With a jerk of his head, he indicated they move on.

Floating over partial walls, they kept their eyes on the GPS device and the ocean floor around them. The sand was patterned in undulating waves, formed by the ever-moving currents. Other than the looming threat of Kherep Amun, the silent world was peaceful, beautiful in its undisturbed state.

Matt stopped to trace his fingers over an inscription on a broken piece of stone. "Obelisk?"

Erica was beside him, inspecting the piece as well. "Yes.

Definitely hieroglyphics. The Egyptians always left a unique fingerprint when they inhabited an area."

Matt twisted to face Erica. "We've got a while left. Do you want to break or stay down?"

"I'm fine." She looked at her gauge to be sure she wasn't using too much air. "I could lose track of time down here, though. This is amazing." She moved to swim off in the lead, but Matt tapped her elbow to gain her attention.

"Over there."

Expecting her to follow, he kicked off in the direction of one of the colossi they were interested in. It was difficult to be sure from a distance, since the statue was overturned in the sand.

Erica caught up and swam beside him, both focusing solely on the monstrous figure. As they floated up to the back, Erica allowed herself to settle for a rest on the broad torso. "It's not one of the three main red granites but is pretty large and could be made of a red granite mixture."

Something about the form tugged at her. "We may as well look. If we keep passing up statues, they'll be spread out and we could forget to revisit one. What do you think?"

Matt looked uneasy. "Fine. This is the first one covered by so much sand."

"We have a dredge on board, right? It won't expose the bottom, but it will help some."

"It's worth a try. But there goes our pristine environment."

Erica turned her mouth down. "It's nice, but I want to see what this big guy is hiding."

Matt pointed toward the statue's hips. "I think it's a big girl."

In no time Matt had made it to the surface then returned with the large tube. The dredge would gently vacuum sand away from the body lying half-hidden by the seabed.

Considering the task at hand, they chose to stay together, Erica scouring any newly exposed surface for a hint of what they were looking for. She had to wait for the disturbed debris to settle, so she stayed several feet behind Matt as he worked.

One time around led to nothing of significance, but Erica's attention was captured by the very female statue's left arm. It appeared to be bent, the point of the elbow protruding at a slight angle from the waist.

Erica and Matt contemplated the form and its position. After clearing more sand it was evident the woman was lying more on her right side than they had originally thought. Erica skimmed her hand under the exposed left elbow. "I'd like to try to clear this area more. Judging by the width of the base under her feet, I don't think she'll roll if we remove more sand here."

Matt resumed dredging, clearing a stretch of the giant's arm from the crook of its elbow to what should have been the forearm. A round structure began to emerge.

Erica couldn't contain herself and thrust her hand toward the strange shape before the swirling water had cleared. "She's holding something." Probing unsuccessfully, Erica huffed. "Try some more."

Matt continued, slowly revealing more of the mysterious object. Soon the shape grew in diameter with an odd projection on the side. Erica's eyes were glued to the spot as more came into view. "I think I know what it is."

"What?"

She only shook her head. "I can't be sure yet, and I don't want to get my hopes up."

Suddenly they seemed to hit a hidden air pocket, and several inches of sand cleared at once. Matt stopped the machine as he and Erica stared. Finally he spoke. "That looks like it could be a pitcher or..."

"It's an urn." Erica swept forward to look more closely at the artist's workmanship. "A water urn."

Though it could still mean nothing, Erica's instinct told her they were getting somewhere. And an archaeologist's instinct could be their most reliable tool.

Matt fingered the roughness at the mouth of the urn. "What is that, some sort of inscription?"

"I don't think so. I think it's supposed to be the movement of the water in the urn." She sighed. "Such incredible detail."

"Yes, and why the detail?" Matt asked.

Erica furrowed her brow. "What do you mean?"

"Even the colossi have only so much detail to designate clothing and facial features. The bulk of their surface is smooth granite."

The significance of what Matt was pointing out became clear to Erica. She returned her scrupulous observation to the urn. "Why would they have depicted water when no one standing on the ground would have ever seen it? The statue's arm and the urn it's holding would have hovered far above anyone's view."

"No one would ever see the artist's detail. Unless they had a reason to look." Matt nodded with resolution. "We need to clear as much as we can. I think we'll have to widen the area or sand will start falling back into the hole we're making."

The delay in progress frustrated Erica. After a fleeting moment she looked at Matt. "Is there another dredge?"

"Yes. I didn't think we would both need to be tied up with one, but we'll work faster at this with two." He passed her the tube. "I'll be back."

The two worked in perfect sync with each other, moving their respective vacuums in slow sweeps to form a deep, wide depression that exposed the bulk of the urn. After a while Matt turned off his dredge. "I don't think we can get much more."

In agreement, Erica turned hers off and waited for the sand to settle. Impatient danced in her stomach like a tiny ballerina.

The sun was higher in the sky now, creating shadow in the space beneath the figure. Matt offered to hold both flashlights in place to illuminate the urn while Erica combed over the surface of the newly revealed stone. She was hoping for an inscription of some kind, or at least some symbolism.

At last she gave up and pulled her head out from under the small enclosure they had formed. "Nothing. I don't see anything."

Matt held the lights out for her to take. "Let me have a look."

He went through the same motions as she had, running the pads of his fingertips over the rough texture, occasionally motioning for Erica to bring the light in closer. After a thoughtful pause, he reached for the knife strapped to his thigh.

Erica's chest clutched. "What are you doing?"

He ignored her and started tapping the urn with the knife's handle before pulling out of the hole to tap the statue in other places. Still not speaking, Matt started banging his knife harder. He began at the crook of the elbow and made his way down to the urn.

The change in sound was distinct, so much that Erica heard it at the same time he did. There was a definite resonance when metal hit the urn. Matt looked at her, an unspoken question in his eyes.

Erica knew what needed to be done, but her archeologist's heart broke at the thought. She extended her open palm to Matt. "I'll do it."

Acknowledging she was better skilled to handle relics with delicacy, Matt gave her the knife and got out of the way.

Erica angled herself in different ways, tapping at the granite to test its feel. Once she established the most promising place, she moved her arm back and forth slowly, then with force and speed brought the butt of the knife down. Amazingly, a small chunk of stone broke free and disappeared inside the urn.

"I take it that's not granite," Matt said dryly.

Erica smiled back at him. "Evidently a different mixture. Hard enough to withstand time, but in such a thin layer that it can be broken. It was probably mixed separately then blended into the stone."

"They did a damn good job." Matt waited, since Erica's attention was back on the small hole. She tapped a few more times then decided to strike her blows in a straight line from the top of the urn down as far as she could get to the base. She made a right degree turn and hit hard, then did the same at the top, hitting just below the first hole. Gently but persistently, she kept at it until a relatively large gap existed.

"This is it." She took a deep breath before reaching her hand in to feel inside. She pulled out quickly. "I think I feel something, but my arm's not long enough."

They switched positions and Matt's hand disappeared inside the urn, his entire arm following swiftly. He grunted once then slowly began to extract himself. He was silent now, and Erica expected the worst.

Then she saw a flash of gold.

Ever so easily, Matt brought forth the cap of a vase. The rest slid into view so quickly Erica felt dizzy, struck in the middle of her chest by the sheer inability to conceive of what they had done.

Matt came away from the statue, balancing the vase in his upturned palms, presenting it to Erica in the royal fashion it had deserved in its day.

Matt caught her astonished eye. "Breathe, Erica."

Realizing she had been holding her breath, breaking the first rule of SCUBA, Erica exhaled in a rush then began laughing. "I can't believe it. Of all places to actually find one of the vases intact."

Her exuberance was contagious, and Matt grinned. "At the bottom of the sea where it was never meant to be in the first place."

Erica reached for the vase, only to have Matt pull it just out of reach. She impaled him with a look that was half confusion, half warning.

Matt spoke calmly. "Now that we have it, we need to go up. The vase may not be watertight, though chances are it's been exposed already."

She gave an acknowledging nod. He was right. It was best to get the vase out of the water in case it had been dry up until they pulled it from its hiding place. Plus, once she got started, she would have a hard time stopping, and they could both use some food and decompression first.

Matt's eyes suddenly lit with a devilish gleam.

Erica was afraid to ask, but she did anyway. "What?"

"I believe we had a deal." His espresso-brown eyes traveled the length of her body down to her fins and back before pinning her with a heated stare. "And technically, I found it first."

22

Once on board and out of her gear, Erica had insisted on taking the time to see if the contents of the vase had endured its underwater resting place.

Unfortunately, it hadn't. The lid had come off all too easily, allowing a brown, cloudy liquid to escape. All that was left of Hatshepsut's lungs. She knew the organs had once resided inside because of the drawing of a baboon on the lid. Habi, the baboon, was associated with the mummification of the lungs.

Erica had begrudgingly agreed to take time to eat something before working on the clue. Then Matt had practically forced her to bathe and change clothes as well.

Now her patience was coming to an end. Granted, she felt recharged after the hot shower and dry clothing, but she couldn't wait another minute to get her hands on the vase and start deciphering the message.

Through the windows of the main cabin, she could see the sun, high and bright, as it glittered on the startling blue water.

Matt, in a move that saved his skin, had the vase resting on a soft towel, ready for her examination. A freshly brewed pot of caramel-mocha coffee didn't hurt either.

Inhaling the tempting aroma as soon as she stepped into the cabin, Erica slanted a look at Matt. "Cheater."

Matt rose to pour her a cup of his version of a bribe. "Have at it, Dr. Conner."

Erica dropped into the chair. "My full title, too? Why do I feel like I'm being worked over?"

"Because you are." He smiled. "I just want you to be on your game."

A flood of warmth gushed through her. All he to do was turn those deep-brown pools on her and she turned to mush. So unfair. She softened her voice. "You'll help me, of course?"

"However I can." He set a steaming red mug in front of her and seated himself to her right.

Erica took a sip then cast a quizzical eye toward the vase. "The clue is on the lid this time. Always a change from the previous disc."

Matt nodded. "First as a necklace on a decoy mummy. Then that same piece was actually the missing portion of a puzzle."

She picked up on his lead. "Off we went to the museum in Amman, where we lucked upon another that had been the bottom of one of Hattie's canopic vases."

"Hattie?" Matt lifted a brow in disbelief.

Erica shrugged. "I'm exhausted, and her name is long."

Matt saw the bruised color under Erica's eyes. She was tired, all right, but he was sure her fatigue was due to more than the just the dive. Every time they found a clue, they drew closer to locating the mummy. But they also increased the chances of running into Kherep Amun.

For now, though, Matt had to put aside any reservations and focus on the clue. And whether he liked or not, Erica had to do the same.

Deciding to leave well enough alone, Matt glanced at the golden circle in her hand. "The clue is there somewhere. What about the bottom?"

"Never hurts to be sure." Erica turned the vase upside down, but found a plain metal surface. Grabbing the penlight, she shined it inside, again with no luck. "No, it's on the cap. Here, look." She handed it to him.

Holding it in his palm, Matt moved his hand slightly up and down as if testing the lid's weight. "Heavier than the others, and thicker."

"It is," Erica agreed. Maybe because it sealed the vase. If the lid were thinner, it would only sit on top. It wouldn't lodge inside the rim."

Matt grazed his fingers over the surface. "Symbols on both sides and no circle for a scytale. No way we're getting that lucky."

Erica smiled. "Senmut never intended for it to be easy to find his lost lady." She took the disc back. "Okay. There is a message on one side, but it doesn't make any sense. The symbols aren't cohesive enough to make a word. They're just a jumble of nouns and biconsonantals."

In response to Matt's raised eyebrow, Erica explained. "Biconsonantals are just symbols that represent a common sound."

"Obviously," he replied with a touch of annoyance. "We're dealing with another encryption."

"Precisely." Erica refilled her coffee then returned her attention to the clue. "The opposite side is more complex. Two rows of symbols circle around the edge, with a line separating the outer row from the inner. Then in the middle of the disc, there are numbers, also encircled by a line."

Erica sighed and put her hands on her temples as if suddenly plagued by a headache. "Great."

"What is it?" Matt asked.

"I think it's an additive cipher."

"Like the ones the computer guys use?"

Erica looked over at him. "You know ciphers?"

"I've picked up a little here and there. I thought those weren't used until Caesar's time."

"He did make the famous Caesar cipher, where letters were assigned numbers. A simple trick, if you know the code."

Matt held her gaze, as awed by her never-dry-fountain-of-facts as he was by her thoughtful blue eyes. He could stare into her crystals and forget about the world.

Eventually. But not today. "This cipher is different how?" he asked.

"There is an algebraic equation that has to be solved, then you add the number or something like that."

"Let's get started then."

Erica shook her head. "No way. I can't do it. It's not our version of algebra. It's ancient Egyptian." She bit her bottom lip before casting him a sheepish look from beneath a wave of inky-black hair. "I was never crazy about math."

Matt stood. "That's why we have backup." Erica thrummed her nails against the table, so he nudged the half-empty coffee back to her nervous hand. "You don't have to do it all by yourself."

She took the warm drink. "I know. Thanks." Tossing her head back to look up at him, she gave him a conspiratorial wink. "Let's call Monroe."

Just as they had decided to call in riddle-solving-reinforcements, another type had shown up in the form of Dan and Clint. The agents entered from outside to say they wanted to relocate farther out to sea. Now that the vase had been found.

Everyone agreed it wasn't worth the risk of being found by Kherep Amun. There was no way of knowing what information the cult had, but they apparently hadn't visited the sunken city of Herakleion, yet.

Yet being the operative word. No need to stick around and risk being found. Or followed.

Matt agreed with the two men, and soon the boat was moving again.

While Dan piloted them toward the horizon, Matt hooked up electronics, and Erica copied the math problem neatly onto a piece of paper they could fax to Monroe.

Her head snapped up when a feminine voice crooned to Matt, "Well hello, lover." She huffed out a breath when she saw Matt laughing along with Karen, whose wicked grin came from the monitor. The comment had been for Erica's benefit, and Matt had enjoyed a proud, male moment when the glint of possessiveness had entered his woman's eyes.

His woman? Matt's laugh faltered. *Aw, hell. Going down that road, all right.*

Oblivious to his inner conflict, Erica picked up the paper and walked over to Matt, pointing a finger at him then Karen. "I think I'm going to regret bringing you two together."

Karen chuckled. "Aw, c'mon, Erica. You're just so much fun to bait. Your reactions are classic."

"Like my reaction to that last guy you dated. What was his name?"

Karen grimaced at Erica's reminder. The women both seemed to know how to push each other's buttons. "Point taken."

Erica settled into the chair next to Matt. "Is Monroe around?"

"He'll be along. I imagine Gus is prying him away from the brandy bottle right about now."

"He tried." The deadpan voice came from behind Karen, just before Monroe's friendly face joined her onscreen. "That man…" He left the rest of the statement up to their imaginations.

Gus spoke out from somewhere in the room. "Just don't spill it on the console."

A distinguished grunt was Monroe's only response.

"Dr. Monroe? Have we driven you to drink?" Erica prodded the man.

"Just trying to open up gateways in my boggy brain." Monroe sighed. "Now what's this I hear about a problem?"

"That's exactly what we have," Erica said. "A math problem. And from Senmut himself."

The older man's eyes widened. "What is it?"

"You should be receiving the scan any minute. I think it's algebra, or whatever they might have called it in 1600 BC." Erica was again shamefaced by her lack of knowledge in that area. She glanced quickly aside to Matt. "I really don't like math."

A moment passed before Gus called from the background. "Got it." The paper appeared onscreen as it was passed to Monroe.

"Hmmm. Yes." He studied the white sheet. "Very simple really." He looked up questioningly at Erica.

She hurriedly stated, "I don't care for math."

"I think we've established that," Matt muttered.

"No matter," Monroe said. "Give me a moment, will you?" He quickly worked the problem before returning his focus to Erica. "It's an additive cipher, then?"

She leaned forward, resting on her elbows. "That was my assumption."

"Yes, I agree. The problem is simple division, and the numerical symbols indicate we are to perform the equation of eight divided by two." He paused only to draw a breath before plowing on. "The answer, four, is then going to be the number of moves subtracted or added. Move that many times from your plaintext, and it will give you the ciphertext."

"Whoa." This from Karen as she lifted a hand. "Say again."

Erica took over. "Once we have the answer to the problem, which is the number four, we have to look at each symbol of the message that's on the lid of the vase. That's our plaintext."

Matt jumped in. "Then look at the other side and move four spaces in one direction and see what symbol that gives us in the other row."

Karen still looked confused. "What row?"

Erica lifted the lid up to the camera in an attempt to give Karen and Monroe a close-up. "What you're looking at now is the encrypted message." At their answering nods, she flipped the object over. "This center of this side has the math problem Monroe just solved. Now look at the edge. See the outer circle of symbols and the inner? We have to figure out which circle of symbols corresponds to the plaintext in the message and go from there."

Monroe leaned forward. "Check to see if all the symbols from the message are included in either row. If any symbol is missing, that can't be your plaintext."

Erica and Matt bent their heads to examine the clue. Again, Erica painstakingly made a copy, this time of the message. It didn't take long to realize all the markings were found in the outer row, the one along the edge of the golden disc.

"I think we have it, but I'm going to check the other, just to be safe," Erica told the others before going through the process again. This time she found several missing symbols. She looked up at Monroe and Karen with a hopeful grin. "The outer row is definitely our plaintext."

Monroe rubbed his chin. "There's no indication in the math as to which direction you should move. Is there any that you can find on the piece itself?"

She and Matt studied both sides. "No, none. I guess I'll just have to pick a direction and see if anything makes sense." Erica tilted her head. "Do I count four spaces and use the symbol in the inner row, the ciphertext?"

Monroe furrowed his forehead. "Who can say if Senmut created his cipher to work in the same fashion as the additive ciphers we know. If he did, you should be able to line up the same symbol, so that the rows match, then move it the appropriate amount of times. You have to have a starting point."

"But you said some of the symbols are missing from the inner row," Karen interjected.

"Line them up." Matt made the statement more to himself than the others. "Wait a minute. Let me see that." He took the lid from Erica then peered closely. He saw something they'd missed before.

"What is it?" Erica asked.

He didn't answer but motioned for the penlight. Retrieving it from the other table, Erica handed it over and watched with brows wrinkled as he angled the light to shine across the surface of the flat sides, first one then the other.

"See that?" Matt asked of no one in particular.

"No." This from a disgruntled Karen. "We don't have the option of leaning in close."

Erica gasped when she saw what Matt had been trying to show them. "It's not just a line." She looked back to the screen. "What we thought was a line between the rows is actually a separation."

Matt worked the object in his hands. "I knew there was something off about this lid." After a moment, a scraping noise announced success as the bottom of the lid moved slightly. Two more turns and the part of the disc holding the message came away.

Matt rubbed his finger over the newly exposed metal. Finally, he paused and smiled at Erica. "Give me your finger."

Without question, she held out her index finger and allowed Matt to guide it to the underside of the disc. Together, they pushed upward, causing a faint click as the inner section rose. Erica spoke rapidly. "It moves. The inner row of symbols rotates."

Monroe sounded equally elated. "Line up the symbols of each row so they match."

"Hold on." Karen repeated her concern. "If some of the symbols are missing from the inner group of markings, how can you line them up?"

Monroe considered the issue. "Good point." Then to Erica and Matt. "Can you line up any of the symbols? Let us keep in mind that this puzzle may not work exactly as we expect it to."

At this point, Matt turned the clue back over to Erica. "All yours."

She tried to turn the inner part in a clockwise direction. After a more aggressive attempt, she shook her head. "It's not turning, at least not in that direction." She met Matt's eyes, her anticipation and anxiety reflected in her gaze.

He inclined his head. "Try the other way."

Taking a deep breath and mentally preparing herself for a letdown, Erica tried to turn it in a counterclockwise fashion. The first small sound made her jump. "It's going. That was one space."

"Three more," Karen encouraged. She and Monroe were literally on the edges of their seats.

Erica clicked three more spaces into the final position, afraid to go too far in case she couldn't get it back. "There." She breathed out in relief.

"Does anything line up?" Monroe asked.

After taking a few minutes to compare the text rows with the original message, Erica had her answer. "The only symbols matching up with their mirror images are the ones *not* found in the message."

"So the symbols from the encryption now each line up with a new symbol," Karen said. "These new symbols form the ciphertext. The readable message."

Three astonished faces swiveled in her direction. "What?" she held up her hands. "I have my moments."

Erica laughed. "You most certainly do my brilliant, co-conspirator." The two women did a mock high-five toward each other through the screen.

Caught up in the revelry, Monroe kissed Karen on the cheek. "Well done!" He returned his attention to Erica and Matt. "What do we have?"

Erica held up a finger. "Back in a sec."

She and Matt moved to the bigger table where the vase still lay. They huddled over the pieces of the lid and translated the plaintext into ciphertext. Gradually they scribbled it onto the paper in an organized fashion.

All Matt saw were simple pictures that consisted of an owl, two snakes, one slithering and one raised to strike, an arm, various other strange markings, and something that looked distinctly like a golf course flagpole.

Erica saw the words as they came together, savoring each

on her tongue until the final image was drawn. Even Matt recognized the last. "That's an ankh."

Erica turned to him and brushed her lips against his. "Yes, it is."

Matt grabbed her and took the kiss deeper before letting her go with a reluctant groan. "So." He looked at her lips then cleared his throat. "What does it say?"

Erica grinned. "Fax it to Monroe." She wanted to let the older man enjoy his reward.

Matt gave one firm nod then pulled her with him to the fax machine. While the cyber communication chirped, he took advantage of their hiding place off screen and held her against his firm chest. He kissed her like a starving man who'd found sustenance.

Finally he pulled away but didn't let go as he called out, "You've got a message coming, Monroe." One final kiss, then he and Erica took their places before the monitor.

Again a paper was handed to Monroe. Looking through the screen to Erica, he gave her a slight bow of gratitude. Then he read the message aloud. "Seek the goddess of the blue stone worker, the presenter of the ankh."

Erica gestured to the older man. "We know who that is."

Monroe took a much deserved sip of brandy. "That we do. None other than the goddess, Hathor." Rolling the last of the brown liquid around the bottom of his glass, he winked at Erica. "And where, *precisely*, was the goddess of the blue stone workers?"

The two archaeologists smiled triumphantly and said in unison, "Sinai."

23

"The blue stone in question is turquoise, of course." Erica laid out the statement as fact.

Matt smiled as he steered the boat. "Of course." They had charted a new course in the direction of Sinai, specifically Serabit el-Khadem, home to the ancient mines that once filled Egyptian coffers with copper and precious stone.

Erica studied her finger, imagining a ring of blue. "The cousin to lapis lazuli, also revered by pharaohs, turquoise has been of high value for thousands of years. In fact it was traded and first came to Europe by way of Turkey, where it got its name."

"How so?" Matt asked, his fierce concentration on the sea ahead.

"The French word for Turkey is Turquoise."

"I could see that." Matt fell silent then, so Erica embraced the fresh, rushing winds as they raced over choppy blue waters. She was content to be in his company. Stealing a glance at Matt, she appreciated the strong line of his jaw and the stubble forming there. She remembered tracing that curve with her mouth the night before.

"How did you and Monroe know right away that the clue referred to Sinai?" he asked, jolting her from sensuality and back to history. Erica had never imagined finding a subject she enjoyed studying more than archaeology.

But that was before Matt entered her life.

"Oh, um…the goddess of the blue stone workers could only be Hathor, protector of miners. The turquoise mines are in Sinai, and Hathor's temple can also be found there. It's also one of the few monuments located in that region." Erica reclined against the gunwale. "I'm sure it's no coincidence Hatshepsut enlarged a portion of Hathor's temple during her reign."

"What's the relationship between Hathor and the ankh?"

"The symbol of life. At least that's the simplest definition. When dynastic rule began, Horus was associated with the king and Hathor with the queen. Many of the scenes in Hathor's temple depict her role in the ascension of rulers to the throne. She played a part in transforming a new king or queen into the deified leader of Egypt. Several scenes on the walls of Hathor's temple show her offering an ankh and therefore control of the land to its recipient."

"Everything had its symbolism," Matt said. "It's amazing how much of that is still around, and people often don't even know it when they see it." He glanced at Erica's hand. "Like that ring you were just thinking of."

"What?" Erica stammered. "She hoped he didn't misinterpret. Then she quirked her mouth to one side. Or would his assumption be wrong? Had she been thinking of Turquoise? Or a big fat diamond?

Ridiculous. She straightened her expression, going for bland and calm.

"You're an easy read," he said, a roll of what sounded like muted thunder coming from his chest. "You need to be more aware of your body language."

"I'll make a note," she snapped as she continued to control her expression. She hoped.

Matt cleared his throat. "Back to the ring that you weren't thinking of." He received a glower for the remark but forged ahead. "Traditionally the ring is a symbol of infinity or eternity.

It binds you with some type of energy. But you probably already know all of this."

"No. I want to hear. What sort of energy?"

"Magic is always a consideration. Then you have the energy of power over others, as seen with royalty. Even your gods and goddesses wore rings." Matt returned his attention to the deep indigo sea. "The most obvious in today's culture would be love."

Erica nodded. "The binding power of love, represented by a ring. It was always just a tradition to me."

Matt remained silent, so Erica decided to steer the conversation to safer ground. "The blue has meaning in its own right."

Matt made a noise that could have been inquiry or disinterest.

Swallowing the lump in her throat, Erica continued. "Blue can also symbolize life, rebirth specifically. Amun was often shown with a blue face, reminding worshippers he was responsible for the birth of the earth itself. Pharaohs were also shown with blue faces when they became associated with Amun."

She stopped and pressed two fingers to her lips.

Noticing the sudden quiet, Matt cast a look over his shoulder at her. "What are you thinking?"

"We already know Kherep Amun wants Hatshepsut's remains so they can perform their ritual and consume a tangible piece of Amun through his daughter's body." Now she tapped those fingers on her chin.

"Go on," Matt said.

Erica sighed. "I don't know. It just feels like there's more meaning behind the placement of the next clue. Hathor's role in presenting the ankh, or new life. The color blue, again a symbol of rebirth." Erica put her hands on her hips in a display of frustration and brushed her hair back. "I'm beginning to see what Monroe means."

Matt throttled back, a signal to the other agents on board that he needed relief at the helm. "About?"

"We're missing something. We have almost every piece of

the puzzle, but I can't see the bigger picture. It's as if there's something on the edge of my visual field I can't quite make out."

Matt turned and crossed his arms, his legs spread in a no-nonsense stance. "Regardless of the bigger picture, my mission is to ferret out members of Kherep Amun and let them lead us to the rest. They are an infestation that has to be exterminated. Completely."

"I agree. But having the whole story may help you find them." Erica returned his tenacious stare with one of her own.

Matt suddenly stepped to her and tucked a wisp of hair behind her ear. He rubbed his knuckles along her cheek. "We will eventually find them. And I'm going to stop them." Then he walked past her, parting words floating in the air as the sky around them darkened. "I just hope it's in time."

It was the following day before Erica, Matt, and the other agents approached the entrance to the Suez Canal. Though still a sensitive area to traverse, it was a fairly safe boating route. As long as they didn't get too close to any military ships.

Throngs of small crafts drifted along the shore, all filled with peddlers waving some trinket or another to the passing cruise boats of tourists. The merchants were boisterous and aggressive, and taking no for an answer was unheard of.

Erica shielded her eyes from the water's glare as she took in the activity. "I hope we don't get stopped. I'm acquainted with the area but would hate to try and explain the guns stashed under seat cushions."

Matt grinned. "I don't think we'll have any problems. My Arabic is good, but you haven't met Clint's alter ego."

"Pretty convincing?"

"Let's just say he could pass for a native."

Erica thought of Clint's brown hair and eyes. Plus, the swarthiness of his skin would fit right in with the Egyptian people. She would have to take Matt's word on the rest and hope there was no need for Clint to use his skills. Even a native would get hauled off for weapons of the sort they carried.

Soon they docked in a long row of other vessels. The Egyptians often lined up boats so anyone disembarking would have to make their way over other yachts and ships before reaching the dock.

The other agents, John and Dan, would be taking the boats to an undisclosed location, leaving Erica, Matt, and Clint to travel by land. Another jeep was waiting for them in a nearby location, but they would have to find a guide willing to take them out to the mines. The place wasn't a point of interest on the average Sinai tour.

The ancient mining complex and Hathor's temple lay on a small plateau north of modern El-Tor, in the mountains of Serabit al-Kadim. It was quite a hike, and their plan was to visit the ruins at night. Their actions needed to be as furtive as possible, though they hoped Kherep Amun was still a step or two behind and nowhere in the vicinity.

El-Tor was a modern city with all the conveniences one would need for a comfortable vacation on the Sinai Peninsula. And if you knew where to go, information could always be bought. For the right price.

The city was not much to look at from the shore. Boxy buildings, a police checkpoint, and large industrial machines were part of a distracting veneer. Odor de fish coated the air, thanks to the seafood storage nearby.

Erica looked down at her olive shorts and white shirt, both of which had seen multiple hand washings since she'd left Georgia. "Too bad we don't have time for the bath."

"You had a shower," Matt said.

Erica grunted. "Moses's bath."

"*Hamman Mousa,*" Clint added with an accent so thick Erica did a double-take. She could imagine how easily he'd blend in.

Matt kept walking, but his tone held a touch of humor. "There's only one Moses that I know of."

Clint grinned. "The bath of Moses has a history. Supposedly, Moses was here at one time, probably on his way to the bush."

Erica laughed. "Who knew agents could be witty."

"Never can tell," Clint quipped before continuing to explain to Matt. "Moses asked a local woman for a drink of water from this spring. When she refused, Moses called on God to bless the water with healing properties, making it undrinkable."

Matt looked doubtful. "Does anyone ever drink it?"

"No way, man, and you wouldn't either." Clint re-adjusted the pack he carried on his shoulder.

Matt shook his head. "I'm not the superstitious type."

Erica walked by Matt's side and almost took his hand. Instead she reached up to scratch the back of her neck and said, "It's not that you would fall down dead or walk the earth cursed or anything. It just tastes awful. The healing properties come from the spring's high content of salt and minerals." She nodded at his look skepticism. "It's supposed to be great for skin diseases."

"No need to stop then," Matt said, lifting his hands palm-side up. I don't have any skin diseases at the moment."

Erica said in a private voice, "I'm well aware."

They turned a corner, and Clint stopped, pointing to a corner cafe. "That's the place. We should be able to find a guide there and find out if anything strange has been going on at the temple or mines."

The café was not as cheerful as its colorful sign implied. Men sat in groups of two or three, huddled in dark corners and carrying on multiple loud discussions. The air was filled with smoke and the rich scent of cooking meat.

Clint turned to Matt and Erica. "I'll ask around. See if I can find a guide."

"In that case, I think I'll wait outside," Erica murmured. She smells and vibe of the place made her uneasy. And a little nauseated.

Through the large plate glass window she could see Clint talking to a pair of men in the back. From the wild gesturing of their hands, it didn't look like he was getting the answer he wanted. It was another few minutes before both Matt and Clint joined her outside.

"It looks like we're going to have to do this by ourselves." Clint flicked his hand against his thigh. "We could, but it would be faster with a guide. Especially since now we *have* to go at night."

"What do you mean we have to?" Erica asked, sliding her sunglasses off. "That was already the plan."

Matt stepped closer and spoke low. "The guides don't want to help us because there have been rumors about the temple. Strangers, probably Kherep Amun, have been here, and they've got the locals terrified. Warnings about taking tourists out to the mines or the temple. Threats of violence."

"But one guy decided to call their bluff," Clint added.

When neither of the men elaborated, Erica prompted, "And?"

Clint clamped his lips together then ground out, "Let's just say he won't be guiding anyone anywhere for a while."

"They're still here. They have to be." Erica tucked her hands in her pockets to keep them still, to keep from giving away her nervousness. "What should we do? We can't give up."

"We find you a hotel room, and Clint and I go it alone." Matt made the statement as if he expected no argument.

He should have known better.

"Forget it." Erica pulled one hand back out and made a slicing motion then walked off down the street.

Matt caught up in a few strides and brought her to a halt with one hand on her shoulder. "Wait. Just wait and stop making a scene."

She sucked in a breath and prepared to tell him what he

could do with his directives. Then she realized he was right. And if she acted like an amateur, he would worry about her even more. Which meant he would try to control her. Even more.

"We'll take a break and sort through our options," Matt said.

Erica opted for cool and unarguable logic. In other words, *Manspeak*. "There is only one option and you know it. You need me, so we all go in together. Carefully and prepared for anything." She cocked a hip. "I happen to know how to use a gun."

Matt cringed but nodded slowly. "We'll have to work with what we've got. Keep our eyes open."

Clint's deep voice came from behind them. "And we just got another set to help watch our backs."

Both Erica and Matt turned to see Clint strolling toward them, accompanied by a teenage boy. "This is Ahmed. He's offered to take us to Serabit al-Kadim."

"He's just..." Erica started

Clint held up his hands to stop her from finishing. "He knows the risks, and I told him he won't have to take us the whole way. No one will ever know he helped us."

"We're standing here talking in the street," Matt pointed out. "Lots of interested parties around."

The boy spoke up. "My people will not say anything. It is only the bad men that I do not want to see me. The guide that was beaten, he talked too much and to the wrong people."

Erica shook her head. "I'm not sure about this. We're trying to save innocents, not put them at risk."

With a smile as bright as the sun, Ahmed touched her elbow. "Don't worry, lady. I have a story to cover me." He whipped out a fabric case that opened to reveal strands of colorful stone necklaces. "You want to buy one?"

24

A star-speckled sky of midnight ink blended into the violet horizon of the Sinai desert. And another day was laid to rest. The group of four, two FBI agents, a female scientist, and a young Arab boy, stood and watched the show, each appreciating the majestic view for their own reasons.

Ahmed was the first to break the silence. "Local tribes protect the sites from looters, but they will be no trouble if they come upon us. Some are my family. I am well known." Again the wide, white smile flashed.

His statement brought a new concern to Matt's mind. "How did the strangers you mentioned manage to influence entire tribes?"

Ahmed simply turned back to the expanse of night, and no one else ventured a response or another query.

Ahmed spoke in a lively, carefree tone, as if he'd all but forgotten the evil men and the threat to his people. "I hope you have enough water. There will be none found on the trail to Serabit al-Kadim." With that said, the teenager set off into the desert night, his sure footsteps indicating knowledge of the terrain.

"Ahmed." Erica spoke into the silence filled only with the brush of their shoes over sand. "Tell us about the mines."

The boy paused then pursed his lips. "You do not know of

the mines?"

Matt grinned in the dark, having gained a new appreciation for their young guide. Ahmed was observant and had already figured Erica out. The kid understood that despite the sweet face and soft curves, the lady was the scholar of the group.

Erica responded without pride or ego, underplaying the extent of her knowledge. "I know some history of the area but always enjoy learning from another's perspective."

Judging by his laugh, Ahmed appreciated her modesty. He pointed his finger as if the mines were just ahead instead of a two hour walk from their current location. "The miners were the first to settle here in Sinai, over eight thousand years ago."

"Eight thousand?" This from Clint. "Did they have dinosaurs for pets?"

Matt and Erica laughed, but Ahmed seemed confused. "No. That was much before."

The boy seemed to be enjoying his role as teacher and continued with his story. "The copper and turquoise found here drew the miners to Serabit al-Kadim in the time you call 3500 BC, when the kingdoms of Egypt were becoming unified under the pharaohs. By 3000 BC, Egyptians controlled the mines. For two thousand years the blue stone was taken from the mountain and carried by boat to Egypt."

Erica followed the line of conversation. "Yes. The Egyptians used the turquoise for many things. Scarabs were carved from the mineral, paint was created by grinding it, and of course there was jewelry."

Matt saw her reach up to finger the blue necklace she was now wearing. He told her he'd bought the jewelry to reinforce Ahmed's cover story. He didn't mention the sky-blue mirrored her eyes or that the stones reminded him of their conversation on the boat. About magic and new life.

The only woman he'd ever given jewelry to was his mother. Unless he counted the lollipop-ring he'd given Stephanie what's-her-name in fourth grade. And he didn't.

No, Matt could no longer avoid what continued to land squarely at his feet, on his shoulders, and in his gut, at its deepest and darkest hiding place. He was going down and there was no stopping it. Falling hard and irreversibly for Dr. Erica Conner.

He'd been protective of her when she'd been nothing more than a risky hindrance. An additional life to guard. Nothing but an assignment. But now that she was…hell…now that she was *Erica,* he was afraid to let her out of his sight.

He'd considered a million and one things that could have gone wrong on this expedition, but falling in love? Never. Not in a million and two.

With a growl for his ears only, Matt rejoined the conversation. "What about the temple?" he asked.

Ahmed pursed his lips again. Matt noticed the kid did that when he was thinking, just as Erica got that cute little wrinkle…*dammit. Stay on track. Pierce.*

Ahmed held up a finger and spoke. "I know the oldest stones were laid during the twelfth dynasty."

"Approximately 2000 BC to 1800 BC," Erica supplied.

"Right," Ahmed said. "Although, I do not go to the temple as often as the mines."

Matt didn't like the sound of that. "You're sure you can get us there?

Ahmed waved a hand and blew air through his lips. "I can get you there. I enjoy the mines more, because I like to see how far in I can go. I have a list and mark them off by pharaohs."

"You mean the inscriptions?" Erica asked.

"Yes."

"How's that?" Clint asked with renewed interest.

Erica took over for Ahmed and explained. "The mines were made by creating entrances into the sides of the mountains. Each entrance had the name of the reigning pharaoh at the time. But I thought the British destroyed the pharaonic reliefs at some point."

Ahmed puffed out his chest. "We keep our own history."

"And a very valuable history it is." Erica smiled at the young, proud, male. "After all, even our alphabet can find its origins here."

Ahmed's big, brown eyes slid to the side to study her. "Truly?"

"Yes. Some of the scientists that found the temple in 1905 found the Sinaitic script there. The script consisted of hieroglyphics used to keep track of the names of the people who worked the mines as well as an accounting of their labor. This led to the development of their *Alef-Bet*." Erica shrugged. "You be the judge."

Ahmed produced a new smile, one that bespoke of pride and that he had another fascinating tidbit to impress other tourists with.

The group walked quietly for a while. Though the ruins were still far away, the closer their group got to the site, the higher the likelihood they'd encounter Kherep Amun. Voices might attract unwanted attention, so no one objected to the silence.

Finally, Ahmed spoke in a muted voice. "We go that way to the mines." He pointed his arm one way then reversed directions. "That way to the temple."

"Can we make it the rest of the way by ourselves?" Matt noted the growing fear in the boy's eyes.

"Yes." Ahmed produced a paper from his pocket. "I have written down very specifics. You should have no trouble. Even in the night."

Ahmed had never intended to travel too close to the sites. The map had been prepared for this moment, but Matt couldn't blame him. He had every reason to be afraid.

"Thank you for your help, Ahmed." Matt handed the boy his promised wages and a tip.

The kid had a bright future ahead of him if he could find the right opportunities. He did not insult Matt and the others by counting the cash in front of them, so the surprise would be that much greater when he finally did. Matt's tip had been generous.

Bowing and gesturing in a way that offered peace and fortune, Ahmed treated Erica to one final smile then he turned to disappear into the dark.

Clint took the lead, translating the notes Ahmed had written down. They were a mixture of English, Arabic, and artwork. Measurements were given in footsteps, and landmarks were provided in both description and a drawing.

It wasn't long before the beams of their flashlights revealed what could best be described as a russet colored cemetery. The stones in the area looked like grave markers, yet were longer and thinner, some tilted, overturned, or broken into pieces.

"We're here," Erica whispered. "Those are the stelae I saw online."

"Online," Matt said. "Isn't that a little like archaeological cheating?"

Erica only turned her lips up at the corners.

"Looks quiet." Clint said to Matt. "You want me to take a look first?"

"No. We need to stay together." He motioned for Erica to fall into step behind Clint, so he could take up the rear. So he could keep her in sight.

As they drew closer to the center of the rocks, Erica shone her light on two stones in particular. "Those are two of the stelae that lead the way to the entrance of Hathor's underground chapel. There should be more pairs like that."

"Should we search outside first?" Matt asked as he surveyed the surroundings. The site had been almost completely destroyed, as if someone had done so on purpose. Long ago.

It was Erica's turn to pull out a handful of papers that had been pressed into a square. She unfolded them and huffed out a breath. "I'm not even sure what we're looking for. Any drawings of the things mentioned in the clue should be carefully scrutinized."

"Like the ankh or any pictures of Hathor." Matt was getting

more used to the process. "Let's find the entrance."

Erica returned her gaze to the paper and traced a finger over the outline of a structure. "According to this there are two caves. One for Hathor's chapel and another that leads to the one belonging to Sopdu. He was another deity, male to balance Hathor's female presence. The temples were originally built for the miners' spiritual needs. When facing the entrances, Hathor's will be on the right side."

"Let's start there then we can work our way around the stones." Matt headed for the upright stelae and called to Clint. "Take that side. See if you can find the other cave."

When Clint waved back, Erica walked to the opposite side of Matt. "If we locate both of the caves, we'll know which is the right one."

They spread out in each direction. In bare seconds, Clint was on his way back. "There's another cave back there."

"Then the one I'm facing is the one we want. Would you go get Erica?"

"Right here." Erica's voice was nearby. Soon her flashlight beam bounced into view.

"Erica and I will go in," Matt said to Clint with an underlying message in his stare.

"Right." The other man understood that he needed to stay alert. He should keep watch while Matt was unable.

As they ducked into the black hole, Erica latched onto Matt's arm for support. "You know, most of the relics from here are nice and safe in a museum somewhere. All that's left are the inscriptions on the markers and some statues. This may be our biggest challenge, yet. "

Matt steadied her as they eased down the slope inside. "I don't know if that upsets me because we'll lose time." He shone his light around when they leveled out. "Or because we may have to make the hike out here more than once."

Erica didn't respond, and when Matt saw her stunned face, he took a more scrutinizing survey of the room they were in.

The chapel was even more barren than they'd expected. The only artifacts left were the ones etched or carved in stone.

"Oh." The despair was evident in Erica's cracked voice.

"It's probably not even worth splitting up." Matt was shocked by how little there was to explore. "We should still work separately. We'll start in one spot and work in opposite ways until we end up back there again." He gave her a nudge and she nodded before spurring into action.

The search took less than five minutes.

"Anything?" Matt asked, though he knew the answer.

"Nothing that made me pause."

"Me either." Cold dread snaked its way into the base of Matt's skull, and he could see the same disappointment in Erica's strained eyes.

She swept her light across the room in a half-hearted manner. "There are references to Hathor, but nothing I could begin to think of as a clue." She kicked a pebble.

"I even tested areas that looked like they might be loose or have moveable parts." Matt said. Then he touched her elbow. "We always knew this was a possibility. If it ends here, it ends here. We'll find another way."

"I know." She tried for a smile but it puttered out.

"They're working the evidence from the rape as we speak. All we need is one break and we'll be all over them."

Erica raised her eyes to meet his. "But you won't be cutting the head off the snake."

"Not right away." Matt pushed his head to one side and popped his neck. The sound was like a gun shot in the small, stony space. "But we will." He decided not to mention the deaths that would occur before they would be able to do any serious damage to Kherep Amun's organizational structure. Erica was already dragging with guilt.

He could see it in her. And he could taste it in his own mouth.

"What do you think will happen if we find Hatshepsut before they do?" she asked.

"I think it will put a crimp in their plans. Slow them down."

"But not stop them?"

"If we knew more about why they've amped up their search, maybe I could predict their reaction. They've had a couple thousand years, but in the last decade their activity has increased tenfold. They started taking chances, which is how we found out about them in the first place."

Erica leaned into Matt then, and he wrapped his arms around her. Offering what comfort he could. She whispered into the shadows. "If there's a chance, then I still want to try."

Matt gave her a squeeze. "I do too. So that means we have to re-strategize."

They rejoined Clint outside and explained their plan to explore the rest of the temple grounds. Erica sketched some symbols to look for and they split up. Designating a central area with their backpacks, they walked out in three different directions, trailing ribbons behind them so they would each recognize the boundaries of their search area.

They worked diligently for over two hours until Clint called them back in for a break. Erica settled onto her backpack, doing her best to avoid the cold, hard ground.

"How about some coffee? Looks like we'll be pulling an all-nighter." Clint handed Erica a tin cup.

"Where did you get that?" She sipped the lukewarm brew. Then again. "Hmmm. Clint, I love you."

"I heard that," Matt said as he strode in to join them, taking a cup from Clint. "I've made you coffee before and don't remember the gushing sentiment."

Erica sipped and grinned. "It's all about the timing."

Matt sat beside Erica, while Clint tossed his coffee back and poured another from the thermos. After drinking the second as quickly as the first, the agent dropped the cup into his pack. "I need a little privacy." Walking away from Erica and Matt, he tossed over his shoulder, "But don't worry, Erica, I won't use your section."

She chuckled. "I'm beginning to think all Feebies have a twisted sense of humor."

"Comes with the territory. If you don't already have one, you will after a couple of years. You need it."

Erica's eyes dimmed as she studied her cup like a mystic reading leftover tea leaves. "I haven't seen anything that was even worth calling you over to take a second look at. I'm beginning to get really scared." Her head fell back on her shoulders. "Why did I think this would be easy?"

Matt spoke with grim honesty. "Because we've been lucky so far. Don't get me wrong. Your expertise made it all happen, but we were fortunate to locate most of Senmut's clues." He tapped the cup against his knee. "Our streak just came to an end."

Erica nodded solemnly. "Not surprising. It has been over two millennia. We were lucky to have made it this far."

Matt tossed his cup toward Clint's pack. "You've done well. We chose the right person for this job."

Erica shifted her eyes, unable to meet his gaze head on. "I can hear it in your voice. This is the end of the road, isn't it?"

Matt inhaled but hesitated. He hated to confirm it out loud.

A male voice from the shadows answered for him instead. "End of the road? Not on your life."

Erica and Matt both jumped up to locate the source, Matt's hand instinctively going to his gun. Just then, Clint stepped forward. "Whoa. It's just me, man. And look who I found lurking around."

"I, dear boy, do not lurk." A figure stepped into the beams of their flashlights.

"Dr. Monroe!" Erica cried. "What are you doing here?"

"We had to come straight away," the older man said before frowning at Matt, "And those phones of yours are obviously not working."

"We turned them off to reduce the chance of noise," Clint explained.

Erica picked up something else Monroe had said. "What do

you mean *we*?"

"Hey." Karen walked up to stand behind Monroe.

"Hey," Clint said, drawing out the word with an appreciative quality.

Karen probably always brought that out in the opposite sex, but Matt punched Clint in the arm anyway.

Erica's breath left her in a dramatic sigh as she ran to hug her friend. "You have the best timing," she said over Karen's shoulder.

Matt moved to shake Monroe's hand. "It is good to see you. I take it you've made a break?"

"We did indeed," Monroe said. "And with you out of contact for most of the day, we decided it would be faster to join you in person."

"And more fun," Karen added. "For all we know you could have camped here until you found something, and we couldn't afford to waste that much time. Plus, Monroe here has been chomping at the bit to get back into the game. I think he's come back out of retirement."

The silver-haired man sniffed. "And you tried so terribly hard to dissuade me, did you?"

Karen cocked a shoulder and grinned. "I couldn't stand not being around to keep an eye on things." She held up a hand. "Not that you weren't doing a good job, Matt."

Matt shrugged on his gear and smiled. "Right now, I couldn't care less. As long as you've got good news."

"Yes, we do. Yes." Monroe waved his hands. "Get your things. I'll explain it all back at the hotel. I've got us a suite or two."

Erica looked at the man in concern. "You've just made a two mile hike. Are you sure you don't need to rest?"

Monroe scowled at her.

Karen patted Erica's arm. "Don't waste your breath. Already been there."

"How did you find us so easily?" Clint asked. "Did you find a guide?"

"We were all set to trek it ourselves," Monroe explained. "I have been here once before, but just as we set out, we encountered a guide willing to take us directly here."

"Really?" Erica shook her head. "We were turned down at first, but then..." She stopped and pointed at Karen's colorful stone bracelet.

Matt smiled as the connection clicked.

"Yes," Monroe continued, "we ran into him on the trail. A very enterprising young man named Ahmed."

25

It was easy to see why Monroe had been so eager to come back to the town of El-Tor. The accommodations he had waiting for them were deluxe suites. Opulence, prompt service, and more than enough space for them all.

As he brought out the brandy from a gold lacquered liquor cabinet, he addressed the group. "Would you all care for showers and a meal before we begin?"

"Not this time," Erica answered Monroe, but looked pointedly at Matt.

Clint lifted a finger. "I could stand some food, though.

"Excellent." Monroe was immediately on the phone ordering enough for an army.

Matt and Erica settled onto a sapphire, velvet loveseat, while Karen and Clint sat on opposite ends of a matching sofa. Monroe cleared a lavish flower arrangement from the large circular table in the center of their conversation area. He soon covered the glass with papers and maps and took a seat in the leather armchair.

Erica sat forward, anticipation and renewed hope strumming through her like a burgeoning symphony. "Tell us." She tapped a finger in the middle of the papers and wanted to turn them to face her. She resisted. Barely.

Unruffled, Monroe took a leisurely sip of brandy and started to speak. "It all came together this morning in the library. I guess now it would be yesterday morning." He looked at his watch, noting the late hour.

"What came together?" Erica asked.

Monroe mimicked her body language and leaned forward. "The locations of the clues have not been random at all. They are connected to a very specific and reliable diagram."

"Diagram? What do you mean?" Karen tucked her feet up under her on the couch, a much more relaxed pose than the two doctors facing each other at the table.

"You don't know what's going on either?" Matt asked in response.

Karen gave her best imitation of a pout. "No. I couldn't pull it out of him. He said it was only right that Erica hear it first."

Erica shot Monroe a we're-in-a-secret-club kind of smile.

The older man winked back at her. "Well...saved me from telling it twice, didn't it?" He tipped his glass in a silent *cheers* to the group. "At any rate, the diagram I'm speaking of is actually a constellation."

"Stars?" Karen asked.

"Yes, stars. The Orion constellation to be exact. At least that's what the Greeks called it."

"Who called it something else?" Clint asked.

It was Erica who answered. "The Egyptians." She turned to Matt. "They called it Osiris."

One side of Matt's mouth lifted. "As in Osiris, Isle of Fire, god of plagues and destruction? That Osiris?"

"One and the same." She slapped her hands together and turned back to Monroe. "What else did you find?"

Monroe set his drink aside and rolled open a large paper. It had a picture of the constellation with handwritten notes all around the border. "I was racking my brain in the library, attempting to determine what I was missing. Memories locked inside from many years ago were desperately trying to come together. Then it hit me. In my younger days, I attended a lecture on the symbolism and legend that accompanied the Osiris assemblage of stars."

Erica came around the table and dropped to her knees to get a better look. "I still don't see. I know the Egyptians placed great faith in astronomy, but how does it connect to Hatshepsut?"

"Not Hatshepsut." Monroe met her stare. "It's all about Senmut. He was the one who orchestrated everything. To say he loved Hatshepsut is an understatement. He truly believed she was divinity itself."

Erica's eyes followed Monroe's finger as he placed it on the starry map and spoke. "To the ancient Egyptians, the Orion constellation was the prime meridian of the celestial world. During a certain time of year, the heavens align correctly so the stars in the constellation correlate with areas on earth. These places on our planet have been called star points."

"Yes, I've studied this." Erica said then crushed her mouth closed. She wanted Monroe to continue.

"These star points are the meeting places of the earth's magnetic fields. The Egyptians built many of their pyramids and other great structures on spots where the magnetic fields crossed each other. They believed energy from outer space would enter the earth in these areas."

Erica knew she was close to a eureka moment. She stared at the diagram then placed her fingertip on one of the stars. Matt, Karen, and Clint all leaned in when she did. "The nebula." Erica was focused now, speaking in a low, clear voice. "It correlates with the Petra region."

"Yes," Monroe whispered as the air grew heavy with expectation.

Matt nodded. "Where we found the second clue. The land of Punt."

"Exactly," Erica said, sliding her finger across the paper until it rested on another star. "The head of Osiris correlates with..." She didn't finish the sentence but clenched her eyes shut to concentrate.

Monroe gave her a hint. "Remember the water."

Her eyes popped open. "The head is where the Nile meets the Mediterranean."

"The Canopic branch," Matt added.

"In the Mediterranean Sea. Clue number three." Erica repositioned herself and began speaking more quickly. "And Sinai. The belt of Osiris lines up with Sinai. Where we are now."

"You've got it!" Monroe exclaimed with a raised glass.

Matt rubbed his hands together. "So we should be able to figure out the location of the last clue. What point in the constellation fits up with the Valley of the Kings, where the original amulet sent us?"

"Nothing," Monroe said with a grin.

The others all looked at Monroe, confused by his answer.

"It's all right." He leaned back in his chair and crossed his legs. "I was afraid I had it all wrong at one point. Just as you think now. But it still makes sense. The only significance of the first location is that it was Hatshepsut's temple. Senmut had already dedicated so much of the intricate artwork and décor to his queen that he was easily able to return and install the clue in the wall. Hidden in plain sight."

"The space where the necklace fit pointed us in the direction of Pella." Matt stood and started pacing, his fist pressed to his mouth. Erica had never seen him this agitated. But then, she was extra twitchy, too. They had both believed their quest was over when they'd found nothing at the mines. Now Monroe had infused their mission with new possibilities. A new direction.

Energy seemed to pulse and shoot between the people gathered at the table. They might still be able to stop Kherep Amun. They might still saves innocent lives.

And find Hatshepsut. Erica wanted that more than ever, but for a different reason. There was no way those murderous bastards were getting their hands on the mummy. The lost queen deserved better.

"That actually that makes sense," Matt said, referring to the constellation and how it didn't line up with the first place they'd visited. "We didn't find a vase in Hatshepsut's temple."

"You've been to three locations where vases were located," Karen said. "Or should have been," she added, since nothing had been found there in Sinai. "So there's one vase left before you learn the final destination?"

"I don't think so." Monroe drew their attention again. "I think the final vase will be in the arms of Hatshepsut herself."

"What makes you say that?" Matt asked.

"Why don't we let Erica explain?" Monroe motioned for her to take over.

Erica licked her lips. "We've accounted for the head and the belt of Osiris, as well as the nebula. That leaves only Betelgeuse."

"Betelgeuse?" Karen piped up with a laugh. Seeing the looks on their faces, she erased her smile. "Sorry. Sorry. I won't go there."

Erica continued. "Betelgeuse correlates with..." She looked to Monroe for confirmation. "Giza?"

The older man spread his hands as if performing a magic trick. "Absolutely."

"And now you're going to explain why, right?" Matt asked Monroe, but a knock at the door prevented the older man from responding.

Matt, Karen, and Clint all drew their weapons and moved to various positions around the door.

Seeing them respond that way was too much for Erica. "Oh, for pity's sake. It's the room service."

Matt shot her a look after he'd checked the peephole. "You want another snake in your bed?"

Point taken. She kept quiet and waited.

But it was only room service. Two young men stood there, since the food was more than one person could transport. After the carts were wheeled into the room, Clint tipped them generously and saw them out.

Erica and the others arranged trays of appetizers on any available space then poured drinks. They took a brief moment before returning to the discussion.

"Your question is sound, Matt, and one I fully intend to address." Monroe paused to finish a fried mushroom. "One reason I believe both the vase and Hatshepsut will be found in Giza is the absence of a fifth star point."

"I think Monroe is right." Erica joined in as she nibbled on a small shrimp salad. "There are only four points that correspond with locations on earth, and Giza holds great astrological significance. The great pyramid falls on the prime meridian." She turned to Monroe. "That can't be a coincidence. Osiris is the prime meridian of the sky, and the Giza pyramid is associated with the one here on earth. At least as far as Senmut and his followers were concerned."

"Yes," he said. "Not only that, but I believe you've hit on the very thing."

Erica reached for an éclair but stilled at his words. "What thing?"

"The Great Pyramid of Giza. The only remaining monument of the Seven Wonders of the Ancient World. Are you at all familiar with the details of its construction?"

She furrowed her brow. "You mean the code?"

"That's part of it, but I believe the geographical placement of the pyramid is just as crucial."

Karen waved a hand. "You've lost me. Again. What code?"

"We'll get to that," Monroe said. "I'm talking about the use of the pyramid as the focal point in relation to other ancient sites in a globally coordinated system."

Karen didn't have to say a word this time. The look on her face said it all.

"Let me put it this way," Erica cut in. "The earth is divided into 360 degrees around the equator. That's how we get longitude coordinates. Latitude coordinates are figured using

90 degrees. Basically, the ancient Egyptians could start from the great pyramid and give a set of instructions that stated how far to go in longitude and latitude to reach any place on earth. Today we recognize Greenwich, England as this point."

"You left out the part about dividing degrees into minutes and seconds." Matt made the comment with a grin.

"I'm thankful she did," Karen was quick to mention. "My brain is on overload as it is. But I get the gist. No need for any more star talk. If I'm hearing you all correctly, Giza is the only place that makes sense. It's the fourth location."

"Giza it is," Matt said. "We'll leave at daybreak." He stretched his legs out in front of him, more content after the meal. "I hate to always be the one to bring it up but..."

"Kherep Amun." Erica and Karen said together.

"Anything new?" Matt asked.

Karen frowned. "Nothing so far on the girl. It takes a while to get the DNA samples crosschecked with all the systems, but that's being done." She locked eyes briefly with Monroe then continued. "There were also two more murders."

"Damn. When and where?" Matt's easy posture was gone. He pulled his legs back in and sat forward, arms propped on his knees. Hands in tight fists.

Erica put her face in her palms but listened intently. She didn't want to hear. But she had to.

"An older couple in the Philippines," Karen said. "They lived in a small rural town. It might not have gotten our attention if the murders hadn't been so extreme."

"Oh no." Erica pressed her hands against her forehead, dreading the details she knew were coming.

"There were Egyptian symbols painted on their bodies in blue." Karen took a long, deep breath. "And they were burned. Just like the reference to incense in the Cannibal Text."

"So they've gone through the ages mentioned in the text." Matt said. "We can't be sure what they'll do next, but whatever their plan, I'm sure the violence is going to escalate."

"Why now?" Clint asked. "What the hell has made them break loose after all this time? We're talking thousands of years they've stayed quiet."

"I believe the answer is in the pyramid." Monroe sighed and rubbed his forehead.

"Why?" Erica questioned the older man as she moved to sit beside Matt.

Monroe slowly raised his head and fixed them with a stare. "The code."

26

Tokyo, Japan

The man was stylishly dressed in an Armani suit, but beneath the dark clothing his body was a colorful map of tattoos. He was a member of a very old society in Japan, one whose origins were believed to be traced back to the days of the Samurai. He walked with authority, carrying himself in a way that stated his position, both a proclamation of pride and caution. A wise man would not trifle with him.

His given name was Kei. The name, chosen by his father, meant reverence, something the man felt his firstborn son naturally deserved.

Kei moved through the city streets in what could only be described as a swagger, the crowds on the sidewalk parting before him, no one willing to cross his path. Normally he would have traveled by limousine, escorted by an entourage of men who could kill with one swipe. But not tonight.

He was a little drunk and impatient to get to the brothel. Where women who would do whatever he wanted. Kei was tired of the playacting, having the prostitutes dress as anything from police women to schoolgirls. Tonight, he wanted to try the paint.

Looking forward to it, he'd left the nightclub while one bodyguard was in the bathroom and the other diverted by a lap dance.

This had given those watching him the opportunity they'd been waiting for. The foolish man let his position and unquestionable authority cloud his judgment. As next in line as boss of a local Yakuza crime organization, Kei was both a worthy sacrifice and an opportunity to send a powerful message. That no one would be safe from what was coming.

The group of men from Kherep Amun waited until Kei went inside. There wasn't much time. As soon as the bodyguards noticed Kei's absence, they would look for him at the whorehouse.

Most people of the night feared the Yakuza, also known as *gokudo* or the violence group. But some things were to be feared even more, as the young girl waiting at the door had been shown earlier in the week. She would risk everything and do as the strange, dark men had asked. She did not want them to visit her little sister. Did not want them to do the things they had threatened. Her sister was only a child.

She was waiting for Kei and had been alerted to his presence, knowing exactly how to gain his attention. The girl had assured them the plan would work.

The beautiful, little *joufu* grabbed Kei's hand and whispered in his ear, ensuring he would follow her to a room. A room where she would mix him a special drink. A room that had a secret exit known only to the girls who worked there.

Kei's men would think him safe. Even if they came to the brothel, they would not disturb him behind those closed doors. Kei did not like to share.

There would be plenty of time for the dark men to come for Kei. Then they would give her the money they had promised, and she could take her sister somewhere to a better life.

The girl waited only a few minutes before the drug worked its spell. Kei was already intoxicated, so all the better. Once

Kei was unconscious, she pulled out the phone she had been given and dialed. The dark men appeared shortly from behind the secret door.

While two of them retrieved Kei's limp form, another reached out and took the phone from the girl. With his other hand he pulled something from a pocket. The girl assumed it would be her payment.

She was wrong.

Too late, she realized her naiveté and knew there would be no one to take care of her sister. These men would leave no money behind. Only death.

St. Petersburg, Russia

The woman's full, crystalline voice filled the shadows of the darkened opera house. Stage lights shone down on her graceful figure as many in the audience wept, enraptured by the emotion of the moment.

The man behind the curtain sneered. How these *aristos* loved their entertainment. They believed themselves so cultured, so refined. They knew nothing of power or society. But they would learn soon enough.

He looked to the stage. Svetlana had been at her best tonight, and the performance would be remembered. Not only because it was the last show of the season, but because it would be the last of her lifetime.

The willowy blonde waved to the crowd. Tears, both genuine and manufactured, fell from the corners of her lovely green eyes as roaring fans stood in ovation.

With a final wave, she gave a graceful turn and strode regally from the stage, searching now for one face in particular. There he was, waiting for her. Yerik. His black eyes smiled at the corners, making her feel even more special than the adoring spectators shouting their cheers. She had known many lovers, but this man held a certain amount of mystery. He had places in him she couldn't seem to touch.

But then, she had always loved a bad boy.

He took the hand she offered and kissed it through her long glove. His warm lips sent sensations up her arm and caused her groin to pulse in expectation. She couldn't wait to be alone with him.

"Svetlana," he purred her name, a steely glint in his stare. "I hope you don't mind, but I've made arrangements for tonight. In …celebration."

With her usual imperious manner, Svetlana nodded acquiescence, though Yerik had known she would have no objection. He let her believe she was controlling the game. What would it hurt? She would know the truth before the night was out.

The pair made a swift escape through a back door to the car Yerik had waiting. With a word to the driver, they were on their way. The lights and noise of the Nikolaevsky Palace and the opera attendees faded into the dark of night as they sped toward the Russian countryside.

Svetlana rubbed against Yerik's side, but he remained distant, stiff. Twining her fingers in her hair, she gave him her best pout. "Is something the matter?"

Looking straight ahead, Yerik smiled icily. "No. Everything is just as it should be."

Taking his statement as encouragement, she rubbed her fingers along the inside of his thigh but gasped as his hand pinned hers in a viselike grip.

"No." Yerik released her. "Not just now." He faced away from her with a dismissive gesture. "I have something else in mind."

With an unexplained stirring of fear, Svetlana inched back, putting a small space between them. "What do you have planned?"

The eerie smile returned to his lips. "I have some friends I'd like you to meet."

London, England

Detective William Doyle turned the deadbolt behind him as he entered the flat. After another fourteen-hour day, he was more than exhausted and glad to be home where he could get some sleep. Over the last two weeks, the search for a particularly depraved murderer had consumed his every waking hour and most of his dreams as well.

He dumped his jacket and gear before heading straight for the icebox and a bottle of cold porter. He grabbed blindly for a microwavable meal, not really caring what it consisted of. He simply needed sustenance.

Doyle was highly decorated and well respected among the ranks of the Metropolitan Police. He'd already turned down two promotions that would have meant a higher salary but would also have entailed the slavery of desk work. Doyle was at his best on the streets and on the hunt. He knew where he belonged, and most of his superiors were finally beginning to accept that.

Kicking back on his recliner, Doyle switched on the television, hoping to catch the last of a football match. It was over, so he settled for a lively game show and debated whether to call Cheryl, the latest in a long line of temporary girlfriends.

Most women wanted commitment and beyond that, children. William Doyle could promise neither, so eventually the women he dated moved on to more promising prospects.

A noise roused him from where he had fallen asleep in the chair. At first he wasn't sure what time it was or what had woken him, though something was tickling at the back of his mind. Then he heard it again. The softest of scrapes, like a door being opened slowly somewhere in the flat.

Most people would never have picked up on the sound, but Doyle was always on alert and trained to notice anything out of place. The slide of a door was definitely out of place. If he were alone as he should be.

Instantly awake and at full throttle, Doyle moved to where he had dropped his holster and gun. They were both gone. Registering the absence, he took a moment to replay his movements since entering the apartment. Yes, he was sure he had put everything on the hallway table.

Slowly he looked around the room and toward the kitchen, where he kept a backup in the drawer under the toaster. He moved like a man with experience and the fearlessness of one who knew death by name.

The gun was gone. The sight of the empty space where the weapon should have been froze him in place. How the hell would an intruder know the location of his gun? Unless they had been here long enough to search thoroughly before he had returned.

A new sound caught his attention. He jerked around to find several men in black clothing. Their eyes all held the cold blank stare he'd come to recognize over the years. These were men who could kill with no remorse. They probably already thought of him as dead, a handy trick that absolved one of guilt.

Possibilities of who the men represented flashed through his head. He had his share of enemies, but none he could think of would be this organized. Perhaps it had nothing to do with him personally. He doubted he would ever know.

The tallest man, in the middle of the bunch, raised his arm smoothly and swiftly. Doyle expected to hear the crack of a pistol, but instead heard nothing. He was aware only of a sharp stab in the right side of his chest. Looking down in shock, he saw the spines of a dart protruding from his torso.

Poison? Unlikely. It was probably a drug meant to disable him, but he would die before he let himself fall into the hands of these assassins. God only knew what they had planned for him. Ransom? A trade for an imprisoned member of their group? Torture?

As the ideas fought alongside each other in his bewilderment. Then something else caught Doyle's attention. A strange smell. Was that incense?

He meant never to find out. Doyle made a move toward the men. He would fight his way out or die trying.

Another dart hit him, on his left and closer to his neck. He paused long enough to try and pull it out. The drug had entered his bloodstream because the men were beginning to blur.

His hands reached blindly for the second dart. He couldn't find it. His arms were lead now and refused to lift. Then his legs were the same. He knew he was going down.

If he could just get his hands on something, anything, he would end his own life before they touched him.

As Doyle lay immobile and twitching on the linoleum floor, one of the strangers spoke in a foreign tongue. "Fear never lived in his eyes. Not once."

The larger man who still held the gun said, "That is why he is worthy."

Eldoret, Kenya

The sounds of crying and moaning filled rooms and hallways. It never seemed to stop. There were always more sick or wounded coming through the doors. When those died, more came to fill their spots.

Dr. Thomas Mosen was working diligently today. Only half of the nurses were able to make it to the hospital, since roadblocks were back in place after a recent conflict. Chaos was the only constant in many parts of Africa, but Dr. Mosen functioned as smoothly in calamity as most physicians did in the calm of a clinic back home.

He had spent a long time in school then in resident programs before joining *Medecins Sans Frontieres*, also known as Doctors Without Borders. Many questioned the length of time he'd spent serving in Africa. They wondered if he would stay until he was killed. Most volunteered their time for several years but eventually returned home for the sake of their own sanity.

Not Thomas Mosen. He was as committed as they came.

They said he would probably die in the very hospital where he had healed so many, for he would never leave. His gentle hands had inoculated many a small child, soothed the young men and women wasting away from AIDS, and removed limbs that had barely survived the machete.

The machete. A favored weapon among fighters. It cost no bullets and sharpened itself on the bones of helpless villagers.

Dr. Mosen pulled himself out of his own memories and gazed around the large white room, filled to capacity with cots. Perhaps it was destiny that the hospital was short staffed today. He had so much work ahead of him, yet only he could perform the task at hand.

His footsteps echoed down the corridor as he briskly made his way to the supply room. He unlocked the medicine cabinet and removed the package received just yesterday. He had been waiting for the vials inside the box. They contained a miracle cure. At least, that's how he saw it.

Dr. Mosen took his time, drawing up each and every vial, carefully calculating the dosages needed for the largest man and the tiniest infant. Not a drop would be wasted.

He settled the filled syringes into trays, separating them by dose. The trays were then loaded onto a cart, enabling him to consolidate his trips from room to room without returning to the medicine cabinet. Pushing the supplies into the hallway, Dr. Mosen decided to visit the strongest patients first. The ones who were not as ill or as badly injured. That made the most sense.

He stopped the cart to turn his ear toward a nearby window. What was that sound? Were the nurses here now? Perhaps the roadblocks had been taken down. He doubted that, however. The other nurses would probably not arrive until tomorrow at the earliest.

Unwilling to waste any more time, Dr. Mosen wheeled the cart into room 2A. It housed rows and rows of patient beds. The healthier people could afford to be packed in together.

Greeting each with a smile and a cup of orange juice, Mosen delivered intramuscular shots of the miracle cure into the hips of the men and women with no intravenous access. He would inject those with IVs afterwards. The ones with lines directly to their veins would feel the effects of the drug much more quickly than those who had received shots.

The children, of course, would be last.

Mosen took a deep breath and picked up his pace as he began delivering the drug. He could push the miracle cure in quickly. It would work just the same.

As predicted, the patients who'd received shots began falling back onto their cots as if suddenly very sleepy. The ones with IVs began to do the same, most having never risen from their pillows.

As Dr. Mosen moved to the group of children playing with a picture book and balls, one small boy came to his side. "Dr. Mosen. Everyone is falling asleep. Are they all sick again?"

Mosen would normally have placed a hand on the boys head and offered a smile. Today his tone was clipped and robotic. "You must have the medicine as well. They were all meant to sleep as the drug works. It is necessary."

With confusion still twisting his face, the child allowed Dr. Mosen to deliver the shot. He had no reason to mistrust the doctor. He was the same man who had saved the child's mother and baby sister.

The boy sat on the floor with his knees folded, watching as Dr. Mosen continued with the others. Soon his tiny lids began to droop, but he was not afraid. He trusted the doctor.

Taking one last look around the room, Mosen made sure he had visited them all. One by one the children stilled and lay down to take a *nap*.

Dumping the used syringes into a container at the door, Dr. Mosen smiled to himself. He would never answer to the name Mosen again. He would be known by his true surname, Moussa. His father had legally changed it years ago, so they would fit in. So they would be accepted.

Now, after many years of service and preparation, he would take his place among the privileged. After this deed, he would be accepted into a higher ranking group. He could begin his training for the ceremony.

Once again, he considered his strategy. The next few wards would consist of much sicker, much weaker patients. They would be no trouble. He knew force would be required to take out any nurses he found on the grounds, but the element of surprise would aid him.

Lastly he would visit the nursery. Babies would be the easiest kills. The tiny needles used on infants would pierce their thin skin, but the crying would not last for long.

The second stage of Kherep Amun's grand design was in action. Some might call it mass murder, but he knew it was more of a cleansing. The removal of refuse.

Besides, not everyone who needed to die deserved to die by the ritual.

27

They came at each other in the dark, fiercely, desperately. The room was cast in soft blue as light from the full moon fingered its way inside. But even in the shadowy realm, Matt's flesh burned. Enflamed whenever he brushed against Erica's silken skin. She was a woman of fire, and her heat was all he craved. All he wanted.

Needed.

He had become vulnerable after all, to her witty charm and stubborn-as-hell personality. The way her eyes shadowed over when she learned of more death. And the way she was able to laugh with him, live with him, even as they stood on the precipice of anarchy, staring terror in its bloody face.

He knew Erica was filled with the same urgency as he was, and he reveled in her feverish exploration of his body. There was no hesitancy this time as he ripped away what little clothing she'd worn to bed. His hold on her hips was firm while the assault on her mouth was invasive. He consumed her for his own sanity. He claimed her for his pride.

And the rush of emotion? The stirring of peace that traveled through him on the tails of pure, animal lust? He wouldn't give it a name. Not just yet. Instead he would take the moment they were lucky enough to steal in the middle of all the chaos.

And he would love her body, even if he wouldn't allow his

heart to do the same for the woman beneath him.

As he raked his fingers down her sides, Matt pressed his face to the hollow of her throat. "Erica." Her name caressed his tongue, just before he used his mouth to carve a path down her body, paying special attention to her breasts. He knew she enjoyed the feel of his lips there, and she lifted off the bed when he took one then the other in his mouth.

Matt imagined his body covering her like a protective force, a shield from the cold and cruelty they both knew existed. He would protect anyone with his life if he had to. That duty came with the job.

But with Erica he would guard more than just life and limb, as lovely as those limbs were. He would do everything in his power to protect her mind from knowing any more of the cult's depravity. Her heart from the loss of another victim.

If Matt didn't know any better, he would say he'd fallen in love. But no. He wasn't ready to give it a name.

Desperate to reign in emotion, he kissed Erica hard, touching her between her legs until she whimpered with pleasure. Until she begged him to come inside her.

Still he spared nothing. Every glorious inch of her skin was treated to the promise of his lips, and when he was as crazed as she was, he slipped between her thighs and pressed himself against her core.

In one thrust he took her, and as she cried his name, he shook with vicious pleasure. The fever took him completely then, filling him with an exquisite, almost painful ecstasy. They moved together in their own unique rhythm, holding onto each other as if their lives depended on the connection.

As Matt moved in long, languid strokes, Erica threw her head back and stared blindly into the cool, moonlit room. Her total abandonment was more than Matt could take. He let himself go, the release more volatile and consuming because it came in time with hers.

Their breaths were quick and shallow as they lay intertwined, and soon he returned to the reality of a darkened hotel room and the sweet scent of the woman he...cared about.

His gut churned as the fear rode back in. Self-preservation battled against a truth he refused to acknowledge.

He had fought hard against Erica. From the start. Because he'd felt the pull long before he'd ever let himself acknowledge it. So he'd acted like an ass. He'd been trying to push her away.

Epic fail, that.

Erica was his own version of Chinese handcuffs. The more he struggled, the tighter her hold became. Now here he was, wondering if he was in love with her.

Damn. He needed to focus on the next day's plans. This was no time to get soft or be distracted. In fact, it was the worst possible time.

If his motivations were in the wrong place, he would be worthless to them all. They would all be put at greater risk, and Matt couldn't let that happen.

Rolling to Erica's side, he pulled the white sheet over them both to create a shelter from the cool night. She moved closer, placing a light kiss on his cheek before letting her eyes drift closed.

Matt stared into the dark, stroking her velvety skin and branding the sensation of holding her into his memory. Tomorrow they would ride toward Giza and possibly find the remains of the mummy. The relic that was a catalyst for mass murder.

They would go tomorrow, even at the risk their own lives. At the risk of Erica's life.

Matt knew there would be no talking her out of going. Professionally, he also had to admit they needed her. But he didn't want her there. He wanted her back in Georgia and the safety of her own home.

That wasn't going to happen. Erica would see this to the end, and so would he. But he would be there to make sure nothing happened to her. The idea of anything else was unthinkable.

Finally, Matt closed his eyes and succumbed to exhaustion. Yet he held her tight, even in sleep.

It was late afternoon the next day before they all walked out to find their newest method of transportation. The gold SUV glimmered in the sun.

Karen paused to scrutinize the vehicle while shielding her eyes from the glare. "I thought you guys all drove black. That doesn't look like a government vehicle."

"Exactly the point," Clint stated as he walked past her with bags.

Once their things were loaded, the clan took their seats. Clint drove with Karen beside him, Monroe and Erica in the middle seats, and Matt in the rear.

"Speaking of government endorsement," Clint said, "how much leeway do we have?"

Matt answered with a nod. "We have clearance to inspect any area of the Giza complex and will be able to stay throughout the night. But..."

"There's always a but," Clint grumbled.

"We can't perform, and I quote, 'any act of destruction' on the grounds."

Erica turned to face him. "Meaning?"

He made a harsh sound. "If we believe we've located the remains of Hatshepsut, the Egyptian team must be called in immediately."

Erica's previously-pink and shiny bubble exploded. After all of their hard work, she and Monroe would be handing over their positions as lead archaeologists.

As if reading her thoughts, Monroe patted her knee. "We will still be involved, and I've been assured the canopic jars will still be yours."

Erica didn't have the heart to tell the kind, older man how little that mattered to her anymore. "And Hatshepsut?" Erica asked, "What will they do with her?"

He fingered his silver moustache. "All things considered, she will have the utmost protection. After all, Kherep Amun will still want her."

Karen also turned around in her seat to face the others. "Why the interest now? Where was Egypt's support in the beginning, while the two of you were risking life and limb?"

Matt met her questioning stare. "Frankly, they didn't think we stood a chance in hell of finding any of the vases, much less the woman herself. After the success we've had, they've decided to protect their assets."

"Of course." Karen's tone told them what she thought of that.

Monroe sighed and said, "It's all too common today for a country to stake its claim on any archaeological bounty, so to speak. Even sunken ships found two continents away from their origins are being claimed by the modern government. No matter who finds them."

"Leaving the worker bees with only a percentage of the take," Erica murmured, thinking of Cameron and his new career path.

"Then there are the murders," Matt said. "The fact that Kherep Amun seems to be targeting symbolic places makes the administration nervous. Egypt could be safe since the cult originated here or they could be targeted for a coming-out party."

"Their own country?" Erica asked.

"The prevalence of Islam could be seen as a betrayal of the worst kind. Heresy in the eyes of the terrorists."

"Well isn't that a switch," Karen supplied with a smirk.

Clint grinned into the rearview mirror at Erica. "On a positive note. I don't think the removal of sand is considered destruction. We can always hope your mummy is resting close by."

Erica smiled gratefully at the agent. She was glad Clint, Monroe, and Karen were here. Even temperaments would be valuable as they got closer to the end game. Especially since she and Matt had come up with their own diversion. She used the rear view mirror for herself this time, hoping for a peek at Matt's steady, brown eyes.

No joy, as he'd taught her to say. He'd slipped on his sunglasses.

"Now. Onto the next." Monroe drew Erica's attention as he shifted his satchel and removed some wrinkled and coffee stained papers. "The code," he said.

Karen's interest was piqued again. "A code that needs to be deciphered? Like the last clue?"

"Not exactly. The code of the Great Pyramid of Giza is actually a reference to a timeline. The internal structure and passages of the pyramid form a diagram. It not only lays out a time scale, but marks specific events in the world's history. Or future, depending on the present time."

Monroe chuckled at the skeptical tilt of Karen's eyebrow. "Yes, some of them have come true," told her.

"According to various interpretations," Erica added, "the pyramid predicted vital episodes of societal evolution like the Exodus, the crucifixion of Jesus, American independence, the industrial revolution, and Hitler. Just to name a few."

Monroe gave her an appraising glance. "You know the history well. That will be of great benefit today."

"Well, how exactly does the pyramid do this, and will we actually be able to, I don't know, read it?" Karen pursed her lips, still not convinced.

Monroe cleared his throat, preparing them for a complex explanation. "The architecture of the pyramid is incredible. It's unknown how people of that time managed to position stones that weighed up to seventy tons with such precision. They fit together perfectly, with less than a fiftieth of an inch between them. And the entire structure has more mass than double the Empire State Building."

Erica felt the familiar hum that was love for her chosen field. She tapped Karen on the shoulder and said, "Many measurements found in the temple correlate with the size of our planet and its movement within the solar system. The units used are related to the diameter of earth and the number of days in our calendar year."

Erica sat on the edge of her seat, her growing excitement making her edgy. "The entrance of the pyramid holds the starting position, and from a specific point you can begin your measurement of inches."

"Yes," Monroe added. "Approximately twenty-five inches represents twenty-five years. Whether the passage is rising or falling depicts the current turn of events for civilization."

"What are we on now? At the present time?" Karen asked.

Monroe referred to his notes. "Hmm…we are in the pit."

Karen jerked her mouth to one side. "That can't be good."

Erica nudged her friend. "I thought you were a skeptic."

"Hey, only half of me. The American half." Karen shrugged. "The other is Chinese. Enough said."

"The pit is irregular and therefore unable to be measured precisely," Monroe read aloud. He looked up at Erica. "That might present a problem, but we'll see what we have to work with once we're there. I have a rough outline of critical events and predictions I thought might come in handy."

"This all sounds like it's going to take time," Matt said, his eyes were still hidden but his voice sounded stern. "The pyramid is intricate, not to mention huge,"

Monroe sighed again. "I've consulted some colleagues who are more familiar with the code. They provided us with some very specific locations and corresponding dates." He straightened his papers. "I propose we begin our search in the time span of Hatshepsut's life."

Erica brushed her hair back. "Her birth and death,

particularly. Senmut would have wanted the clues to be meaningful."

"The pyramids of Giza have all been thoroughly searched over the years. We can't expect to find any vases lying around," Karen said. "What exactly are we looking for?"

Now it was Erica's turn for doubt. "Anything."

Matt touched her on the shoulder to get her attention. "We obviously won't get much done until the tourists leave for the day, but we can use the next few hours to get acquainted with the layout."

"What about security?" Karen asked.

"The normal night guards will be around," Matt said. "They know to expect us and to stay out of the way, unless we ask them for assistance. The surveillance cameras will still be in operation, too."

"No blasting a hole and patching it up by morning, huh?" Clint was joking, but Monroe looked at him in horror. Karen laughed at the older man's expression, earning herself a reproachful glare.

"Will Gus be staying in Lyon or coming here as well?" Erica wondered how far out of the loop she would be by the next morning if she and the others found anything during the overnight search. If the government bodies would still share anything with her and Monroe once they'd served their purpose.

"Not that I'm aware of. He can pull more strings from where he is," Matt told her and Monroe, giving them some assurance. "He's working hard to keep us all involved and informed."

"John and Dan will be back, too" Clint said. "Gus agrees with Matt and me that the closer we get, the closer Kherep Amun will get."

Karen scowled. "Do you think they know about Giza?"

"They showed up in Jordan and the ruins in Sinai," Matt answered. "We can't be sure what information has been passed down through the years. Most members had fathers and grandfathers who raised them with the teachings. The stories of Senmut and Hatshepsut could be as familiar to them as Bible study is to Christians."

"Yet Senmut wanted to keep her location a secret from her enemies. Hopefully some facts have been confused over time." Erica looked out the window at the expansive sand dunes, burnt umber in the waning daylight. "They can't have all the pieces, or they would have found her by now."

"Don't forget we had the first clue, which led to the others that followed. The details found within them are crucial for knowing where to search for the next." Monroe cast a determined look her way. "And we're almost there."

Everyone became thoughtful, as the distinguished man's words hovered over them in the air-conditioned vehicle.

After a moment of contemplation, Matt gritted his teeth and echoed the statement. His voice was cold and somber. "Right. We're almost there."

28

Tourists in hot weather clothing milled around the Giza complex. Over the noise of the crowds, serious monotone voices of pyramid guides punctuated the air, sharing the area's history with visitors.

Erica came to a standstill beside Karen and Matt. They were all thinking the same thing. "We won't be able to do much until the site is closed for the night," Karen said, voicing their concern.

Erica crossed her arms. "No. The passages inside the pyramid are narrow. Groups of people passing through will be a constant interruption."

"We can at least familiarize ourselves with points of interest in the timeline. Maybe save ourselves some work later." Matt made the statement then turned to his left as Clint sidled up to stand with them. "And you know what to do."

"Right," Clint responded. The two agents had agreed earlier that Matt would focus on assisting Erica and the others with the search while also keeping an eye out for suspicious characters or activity.

Clint, meanwhile, would concentrate solely on the latter. They had to be vigilant in the final hours. Members of Kherep Amun could be anywhere, blending into the hordes of sightseers.

"I've always wanted to come here, especially after hearing

some of your stories," Karen said to Erica. "The sheer amount of labor it must have taken to build a structure of this size so exactly...well, it's staggering."

"Over two million blocks of limestone were shipped from quarries all along the Nile." Erica gazed at the pyramid in awe with her friend, as if seeing it for the first time as well. "The outside was once covered with limestone casings, all polished, white stone. Some have fallen away, but many were removed during the Middle Ages. Imagine how it must have shone in the sun."

"It was built for a pharaoh, right?" Clint asked.

"For the king of the fourth dynasty, Khufu. It's believed to have been built as his tomb. There are three main chambers inside, and outside are the additional mortuary temples, smaller pyramids for Khufu's wives, and even smaller tombs meant for the nobles of his time."

"They prepared for death more than life," Clint observed grimly.

Monroe was the last to join the group. Without preamble, the older man laid out the plan. "We will begin near the original entrance. Lines are scored into the rock and are aligned with the pole star, formerly known as Alpha Draconis. The alignment occurred in March of the year 2141 BC."

"Which is how we will find our initial point in the timeline," Matt said.

"Yes. The Giza pyramid is the only one to boast both ascending and descending passages, so I suggest we become acquainted with the overall design of the internal structure. We can take exact measurements later tonight."

They decided Karen would stay with Clint for the time being. The two would blend in more easily as a couple, and Karen was experienced in undercover surveillance. If any Kherep Amun members were on the grounds, Erica and Monroe would be recognized. There was no help for that, and the search for Hatshepsut needed to be completed.

As Monroe, Erica, and Matt neared the pyramid, Monroe pointed at two large holes, one more neatly hewn than the other. "The upper entrance is the original. Once the structure was completed, the entrance was sealed and covered with limestone facing. The cruder entrance below was created by Arab Al Mamun in 820 AD. Since no one knew where the passages were, he and his men heated the stones then doused them with vinegar to cause cracking. Eventually, enough was broken away, and they found a corridor. He urged his men on with promises of unimaginable treasure stored inside, though some say Al Mamun only wanted access to the code."

"The code was well known?" Matt asked.

"Yes," Erica said, "The tomb that reportedly held the history and future of mankind." She walked forward as if in a trance. An aura about the pyramid disturbed her. It always had. Knowing what she did now, she couldn't help wondering if some sixth sense had forewarned her. Chill bumps raised on her arms despite the warm sun beating down. "Have you considered the other shaft leading out of the Queen's chamber?" she asked Monroe.

"It occurred to me. However, considering the difficulty accessing it, I had hoped to find a clue that would point somewhere else."

"What kind of shaft are we talking about?" This from Matt. "Will we be able to search it, if need be?"

"Therein lies the difficulty." Monroe straightened his field hat. "The shafts lead up and out of the queen's and king's chambers, supposedly to allow the Ka, or spirit, an escape route upon death of the mortal body. A team of researchers used a robot to drill a hole into one door so it could take some pictures of whatever was on the other side."

"They only saw another door," Erica interjected. "Anyway, those shafts were obviously created when the pyramid was built."

"But Senmut was a man of means, both financially and

mentally." Monroe made the statement with surety.

Matt saw the look in the other man's eye. "You admire him."

The professor furrowed his brow in thought. "I do, yes. He was an exceptional man. It's no wonder he chose to secure the location of his lost love in the manner he did. He was well known as a master of concealment."

"What else did he do?" Matt asked.

"Many of his buildings and sculptures held puzzles, pictures with hidden meanings. It was his trademark." Monroe looked up. "He was also the first person to record an accounting of the stars as a horoscope, known as a reading of the sky. The ceiling of his own secret burial chamber is covered with a celestial map, detailed in both astronomical and astro-mythological information."

Matt followed the man's gaze to the blue sky above, as if able to visualize the stars. "He built a secret tomb for himself?"

"Two, actually. It is the second that contains the map. However, construction stopped abruptly for some reason. Perhaps when Senmut decided to hide the vases of Hatshepsut. The sudden departure from such a personal piece of work suggests a certain urgency."

"Maybe he got wind that the new pharaoh had plans for him" Matt said. "If he was a well-known supporter of the deceased Hatshepsut, he must have had a pretty big target on his back."

"True, true." Monroe contemplated the younger man. "Still, he did what was necessary to protect her name and her body after she died. I tend to believe Senmut appreciated her for the woman she was, not simply for her position and title." He tilted his head with meaning. "Only true love can drive a man to do what others say is impossible."

Matt continued to study the sky and the hazy line of the horizon where blue met torrid orange. He mulled over Monroe's words, but refused to let his expression reflect his inner turmoil. He would do what he had to do. It was his job, his duty. And nothing else.

Erica had remained silent during their discourse, strolling away as they spoke so she missed the last things Monroe said to Matt. She was busy imagining how the cities of Egypt must have looked in those days. The elegant and colorful riches that adorned the temples as well as the royal family.

Picturing a heartbroken Senmut and his determination to ensure that his queen's name was remembered with honor, she experienced a sharp little clutch just under her ribs. She could almost feel his mourning.

Erica was suddenly filled with renewed energy. She wanted to finish what Senmut had started. "Let's go," she called. Without waiting for a reply, she started toward the pyramid. Matt and Monroe fell in behind her.

Only one entrance was in use. Oddly enough, it was the second hole formed by the invading Arabs, now considered a shortcut. The temperature fell several degrees as Erica entered the gloomy recesses of the thief's doorway. Modern tracks of lighting filled most of the space with an amber glow, and metal braces added support in some spots.

Walking down the descending corridor, Erica measured approximately forty feet with her stride and began to look for the scored lines. Easily able to reach both walls with her arms outstretched, she ran her hands along the cool stone and explained to Matt. "There will be carved lines from floor to ceiling on both sides. This is the origin of the timeline. The place that lines up with the Pole Star."

"Only once every thousand years," Matt said.

Erica stopped in her tracks, facing him. "I want to thank you."

Matt to looked over his shoulder for Monroe, but the man was seemed engrossed in a map he was reading. "Thank me?"

She nodded and held his gaze before speaking. Her voice thick with a nameless emotion. "You've been more than just a bodyguard on this trip." She held up a hand as he prepared to speak. "I know it's your job, and you are the expert on Kherep

Amun. You were the best choice to accompany me. But more than that. You've respected both my judgment and expertise. You've been patient with the sentimentality that often follows me on any expedition." She smiled now. "You've listened to countless history lessons."

Matt's jaw tensed. "I've had a good professor."

Erica stared down at the toe of her boot as she tapped it on the floor. "What I'm trying to say is you've made this much easier than it could have been. Than it should have been. So, thanks."

"And you, Doc." Matt placed a finger under her chin, drawing her gaze back up to his own, "You have really mellowed out."

She saw the laughter in his eyes and was grateful for the return of their casual banter. "I had help from the most talented smartass Washington had to offer." A look passed between them, full of moments shared and remembered.

Arguing in the sands outside of Hatshepsut's temple. Buried beneath mounds of newspaper in the museum and the elation they had felt when the scytale finally worked. Their mutual fear that they'd lost the trail of Hatshepsut at Mount Sinai.

Moments that had come to mean so much more than either of them had expected.

The sound of Monroe's shuffling papers caught up to them. Matt pulled away and cleared his throat. But he gave her a special grin when he said, "We'd better find those lines."

Hours later, after the last of the tours were gone, Karen appeared back at the entrance, the designated meeting point. She was accompanied by a guard and Clint, the two men speaking quietly to each other in Arabic. Once the discussion was concluded, the uniformed man nodded to Matt and turned to leave without speaking.

"The guards all understand to watch but stay out of our way," Clint said. "They'll probably be grateful to have some entertainment on their monitors tonight."

"I'm glad they'll be watching," Erica said as the chilly night wind blew in from the desert. "The more eyes looking out for trouble, the better. We're getting close, and I have to believe that Kherep Amun is close. They would also know Giza's history, so it's probably on their list of potential sites. With or without the clues."

"Maybe." Matt eyed the lights of the distant city. "We haven't had trouble with them since Jordan, but they do have enough man power to scout any significant area. Hopefully they won't be around tonight."

Karen stepped closer and rubbed her arms, bare in a T-shirt. "I can't believe how the temperature drops." She shivered. "You didn't see them near the dive sight or in Sinai. Maybe they're at a dead end. For the moment. If they haven't found Hattie in two thousand years, surely we'll do so before they get back on track."

Matt shook his head. "But they had been in Sinai before we got there, so they know something. And the sunken city...well, no one would have looked there if not for the clue we found. The message was specific enough to narrow our search, and that's where we got an edge on them."

"There are multiple monuments of significance here in Giza. Maybe they haven't had the opportunity to devote their time to this pyramid, yet," Erica said with hope in her voice.

Monroe joined the group from the steps below the entrance. "I've had a bit of sustenance and have found my second wind. Now let's verify those locations."

The others knew he was referring to the places in the temple they'd become familiar with that afternoon. More precise measurements would now be needed.

One by one they moved down the passageway, heading

toward the forty-foot mark. Once there, Monroe and Erica crowded around the lines scored into the stone walls. The marks indicated the first year of the timeline.

Monroe began. "From here we should count our way down the descending passage until we reach the year of Hatshepsut's birth, approximately 1502 BC. One of the more likely places for any information to be hidden."

"It's also the first date we'll come to." Erica pulled out a diagram. "Luckily, the dates of her birth, assignment to the throne, and her death can all be found on this main path."

Matt pulled out two measuring tapes, one typical American version and another that measured in the precise unit of the Jewish inch. "We should take turns as teams of two, each team measuring with both tapes. Four tries will tell us if we're accurate. Clint and I will work together. Erica?"

"Dr. Monroe and I will measure as well," she said before glancing to her friend. "Karen, will you mark the distance?"

"Sure. What should I use?"

In response, Erica handed her a roll of neon yellow masking tape and blue chalk. "I'm not sure if the tape will stay put. Back it up with a chalk mark, just in case."

Karen took the items, slipping her hand through the roll of tape so she could still hold her flashlight. "See you down under," she quipped and faded into the shadows.

"The light sources are not sufficient, so we will all need to use our torches," Monroe explained.

Clint pulled them out of his bag. "New batteries and more on hand."

"You expect this to be a long night?" Erica asked, one side of her mouth pulling into a grin.

"Never can be too prepared." He shrugged and turned to Matt. "You hold, I'll drag. How many inches are we going?"

Erica didn't need to check her notes. She knew all the measurements by heart. "Six hundred and thirty-eight inches, or a little over fifty-three feet."

"Okay. We'll have Karen mark the points found with both measuring tapes, then we'll have a more specific area. You and Monroe can start when we've marked our first point. Then we'll go again."

Matt knelt at the base of the wall and put the tip of the measuring tape at the line chiseled in stone. He looked up at Clint. "Let's keep it up against this side for now."

The two men carefully stretched the tape out as Clint descended into the tomb. Erica decided to follow behind him, ensuring no kinks in the line or imperfections in the rock that might affect accuracy. Once Clint and Matt were finished and their spot noticeably marked, Monroe and Erica followed suit.

They decided to lay the tape along the other side of the passageway. After both teams had repeated the process down the center, they had four pieces of tape that fell within inches of each other.

Erica kneeled with her flashlight. "Let's mark our boundaries slightly farther out on each side then remove the tape. I don't want to miss something because it's covered up." Tapping a finger to her chin she said, "Let's extend the tape up the walls, too. If there is an inscription it could be anywhere." She turned expectant eyes to the still standing Monroe. "You're not joining me?"

He sighed and adjusted the hat perched on his head. "A wise man knows when to turn the task over to younger eyes."

Nodding to the older gentleman, Matt lowered to the hard stone floor with Erica. A tap on the shoulder brought his attention around to Karen, standing behind him with a towel in her outstretched hand. "You might need this."

With their knees cushioned and flashlights on full beam, Matt and Erica repositioned the bright yellow tape. The others held their lights over the area as well, purging the darkness as much as possible.

Before beginning the inspection of the limestone, Erica surprised them all by closing her eyes and whispering into the eerily quiet gloom.

"Queen Hatshepsut. Help us. Help us find you."

29

Erica focused her attention on a corner of the field they had cordoned off, only a few square feet in total. "Let's do a visual survey first then we can use our fingertips." She paused and remembered the great esteem Hatshepsut's lover had held for his queen. "I really wouldn't expect Senmut to have placed an inscription on the floor."

"Afraid the treading of feet would wear it away?" Karen asked as she bent down to peer over Erica's shoulder.

"There is that. And if he mentioned Hatshepsut, it would be…"

"Disrespectful," Matt finished. He spoke to the ground, but his words touched Erica inside. "I can understand that."

"Right," Erica said in a broken voice." She swallowed the emotion. "The written word was held sacred and believed to have been very powerful, especially someone's name."

"That's why that wily bastard, Tuthmose III, had Hatshepsut's name scratched from so many of her monuments." The heat in Monroe's tone was uncommon for the dignified man. "The Egyptians believed that erasing a person's written name could erase their very existence."

"So he not only went after her memory and reputation, but the very essence of her spirit." Karen also seemed to have become more emotionally involved. They all had. The US

Marshal took a wide stance and put her hands on her hips. "Let's find her, Erica, and shout her name from the rooftops."

Erica tilted her head back and flashed an indomitable smile at her friend's upside-down face. "Yes, why don't we?" She pointed her light to the unyielding rock floor, scouring over every inch. Whenever she felt an odd texture under the sensitive pads of her fingertips, she would move in even closer. After she and Matt had switched positions with no results, they cast their attention to the scrutiny of the walls.

"How high should we look?" Matt asked after another thorough search produced nothing.

Erica looked to Monroe for confirmation. "I think we should do a cursory inspection of the ceiling, then move to the next date."

"Agreed." Monroe slapped his hand against the wall. "Finding the exact location of a clue in this mausoleum would be difficult enough. No need for Senmut to have made it physically challenging as well. It's all about the clue, which we don't actually have."

"But we're right. I know we are." Erica put her finger to her lips. "The location makes sense according to the constellation. And the presence of the code..." She trailed off but regained calm after clenching her hands into a ball then releasing. "I just know we're right."

Matt stood from where he had been going over the floor and dusted off his knees. "We're in the right place. We just have to find the right time."

Erica nodded. "Let's move on to the time of her ascension to the position of pharaoh. It's only a matter of inches now. Her life spanned about forty-four years, so all total, we have to cover almost four feet of the passageway lengthwise."

"Not so much." Clint folded his arms across his chest.

Monroe smiled. "That depends on the size of the inscription."

"And if an inscription is how Senmut even chose to leave the message." Erica huffed out a breath. "The last vase, which we didn't find, could have led us to a very specific spot in this very large pyramid. A spot that might not be where we're looking."

"None of that, now." Karen patted Erica's shoulder. "Tell me again why you think it's here."

Erica took a deep breath and recounted her rationale. "Because Senmut often used hidden messages, including inscriptions. The Giza pyramid is the only place that fits the star points. And the presence of the timeline is why Senmut chose this pyramid."

"Why?" Karen pushed her to continue.

"Because you can locate any point in time by its position in the pyramid. And the only times he would have used for a clue are those that were noteworthy in the life of Hatshepsut."

"Great." Karen clasped her hands together with a slap. "I'm duly convinced."

"You do realize you're transparent as glass." Erica's said, poking her friend in the stomach.

"Hey." Karen spread her arms wide. "As long as we're back in the game."

"We are. And thanks for that." Erica sent a questioning look to Matt. "What do you think? Should we map off the four feet of the passage and hit it as a team?"

"Yes, but we should extend to five feet. Just in case."

"Just in case," Karen echoed. "I'm beginning to despise that expression."

Erica still looked at Matt but with a twinkle in her eye. "We have a plan, then. Five feet." Her smile was for Karen. "Just in case."

They made their marks, removing the old pieces of tape after placing the new. The neon strips stretched across the floor, up both walls, and across the ceiling in two places, five feet apart from each other.

They began looking in earnest, putting their lights and their noses close to the stone. After more than half an hour of searching, Erica stood abruptly. Her gut was tingling, and she couldn't say why. "Matt, I want to measure again."

"Why? You know we're in the area that represents her life. We haven't looked enough, yet."

"I know. I know. Just humor me, okay?" She walked up the incline to Matt's bag and began rummaging inside. "I want to measure dead center of the passageway, using the tape with the sacred inch."

Matt must have recognized her determination, since he followed her back to the scored lines. When he reached her, he took the measuring tape from her hand. "What's going on?"

She shrugged and appeared agitated. "I'm not sure. Call it a hunch, my gut, even women's intuition. I just feel compelled to do this."

"I'll hold it for you but promise me this."

She didn't know the odd look on his face or what he was about to say. "What?"

"Just because it worked this time, don't try that women's intuition thing on me ever again."

She laughed with relief as his mouth broke into a shameless grin. "Got it."

They fell quiet as Matt squatted and held the tip of the measuring tape in the exact center of the aisle and in the exact middle of the two walls. Erica backed slowly down the corridor, being careful to stay appropriately aligned.

No sound came from the others below, as if they too felt an unexplained current in the air. Shadows seemed to dance with eagerness at the edges of the yellow thrown out by the flashlights.

Erica finally reached her intended destination. "Karen, could I have a piece of tape?"

"Sure." Her friend ripped off a fresh piece. "Where do you want it?"

Erica pointed then stood while Karen marked the spot. "That should be 1458 BC."

"The year of her death," Monroe whispered in reverence.

"Yes." Erica dropped to her knees again, foregoing the towel offered by Karen. Matt had joined them by now, and they all waited and watched as Erica flashed the beam of her light across the stone from various directions.

It wasn't until she was midway up one wall that she called for more light and another set of eyes. "Someone come look at this."

Karen was the first to see what Erica did. "Those scratches look different. They're more uniform in size and...by God... they're in a straight line."

"Let me see." Monroe moved into the spot Karen had quickly vacated. He brought forth a magnifying glass from the brown leather satchel at his side and studied the tiny indentions in the rock. "I believe you have something here."

He reached again into his bag to remove a small bottle and what looked like a lipstick brush. He twisted the lid off the bottle and dipped the brush inside before handing it to Erica. "You found it. You do the honors."

With no need for an explanation, Erica started with what she thought was the first symbol. Gently she swirled the brush over it, leaving behind a white film of powder.

"What is that?" Karen asked as Erica continued with each symbol.

"Just a bit of magnesium silicate," Monroe replied.

Erica spared a glance back at her friend. "Talcum powder."

"Oh." Karen nodded as if she understood perfectly, then stopped and cocked one brow. "And we're doing this so they'll be more visible?"

"Just wait. You haven't seen the real show, yet," Erica said after accepting another brush from Monroe. This one was slightly larger, but with a blunt, flat head. She began to move it over the markings, again with delicate sweeps.

While the women were engaged in that process, Monroe took Clint aside for a brief conversation. Afterward Clint walked away, heading toward the entrance.

"Where's he going?" Karen asked.

Monroe rubbed his hands together. "You'll see. He'll return shortly."

Monroe was true to his word. Clint rejoined them within a few minutes, just as Erica stood to report that she was finished.

"Everyone gather around." Monroe fished in his pack again. "Clint, are we ready?" At the younger man's nod, Monroe held up a small black box.

Clint made a motion to one of the surveillance cameras.

"Hold still everyone," Monroe said. "And turn off your flashlights."

The suspense lasted only a moment before they were thrust into total darkness.

"Hey, now," Karen whispered in the black.

Monroe could be heard jostling. "Ready, Erica?"

"Most definitely," she answered. Her heart was thundering so loudly she was afraid everyone would hear it.

A small click and the passage erupted in pale violet light, coming from the box in Monroe's hand. He swung it toward the wall and the newly powdered inscription. Karen gasped and the others made various sounds of approval.

Erica carefully placed her finger under the etchings, now glowing brightly in the black light. "And there it is."

Matt placed a hand on her shoulder. "There it is." The spark of unity between them was stronger than ever.

"What does it say?" Karen was poised with pad and pen, both extracted from the pocket of her olive cargo pants.

Erica blew out a slow breath and began. "Truth will be found in the kingdom of the soul."

They remained silent, but Erica said no more.

Karen chewed her lower lip and said, "I certainly hope that means something to you."

"Um, not yet, really." Erica slipped the pad from Karen and sketched the hieroglyphics for further use.

Clint waved to the camera again, and the lights came back

on. Monroe and Erica huddled together, studying the writing on the paper. "Look at the choice of symbol he used for truth," Erica pointed out.

"Hmmm. *Maat*." Monroe said the word again thoughtfully. "Of course. *Maat Ka Re*."

"Care to enlighten us?" Matt stood beside them.

Erica brushed her hair back. "Maat Ka Re was Hatshepsut's throne name. Pharaohs held various names, each with a different purpose. Maat Ka Re translates into Truth is the Soul of Ra. Ra being the sun god, chief of all cosmic deities."

"Another astrological connection." Matt said then pointed to the words Karen had written. "You said the word soul, which is also in her throne name. Any connection there?"

"Could be. Whether it is or not, I don't understand what this means." Erica formed her think-wrinkle.

"You said the symbol for Ka in her name translated to soul?" Karen's asked.

Erica didn't look up from the writing pad. "Yes."

"I always thought the word Ka meant spirit. I guess the two are fairly synonymous, though." Karen dropped her hands to her sides. "Probably not important."

"Wait." Monroe gripped Karen's upper arm. "That's it. That's what he was referring to."

They all looked at the older man as he scrambled around for some papers. "The way we read the inscription is correct, or rather, it is one possibility. If we change the word soul to spirit, we have something else entirely."

"I don't understand." Erica gaped at him. Whether she was over-tired or over-stressed, she wasn't catching his meaning. "The symbol in reference to Hatshepsut meant soul."

"Yes, but let us not forget the author." He looked at her expectantly.

Erica groaned as the light in her head dawned. "Senmut, the riddler. It's a play on words. If we replace soul with spirit, the inscription reads 'Truth will be found in the kingdom of the spirit.' If the symbol used here for truth, maat, implies Hatshepsut's throne name...we could surmise that either truth or Hatshepsut is to be found in the kingdom of the spirit."

"That's what I'm thinking." Monroe smiled triumphantly.

"How does that help us?" Still baffled, Erica threw up her hands. "Where is this kingdom?"

Monroe motioned her over with a crook of his finger, then pointed to a spot on the diagram he was holding. "It's right here."

Erica stared at the map.

"Where is here?" Karen asked.

Erica spoke softly, a glorious warmth spreading through her. "It's here. In the pyramid. According to the timeline and the prophecies, the year 1999 was the start of," she looked up at the others, "The Kingdom of the Spirit."

30

"Does this mean we're going into the pit?" Karen asked the question in a voice that was a mixture of fear and anticipation.

"Not quite, my dear, ghoulish girl." Monroe's mood had been significantly improved by their revelation. "The pit begins just a bit later, somewhere between the years 2004 and 2025. Though in reality, that's only a couple more feet. So, feel free to dance around in it if you feel the urge."

"Maybe after we find Hattie." Karen grinned. "I'm not going to be the one to tempt fate before then."

Erica opened her mouth to comment, then snapped it shut. She held up a speculative finger. "Good idea. Let's save the pit dance for later."

"We need the year 1999. That means we enter the room farther down." Matt hefted his backpack and started descending. His main concern was still defeating Kherep Amun, but Erica's elation was contagious. Yes, he ready to find and stop the murderers, but he was also happy. Happy for Erica.

"Correct." Monroe said, walking right behind Matt and reminding him of their goal. "The decline will level out at about 1521 AD. That way leads us to the room with the pit."

"The floor is irregular in shape and uneven," Erica said as she turned her light back on. "Getting an exact measurement will be difficult."

"We'll start from the year the entrance to the room represents and do our best from there." Matt stopped to allow Erica to catch up. She looked pretty good in those shorts, now that he could allow himself to relax some and appreciate the view. "We may have to block off another large area and each take a portion. At least we have an idea what we're looking for, assuming it's another inscription."

They carefully ducked under the doorway as they entered the room, Matt guiding Erica with his hand. "Why do you think Senmut changed the method for the last clues?" he asked.

She paused. "That was his way. Even the other messages were found on slightly different objects. A medallion, a vase lid, and a bottom. And don't forget the inscription on the wall of Hatshepsut's tomb."

Matt was impressed all over again by the complexity of Senmut's elaborate scavenger hunt. The man had loved his woman, even after she'd died. "He wanted to mix it up some."

"Precisely." Erica gave him a sweet smile. "Besides, anyone who wanted to follow the path he laid out would have to know Senmut's unpredictability and his penchant for cryptography. The minute you think you know what's coming next and get too confident, he throws you a curveball."

"He didn't want just anyone to find her." Matt's lips thinned into a serious line. "I think he would approve of us. Of you. He obviously appreciated strong women."

The last remark made Erica stop to meet Matt's eyes. He would swear those crystal blues watered a little. She spoke slowly. "That, Agent Pierce, is one hell of a compliment."

He chucked her under the chin to hide his reaction before shuffling his pack to the front. "I'll go help line off the work area." As he walked away, he spoke only to himself. "And you, Erica Conner, are one hell of a woman."

Soon the group realized how complicated the search would be in this part of the pyramid. Even the act of placing the tape proved to be tricky, impeded by the rise and fall of the floor. The space they designated for exploration was wider than they had originally planned, but everyone agreed they would rather be cautious than miscalculate. A delineation that was too narrow might leave the message somewhere outside the guide lines.

They looked for anything resembling the scratches they'd seen before, all of them on their hands and knees, despite the hard, uneven floor. After an hour of searching, Clint stretched his arms and back. He moaned in relief. "Anyone up for some coffee?"

"Do you have the same as we drank in Sinai?" Erica asked. "That was some good stuff.

"Not quite, but I promise you'll like it," he said with a wink. "Trust me."

She laughed and went back to searching. "I don't trust you, but get me some anyway. You know what they say. There's no such thing as bad coffee."

"You're misquoting." Karen joined in the teasing, still brushing her fingers over a crevice in the wall. "I think that was supposed to be sex. No such thing as bad sex."

"My version is rated for all audiences," Erica said with a shy grin for Dr. Monroe.

"In my opinion, neither one is ever bad, and they're even better in combination." Clint laid his flashlight on the floor and started to rise, but something caught his eye in the illumination. "What's that?"

Matt picked up on the tone. "You got something?"

"Maybe. Hey, professor, you still have your magnifier?"

Monroe and Erica were beside Clint in the space of a heartbeat. They shone their lights to the spot he indicated. "I don't know why, but when my eye fell across this area, something in these marks made me think of the symbol Erica drew on the pad." He dragged his finger across the limestone. "I swear it was just here."

Matt moved up behind them and saw the problem. "Everyone stay where you are. Erica and Monroe, turn off your lights."

They did as he suggested, still staring hopefully at the base of the wall. Clint blinked a few times before pointing again, with more insistence. "There it is. Do you see it?"

Erica stood behind him, her line of sight following his. "Where do you…" She broke off and squinted. "Yes, I see it. We were flooding it with too much light. The indentations were lit from all sides, so there were no shadows."

Before she could ask, Karen was at her side with a piece of tape. "Here, mark it." They all feared the inscription would disappear again.

"That's the same symbol the other one started with, isn't it?" Clint asked.

"It is." Erica moved in closer, while Monroe laid the bottle and brushes out on a cloth next to her. "It's the hieroglyph for maat. I can't make out the rest."

She immediately began the powdering process, precision in every stroke. She made sure the reflective powder fell only on the inscription. It wasn't long before she spoke to Clint over her shoulder. "We're ready for the lights."

Clint found the nearest surveillance camera and motioned to the guards watching in the control booth.

Matt waited anxiously. What would the writings tell them? Were they at the end of their journey? The idea of finishing this thing and getting Erica out of harm's way once and for all was too tempting. He could almost taste the relief he would feel when she was tucked safely behind her museum walls and the security system there.

He'd make sure she had one at home, too. He'd gotten in much too easily.

The lights were still on. They waited, but Matt was sick of the tension. "Maybe they weren't watching. Flag them again."

"I'll do better than that. I'll run up to the entrance and call them over the radio." Clint left with hurried steps.

No one broke the silence while he was gone. They stared at the marks, giving each other the occasional nervous smile, or glancing impatiently at the passageway.

Finally, Clint reappeared in the doorway. "Sorry. Took me a minute to raise them. Probably disturbed their nap." He waved at the camera. With all of their flashlights already turned off, the room fell into blackness. Then there was a purple blush on the wall from Monroe's special light.

Monroe raised his magnifying glass. "The first symbol is definitely maat."

"Again he used the part of her throne name that means truth. The truth will be found." Erica touched Monroe's arm. "It's unlike him to repeat in any way."

"Remember what you said about Senmut and his curveballs," Matt said. "If he's changed the rhythm, it was on purpose."

"Maybe he used that particular word for a reason." Erica looked again to the brightly shining symbols. "Dr. Monroe, I can't make out the rest. The scale is uniform, but they aren't hieroglyphs."

"No, they most certainly are not," he replied with meaning in his voice.

"You recognize them?" Erica asked.

"Not specifically but in general." He turned to Karen. "Might I borrow your writing pad?"

She handed it over without question.

Monroe scribbled on the paper, looked back to the wall then gave his attention to his own writing once again. "I've seen something like this before, but it's been a long while."

"What is it?" Erica seemed disappointed. Matt knew how she hated being unfamiliar with anything having to do with Egypt's history.

"At first I thought it was some type of math problem, like before," the older archaeologist said. "But the structure wasn't quite right. Then I remembered an example I once saw in a book."

"An example of what?" Erica asked.

The older man stood. "You know the Giza pyramid was once

the prime meridian, designated zero degree longitude, from which all other longitudes were measured."

"Yes," Erica answered hesitantly.

"Are you going where I think you are?" Matt asked Monroe.

The silver-haired man took a moment to look them in the eye before answering. "What we have here are coordinates."

They all processed the information before Erica spoke, her voice incredulous. "Coordinates to a specific location."

Monroe nodded.

"Wait." Matt held up a hand. "What we have are Egyptian coordinates that correlate with a now defunct prime meridian."

"We have ancient coordinates. On that you are correct." Monroe spoke with care. "What we also have is a contact person with a computer program capable of translating the former coordinates into current ones."

Matt was ready move. "Where is he?"

Monroe gave him an address in London. "I should call him."

"No." Matt was already walking toward the passage that would lead him up into the open air. "We can't take any chances. We'll have an agent there immediately, and we'll use protected lines of communication. I'll go set up."

The others remained to gather their equipment, leaving no trace of yellow tape or white powder to mar the historic building. As they exited into the cool night, Matt was busy at the computer.

The monitor was out of place atop the ancient stone, but he spared no time for reflection. "We're waiting for a reply. A man is on his way now with a copy of the inscription." Matt turned to Monroe. "You can vouch for your contact's discretion?"

"Absolutely. Especially if the situation is explained."

"He'll be told as little as possible, but the existence of jeopardy and the need for his cooperation and secrecy will be made clear." Matt watched Erica as she sat with Karen on the edge of one of the massive stones. Blue, pink, and yellow lights of the distant city danced on the midnight horizon.

Too far away for Matt to hear, Karen studied Erica's profile before asking, "Are you okay?"

Erica murmured, "Sure." Only the sweeping winds spoke for a moment. "It's a little overwhelming. And the rush, the need to hurry. Can you feel it?"

"I can, and so can everyone else. Matt seems especially determined to see this thing finished."

"I know."

"I think he's scared for you. He wants this over and done and you in a safe place." Karen returned her gaze to the brilliant lights. "He has feelings for you, but I bet he's fighting them with all he's got."

When Erica said nothing, she pushed ahead. "And if I'm not mistaken, you don't think he's too bad either."

Erica looked her in the eye and said nothing. No words were needed with a true friend.

"You love him," Karen whispered.

Erica didn't have time to respond as they were interrupted by Matt's announcement that the results were back. It didn't matter. Karen knew the answer.

The women gathered around the computer screen. "Where is it?" Erica asked.

Matt handed her a scrap of paper with numbers written on it. "The website we need is already pulled up. All you have to do is type these in."

She heard satisfaction in his voice. They both knew this was it. Hatshepsut would be located after a two thousand year departure from her rightful place of honor.

Erica spoke the words from the inscription. "The truth will be found." Her eyes met Monroe's for confirmation. "The truth translates into maat. Maat was part of her name. Maat will be found. Hatshepsut...will be found."

She took the note in her trembling hand and sounded out the coordinates as she typed them in. "Twenty-five degrees, forty-three minutes, and five seconds north. By thirty-two degrees, thirty-nine minutes, and thirty seconds east." Her finger hovered over the enter key.

Erica held her breath, gave Matt one final grin, and pushed the button. "Hold on everybody. Here she comes."

31

The online program worked quickly, flashing an actual photograph of the location onto the monitor. Having been taken via satellite, the images were grainy and in various shades of gray. Erica rolled the cursor and tapped two times, zooming in for a better view.

The name of the location was listed under the coordinates at the top of the screen, but Erica recognized it by sight. "Of course. One of the few places left that Tuthmose III wasn't able to destroy or desecrate. The monument where Hatshepsut's very own words tell the people not to forget her."

Erica stood back from the computer and fought the tears that threatened. "Her obelisks at Karnak."

"Perfect. Absolutely perfect." Monroe wiped suspiciously at the corner of his eye as well. "I have to ask myself how I didn't see this coming."

"Because they are obelisks, and one of their claims to fame was their lack of seams. They were built as whole structures. They aren't buildings, tombs, or temples." Erica grasped his hand. "We would never have imagined it. Even now, I'm wondering how Senmut managed it."

There was a brief hug and mutual congratulations as the two archaeologists basked in the what they had accomplished. The group as a whole experienced emotions spanning from relief to exhilaration.

Erica turned to Matt and threw herself into his arms holding him tightly and kissing him full on the lips. Propriety could be damned as far she was concerned. "We did it. I can't believe we actually did it."

She felt his heart beating against hers and wanted to tell him everything. That she didn't want tonight to be the end for them, but the beginning. That she wanted to be with him, needed him. Her chest was bursting with a riotous mix of feelings.

She wanted to tell him that she loved him.

She felt herself falling into the velvet brown of Matt's eyes and thought he might just let her. He needed her, too. No words were necessary. It was evident in the way he held her and caressed her cheek. How he gave her that roguish half-smile.

There will be time. Deciding to enjoy the glorious moment with Matt and the others, Erica composed herself and pulled out of his arms. "Should we inform the Egyptian government?" Erica asked.

"Not quite yet." The voice that spoke behind them was unknown. It was accompanied by the shuffling of many booted feet as a large number of men dressed in black surrounded them. They all held guns.

Erica's throat ran dry, and her hands clenched into fists. These were the men of nightmares, who spared no mercy to their victims. Erica and her friends were outnumbered, and her stomach filled with cold nausea. She'd lost Hatshepsut again. And the lives of her friends.

Sparing a glance for Matt, she clamped her jaw against the paralyzing fear. This couldn't be happening. Not now. Not now.

Erica felt Matt tense beside her and knew he was blaming himself. They had been caught up in the celebration and had let their guard down. And Kherep Amun had walked right in.

"That's why the guards didn't respond to your signal the last time," Matt said calmly, his words for Clint.

"Right. These guys didn't know what I was doing until I radioed them," Clint said. Both he and Matt wore chiseled expressions of anger.

Matt nodded, still facing the man who had spoken, evidently the one in charge. "So they decided to play along and let us finish the job."

"Because they couldn't do it." Erica surprised herself with the harsh words. The menacing man who'd spoken to them narrowed his eyes as she continued, her tone scathing. "You couldn't find Hatshepsut, even with all your extra information. You had to sit back and follow us."

The man stepped forward. "When you survived in Jordan and made away with the clue, we decided to use you for our own benefit." He offered a cruel smile. "We would have found a way to utilize your skills Dr. Conner. It was unfortunate your government got to you first. Our group needed a fresh set of eyes, then we were made aware of your new association with Dr. Monroe and Agent Pierce."

"How did you know?" Erica could feel the furious pulse in her neck. "Were you spying on me?"

The man's face fell into serious lines again. "We didn't need to. You have no idea the extent of our reach. The positions of power that are housed by one of our own."

He turned his head slightly at the sound of an approaching engine. "We will gladly enlighten you further, Dr. Conner, but first tell us where she is."

"You don't know?" Matt asked. The intruders must not have overheard the earlier discussion.

Without answering, the man motioned another of his team to the computer. The second man quickly moved to the machine and typed a few strokes on the keyboard before speaking to the leader in a dialect of ancient Coptic Egyptian. Erica was amazed to hear the words so many believed were long dead.

The leader turned a hard gaze to Matt. "Sign on to your computer. Remove the encryption."

"I won't do that." Matt knew as long as they held back the location of the lost queen, they had a bargaining chip.

The man took several quick steps toward Matt, pushing the tip of his gun forward. He made no further demand, instead he appeared to be reconsidering his options.

He finally spoke. "You and the other operative. Move there." He gestured with his free hand to the entrance of the pyramid, while another of the intruders pushed Monroe against the wall, his face pressed to the stone.

Matt glanced at Erica. He didn't want to be far from her but knew he had to put aside his personal motives and follow through as his experience dictated. He couldn't risk a confrontation while they were all vulnerable. He jerked his head at Clint, indicating he do as instructed. They moved in the specified direction, keeping their backs against the stone exterior and their eyes on the man giving orders.

"Get down on your knees, hands behind your heads." The leader shot a look at Erica and Monroe, then back to Matt and Clint. "If you value the lives of your companions, you will stay where you are until otherwise directed." He studied Erica, rubbing his lips together before speaking. "Do you know where we need to go?"

She stared back, giving no response.

The man spoke again in the other language. Another from his horde unsheathed a knife at his leg and moved behind Karen.

"Shit," Karen muttered. "Don't let them play you, Erica." The resolve was evident in her eyes. She would die before giving anything up.

Erica tossed a look to Matt then to Karen. She was afraid to risk either of their lives and felt sure she and Monroe would be the last ones in any danger. The Kherep Amun members would keep one of the archaeologists alive. They needed to find Hatshepsut and would ensure that discovery before ridding themselves of the people who held any useful information.

She took a step in his direction, drawing a look of perplexity from the man. "I'll tell you, but not here. Not until we are far away from here." She tossed her head toward Matt and Clint. "And I want them all left behind."

"You seek to bargain?" He lowered his gun and laughed. "I will have what I need." He threw words at his men, causing several to rush forward, surrounding Matt and Clint. Others quickly subdued Monroe and Erica, then Karen who had already been relieved of her weapon. Their hands were tied roughly behind their backs.

Erica was forced down the steps then shoved off the last. She fell face down in the sand. Noises of protest told her Karen was close behind, but she had no idea what was going on above. Rolling onto her back, she looked about wildly for Matt and the others.

The leader suddenly loomed over her. He spoke in English, giving orders in a low voice to another man. "We bring these two with us." He looked intently at Erica as the words fell from his tongue like venom. "Kill the others."

"No!" Erica tried to scream a warning to Matt but was silenced by a coarse hand across her mouth. She tasted blood as her lips were crushed against her teeth. She was gagged and tossed into the back of a van. Hitting what felt like another body, she pulled herself upright to find Karen crumpled beside her, unconscious.

"Don't worry. She'll wake up in time for the ritual." After sneering those words, another man climbed into the back of the vehicle and slammed the doors closed. He sat near the doors and leered at Erica.

Terror, icy and unrelenting, clawed its way into her chest. Tears battered for release as she worried for Matt, Clint, and Dr. Monroe. She moved closer to Karen, trying desperately to cushion her friend's head as the van started a bumpy ride over rough terrain.

She had no idea what she should do. She couldn't let these

madmen find Hatshepsut and use her remains as a launch pad for an international killing spree. But she knew she wouldn't be able to sacrifice Karen to keep the secret of the mummy's whereabouts.

Erica closed her eyes. She had to concentrate, to think of a way out of this mess. All she knew was that she and Karen were still alive, and it was up to her to keep it that way.

Without giving in to Kherep Amun.

She shivered, envisioning what the man might have meant when he'd promised a ritual. What would happen to her? To Karen? And, oh God, she didn't want to think about what was happening to Matt back at the pyramid.

Matt was fighting to control himself. The men had taken Erica and Karen, but he knew he had to remain calm and wait for an opportune moment. The number of would-be assassins had been reduced by half. Still, he and Clint were outnumbered.

Several minutes passed with no movement from the men left to guard them. Vehicle lights came to life in the distance, telling Matt that the other intruders were on the move. With Erica and Karen.

He had to do something.

"Pierce." His name came as a graveled whisper from Clint's unmoving lips. "The chest of the guy on the far right."

Uncertain of his meaning, Matt looked to the right. At first he saw nothing, then a small red dot appeared on the black of the man's shirt. It flickered on and off briefly, but that was enough. Matt recognized the laser. It emitted from a sniper rifle and was trained on the enemy.

Matt also recognized the signal. Dan and John had finally made it.

Matt gave a quick, stilted nod, letting whoever was behind the gun know he was aware. He watched again as the laser flashed in sequence. The sniper would wait for a move from Matt and Clint then take down as many as he could.

Their chance came sooner than expected as the two men closest to the steps gave their attention to someone climbing up. Matt grunted to Clint then held his hand out to the side, counting down with three fingers. He and Clint sprang at the sound of the rifle fire that swiftly felled the man to the right then another who still had his gun trained on the captives.

No one had to warn Monroe. He immediately dropped to the ground.

The two men at the top of the steps turned at the sound of the commotion only to be met by the rapid strikes of skilled agents. Neither Matt nor Clint showed any restraint.

The final member of Kherep Amun was near the entrance of the pyramid. He raised his pistol but stilled when a bullet pierced his temple.

Matt looked down at the man who had been ascending the stairs. This was the one who'd been with the leader when Erica and Karen had been dragged away. Matt wouldn't kill him, but he would make him talk. He was their only link to the intended destination of the killers who held the women.

As if reading Matt's intentions, the darkly clad assassin swiveled to rush down the platform. Another sharp retort rang in the night and the man's knee crumpled beneath him. Matt was on him in seconds, flipping him on his back. "Where are they taking them?"

"Never," the man spat out before groaning in agony.

Matt grasped his shirt and shook him savagely. He started to reach for the injured knee when he heard his name shouted. He looked up to see John running toward him.

"Don't waste your time." John came to a halt some distance away, motioning for Matt. "Dan has a lock on them. We'll follow in your vehicle."

He tossed two sets of handcuffs to Clint, who had joined Matt beside the fallen cult member. They promptly secured his hands and feet before hauling him to the nearest fencepost where he could be hooked up and left behind.

They jumped into the waiting SUV, John already at the wheel. He spoke into a cell phone before clicking it shut and apprising Matt and Clint of the situation. "He's still behind them, keeping a discrete distance. Wherever their going, they've headed away from the city."

Matt checked and loaded a gun, then focused his attention on the gravel road ahead, but all he could see was the blue of Erica's eyes. "Whatever happens, we can't lose them."

32

The van raced through the night, destination unknown. At one point during the drive, the man in back reached over and tore off Erica's gag then held out his arms and crooked his fingers as if inviting her to scream. That scared her more than anything.

"Where are we going?" she rasped, the edges of her mouth sore from chafing.

He shook his head in reply.

The van had no windows that would allow Erica to see the surroundings, but she surmised they had been driving for a little more than an hour. She startled when Karen issued a moan. She looked down to see her friend's lashes moving. Karen was waking up.

"You see," the man said in a tone that mocked her. "I told you she would be awake in time."

Erica didn't ask what he meant, afraid she wouldn't want to know.

By the time the vehicle came to an abrupt halt, Karen was fully awake and sitting up beside Erica. Wincing at the sudden stop, Karen asked, "What did they give me? My head is still foggy, and it aches."

"I don't know," Erica replied softly. "Do you feel sick?"

Karen shook her head slowly. "No. I'll be fine in a minute."

Their co-passenger opened the back doors and jumped out, leaving them alone. He evidently felt safe doing so, as they were both still trussed. Erica had the feeling they were isolated as well. The air lacked suburban smells and sounds, and lush foliage surrounded the area. She guessed they had traveled northeast, possibly toward Alexandria or the new October City. The road leading to both places boasted a much greener landscape.

Soon their unpleasant watchman returned with two other cult members. The men didn't motion or try to speak to the women. They simply grabbed them by their arms and legs, pulling them out with no regard for their comfort.

Erica took in her surroundings as she and Karen were escorted to a large house of dark wood and stone. Yellow lighting illuminated the windows from inside. Gentle breezes were all that answered the lonely cry of a bird.

Erica was disappointed to see her worst fear confirmed. They were in the middle of nowhere.

As they were ushered into the house, Erica and Karen looked into each other's eyes. Erica saw her own dread reflected in her friend's stare. They were taken through a large door that opened to wide stone steps. Actual torches lit the way, flickering on the stonework of the walls as they walked down in a spiral.

Their feet touched ground, and they found themselves in a massive room that appeared to span the length of the house. Great square columns and beams supported the floors above. More torches filled the corners of the room, with several placed in a curved structure that encircled a huge granite table. The wooden configuration that held the torches undulated up and down, allowing the fire to burn at various heights. Some sort of wicked candelabra.

Beside the table was a smaller stand. This one was even more frightening because of what it held. There were candles, already lit in preparation for whatever was to come, some type of rope coiled on the far corner with several strange utensils lined up beside it, and silver bowls reflecting the snapping flames.

The last items were the knives.

Erica managed to tear her eyes away from the gruesome display. Surely this was all a nightmare. How had they gotten themselves into this? She swallowed hard and looked at her friend, who seemed to be unaffected by it all. Karen had her cop face on with fury burning just beneath the surface.

Taking courage from this, Erica shook off the hands of one of her captors. When the man attempted to restrain her again, a commanding voice echoed throughout the open basement. The man on her other side released her in response, and Erica searched the back of the room for the source of authority. She hadn't noticed the far wall before or the long benches that sat in angled rows facing that direction.

Five large chairs, reminiscent of thrones, sat on a dais adorned with Egyptian hieroglyphs and carvings. A single man stood in the middle of the platform. He wore a black robe; hieroglyphics embroidered in blue ran down the left sleeve.

"Your attire is remarkable," Erica commented drolly. She made out the symbols of a viper, two vultures and what looked like a lion. "I can't read it in its entirety."

The man paused with a frown. Unwilling to defer anything, he did not offer her a full view of the garment but explained himself by way of an introduction. "For the ultimate ritual, I am the designated vessel."

"Vessel," she repeated. "Interesting name."

Her sarcasm was not lost on the man. "Dr. Conner, while I respect your knowledge of the lost kingdoms, do not overestimate your value. We have extended more courtesy to you than any non-believer deserves."

The set of his chin warned Erica more than his statement. She had to keep in mind that he was an authority figure, and the room was full of subordinates. He would not allow himself to be embarrassed by anyone. She bowed her head with a respect she did not feel before casting her arm out in a sweep. "I'm sure you've brought us here for a reason, and I don't think it's one I should look forward to."

The man put his hands together and tapped his fingertips. Erica thought of him as the vessel, since it was the only name he had offered.

"We have brought you here to give you answers. Once you understand our mission, we hope to have an answer of our own." He indicated the chairs behind him. "I regret that the rest of the esteemed could not be here for this. I assure you they are traveling here from around the globe as we speak. Now that the resurrection of the queen is at hand."

"Resurrection?" Erica choked on a breath. "You think to bring her back to life?"

The vessel waved his hand. "Not in the manner you might imagine."

Erica heard a sound and saw Karen had been released and had moved into Erica's peripheral vision. It seemed the man was trying to make them feel safer.

Erica knew it was a lie.

That was the only answer that mattered. It was a foregone conclusion that their time was limited. For Karen's sake she would stall as long as possible, and if forced to give information, she would tell them a false location.

No matter what, these heathens could not be allowed to find Hatshepsut and perform their ceremony. They had committed horrible acts of cannibalism and murder already. She shuddered to think of their plans once they consumed Hatshepsut and believed they were imbibed with the power of the god Amun.

Erica gave her attention to the tall man on the platform. He was younger than she would have expected, and the idea of what he must have done to achieve his rank was unsettling. She had to keep him talking as long as possible. Maybe he would give something away. Something she could use. "Why are you doing this?"

He looked at her, taking stock of her worth, then turned and sat in the middle chair. "Do you know how our order began? No, of course not." He laughed, but there was no humor behind it. "If you did, you would not be alive today. Our secrets have been protected for centuries and by any means necessary."

In response to Erica's silence, he continued. "Senmut was not the only man that cherished Hatshepsut. He was, however, the only one weak enough to fall in love with her in the carnal sense. It blinded him to her true value."

Erica disagreed but didn't think it prudent to voice her opinion. "What was her true value?"

The man slapped a hand down on the wooden armrest, his features hardening. "Do not insult me further. There are other methods of retrieving information." He slid hooded eyes over to Karen.

Erica heeded the message. "I meant no offense. Please continue."

His voice still held a hint of irritation. "We do not simply believe. We are the recipients of sacred instructions, originating from Hatshepsut's very own priests. They are the ones who discovered the way to possess divinity and the inherent benefits." He jumped to his feet suddenly, one hand raised in a fist. "But that fool Senmut stole her from them before the sacrament could be received."

Erica realized she'd been wrong all along. "He wasn't hiding her from Tuthmose III, but from your founders." She shook her head, trying to stay calm, but her throat tightened from the injustice. "Don't you think Senmut would know her wishes more than anyone else? He didn't want her to be desecrated."

"The power of Amun was not given to her for her use only. It is in the priests' edicts that her worshippers and their descendants inherit the force to withstand the days that follow the Kingdom of the Spirit."

The man's face was contorted, his obsession evident. Erica knew then they would never be allowed to leave the house alive.

"Now." The vessel smoothed his hands down the front of his robe. "I have said enough. I will know the resting place of Hatshepsut."

"I still don't understand..." she stopped when the fearsome man sliced his hand through the air with impatience.

"We will have what we ask from you. Please do not make us show you what we are capable of." He flicked his fingers and several men surrounded Karen.

"Wait," Erica said. She could hear the desperation in her own voice.

The man ignored her, his full attention on the beautiful Asian woman instead. "This one is some sort of authority figure?"

"A U.S. Marshal." The man who had led the members of the group at the Giza pyramid stepped up to answer. He literally licked his lips. "Two strong, intelligent women. Hatshepsut would have approved."

"You're wrong." The vehemence in Erica's words took the men by surprise and had Karen's head jerking in her direction. "Hatshepsut would not approve. She deserved better than to have jackals trying to steal her power or her divinity in such a disgusting way."

The vessel revealed a malicious smile. "Our ancestors did not think so and neither do we. We have passed the sacred rituals and preparations down through many generations of believers so we would be ready for this day."

Waving his hands in the air, the vessel continued to rant, clenching and unclenching his fists. "Senmut failed. He naively thought we would give up our search. That the first clue would pass from Hatshepsut's trusting servant to others of a like mind. Our forebears did overlook the peasant but knew Senmut had left a trail. After many long years, we followed. He unknowingly led us along the pathway of godly protection. It is our destiny. We cannot be stopped."

"Senmut wanted Hatshepsut to be remembered and revered." Erica spat the words at him. "He never intended to have her bones chewed on by animals like you."

"Enough!" The man breathed deeply then held his arm out, pointing at Erica. "Where is the queen?"

Erica met Karen's eyes. They both knew they were out of time.

Erica called out in a forgotten language. Her blood burned with intensity, and the air seemed to pulse as her heated words in an ancient, mystical dialect cursed Kherep Amun for their blasphemy.

The men stood in shocked stillness, the unexpected chastisement in their sacred tongue holding them at bay for a moment. Indecision on their faces battled with the desire to have the information they sought. More than one man looked at Erica with apprehension. They were a superstitious culture and might believe they'd witnessed a transformation.

Or a possession.

The vessel snapped out of his daze and shook with resentment. "We will waste no more time." He spoke to the others tersely, shocking them out of their stupor.

The men around Karen took hold of her and forced her to the table. She tried to fight her attackers and landed several good hits before another joined the fray and subdued her.

"Leave her alone! She has nothing to do with this!" Erica cried out to her friend and made a move toward her but was restrained by two cult members.

The men bound Karen to the table, forcing her on her back with arms out to each side. They secured her wrists. Once she was tied completely, the men backed away, looking to the vessel for instructions. He nodded to the leader from Giza. "Get what we need."

The leader spoke quietly in their dialect. He and three others removed their shirts and folded them neatly on a shelf to the side of the room. They moved to a bulky stone basin and began to wash their torsos while other members of the group assisted them with silken towels. They began to chant.

"No. Please," Erica whispered. She looked at Karen, still struggling against the willow ropes.

"Don't tell them, Erica. It will all have been for nothing."

A man swiftly filled Karen's mouth with leaves and tied a linen strip around her as a gag. Karen continued to use her eyes to plead with Erica. She too realized what would happen if Kherep Amun was successful.

Chaos would be unleashed on the world with soldiers bent on the most horrible of all holy wars. They would seek to gain more power through their cannibalism. If their numbers were as extensive and integrated as they claimed, no one would be safe.

The newly cleansed men walked to the table. Each of their abdomens sported the falcon tattoo with the pattern that veiled the name of the pharaoh Unis. Their muscled chests glistened in the light of the torches.

One man picked up a knife, the handle encrusted with blue stones. He stepped in to hover over Karen before sliding the blade under her white T-shirt.

Erica saw her friend flinch, and in response, she jerked against the imprisoning arms that held her. "Wait." The man ignored her. "Wait! I'll tell you!"

Still, he brought up his other hand and gripped Karen's shirt. The knife sliced cleanly through the material with a muffled ripping sound. The cloth fell away, leaving her exposed except for her bra.

The vessel spoke and the man finally ceased. He stepped away and returned the knife to the stand.

The vessel caressed his robe and looked down at Erica from his position on the dais. "Do you have something to impart, Dr. Conner?"

"Yes. I'll give you what you want." She stared back at him. "But first, I want her released."

He studied Erica's face, searching for any indication of deceit.

"She means more to me than keeping the secret." Erica saw

he was beginning to relent so she added more to the teaser. "We found coordinates in Giza. We have an exact location."

The truth in her words was apparent. The vessel clapped his hands twice. "Release the woman."

Erica didn't want to waste the opportunity. "When she drives away by herself, I'll tell you." Erica knew they would pursue Karen as soon as they had what they wanted, but at least her friend would have a fighting chance.

The man's demeanor had changed completely. It was as if he could smell the looming triumph. He spoke to the leader from Giza with urgency. "Take them both upstairs and allow the woman to leave. Remove any communication devices from the vehicle. Once she is gone from the property, return with Dr. Conner."

After her bonds were cut, Karen clutched the remnants of her shirt. Had her eyes been weapons, the shirtless men would have fallen around her. She rushed to Erica's side as they climbed the stairs with the leader and several others. "What are we doing?"

"Just go, Karen. Don't look back." Erica was near tears with the hope her friend would make it out alive.

"I'm not leaving you."

The leader elbowed Karen in the stomach. She crumpled over but quickly regained her full height. She held herself in check, clearly wanting to strike back.

The man gripped her arm. "No more talking. You would be wise to take this opportunity and flee as quickly as you can." The way he spoke told Erica her assumption was correct. Once she named a place, she would be dead and Karen would be hunted.

The men hustled Erica and Karen out of the house and into the front yard. The van sat parked in the same spot, but now a small red car was beside it, engine humming.

The cult members seemed to sense the pressing need to complete their task and return to the basement below. They believed Erica would reveal the resting place of Hatshepsut. Many allowed their weapons to dangle at their side, while others grappled with Karen, pushing her toward the car.

Their impatience and confidence were their undoing.

A flurry of activity erupted in the night. Two men to Erica's left fell in unison while others started shouting.

Looking for the source of the commotion, she saw Matt. He strode in at a measured pace, gun drawn and firing. Stunned, she started toward him only to find herself confronted by Karen who grabbed Erica and shouted for her to run.

"Come with me! You'll only distract him!" Karen yelled, still pushing Erica to the side.

Recognizing the importance of removing herself from the fight, Erica nodded to her friend.

The two women were headed for the relative cover of the van when a flash of movement caught Erica's eye. The man who had been at Giza, the same man who had hit Karen in the stomach, was coming at them fast.

Erica didn't have time to cry out before he brought Karen down from behind. She and the man hit hard in a cloud of dust then started grappling on the ground.

Erica made a move to help her friend, but an arm wrapped around her throat, choking her and dazing her with instant pain.

The vessel was at her side, directing the man who held her neck in a vise-like grip. "Quickly. Take her back down." He marched to the front steps, apparently unafraid of the melee going on around him or the possibility of a flying bullet.

Erica was dragged behind him mercilessly, the edges of her vision darkening from the chokehold on her throat. Fleetingly, she realized he might unintentionally kill her in his haste to force her back inside.

Lungs burning, she felt her legs losing their ability to hold her weight, but soon she didn't need them. She had no more need to stand when her captor flung her into the foyer of the house and onto the floor. The vessel slammed the large wooden door shut behind them, bolting it and heading toward the basement.

Another cult member appeared at the top of the stairs. "The preparations have been..."

"Never mind that." The vessel shot the words out in a rage. "There is no time now. Can't you hear what's happening out there?" He backhanded the subordinate. "Open the tunnel. Immediately!"

The man hastened down the stairs, shouting to the others who had stayed below, obviously preparing the ritual table once again.

Erica might still die this night, but at least she wouldn't be cut open as their latest worthy sacrifice. The image of these heathens eating her organs and flesh made her stomach revolt. She breathed heavily through her sore throat, attempting to regain strength before they came for her again.

Too late. The one that had dragged her in was jerking on her arm, yelling at her in Arabic. Evidently their sacred language was forgotten amidst the panic. She pretended confusion, taking the opportunity to stall.

Belatedly he switched to English. "Get up. Now."

It was either stand up and move or have her shoulder wrenched from its socket. Any physical harm the man might be inflicting was unimportant to him. His eyes were wide with fear, yet his mouth tightened with fury. "We should have killed you at the pyramid. You have brought a curse on us all with those demon words."

Erica remembered her use of Coptic Egyptian earlier as she'd admonished the group. He obviously thought her directives to the underworld were coming true. Somewhere in her stomach a flame of retribution flickered. Good. I hope you all piss your pants before you die.

The push down the stairs swept away any satisfaction she might have knowing she'd spooked them. The journey was doubly terrifying this time. She knew what was down there but also that the cult was backed into a corner.

They would do anything to survive, and right now, she was their only advantage.

Outside, the fighting had died down considerably. The first few members of Kherep Amun who'd been shot still lay where they fell. Matt and the others had taken no chances. One kill shot each.

Matt called to Dan. "What's it looking like?" He was scanning the area, searching for Karen and Erica. He'd seen them running for safety when the shooting started and knew they were probably keeping low.

He turned at the sound of footsteps. Clint was approaching, dirt smeared across his arms. "The ones that are still alive won't be going anywhere," he told Matt, referring to their new prisoners. "Dan and John are taking care of them, and the Egyptian authorities are on the way."

Nodding, Matt continued his search of the area, a his teeth grinding together. Worry was beginning to work its way in past the adrenaline rush that lingered. The fervor had quieted down, but there was still no sign of the women.

He was about to verbalize his concern to Clint when Monroe sidled up and beat him to it. "Where are the girls?" The older man asked, glancing about the scene of carnage with wide eyes.

Matt issued a terse order to Clint. "Let's go. I saw them head in that direction." He gestured toward the van just as a figure appeared around the back side of it.

Dirty, bloody, and disheveled, Karen headed toward them, a knife dangling from her hand. Looking at the men with anxiety in her eyes, she moved with more speed to join them. Matt could feel the darkness rising in his chest before she ever spoke.

Karen glanced at him, back toward the house, then again to Matt's troubled stare. "Where's Erica?"

33

Solid wood and inaccessible locks met them as they tried to get past the front door. Dan and Clint had gone around to the sides of the house, looking for an entrance. Karen was now wearing a borrowed T-shirt, and she and Matt were reviewing their options on the porch when Clint crept silently around the corner of the building and motioned for them to join him.

"Dan and I will secure the exits," John said, walking to let the other agent know what was happening.

Matt and Karen moved with stealth and speed, catching up with Clint at a side door. "I don't hear anything," he told them as they crouched below the window of the door.

"They've got to be making a run for it." Karen accepted the pistol Clint offered in lieu of the knife she held. Blood still stained the blade from where she'd ended the life of at least one murderer.

The leader of the group from Giza had been left in the dirt where he'd fallen, his own knife turned against him. Thinking Karen would be an easy target had been his first mistake. Trying to kill her had been his last.

"We don't have time to waste." Matt rose and tested the doorknob. Amazingly, it was unlocked. The group hadn't been expecting the turn of events that had reversed their position. The hunters were now the quarry.

Matt, Karen, and Clint fell naturally into their training, each checking alternate rooms and motioning when the space was deemed clear. Karen jerked her head then proceeded to the cellar staircase with the two men allowing her the lead.

"This will take us to the basement," she said in a low voice when they gathered at the closed door. "It runs the length of the house. My bet is they're down there."

"We need to make a quick survey of the upper floor. Can't let ourselves get stuck between them," Clint said and crept up the stairs after the others nodded a silent agreement for him to go.

Matt blinked slowly, thinking only of the proper course of action. Completing the mission with minimal casualties was the ultimate goal. He couldn't allow personal feelings to affect him, so he tried to push Erica from his mind. Tried not to imagine the terror she must be experiencing.

If she was still alive.

Karen was stone-faced, but her eyes told a different story. She was scared for her friend and knew the odds were not in her favor. Erica was in the hands of killers, and now those killers were desperate.

Clint reappeared and motioned that the second floor was empty. They opened the cellar door slowly, with only a slight scrape to announce their presence, and glided down the stairs.

Matt went first, ready for anything. They were at a disadvantage and knew there would probably be members of Kherep Amun lying in wait for them at some point.

The basement appeared empty, torches and candles still burning and casting an orange glow on the surroundings. Matt caught a scuffling sound like someone scraping their shoes across dirt. He and the others all reacted, taking cover wherever possible just as three men came out from behind the support columns.

One of them dropped before he he'd ever raised his gun. He'd taken a direct hit to the chest. Clint and Matt turned to look at Karen with new appreciation.

Leaning around the stone table she'd hidden behind, Karen fired at one of the other two men. She hit his knee just as Matt's bullet found its way into his stomach.

The remaining cultist backed into a hiding spot, firing wildly from behind the massive column. Soon an empty clicking echoed throughout the chamber. He was out of ammo. Now was their opportunity, so they closed in swiftly. Clint took the man out with a striking blow, and the empty gun clattered to the floor.

While Clint made sure the man was restrained, Karen and Matt surveyed the room.

"Something's off," Karen stated in a flat voice. It was then she noticed what was different. "Look." She pointed to the front of the room and walked that way. "The dais has been moved. It wasn't this close to the pews before."

Matt saw what she meant. The stage was so close the pews, no one could sit in the front rows. He and Karen both understood immediately and went to the side of the platform. Behind it, they found an entrance into the wall.

"There's a tunnel." Matt spoke while sliding down the wall and peering into the passageway. "Let's go," he said as Clint joined them.

Again they headed into darkness, unsure what might burst from its depths at any moment. The tunnel was archaic; cobwebs and the stale scent of mildew spoke of its neglect. Torches lined the walls but remained unlit, so Clint and Matt pulled out flashlights. Clint gave an extra one to Karen.

"Thanks. I'm glad you came prepared," she said, positioning the light in her hand so its beam illuminated the path her gunfire would travel.

They were all grateful for the extra light when they moved another twenty feet and discovered the tunnel splitting into three directions.

"Looks like we go ahead alone from here," Clint said in a tight voice.

Matt wasn't afraid to face the men by himself but was worried he might pick the wrong direction. He hated the thought of going the wrong way and losing Erica to these lunatics. Karen and Clint were capable, but he needed to be sure she was safe.

She was still his responsibility, and he told himself that was the only reason he wanted to get her back safely. Thinking of her dead or injured would serve no purpose and would only cloud his judgment. He had to think and act rationally.

Without further talk, they each took the closest opening and pressed on. There was nothing else to be done. None of them knew how far the corridors stretched or how long it would take to search them, and Erica might not have much time.

They were forced to split up.

Determination in every step, Matt made his way forward until he felt the ground beneath him start to slope down. The shaft grew cooler and the air felt damp. He was going deeper into the earth with no sense of how far below he actually was.

A voice carried to him from the blackness, beyond the beam of his light, alerting him to the presence of others. Hearing the faint sound again, Matt turned off his flashlight, allowing his eyes to adjust. After enough time, a yellow glow appeared ahead.

The corridor curved gently and opened into a cavern. Kherep Amun had utilized the naturally existing cave as part of their underground system. Wooden chairs, tables, and crates were spread about but were dusty from lack of use.

"Where are we going?" Matt heard Erica ask her abductor. The urge to run to her was strong, but he didn't have the situation in hand. Exposing himself could cost both their lives.

He waited and listened as someone issued instructions. The sharp, smug tone implied the man was used to authority. "Make sure that ladder is strong enough. Climb all the way and open the hatch."

A deep, hollow noise reverberated in the air, the sound of boots on metal ladder rungs.

Matt listened and judged the number of group members

present. The leader would want to extricate himself and Erica first, so he had to take action soon,

Matt couldn't afford to lose sight of Erica while fighting his way through the men. For all he knew, a vehicle was waiting at the top of that ladder.

The man who'd climbed up was yelling, asking for help with the hatch. Matt knew this was his best chance. With two men off the ground, the odds were more in his favor.

He peered around a massive rock form and saw two men. One was holding Erica while the other looked above. Moving as quietly as possible, Matt eased forward, his gun ready to take out any threat.

The man standing alone turned to pick up something from the ground and saw Matt right away. Matt's aim was lethal, and the man fell before he could issue a warning.

The gun's retort alerted the others anyway. Shots rang out from above, the second man on the ladder shooting in response to the surprise attack. Matt fired back but was unsuccessful. He heard a commotion before light blasted in from overhead. The two men disappeared through the opening at the top of the ladder.

The two could return with help, but for now Matt had to keep an eye on the ones who were still in the cave with him. The man who'd spoken with authority had Erica. The bastard held her in front of him, a knife to her throat.

"This has gone far enough," the man said, temper flaring in his eyes. He looked at Matt as if he were nothing but an inconvenient disturbance. Even with the wolf at his back, the man spoke with an imperious quality.

"You're right about that," Matt replied, the strength of steel in his tone. "Let her go."

An obnoxious smile spread across the face of Erica's captor. "You want her back? Of course." His words dripped of evil and deceit. "I'll give you your queen when you give me mine."

"Don't tell him, Matt. He'll slit my throat as soon as he knows where she is." Erica grimaced when the man yanked her hair.

The man held her head back, exposing the length of her neck. Madness danced behind his eyes as he spoke to Matt. "I think that's a brilliant idea," he said before sliding the knife across Erica's skin, leaving a line of blood in its wake.

Matt froze, unable to believe what he was seeing. Helpless to do anything but watch and wait for Erica to crumple to the ground, he stood immobile, feeling the painful force of his heart squeezing inside his chest.

Images assaulted him and blurred the lines between the past and present. It wasn't Erica he was seeing but the young girl who'd been shot while under his protection. He saw her falling to the floor, eyes wide with shock. He couldn't save her.

No. That's not right. Matt clenched his jaw, putting aside the memories. He looked instead to the woman before him, still standing, with a thin line of red on her soft, golden skin. *Erica.*

The cut on her throat was only superficial, a tactic employed to instill fear in both Erica and Matt. It had worked, but not for long. The move told Matt a great deal about the person he was dealing with.

The man was insane. And dangerously unpredictable.

"You want to see your queen," Matt said in a cold, flat voice, raising his gun once again. He caught Erica's eye, willing her to keep still, then directed his attention once again to the man behind her. "I don't think she'll want you."

He fired once, striking the man in his right eye. The cult leader stood for several seconds then fell easily to his knees, like a film in slow motion.

Erica felt his hand sliding off her shoulder and down her back. She stepped away and turned to make sure the vessel was no longer any danger. Anger still twisted his features as he took his illusion of entitlement with him to his death.

Breathing a sigh of relief, she pivoted and ran to Matt. She couldn't get into his arms fast enough.

He held her tightly but only for a brief embrace. "We need to move. The others might be coming back." Pulling her after him, he explained, "We'll go back the way I came. At least I know it will be clear."

Her eyes remained riveted on his back as they made their way through the tunnels and back toward the basement of the house. Numbness and relief raged through her body, disguising the pain she should have been feeling.

Karen and Clint met them just before the split passages merged back into one. Karen wrapped Erica in a hug as Clint spoke to Matt. "We heard the shots, but it took us a minute to get back. Good to see you're both safe."

"They're not," Karen said. "Erica, you're bleeding."

Erica reached a hand up to her throat and felt a sticky streak on her throat. "It's not as bad as it looks. Let's keep going. I just want to get out of here."

In complete agreement, the four found their way back to the house and up to the entry level. Clint unlocked the front door while Karen looked for anything she could find to clean Erica's wound. Moments later she returned with a wet rag.

Erica was still dabbing her tender skin when the roar from multiple cars rushing up the road drew her attention. Sleek black sedans and powerful trucks resembling American SWAT vehicles skidded to a halt, spraying sand in their wake. The official emblems embossed on the doors announced the arrival of the Egyptian government.

Monroe was suddenly in the doorway, Dan and John trailing behind. The older man looked them all over with wide, searching eyes. "You're both all right. Stand back and let me see you."

The sight of her colleague shook Erica from her daze. "Monroe." She stated his name in disbelief then looked to Karen.

Karen smiled broadly, offering the man words of comfort. "We're fine. We're both fine."

Officers in black swarmed the house, ushering the small

group out for their own safety. Clint went with Dan and John to brief the new arrivals.

Erica tilted her head in concern as she walked with Matt to the waiting vehicles. "What's the matter? Is there something else going on that you haven't told me?"

He shook his head. "I'm just thinking about where we'll go from here."

Erica wasn't sure what he meant, but his gaze was distant. In fact, it was anywhere but on her. He wouldn't look at her.

"What happened here will open up a lot of leads for us. We're going to be all over the rest of the leaders of Kherep Amun." He finally spared her a glance. "It's going to be pretty busy the next few weeks."

She didn't know why the words stung, but they did. He was right back on the job. Agent Pierce reporting for duty with no time for niceties. Was it too much to expect him to show a little emotion, some relief that she was walking beside him instead of lying dead in an underground cave?

Erica swallowed the lump in her throat and steadied her voice so it wouldn't shake. "Where are we going?"

"Back to the hotel for now. We could all use some time to recover." Matt steered her forward with his hand still clamped on her arm. "I'll know more after I speak with Gus."

They went straight to one of the black government vehicles. Matt opened the door and stood back to let her in. "They'll give you a ride back, and Clint and I will follow soon," he said. "We need to tie up the loose ends here before we go."

She wanted to speak, but only nodded in silence, sliding into the back seat as Karen came in from the other side. Erica hazarded a glance at Matt, but his face was impassive, a faraway look in his eyes.

"I'll see you at the hotel," he said and slammed the door.

Erica watched him walk to where Clint stood with several other men. As the car pulled away, she faced forward to stare at the leather headrest of the front seat.

Wondering what had just happened.

34

Almost a day later and the group had yet to discuss all that had happened since Giza. With the search all but completed and danger still looming, Matt's superiors wanted them back in France for immediate debriefing.

Quick showers and changes of clothes were all they'd managed before boarding one of the U.S. government's jets headed for Lyon, France and Interpol headquarters. With the sun rising on the horizon, Erica and the others got what sleep they could onboard the aircraft.

Matt was occupied with Gus and other members of their team as they worked frantically to follow the leads they'd gotten from the previous night's arrests. Kherep Amun was still largely functional, and he was doing his best to stay one step ahead of the cult. So he didn't have time for a real conversation with Erica.

At least, that's what he told himself.

Everyone involved in the rescue and resulting confrontation at the house had been summoned. Sleek cars met them at the terminal and secreted them away to the safety of Interpol. Back in their professional clothing, they now rode up in the silver elevator and were directed to the designated board room.

They were presented a hero's welcome that consisted of a smorgasbord of breakfast foods. And to Clint's and Erica's particular relief, coffee.

Matt had no interest in food or beverage, though. He was ready to move forward. There was still work to be done. For him, this was go time.

Gus entered the room, accompanied by two men and a woman. Introductions were made all around. The woman was an Interpol officer from France and the two men were an Egyptian government official and a liaison for the museum in Cairo.

Despite being partially informed, the three required a full accounting of the archaeological discoveries that had been made in their country, as well as the information obtained about Kherep Amun.

After Monroe had briefed them on the various sites involved in the hunt for Hatshepsut and the resulting discoveries, he looked to Matt and Erica to take over.

Erica placed her hands flat on the table. "Agent Pierce is the expert on Kherep Amun, but I'll share what I learned from the man at the house. He was one of their highest ranking members, referring to himself as one of the esteemed." She looked to the Egyptian official. "Was his body recovered last night?"

The handsome, dark-skinned man coughed. "It was. Though many others were killed in the skirmish that resulted, we were able to apprehend two of the other expected guests, these esteemed ones as you call them. Men are still stationed at the house in case the others show."

He looked to Matt. "We will extend Agent Pierce every courtesy and welcome his involvement as we continue our investigation into this organization."

Matt nodded in return, the knot of concern he hadn't known he carried dissolving in his gut. Things would run much smoother and faster without political obstacles. "We have never had the opportunity to question any of their members," he said. "Hopefully we can start unraveling their network."

The museum liaison, an archaeologist as well, leaned forward. "Dr. Conner, please tell us about the formation of Kherep Amun. How long have they been in existence?"

Erica ran her hands over her thighs under the table. "According to the vessel, that's what he called himself, and I have no other name for him," she told them before pausing, waiting for them to clarify his identity. When they didn't, she continued. "According to him and his accounts of the Kherep Amun history, the foundation of their group began during Hatshepsut's lifetime. Of course, Amun had long been considered a deity, and I can only assume Hatshepsut's claim to be his earthly daughter prompted certain members of society to worship her in a religious fashion as well."

Erica took a moment to sip her coffee. "The priests that surrounded her during her reign as pharaoh, must have been planning the use of her body for their own purposes before she died." She tilted her head. "What bothers me is that either Hatshepsut never endorsed their concepts of cannibalism, or if she did, Senmut decided to prevent that. Frankly, given the ancient Egyptian's belief in preparing a corpse for the afterlife, I don't believe she would have wanted her body to be consumed."

The liaison pursed his lips. "I agree. If Senmut gained knowledge of the priests' plans, that could very well explain why the work on his own burial tomb was halted so abruptly."

"We had that same thought," Erica said with a nod. "Which makes it even more ironic that Senmut's work may have contributed to the prophecy that Kherep Amun and others have clung to for many years."

Matt didn't know what she was talking about. "How did his work support the prophecy?"

Erica spoke directly to Matt now, and he did his best to deny the flash of pain he saw cross her face before she schooled her features. "Painted on Senmut's ceiling, in addition to the zodiac, are references to an even more prehistoric ceremony called 'the drawing of the cords.' It was performed by educated men who were trying to determine the polar axial tilt. This was important, because they had accounts in their history of times when the polar axis coincided with great climate changes."

"Like transforming your American Midwest from a frozen block of ice into what it is today," Monroe interjected. "Or in some places, the exact opposite."

"Which would be considered a disaster of great magnitude." Erica allowed them a moment to register the information. "Senmut's charting of the ceremony on his astrological ceiling could have been construed as prophecy."

"The End of Days," Monroe muttered.

"Wait a minute." Karen reached over to tap Monroe's shoulder. "That was on your guide to the code from the pyramid, wasn't it?"

"Yes." Monroe shifted in his seat to sit taller. "The End of Days follows swiftly after the Kingdom of the Spirit. It has been foretold many times in the past by those claiming to be oracles or prophets."

Matt motioned to Erica. "Didn't you say the vessel mentioned something about surviving the times that come after the Kingdom of the Spirit?"

"He did," Erica said. "Which is why Kherep Amun became more visible in the last several years. They thought they were running out of time. We are currently experiencing the Kingdom of the Spirit, according to the code."

"That and they picked up on Dr. Monroe's research regarding the necklace found on the mummy. The first clue." Matt sent an apologetic look to the older man. "Just like we did."

Monroe only laughed and shrugged. "Who could have guessed that poking around on the Internet would lead to all of this? Now that it's done, though, I'm happy to have been a part of it. Unfortunately, they were already beginning their barbaric rituals. I'm only sorry anyone had to suffer at their hands."

"Let me see if I've got this straight," Matt said. "Kherep Amun thought if they cannibalized Hatshepsut's corpse, they would be consuming something of the god Amun, since he was supposedly her father. And that would...what? Afford them some sort of power or protection?" Matt frowned, feeling both disgusted and skeptical. "How did that turn into a religion that survived for two thousand years?"

Monroe spoke up. "Fear is a powerful motivator. That and the belief in redemption from hell in the afterlife. Or a hell here on earth."

"The priests that founded Kherep Amun believed they could gain the powers or gifts of others by eating them," Erica stated simply. "It is clearly referenced in the Cannibal Text written for Pharaoh Unis a thousand years before their time. Those teachings combined with a prediction of catastrophe and a queen who was supposed to have been divine. The result was a cult obsessed with preserving their lives and their souls."

"And they called it their religion." Matt's statement was followed by silence.

Erica directed a question to the museum's liaison. "What is your country planning to do with Hatshepsut's remains?"

"That has yet to be decided. Advanced imaging equipment was flown to Karnak this morning." He paused. "The presence of a body has been verified. Even more remarkable, it is located under the only obelisk of the original four that still stands. Whether we leave her in her present place of rest or install her in a museum will be discussed at length by the council. Whatever we decide, there will be significant security precautions. That is one reason we may move her to a museum. We don't want Karnak to become inadmissible to the public, and it will be difficult to guard otherwise."

"Our agreement still stands?" Monroe asked the liaison.

"The artifacts recovered in your quest are the rightful property of Dr. Conner." The man smiled at her. "I hope to visit your museum in its completion."

"You are always welcome," Erica graciously responded, though Matt noted the lines of strain around her tight smile.

"I'm sure the council will make the right decision regarding the queen," Erica added, "though I feel the obelisk is a fitting resting place."

"Why?" the liaison asked. He looked genuinely interested in her thoughts on the matter.

Erica leaned forward, passion in her gaze. "It's been theorized that obelisks were erected to symbolize a *djed* pillar, the Osirian representation of a channel for spiritual travel. The belief is that one's Ka, or soul, could rise up through it and return to its creator."

"I see where you're going with this," Matt said, offering his support of Erica's view. It was the least he could do. "Considering Senmut's love for both Hatshepsut and astrological influences, the obelisk is an honorable burial, even if not the norm."

Erica's took her time and encompassed everyone in the room with her eyes. "We all know Hatshepsut was the queen who would be king. A woman who claimed divinity as well as the position of pharaoh, though that was unheard of. What many seem to forget is the compassion with which she ruled and the prosperity she brought to her people."

She paused, but the others looked to her for more. "Hatshepsut was one of the most extraordinary rulers in Egypt's history. During her reign the culture progressed in many ways. There is evidence that she encouraged education in the art of medicine while accomplishing extensive projects in architecture. She was also a proponent of peaceful trade instead of forceful conquests, though an army of warriors was ready to serve at her command."

"Hatshepsut's hopes for her remembrance were inscribed on one of the now fallen obelisks." Erica's voice grew softer. "It reads, 'As I shall be eternal...like an undying star.'"

The liaison smiled then nodded in respect for both Erica and the forgotten queen. "She deserves for her story to be told, and you have given us a new opportunity to do so."

Gus spoke for the first time since the meeting had begun. "You have all performed exceptionally, especially given the unique circumstances." He addressed the Egyptian representatives as well as the Interpol officer who would be informing other agents about Kherep Amun and the new intelligence concerning their members. "Do any of you have any questions?"

At the shake of their heads he said, "If you do, I'll be in ready contact with Dr. Monroe, Dr. Conner, and Agent Pierce."

After the small talk was over, Gus and his three guests left the conference room. The others returned to their relaxed demeanor. Except for Matt and Erica. Neither seemed to know what to say to one another, and Matt knew he was to blame.

Not only for the way he'd shoved her away last night, but for ever getting close in the first place. How many times since he'd met her had he reminded himself to keep things clean? To keep it professional?

And when he'd seen her in the hands of a murderer, the reasons, all good ones, had come roaring back into crystal clarity. The crushing fear he'd experienced as he'd looked into her terrified eyes had been...

Incapacitating. And he'd almost lost her.

That's when he'd known. When he'd realized his heart had made him a fool. The overwhelming emotion he'd felt for her, hell, the love he'd felt, had almost stolen his mind from him.

And he was no good to anyone in that condition. Least of all Erica.

Movement on his left snapped him back to find Erica at his side. She still had a hint of wounded in her eyes, though she firmed her lips and lifted her head valiantly. His tough little archaeologist with the crystal eyes.

She sniffed before meeting him head on and asking, "I hate to sound clichéd, but what do you do next?"

Matt breathed in deeply, inserting his hands into the pockets of his pants. "Follow up work still needs to be done on Kherep Amun. Interrogations, background checks, tracking down every last affiliation that might be involved."

"In other words, you'll be pretty tied up," she said with a look that told him she'd heard the underlying message in his words. His excuse.

"Looks that way."

They both fell quiet. A nervous tension hung between them that hadn't existed before. Erica didn't know what to make of it or the stilted conversation they somehow managed. She was grateful when Monroe and Karen joined them and interrupted the terrible silence.

Karen looked between Matt and Erica cautiously. "Any plans for the trip home?"

Erica glanced at Matt but saw no encouragement there. No warmth. She cleared her choking throat and said, "I need to get back to the museum." She'd hoped he would ask her to stay for a while. To stay close so he could spend more time with her.

She could see now she'd been too optimistic.

Matt finally spoke. "I'm afraid I'll be stuck here for a while. If not, I'll be traveling back and forth to interrogations."

Erica looked over Karen's shoulder, unsure what to say to any of them. She knew Matt would be needed now more than ever, but even big, strong FBI agents had to eat. To sleep. Why wouldn't he let her be there for him? Even in small doses?

Matt was in charge of the task force that would work night and day to put Kherep Amun out of business before any more lives were lost. But she wasn't asking for much. A word, a gesture, a look. Anything.

But he was colder now than she'd ever seen him. And none of it made any sense.

Clint walked by and slapped Matt on the back as he passed. "I'm heading down to the office they've allocated for us. The leads are beginning to trickle in, and we need to make some assignments." He looked to Erica with a sheepish grin. "Sorry to be in a rush. Still a few bad guys out there."

She surprised him by standing on her toes and planting a kiss on his cheek. "Thank you, Clint. For everything."

The tall, muscular man looked sheepish. "No problem." A mischievous glint took hold of him. "And if you ever get tired of Pierce, you can share a cup of my coffee anytime." He headed for the door before Matt could say anything. Backing away, he held up both hands. "Hey. Can't blame a guy for trying."

Clint pointed a finger at Karen as well. He winked and said, " See you around, legs. And keep shooting."

Erica turned to Matt, cheered by Clint's playfulness. Then she was jolted when Matt rubbed a finger down the back of her hand. "I'll walk you down to the car," he said.

Once they exited the building, Karen and Monroe did their best to appear distracted and climbed into the waiting vehicle to give Matt and Erica some privacy.

The day was clear and sunny as the French city bustled around them. Matt took Erica by the hands. "Before you go, there's something you need to be told."

She tried to smile but couldn't find one. Instead she lifted a shoulder. "I'm listening."

"You should take the vases. And the mummy if it comes to that." Matt put his finger to her lips when she would have protested. "I saw how you reacted in there, and I know better than anyone the change of heart you've had since this all started. You aren't wrong to take what you've earned."

He tilted his head forward, holding her immobile with his dark stare. "Erica, you helped saved countless lives. And while the images of the people killed will stay with you, with me, and haunt all of us for a long time, those vases still belonged to Hatshepsut. And now to you." He squeezed her hand. "I think the queen would admire you and want you as her guardian."

Gratitude and melancholy wrestled in Erica's heart. "I'm not sure it would be right. I wanted to find them for all the wrong, selfish reasons. I don't deserve them or the praise the museum would receive for housing them."

"No," he said flatly. "You deserve a hell of a lot more. Take them Erica. No one else would treat them better. And..." He trailed off before lowering his voice to a near whisper. "Your father and grandfather would want your museum to have the relics you discovered."

Erica swallowed hard, trying to keep her tears locked up tight.

"The things you've accomplished, the dangers you've faced for all of us." He heaved a breath. "You helped save innocents, Erica," he stroked away a stray drop, evidence of her broken heart, and said, "What better way to honor the men who raised you?"

She was finally able to offer him that stubborn smile. "When did you learn to speak so eloquently, Agent Pierce?" His words had eased some of her conflict over the artifacts, though she would still need to consider everything. Right now she was consumed with grief, and Matt's touching encouragement only backed up her assumption.

She was losing him.

He shook himself and let go of her hands. "I'm not sure how I expected to deal with this moment."

Erica felt devoid of all warmth when she lost the small bit of contact. She spoke quickly now, an attempt to mask the panic that was setting in. "I want to thank you again."

He waved away her gratitude. "We were a good team." He looked at her intently before diverting his eyes. "Erica, about us."

She heard the goodbye in his voice.

"We both came into this with jobs to do," he said. "We knew what was important." He pressed his lips together then continued. "Along the way we lost sight of that and almost threw everything away. You were almost killed."

Her brow creased in confusion while she shook her head against his reasoning. "No, what happened couldn't be helped, but we made it out. The worst is behind us."

"For now." Matt's tone was clipped and hard. "Look, Erica, you know I care about you."

The voice that made its way out of her tightening throat sounded small. "You care about me?"

"But I just can't put myself in that position again," he said as if he hadn't heard her.

"What position?" Her head felt numb, her chest heavy. An aching weight was pulling her down into the abyss that waited to claim her. *Why is this happening?*

Matt took a few steps toward the building. "Take care of yourself."

Erica put her hand on top of the open car door, needing the support of something solid as she watched him walk away.

Karen had heard enough of the exchange from her place in the back of the car. She rushed out and around to where Erica stood. "Erica. I'm so sorry. Here, get in the car." She guided Erica into the car and closed the door. As soon as Karen was back inside, she instructed the driver to go. Quickly.

Karen met Monroe's worried eyes as he glanced over his shoulder from the front. She placed her hand over Erica's, but Erica barely felt it. "We'll be home soon and you can get some rest, " Karen said. "We all just need some time to get ourselves together."

The words were lost on Erica as she faced away from her friend and pretended to watch the splendor of Lyon streak by outside. She couldn't speak with Karen and Monroe just now. She wasn't sure if she could form coherent thoughts.

She just kept seeing Matt's face as he turned away from her. The man she'd come to trust had left without a backward glance. How could she have been so wrong?

They stopped at a busy intersection and Erica gazed out at the sidewalks full of people moving with haste to their next destination. Some strolled or rode by on bicycles. Some alone or in groups. And so many of them seemed to be smiling.

Erica was thankful for the car's tinted windows. The dark glass made it impossible for passersby to see inside.

And she didn't want anyone to see her cry.

35

In the two weeks Erica had been back home in Georgia, Matt had only contacted her one time. The e-mail had been short and to the point.

He had wanted to let her know the advances they'd made in short-circuiting Kherep Amun's activities. Though finding every last member would probably never be accomplished, at least their plans had been interrupted. He let her know they intended to keep after them until all the cells had been dispersed. And if they were on the run, they wouldn't have time for murderous rituals.

She felt sure it was his way of telling her he would be immersed in his work. Indefinitely.

Given the sensitivity of what he was doing with Interpol, Matt couldn't mention anything specific. He sent no polite comments about himself or inquiries about how she was doing. The e-mail could have been written by a computer for all the personality and warmth it contained.

Erica had no idea what had happened between her and Matt. There had been no unkind words in their last hours together, but there had been no promises either. Still, the abrupt transformation from their time together in Giza to the days after he'd saved her life was a mystery.

She had never felt so distanced from him, even when he'd

been a stranger. But he was no stranger to her now.

She'd spent the first few days in bed, crying and sleeping as needed. After that she'd had several heart to heart talks with Karen, midnight brownie binges, and coffee. Lots and lots of coffee.

Sorrow was an ever present shadow, so Erica had thrown herself into the projects she needed to complete before the museum could open. She had been excited about the prospect before meeting Monroe and Matt, but now she worked with a fervency that was unhealthy. Time and again Karen or Erica's assistant, Randie, had to force Erica to stop and eat. Or simply take a break.

Even now, as she put the final touches on the exhibit featuring Hatshepsut's story and the artifacts from their excursion, Erica heard Karen's voice echo through the gallery.

"Come out, come out, from whatever all-consuming project you're working on. I know you're in here. Randie told me."

Instead of yelling out, Erica gave away her position by flipping the switch to turn on the visual effects. She was inside a tunnel, and it instantly transformed into a world under water.

Though not the one she had originally intended.

She had commissioned a photographer to film the dive site of Herakleion. A screen covered the walls and above, so the images curved up and over the ceiling to create the illusion of being in the ocean.

In addition to the vase she and Matt had recovered, the Mediterranean Sea display would also offer information about the relics discovered by her father and grandfather before their untimely deaths. Instead of shying away from their diving accident, she used the aquatic footage as part of their memorial, tying together their work with hers in a tribute that contained photos of the three of them together.

She grinned whenever she thought of it. Everything was as it should be.

At least Matt had helped her with that choice.

Karen poked her head around the corner at the far end. "Wow. This is amazing." She strolled in, looking all around her as a fish floated by and a large, overturned statue came into view. "You told me how it would be, but this is unbelievable."

Karen stopped and looked at Erica in all seriousness. "You realize some people will be afraid to come in here. It's too real."

Erica bounced up and down on her toes in some version of a happy dance. "I know. This is my favorite part."

"The rest is great, too, especially the encryption wall," Karen added, referring to the display that featured imitation sandstone with encoded messages for patrons who liked a challenge. Some of Senmut's work had been included.

"What do you have there?" Erica pointed to the paper sacks her friend carried.

"I thought we'd try out that new Thai place in town." She held up a bag and shook it. "Hot and spicy, just like us."

Erica brushed her hair back from her face and surveyed her dirty clothing. "Yeah. That's me."

"Usual place?" Karen asked.

"Sure. I'll go get some drinks."

Erica retrieved two cold bottles of raspberry vitamin-tea and joined her friend in the center of what they called "the jungle." Another exhibit featured faux but convincingly lush vegetation, and it was their preferred spot for picnicking.

They ate quietly for a few minutes, and Karen didn't ask about Matt. She steered clear of that topic unless Erica brought it up. The last discussion had been a couple of nights ago over too many glasses of wine.

It hadn't been pretty.

Soon Erica noticed the other woman's blank stare. "Hey. Is something the matter?"

Karen tried to fake a look of nonchalance. "Uh-uh. Just a long day."

Erica wasn't fooled. "Okay. What gives?"

"It's not a big deal." Karen huffed out a breath. "And I didn't want to burden you with everything else that's been going on."

"There's nothing going on with me."

Karen gave Erica a look that called her a liar.

"Fine. But you know you can talk to me." Erica dug into her Panang Beef. "Lord knows, I owe you some ear time."

Karen gave a long-suffering sigh and rolled her eyes. "My mother..."

Unable to stop herself, Erica chuckled. Karen and her mother didn't see eye to eye on many things. "Don't tell me she's found you a husband."

"If only it were that simple. Running off men has never been an issue for me." Karen's expression grew sober. "I have to fly to Texas. I'll be taking more time off from work. Whether it will be vacation time or a leave of absence remains to be seen. I'm not into any heavy cases at the moment, so it's doable."

Erica put her hand on Karen's arm. "No one is sick?"

"No. No. I don't even have the whole story myself. All I know is my mom is insistent that I come home right away. She has something that she has to give to me and only to me." Karen held up a palm. "I swear, that's how she put it. Then she pulled out a speech about disgracing my ancestors."

"Has she ever talked like this before?"

"No. Not even when I told her I was going into law enforcement. I only got the, 'proper Chinese lady' lecture. She thinks women of our culture shouldn't carry guns and chase criminals."

"Oh, yeah. That argument. I was there, remember?" Erica lifted a brow. "You told her most women of your culture didn't marry Texans either."

"Ouch. Yeah, she hasn't let me forget that one, but my dad still gets a kick out of it." Karen smiled, but it was weak.

"What does he say about what's going on now?" Erica asked.

"That was even worse. He got on the phone and told me to get myself home. Pronto."

"Did you tell them we've been trying to stop a murderous,

cannibalistic cult from carrying out their international coup de' grace on civilization as we know it?"

Karen grimaced. "I honestly don't think it would have mattered. You know how my mother can be. She had that whole don't-disrespect-the-ancient-ways tone in her voice." Karen dropped her eyes to the floor.

And as any good friend would do, Erica thumped her. "What?"

"I don't know." Karen tossed her hands up. "This time she was calm, missing the usual frustration she has when dealing with the daughter she thinks is too modern. And unmarried. Still."

Erica smiled at her friend's attempt to joke but knew Karen was worried. "She didn't say anything more?"

"Nope." Karen put aside her food and fell back to lie in the fake, green grass. "She said she didn't want to discuss it over the phone. On an open line."

She swiveled her head to Erica. "An open line. Can you believe that? My mother has been watching too many cop shows."

"You'll be going home tomorrow, then?"

"Tonight. As soon as I leave here I'm going home to pack."

"Do you want me to go with you?" It was Erica's turn to have her friend's back.

Karen gave her an appreciative look. "I'll be fine. Besides, I think you need a little time off yourself. A vacation from your most recent vacation."

"Probably true. I can't wait to open, especially now that we've added the exhibit for Hatshepsut." She put her hand on Karen's arm. "But seriously, if you need me, just call."

"I will. Promise." She stood, cleaning up the mess they'd made. "I'll let you know as soon as I know. Are you closing up for the night?"

"I need to make a few more adjustments."

Karen shook her finger. "Go home and get some sleep. The museum will be here in the morning, just like you left it."

The two women hugged and Karen made her way out.

With a worried mind, Erica went back to the underwater display to turn it off. Instead, she found herself caught up in the scenery. And the memories.

The statue of Hapi loomed large against the background of jewel blue water, and Erica remembered swimming around the great stone giant with Matt.

They'd been diving for remains and racing to stop what seemed like an insurmountable force, yet they'd found a way to laugh. In the worst of times.

She stood in the pale light for a long while, wondering if she would ever see him again. He had occupied too many of her thoughts since they'd parted in Lyon, and being without him was harder than she'd ever expected. So hard.

She shook herself and let her hands fall to her thighs. Once the museum was up and running smoothly, she would have to find an expedition to go on. Maybe plan a garden. She had to have something to keep her busy. Better make that garden a labyrinth.

She rubbed her hand over the screen as the images took her through a school of darting silver fish and floating sea plants. Caught up in the view, Erica didn't realize she had company until she was startled by a familiar voice.

"I remember this place."

Erica thought she might have conjured the sound from her imagination. After all, she had just been thinking about him.

She pivoted. And there he stood.

Matt wasn't dressed for work in his dark jeans and white shirt. So why was he here?

"Matt?" She rubbed a hand across her brow. "Sorry, I'm... just surprised." Staggered was more like it. "Why didn't you let me know you were coming?"

He rocked back on his heels and dodged her question. "We've made a good deal of progress tracking down the leaders and the higher level members of Kherep Amun." He stopped as if at a loss for words. "And I had some time."

"You should have given me warning." Erica rubbed her palms over her shirt. Then she patted her hair. She had Matt had worked long dirty hours together in their search for the vases, but her smudged and dusty clothing felt awkward.

Matt started to speak then stopped. He drew a breath and tried again. "I can understand if you're not happy to see me. I hoped we could talk, in person. I left a lot unsaid."

"Did you?" The fire was suddenly back in her tone. "I would never have guessed. You seemed to sum it all up in a few words. Because that's all it was worth to you."

"I'm sorry for that," he said.

The apology caught Erica by surprise, so Matt took advantage of her gaping expression. He moved forward, hands out in front of him. If he appeared weak to her, then so be it. He deserved worse than a knock to his pride. "I know I was hard on you before. At the time, I had to be."

"Why?" Erica sliced her hand into the air in a rare show of temper. "No one was around. No murderers, bosses, or even friends. You could have given me some idea of what was going on with you. Explained yourself."

She shook her fists in front of her. "You sent me away like a play thing you'd tired of. You could have told me...*something*!"

"No. I couldn't. Because I didn't know what I was doing." Matt was glad to see the sadness leave her eyes. The anger was healthier. And at least he knew how to deal with it. "After the night you were taken, I realized I just couldn't risk it anymore. The thought of losing you was too hard. Too painful. You were a distraction."

She gaped at him.

"That's not how I meant it." He paced to the wall, cerulean light shimmering around them from the display. "Once we were back in France, I was more determined than ever to hunt down every last Kherep Amun member." He whirled on her. "And I wanted you gone. I wanted you safe."

She crossed her arms over her chest, nails biting into her flesh. He was stirring everything back up again. Not that it had ever settled. She had just been able to put a bandage on the wound, and now here he was, ripping it back off.

Erica accused him with her eyes.

"I was barely able to let you go in Lyon that day, but I thought I had to. That to do my job completely I had to cut you loose." His face was set in hard lines, as if he could force her to understand.

Erica's heart tripped over the painful reminder. "And you did. You cut me off completely."

"I tried," he said. "But you were always there. Your smile, your laugh. Hell I even missed your sarcasm and the way you switch from girl next door to uptight professor in a heartbeat. Being away from you...it killed me."

Erica took a step toward him but was still cautious.

Matt gave her a look she couldn't interpret. "You've really interrupted my life, you know. I never thought I'd get involved with you when this all began. I did my best not to."

Erica thrust her chin out and responded in a cool voice. "I remember."

Matt's expression relaxed as he stepped closer. "Erica. I don't regret anything. Not now. I used to be afraid you'd be hurt or worse. That I'd lose you." He ran a hand through his coal black hair and sighed. "And now I have."

She raised her eyes to meet his. "If you believe that, why did you come?"

Matt held her gaze, his eyes fierce but imploring her to hear him. "After you left I started thinking about Senmut."

"Senmut?" She dropped her arms, hands spread wide in question.

"Yes. I thought about the lengths he went to for the woman he loved. He must have been destroyed by her death, but he went on to do amazing things in her honor. He evaded her nephew and was able to hide her from the priests who wanted to use her body. He protected her to the end. He never abandoned her." Matt grew somber. "Like I abandoned you."

He took one step in her direction. "You deserve better. To be loved by someone you can count on. Someone you can trust, with everything that's important."

Unable to speak through the churning in her chest, she nodded, never breaking eye contact.

"If you let me, I can give you what you need." Matt moved in closer.

"How do you know what I..."

He silenced her by reaching out and crushing her to him. "Straight talk. I knew when I saw you again that would be it. No more separations." Matt's locked his dark eyes with hers. "You can trust me, Erica. I know how it feels to let you walk away. And it will never happen again."

Taking advantage of her silence, he pressed on. "How would you feel about my being closer, working for a local division?"

She felt hope spring to life in her chest but remained calm. "How close?"

"Atlanta. Close enough for me to live nearby." He kissed her on the forehead. "I'd like to be able to keep an eye on you at all times. At least until the risk of any cult members resurfacing has passed."

She huffed. "Still think you need to protect me?"

He kissed her again, this time letting his lips linger before he said, "I'll always protect you."

Erica tried to pull away. "I need more than that. I've had you as a bodyguard, and it's not enough. Not nearly."

His arms tightened, keeping her firmly in place. The warmth of his chest was like coming home. His heartbeat a beacon.

Matt whispered against her cheek. "I love you, Erica."

The soft words were her undoing, and her hands slipped around him as if they knew exactly where they belonged. She'd been around the world a few times, but here, in her arms, was the most precious thing on earth. The most glorious discovery she'd ever made.

She buried her face against his neck. "I guess you know I love you, too," she mumbled.

Matt held her tighter and closed his eyes. "Good to hear. Or I'd have wasted a plane ticket for nothing."

She reared back and gave him a haughty look.

He'd never seen anything more beautiful in his life.

"Now I'm going to kiss you," he said. And did. Until the floor seem to buck beneath them and they ended up clinging to each other.

Between ragged breaths, Erica licked her lips. "Before I let you haul me off to bed again, I want to make sure I've got this straight. You admit you were wrong. Very wrong. You should never, ever, ever have let me go. But you've seen the error of your ways, so now you're going to relocate and start a life with me." Her eyes shone. "And...what was that last bit? Oh, yeah. You love me."

He slid possessive arms around her waist. "Yeah. That's it." As he fingered the blue stone necklace she still wore, Matt silently thanked each and every deity Erica had taught him about. "That's it, Doc." Then he nodded and gave her his best wicked grin. "Precisely."

Author's Note

In June of 2007, a female mummy known only as KV60 was identified as the lost Queen Hatshepsut. I was in the middle of writing, *She Who is Hidden* at the time and had to revisit portions of the book to accommodate her discovery. Kherep Amun and the surrounding plot are fictional, but I tried to maintain as much accuracy as possible when dealing with historical sites and facts.

Queen Hatshepsut lived quite a story, and I hope the one I've written for her continues to spread her good name. It amazes me that she'd been lost for over two millennia but was finally located in the few years I spent writing a book about her.

I like to think of it as her blessing.

Suza Kates writes both paranormal romance and romantic suspense. She lives in Savannah, Georgia with her family and four ridiculously spoiled cats.

For more on Suza and her books visit

www.suzakates.com